THE
BOOK
OF THE
LIVING
DEAD

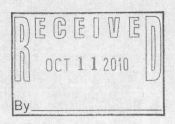

THE
BOOK
OF THE
LIVING
DEAD

EDITED BY
John Richard Stephens

BERKLEY BOOKS, NEW YORK

THE BERKLEY PUBLISHING GROUP
Published by the Penguin Group
Penguin Group (USA) Inc.
375 Hudson Street, New York, New York 10014, USA
Penguin Group (Canada), 90 Eglinton Avenue East, Suite 700, Toronto, Ontario M4P 2Y3, Canada
(a division of Pearson Penguin Canada Inc.)
Penguin Books Ltd., 80 Strand, London WC2R 0RL, England
Penguin Group Ireland, 25 St. Stephen's Green, Dublin 2, Ireland (a division of Penguin Books Ltd.)
Penguin Group (Australia), 250 Camberwell Road, Camberwell, Victoria 3124, Australia
(a division of Pearson Australia Group Pty. Ltd.)
Penguin Books India Pvt. Ltd., 11 Community Centre, Panchsheel Park, New Delhi—110 017, India
Penguin Group (NZ), 67 Apollo Drive, Rosedale, North Shore 0632, New Zealand
(a division of Pearson New Zealand Ltd.)
Penguin Books (South Africa) (Pty.) Ltd., 24 Sturdee Avenue, Rosebank, Johannesburg 2196,
South Africa

Penguin Books Ltd., Registered Offices: 80 Strand, London WC2R 0RL, England

This is a work of fiction. Names, characters, places, and incidents either are the product of the authors' imagination or are used fictitiously, and any resemblance to actual persons, living or dead, business establishments, events, or locales is entirely coincidental. The publisher does not have any control over and does not assume any responsibility for author or third-party websites or their content.

PRINTING HISTORY
Berkley trade paperback edition / October 2010

Library of Congress Cataloging-in-Publication Data

The book of the living dead / [edited by] John Richard Stephens. —Berkley trade pbk. ed.
     p.   cm.
  ISBN 978-0-425-23706-9
1. Zombies—Fiction.   I. Stephens, John Richard.
  PN6071.H727B66   2010
  823'.0873808—dc22   2010022755

PRINTED IN THE UNITED STATES OF AMERICA

10   9   8   7   6   5   4   3   2   1

This book is dedicated to Charlotte Cecil Raymond

ACKNOWLEDGMENTS

John Richard Stephens wishes to express his appreciation to Elaine Molina; Martha and Jim Goodwin; Scott Stephens; Marty Goeller and Dorian Rivas; Terity, Natasha, and Debbie Burbach; Brandon, Alisha, and Kathy Hill; Jeff and Carol Whiteaker; Christopher, Doug, and Michelle Whiteaker; Pat Egner; Gabriel, Aurelia, Elijah, Nina Abeyta, and Justin Weinberger; Jayla, Anthony, Sin, and Bobby Gamboa; Anne and Jerry Buzzard; Krystyne Göhnert; Eric, Tim, and Debbie Cissna; Norene Hilden; Doug and Shirley Strong; Barbara and Stan Main; Joanne and Monte Goeller; Irma and Joe Rodriguez; Danny and Mary Schutt; Les Benedict; Dr. Rich Sutton; SK Lindsey; Jeanne Sisson; Baba and Mimi Marlene Bruner; Randi Bendit; Sarah Russo; and his agent, Charlotte Cecil Raymond.

CONTENTS

ZOMBIES, VAMPIRES, MUMMIES, AND OTHER REANIMATED CORPSES

John Richard Stephens

When thinking of the living dead, the first thing that comes to mind is, of course, zombies. The modern idea of zombies is relatively recent. Hordes of wild corpses trying to tear apart the living and eat them is an idea popularized by the 1968 film *Night of the Living Dead* and its sequels. It was in the 1985 movie *The Return of the Living Dead* where zombies first focused on eating brains. The creatures in the Living Dead movies were actually undead ghouls, not zombies, but the public has come to see them as zombies, and bowing to the weight of public usage, the definition of the word "zombie" changed for the second time.

Prior to this—from the 1920s to the 1960s—zombies were largely portrayed as innocent victims of voodoo sorcerers. These people were resurrected from the dead to become blindly obedient slaves. For many people in the Caribbean, freshly liberated from slavery, the idea of an eternity of mindless servitude was, understandably, a tremendous horror.

There was a belief in zombies in the 1800s but, except for the name, they were unrecognizable compared to today's zombies. Back then, they were more like spirits that could possess people, animals, or everyday objects. Lafcadio Hearn, while living on the Caribbean island of Martinique, described a woman who opened her front door at about five in the morning and saw a huge crab walking down the street. The woman was convinced this crab was a zombie.

Things have changed considerably since then. Today zombies are usually undead people who it's okay to shoot, dismember, slaughter, explode, or use as target practice. It's okay to murder zombies since they're already dead. Besides, if you don't, then they'll eat your brains ... so it's self-defense.

Of course zombies aren't the only type of undead. Another extremely popular form is the vampire. These are corpses with class. Modern vampires tend to be young—at least in appearance—suave, sophisticated, well-off, and rather sensual. Vampires are blessed with superhuman and supernatural powers, but they're cursed with a generally unpleasant existence and a need to feed on the living. They are cool, but sultry. This is often contrasted with vampires who are selfish and revel in killing the living. These vampires usually aren't as attractive.

Mummies are another form of the undead. Mummies are kind of spooky to begin with, but when they come back alive they make excellent monsters. Mummies are ancient and visibly decayed, with a desiccated and sometimes geezerlike appearance, making them quite gruesome.

Another form of reanimated corpse is the one created by a scientist. Frankenstein's monster is, of course, the most famous. These creatures are usually assembled from parts of a variety of corpses. Or sometimes just one part from a dead body is what gets reanimated.

Death is creeping up on us all and sooner or later it will strike each of us down. We do our best to ignore it, but our time is running out. Many people are confident they know what will happen after that, but no one really knows for sure. Belief is not the same as knowledge, no matter how much we may want to convince ourselves that it is.

While the idea of life after death greatly appeals to most people, becoming one of the living dead is not, of course, what they have in mind. The tales in this book take the desire for a continued existence and turn it into a nightmare. Everyone also has a strong desire for the return of loved ones who have passed on. These tales also play off that to create some chilling images. This book is about the dark side of life after death.

Hopefully these creepy stories will give you another view of mortality, with the added benefit of keeping you awake late into the dark and lonely night.

THE
MONKEY'S PAW

W. W. Jacobs

This gothic tale by W. W. Jacobs is considered a classic of horror literature. Jacobs wrote primarily satire and humor, but he also wrote some wonderfully creepy stories. This is his masterpiece.

◆ ◆ ◆

Without, the night was cold and wet, but in the small parlor of Laburnam Villa the blinds were drawn and the fire burned brightly. Father and son were at chess, the former, who possessed ideas about the game involving radical changes, putting his king into such sharp and unnecessary perils that it even provoked comment from the white-haired old lady knitting placidly by the fire.

"Hark at the wind," said Mr. White, who, having seen a fatal mistake after it was too late, was amiably desirous of preventing his son from seeing it.

"I'm listening," said the latter, grimly surveying the board as he stretched out his hand. "Check."

"I should hardly think that he'd come tonight," said his father, with his hand poised over the board.

"Mate," replied the son.

"That's the worst of living so far out," bawled Mr. White, with sudden and unlooked-for violence; "of all the beastly, slushy, out-of-the-way places to live in, this is the worst. Pathway's a bog, and the road's a torrent. I don't know what people are thinking about. I suppose because only two houses on the road are let, they think it doesn't matter."

"Never mind, dear," said his wife, soothingly; "perhaps you'll win the next one."

Mr. White looked up sharply, just in time to intercept a knowing glance between mother and son. The words died away on his lips, and he hid a guilty grin in his thin gray beard.

"There he is," said Herbert White, as the gate banged to loudly and heavy footsteps came towards the door.

The old man rose with hospitable haste, and opening the door, was heard condoling with the new arrival. The new arrival also condoled with himself, so that Mrs. White said, "Tut, tut!" and coughed gently as her husband entered the room, followed by a tall burly man, beady of eye and rubicund of visage.

"Sergeant-Major Morris," he said, introducing him.

The sergeant-major shook hands, and taking the proffered seat by the fire, watched contentedly while his host got out whiskey and tumblers and stood a small copper kettle on the fire.

At the third glass his eyes got brighter, and he began to talk, the little family circle regarding with eager interest this visitor from distant parts, as he squared his broad shoulders in the chair and spoke of strange scenes and doughty deeds, of wars and plagues and strange peoples.

"Twenty-one years of it," said Mr. White, nodding at his wife and son. "When he went away he was a slip of a youth in the warehouse. Now look at him."

"He don't look to have taken much harm," said Mrs. White, politely.

"I'd like to go to India myself," said the old man, "just to look round a bit, you know."

"Better where you are," said the sergeant-major, shaking his head. He put down the empty glass, and sighing softly, shook it again.

"I should like to see those old temples and fakirs and jugglers," said the old man. "What was that you started telling me the other day about a monkey's paw or something, Morris?"

"Nothing," said the soldier, hastily. "Leastways nothing worth hearing."

"Monkey's paw?" said Mr. White, curiously.

"Well, it's just a bit of what you might call magic, perhaps," said the sergeant-major, off-handedly.

His three listeners leaned forward eagerly. The visitor absent-mindedly put his empty glass to his lips and then set it down again. His host filled it for him.

"To look at," said the sergeant-major, fumbling in his pocket, "it's just an ordinary little paw, dried to a mummy."

He took something out of his pocket and proffered it. Mrs. White drew back with a grimace, but her son, taking it, examined it curiously.

"And what is there special about it?" inquired Mr. White as he took it from his son, and having examined it, placed it upon the table.

"It had a spell put on it by an old fakir," said the sergeant-major, "a very holy man. He wanted to show that fate ruled people's lives, and that those who interfered with it did so to their sorrow. He put a spell on it so that three separate men could each have three wishes from it."

His manner was so impressive that his hearers were conscious that their light laughter jarred somewhat.

"Well, why don't you have three, sir?" said Herbert White, cleverly.

The soldier regarded him in the way that middle age is wont to regard presumptuous youth. "I have," he said, quietly, and his blotchy face whitened.

"And did you really have the three wishes granted?" asked Mrs. White.

"I did," said the sergeant-major, and his glass tapped against his strong teeth.

"And has anybody else wished?" inquired the old lady.

"The first man had his three wishes, yes," was the reply. "I don't know what the first two were, but the third was for death. That's how I got the paw."

His tones were so grave that a hush fell upon the group.

"If you've had your three wishes, it's no good to you now, then, Morris," said the old man at last. "What do you keep it for?"

The soldier shook his head. "Fancy, I suppose," he said, slowly. "I did have some idea of selling it, but I don't think I will. It has caused enough mischief already. Besides, people won't buy. They think it's a fairy-tale, some of them, and those who do think anything of it want to try it first and pay me afterwards."

"If you could have another three wishes," said the old man, eying him keenly, "would you have them?"

"I don't know," said the other. "I don't know."

He took the paw, and dangling it between his front finger and thumb, suddenly threw it upon the fire. White, with a slight cry, stooped down and snatched it off.

"Better let it burn," said the soldier, solemnly.

"If you don't want it, Morris," said the old man, "give it to me."

"I won't," said his friend, doggedly. "I threw it on the fire. If you keep it, don't blame me for what happens. Pitch it on the fire again, like a sensible man."

The other shook his head and examined his new possession closely. "How do you do it?" he inquired.

"Hold it up in your right hand and wish aloud," said the sergeant-major, "but I warn you of the consequences."

"Sounds like the *Arabian Nights*," said Mrs. White, as she rose and began to set the supper. "Don't you think you might wish for four pairs of hands for me?"

Her husband drew the talisman from his pocket, and then all three burst into laughter as the sergeant-major, with a look of alarm on his face, caught him by the arm.

"If you must wish," he said, gruffly, "wish for something sensible."

Mr. White dropped it back into his pocket, and placing chairs, motioned his friend to the table. In the business of supper the talisman was partly forgotten, and afterwards the three sat listening in an enthralled fashion to a second installment of the soldier's adventures in India.

"If the tale about the monkey's paw is not more truthful than those he has been telling us," said Herbert, as the door closed behind their guest, just in time for him to catch the last train, "we sha'n't make much out of it."

"Did you give him anything for it, father?" inquired Mrs. White, regarding her husband closely.

"A trifle," said he, coloring slightly. "He didn't want it, but I made him take it. And he pressed me again to throw it away."

"Likely," said Herbert, with pretended horror. "Why, we're going to be rich, and famous, and happy. Wish to be an emperor, father, to begin with; then you can't be henpecked."

He darted round the table, pursued by the maligned Mrs. White armed with an antimacassar.

Mr. White took the paw from his pocket and eyed it dubiously. "I don't know what to wish for, and that's a fact," he said, slowly. "It seems to me I've got all I want."

"If you only cleared the house, you'd be quite happy, wouldn't you?" said Herbert, with his hand on his shoulder.

"Well, wish for two hundred pounds, then; that'll just do it."

His father, smiling shamefacedly at his own credulity, held up the talisman, as his son, with a solemn face somewhat marred by a wink at his mother, sat down at the piano and struck a few impressive chords.

"I wish for two hundred pounds," said the old man, distinctly.

A fine crash from the piano greeted the words, interrupted by a shuddering cry from the old man. His wife and son ran towards him.

"It moved," he cried, with a glance of disgust at the object as it lay on the floor. "As I wished, it twisted in my hands like a snake."

"Well, I don't see the money," said his son as he picked it up and placed it on the table, "and I bet I never shall."

"It must have been your fancy, father," said his wife, regarding him anxiously.

He shook his head. "Never mind, though; there's no harm done, but it gave me a shock all the same."

They sat down by the fire again while the two men finished their pipes. Outside, the wind was higher than ever, and the old man started nervously at the sound of a door banging upstairs. A silence unusual and depressing settled upon all three, which lasted until the old couple rose to retire for the night.

"I expect you'll find the cash tied up in a big bag in the middle of your bed," said Herbert, as he bade them good-night, "and something horrible squatting up on top of the wardrobe watching you as you pocket your ill-gotten gains."

He sat alone in the darkness, gazing at the dying fire, and seeing faces in it. The last face was so horrible and so simian that he gazed at it in amazement. It got so vivid that, with a little uneasy laugh, he felt on the table for a glass containing a little water to throw over it. His hand grasped the monkey's paw, and with a little shiver he wiped his hand on his coat and went up to bed.

In the brightness of the wintry sun next morning as it streamed over the breakfast table Herbert laughed at his fears. There was an air of prosaic wholesomeness about the room which it had lacked on the previous night, and the dirty, shriveled little paw was pitched on the sideboard with a carelessness which betokened no great belief in its virtues.

"I suppose all old soldiers are the same," said Mrs. White. "The idea of our listening to such nonsense! How could wishes be granted in these days? And if they could, how could two hundred pounds hurt you, father?"

"Might drop on his head from the sky," said the frivolous Herbert.

"Morris said the things happened so naturally," said his father, "that you might if you so wished attribute it to coincidence."

"Well, don't break into the money before I come back," said Herbert as he rose from the table. "I'm afraid it'll turn you into a mean, avaricious man, and we shall have to disown you."

His mother laughed, and following him to the door, watched him down the road, and returning to the breakfast table, was very happy at the expense of her husband's credulity. All of which did not prevent her from scurrying to the door at the postman's knock, nor prevent her from referring somewhat shortly to retired sergeant-majors of bibulous habits when she found that the post brought a tailor's bill.

"Herbert will have some more of his funny remarks, I expect, when he comes home," she said as they sat at dinner.

"I dare say," said Mr. White, pouring himself out some beer; "but for all that, the thing moved in my hand; that I'll swear to."

"You thought it did," said the old lady, soothingly.

"I say it did," replied the other. "There was no thought about it; I had just—What's the matter?"

His wife made no reply. She was watching the mysterious movements of a man outside, who, peering in an undecided fashion at the house, appeared to be trying to make up his mind to enter. In mental connection with the two hundred pounds, she noticed that the stranger was well dressed and wore a silk hat of glossy newness. Three times he paused at the gate, and then walked on again. The fourth time he stood with his hand upon it, and then with sudden resolution flung it open and walked up the path. Mrs. White at the same moment placed her hands behind her, and hurriedly unfastening the strings of her apron, put that useful article of apparel beneath the cushion of her chair.

She brought the stranger, who seemed ill at ease, into the room. He gazed furtively at Mrs. White, and listened in a preoccupied fashion as the old lady apologized for the appearance of the room, and her husband's coat, a garment which he usually reserved for the garden. She then waited as patiently as her sex would permit for him to broach his business, but he was at first strangely silent.

"I—was asked to call," he said at last, and stooped and picked a piece of cotton from his trousers. "I come from 'Maw and Meggins.'"

The old lady started. "Is anything the matter?" she asked, breathlessly. "Has anything happened to Herbert? What is it? What is it?"

Her husband interposed. "There, there, mother," he said, hastily. "Sit down, and don't jump to conclusions. You've not brought bad news, I'm sure, sir," and he eyed the other wistfully.

"I'm sorry—" began the visitor.

"Is he hurt?" demanded the mother.

The visitor bowed in assent. "Badly hurt," he said, quietly, "but he is not in any pain."

"Oh, thank God!" said the old woman, clasping her hands. "Thank God for that! Thank—"

She broke off suddenly as the sinister meaning of the assurance dawned upon her and she saw the awful confirmation of her fears in the other's averted face. She caught her breath, and turning to her slower-witted husband, laid her trembling old hand upon his. There was a long silence.

"He was caught in the machinery," said the visitor at length in a low voice.

"Caught in the machinery," repeated Mr. White in a dazed fashion, "yes."

He sat staring blankly out at the window, and taking his wife's hand between his own, pressed it as he had been wont to do in their old courting days nearly forty years before.

"He was the only one left to us," he said, turning gently to the visitor. "It is hard."

The other coughed, and rising, walked slowly to the window. "The firm wished me to convey their sincere sympathy with you in your great loss," he said, without looking round. "I beg that you will understand I am only their servant and merely obeying orders."

There was no reply; the old woman's face was white, her eyes staring, and her breath inaudible; on the husband's face was a look such as his friend the sergeant might have carried into his first action.

"I was to say that Maw and Meggins disclaim all responsibility," continued the other. "They admit no liability at all, but in consideration of your son's service they wish to present you with a certain sum as compensation."

Mr. White dropped his wife's hand, and rising to his feet, gazed with a look of horror at his visitor. His dry lips shaped the words, "How much?"

"Two hundred pounds," was the answer.

Unconscious of his wife's shriek, the old man smiled faintly, put out his hands like a sightless man, and dropped, a senseless heap, to the floor.

In the huge new cemetery, some two miles distant, the old people buried their dead, and came back to a house steeped in shadow and silence. It was all over so quickly that at first they could hardly realize it, and remained in a state of expectation as though of something else to happen—something else which was to lighten this load, too heavy for old hearts to bear.

But the days passed, and expectation gave place to resignation—the hopeless resignation of the old, sometimes miscalled apathy. Sometimes they hardly exchanged a word, for now they had nothing to talk about, and their days were long to weariness.

It was about a week after that that the old man, waking suddenly in the night, stretched out his hand and found himself alone. The room was in darkness, and the sound of subdued weeping came from the window. He raised himself in bed and listened.

"Come back," he said, tenderly. "You will be cold."

"It is colder for my son," said the old woman, and wept afresh.

The sound of her sobs died away on his ears. The bed was warm, and his eyes heavy with sleep. He dozed fitfully, and then slept until a sudden wild cry from his wife awoke him with a start.

"*The paw!*" she cried, wildly. "The monkey's paw!"

He started up in alarm. "Where? Where is it? What's the matter?"

She came stumbling across the room towards him. "I want it," she said, quietly. "You've not destroyed it?"

"It's in the parlor, on the bracket," he replied, marveling. "Why?"

She cried and laughed together, and bending over, kissed his cheek.

"I only just thought of it," she said, hysterically. "Why didn't I think of it before? Why didn't *you* think of it?"

"Think of what?" he questioned.

"The other two wishes," she replied, rapidly. "We've only had one."

"Was not that enough?" he demanded, fiercely.

"No," she cried, triumphantly; "we'll have one more. Go down and get it quickly, and wish our boy alive again."

The man sat up in bed and flung the bedclothes from his quaking limbs. "Good God, you are mad!" he cried, aghast.

"Get it," she panted; "get it quickly, and wish—Oh, my boy, my boy!"

Her husband struck a match and lit the candle. "Get back to bed," he said, unsteadily. "You don't know what you are saying."

"We had the first wish granted," said the old woman, feverishly; "why not the second?"

"A coincidence," stammered the old man.

"Go and get it and wish," cried the old woman, and dragged him towards the door.

He went down in the darkness, and felt his way to the parlor, and then to the mantel-piece. The talisman was in its place, and a horrible fear that the unspoken wish might bring his mutilated son before him ere he could escape from the room seized upon him, and he caught his breath as he found that he had lost the direction of the door. His brow cold with sweat, he felt his way round the table, and groped along the wall until he found himself in the small passage with the unwholesome thing in his hand.

Even his wife's face seemed changed as he entered the room. It was white and expectant, and to his fears seemed to have an unnatural look upon it. He was afraid of her.

"*Wish!*" she cried, in a strong voice.

"It is foolish and wicked," he faltered.

"*Wish!*" repeated his wife.

He raised his hand. "I wish my son alive again."

The talisman fell to the floor, and he regarded it shudderingly. Then he sank trembling into a chair as the old woman, with burning eyes, walked to the window and raised the blind.

He sat until he was chilled with the cold, glancing occasionally at the figure of the old woman peering through the window. The candle end, which had burnt below the rim of the china candlestick, was throwing pulsating shadows on the ceiling and walls, until, with a flicker larger than the rest, it expired. The old man, with an unspeakable sense of relief at the failure of the talisman, crept back to his bed, and a minute or two afterwards the old woman came silently and apathetically beside him.

Neither spoke, but both lay silently listening to the ticking of the clock. A stair creaked, and a squeaky mouse scurried noisily through the wall. The darkness was oppressive, and after lying for some time screwing up his courage, the husband took the box of matches, and striking one, went downstairs for a candle.

At the foot of the stairs the match went out, and he paused to strike another, and at the same moment a knock, so quiet and stealthy as to be scarcely audible, sounded on the front door.

The matches fell from his hand. He stood motionless, his breath suspended until the knock was repeated. Then he turned and fled swiftly back to his room, and closed the door behind him. A third knock sounded through the house.

"What's that?" cried the old woman, starting up.

"A rat," said the old man in shaking tones—"a rat. It passed me on the stairs."

His wife sat up in bed listening. A loud knock resounded through the house.

"It's Herbert!" she screamed. "It's Herbert!"

She ran to the door, but her husband was before her, and catching her by the arm, held her tightly.

"What are you going to do?" he whispered hoarsely.

"It's my boy; it's Herbert!" she cried, struggling mechanically. "I forgot it was two miles away. What are you holding me for? Let go. I must open the door."

"For God's sake don't let it in," cried the old man, trembling.

"You're afraid of your own son," she cried, struggling. "Let me go. I'm coming, Herbert; I'm coming."

There was another knock, and another. The old woman with a sudden wrench broke free and ran from the room. Her husband followed to the landing, and called after her appealingly as she hurried downstairs. He heard the chain rattle back and the bottom bolt drawn slowly and stiffly from the socket. Then the old woman's voice, strained and panting.

"The bolt," she cried loudly. "Come down. I can't reach it."

But her husband was on his hands and knees groping wildly on the floor in search of the paw. If he could only find it before the thing outside got in. A perfect fusillade of knocks reverberated through the house, and he heard the scraping of a chair as his wife put it down in the passage against the door. He heard the creaking of the bolt as it came slowly back, and at the same moment he found the monkey's paw, and frantically breathed his third and last wish.

The knocking ceased suddenly, although the echoes of it were still in the house. He heard the chair drawn back and the door opened. A cold wind rushed up the staircase, and a long loud wail of disappointment and misery from his wife gave him courage to run down to her side, and then to the gate beyond. The street lamp flickering opposite shone on a quiet and deserted road.

THE AMOROUS CORPSE

Théophile Gautier

Théophile Gautier was a very talented French author and poet who was highly influenced by his friend Victor Hugo. Sci-fi horror master H. P. Lovecraft wrote, "It is in Gautier that we first seem to find an authentic French sense of the unreal world . . . [it] is recognizable at once as something alike genuine and profound." Gautier was part of the Romantic Movement, which chose emotion and the senses over reason and intellect, while focusing on individual heroism and placing an emphasis on the mysterious and the exotic. All of these elements feature in this supernatural story, translated by Lafcadio Hearn, which the *Encyclopædia Britannica* described as "a gem of the most perfect workmanship."

◆　◆　◆

Brother, you ask me if I have ever loved. Yes. My story is a strange and terrible one; and though I am sixty-six years of age, I scarcely dare even now to disturb the ashes of that memory. To you I can refuse nothing; but I should not relate such a tale to any less experienced mind. So strange were the circumstances of my story, that I can scarcely believe myself to have ever actually been a party to them. For more than three years I remained the victim of a most singular and diabolical illusion.

Poor country priest though I was, I led every night in a dream—would to God it had been all a dream!—a most worldly life, a damning life, a life of Sardanapalus. One single look too freely cast upon a woman well-nigh caused me to lose my soul; but finally by the grace of God and the assistance of my patron saint, I succeeded in casting out the evil spirit that possessed me. My daily life was long interwoven with a nocturnal life of a totally different character. By day I was a priest of the Lord, occupied with prayer and sacred things; by night, from the instant that I closed my eyes I became a young nobleman, a fine connoisseur in women, dogs, and horses; gambling, drinking, and blaspheming; and when I awoke at early daybreak, it seemed to me, on the other hand, that I had been sleeping, and had only dreamed that I was a priest. Of this somnambulistic life there now remains to me only the recollection of certain scenes and words which I cannot banish from my memory; but although I never actually left the walls of my presbytery, one would think to hear me speak that I were a man who, weary of all worldly pleasures, had become a religious, seeking to end a tempestuous life in the service of God, rather than a humble seminarist who has grown old in this obscure curacy, situated in the depths of the woods and even isolated from the life of the century.

Yes, I have loved as none in the world ever loved—with an insensate and furious passion—so violent that I am astonished it did not cause my heart to burst asunder. Ah, what nights—what nights!

From my earliest childhood I had felt a vocation to the priesthood, so that all my studies were directed with that idea in view. Up to the age of twenty-four my life had been only a prolonged novitiate. Having completed my course of theology I successively received all the minor orders, and my superiors judged me worthy, despite my youth, to pass the last awful degree. My ordination was fixed for Easter week.

I had never gone into the world. My world was confined by the walls of the college and the seminary. I knew in a vague sort of a way that there was something called Woman, but I never permitted my thoughts to dwell on such a subject, and I lived in a state of perfect innocence.

Twice a year only I saw my infirm and aged mother, and in those visits were comprised my sole relations with the outer world.

I regretted nothing; I felt not the least hesitation at taking the last irrevocable step; I was filled with joy and impatience. Never did a betrothed lover count the slow hours with more feverish ardour; I slept only to dream that I was saying mass; I believed there could be nothing in the world more delightful than to be a priest; I would have refused to be a king or a poet in preference. My ambition could conceive of no loftier aim.

I tell you this in order to show you that what happened to me could not have happened in the natural order of things, and to enable you to understand that I was the victim of an inexplicable fascination.

At last the great day came. I walked to the church with a step so light that I fancied myself sustained in air, or that I had wings upon my shoulders. I believed myself an angel, and wondered at the somber and thoughtful faces of my companions, for there were several of us. I had passed all the night in prayer, and was in a condition well-nigh bordering on ecstasy. The bishop, a venerable old man, seemed to me God the Father leaning over His Eternity, and I beheld Heaven through the vault of the temple.

You well know the details of that ceremony—the benediction, the communion under both forms, the anointing of the palms of the hands with the Oil of Catechumens, and then the holy sacrifice offered in concert with the bishop.

Ah, truly spake Job when he declared that the imprudent man is one who hath not made a covenant with his eyes! I accidentally lifted my head, which until then I had kept down, and beheld before me, so close that it seemed that I could have touched her—although she was actually a considerable distance from me and on the further side of the sanctuary railing—a young woman of extraordinary beauty, and attired with royal magnificence. It seemed as though scales had suddenly fallen from my eyes. I felt like a blind man who unexpectedly recovers his sight. The bishop, so radiantly glorious but an instant before, suddenly vanished away, the tapers paled upon their golden candlesticks like stars in the dawn, and a vast darkness seemed to fill the whole church. The charming creature appeared in bright relief against the background of that darkness, like some angelic revelation. She seemed herself radiant, and radiating light rather than receiving it.

I lowered my eyelids, firmly resolved not to again open them, that I might not be influenced by external objects, for distraction had gradually taken possession of me until I hardly knew what I was doing.

In another minute, nevertheless, I reopened my eyes, for through my eyelashes I still beheld her, all sparkling with prismatic colors, and surrounded with such a penumbra as one beholds in gazing at the sun.

Oh, how beautiful she was! The greatest painters, who followed ideal beauty into heaven itself, and thence brought back to earth the true portrait of the Madonna, never in their delineations even approached that wildly beautiful reality which I saw before me. Neither the verses of the poet nor the palette of the artist could convey any conception of her. She was rather tall, with a form and bearing of a goddess. Her hair, of a soft blonde hue, was parted in the midst and flowed back over her temples in two rivers of rippling gold; she seemed a diademed queen. Her forehead, bluish-white in its transparency, extended its calm breadth above the arches of her eyebrows, which by a strange singularity were almost black, and admirably relieved the effect of sea-green eyes of unsustainable vivacity and brilliancy. What eyes! With a single flash they could have decided a man's destiny. They had a life, a limpidity, an ardour, a humid light which I have never seen in human eyes; they shot forth rays like arrows, which I could distinctly *see* enter my heart. I know not if the fire which illumined them came from heaven or from hell, but assuredly it came from one or the other. That woman was either an angel or a demon, perhaps both. Assuredly she never sprang from the flank of Eve, our common mother. Teeth of the most lustrous pearl gleamed in her ruddy smile, and at every inflection of her lips little dimples appeared in the satiny rose of her adorable cheeks. There was a delicacy and pride in the regal outline of her nostrils bespeaking noble blood. Agate gleams played over the smooth lustrous skin of her half-bare shoulders, and strings of great blonde pearls—almost equal to her neck in beauty of color—descended upon her bosom. From time to time she elevated her head with the undulating grace of a startled serpent or peacock, thereby imparting a quivering motion to the high lace ruff which surrounded it like a silver trellis-work.

She wore a robe of orange-red velvet, and from her wide ermine-lined sleeves there peeped forth patrician hands of infinite delicacy, and so ideally transparent that, like the fingers of Aurora, they permitted the light to shine through them.

All these details I can recollect at this moment as plainly as though they were of yesterday, for notwithstanding I was greatly troubled at the time, nothing escaped me; the faintest touch of shading, the little dark speck at the point of the chin, the imperceptible down at the corners of the lips, the velvety floss upon the brow, the quivering shadows of the eyelashes upon the cheeks—I could notice everything with astonishing lucidity of perception.

And gazing I felt opening within me gates that had until then remained closed; vents long obstructed became all clear, permitting glimpses of unfamiliar perspectives within; life suddenly made itself visible to me under a totally novel aspect. I felt as though I had just been born into a new world and a new order of things. A frightful anguish commenced to torture my heart as with red-hot pincers. Every successive minute seemed to me at once but a second and yet a century.

Meanwhile the ceremony was proceeding, and I shortly found myself transported far from that world of which my newly born desires were furiously besieging the entrance. Nevertheless I answered "Yes" when I wished to say "No," though all within me protested against the violence done to my soul by my tongue. Some occult power seemed to force the words from my throat against my will. Thus it is, perhaps, that so many young girls walk to the altar firmly resolved to refuse in a startling manner the husband imposed upon them, and that yet not one ever fulfills her intention. Thus it is, doubtless, that so many poor novices take the veil, though they have resolved to tear it into shreds at the moment when called upon to utter the vows. One dares not thus cause so great a scandal to all present, nor deceive the expectation of so many people. All those eyes, all those wills seem to weigh down upon you like a cope of lead, and, moreover, measures have been so well taken, everything has been so thoroughly arranged beforehand and after a fashion so evidently irrevocable, that the will yields to the weight of circumstances and utterly breaks down.

As the ceremony proceeded the features of the fair unknown changed their expression. Her look had at first been one of caressing tenderness; it changed to an air of disdain and of mortification, as though at not having been able to make itself understood.

With an effort of will sufficient to have uprooted a mountain, I strove to cry out that I would not be a priest, but I could not speak; my tongue seemed nailed to my palate, and I found it impossible to express my will by the least syllable of negation. Though fully awake, I felt like one under the influence of a nightmare, who vainly strives to shriek out the one word upon which life depends.

She seemed conscious of the martyrdom I was undergoing, and, as though to encourage me, she gave me a look replete with divinest promise. Her eyes were a poem; their every glance was a song.

She said to me, "If thou wilt be mine, I shall make thee happier than God Himself in His paradise. The angels themselves will be jealous of thee. Tear off that funeral shroud in which thou art about to wrap thyself. I am Beauty, I am Youth, I am Life. Come to me! Together we shall be Love. Can Jehovah offer thee aught in exchange? Our lives will flow on like a dream, in one eternal kiss.

"Fling forth the wine of that chalice, and thou art free. I will conduct thee to the Unknown Isles. You shall sleep in my bosom upon a bed of massy gold under a silver pavilion, for I love thee and would take thee away from thy God, before whom so many noble hearts pour forth floods of love which never reach even the steps of His throne!"

These words seemed to float to my ears in a rhythm of infinite sweetness, for her look was actually sonorous, and the utterances of her eyes were reechoed in the depths of my heart as though living lips had breathed them into my life. I felt myself willing to renounce God, and yet my tongue mechanically fulfilled all the formalities of the ceremony. The fair one gave me another look, so beseeching, so despairing that keen blades seemed to pierce my heart, and I felt my bosom transfixed by more swords than those of Our Lady of Sorrows.

All was consummated; I had become a priest.

Never was deeper anguish painted on human face than upon hers. The maiden who beholds her affianced lover suddenly fall dead at her side, the mother bending over the empty cradle of her child, Eve seated at the threshold of the gate of Paradise, the miser who finds a stone substituted for his stolen treasure, the poet who accidentally permits the only manuscript of his finest work to fall into the fire, could not wear a look so despairing, so inconsolable. All the blood had abandoned her charming face, leaving it whiter than marble; her beautiful arms hung lifelessly on either side of her body as though their muscles had suddenly relaxed, and she sought the support of a pillar, for her yielding limbs almost betrayed her. As for myself, I staggered toward the door of the church, livid as death, my forehead bathed with a sweat bloodier than that of Calvary; I felt as though I were being strangled; the vault seemed to have flattened down upon my shoulders, and it seemed to me that my head alone sustained the whole weight of the dome.

As I was about to cross the threshold a hand suddenly caught mine—a woman's hand! I had never till then touched the hand of any woman. It was cold as a serpent's skin, and yet its impress remained upon my wrist, burnt there as though branded by a glowing iron. It was she.

"Unhappy man! Unhappy man! What hast thou done?" she exclaimed in a low voice, and immediately disappeared in the crowd.

The aged bishop passed by. He cast a severe and scrutinizing look upon me. My face presented the wildest aspect imaginable: I blushed and turned pale alternately; dazzling lights flashed before my eyes. A companion took pity on me. He seized my arm and led me out. I could not possibly have found my way back to the seminary unassisted. At the corner of a street, while the young priest's attention was momentarily turned in another direction, a servant, fantastically garbed, approached me, and without pausing on his way slipped into my hand a little pocket-book with gold-embroidered corners, at the same time giving me a sign to hide it. I concealed it in my sleeve, and there kept it until I found myself alone in my cell. Then I opened the clasp. There were only two leaves within, bearing the words, "Clarimonde. At the Concini Palace."

So little acquainted was I at that time with the things of this world that I had never heard of Clarimonde, celebrated as she was, and I had no idea as to where the Concini Palace was situated. I hazarded a thousand conjectures, each more extravagant than the last; but, in truth, I cared little whether she were a great lady or a courtesan, so that I could but see her once more.

My love, although the growth of a single hour, had taken imperishable root. I did not even dream of attempting to tear it up, so fully was I convinced such a thing would be impossible. That woman had completely taken possession of me. One look from her had sufficed to change my very nature. She had breathed her will into my life, and I no longer lived in myself, but in her and for her. I gave myself up to a thousand extravagancies. I kissed the place upon my hand which she had touched, and I repeated her name over and over again for hours in succession. I only needed to close my eyes in order to see her distinctly as though she were actually present; and I reiterated to myself the words she had uttered in my ear at the church porch: "Unhappy man! Unhappy man! What hast thou done?" I comprehended at last the full horror of my situation, and the funereal and awful restraints of the state into which I had just entered became clearly revealed to me. To be a priest!—that is, to be chaste, to never love, to observe no distinction of sex or age, to turn from the sight of all beauty, to put out one's own eyes, to hide forever crouching in the chill shadows of some church or cloister, to visit none but the dying, to watch by unknown corpses, and ever bear about with one the black soutane as a garb of mourning for oneself, so that your very dress might serve as a pall for your coffin.

And I felt life rising within me like a subterranean lake, expanding and overflowing; my blood leaped fiercely through my arteries; my long-restrained youth suddenly burst into active being, like the aloe which blooms but once in a hundred years, and then bursts into blossom with a clap of thunder.

What could I do in order to see Clarimonde once more? I had no pretext to offer for desiring to leave the seminary, not knowing any person in the city. I would not even be able to remain there but a short time, and was only waiting my assignment to the curacy which I must thereafter occupy. I tried to remove the bars of the window; but it was at a fearful height from the ground, and I found that as I had no ladder it would be useless to think of escaping thus. And, furthermore, I could descend thence only by night in any event, and afterward how should I be able to find my way through the inextricable labyrinth of streets? All these difficulties, which to many would have appeared altogether insignificant, were gigantic to me, a poor seminarist who had fallen in love only the day before for the first time, without experience, without money, without attire.

"Ah!" cried I to myself in my blindness, "were I not a priest I could have seen her every day; I might have been her lover, her spouse. Instead of being wrapped in this dismal shroud of mine I would have had garments of silk and velvet, golden chains, a sword, and fair plumes like other handsome young cavaliers. My hair, instead of being dishonored by the tonsure, would flow down upon my neck in waving curls; I would have a fine waxed moustache; I would be a gallant." But one hour passed before an altar, a few hastily articulated words, had forever cut me off from the number of the living, and I had myself sealed down the stone of my own tomb; I had with my own hand bolted the gate of my prison!

I went to the window. The sky was beautifully blue; the trees had donned their spring robes; nature seemed to be making parade of an ironical joy. The *Place* was filled with people, some going, others coming; young beaux and young beauties were sauntering in couples toward the groves and gardens; merry youths passed by, cheerily trolling refrains of drinking-songs—it was all a picture of vivacity, life, animation, gaiety, which formed a bitter contrast with my mourning and my solitude. On the steps of the gate sat a young mother playing with her child. She kissed its little rosy mouth still impearled with drops of milk, and performed, in order to amuse it, a thousand divine little puerilities such as only mothers know how to invent. The father standing at a little distance smiled gently upon the charming group, and with folded arms seemed to hug his joy to his heart. I could not endure that spectacle. I closed the window with violence, and flung myself on my bed, my heart filled with frightful hate and jealousy, and gnawed my fingers and my bedcovers like a tiger that has passed ten days without food.

I know not how long I remained in this condition, but at last, while writhing on the bed in a fit of spasmodic fury, I suddenly perceived the Abbé Sérapion, who was standing erect in the centre of the room, watching me attentively. Filled with shame of myself, I let my head fall upon my breast and covered my face with my hands.

"Romuald, my friend, something very extraordinary is transpiring within you," observed Sérapion, after a few moments' silence; "your conduct is altogether inexplicable. You—always so quiet, so pious, so gentle—you to rage in your cell like a wild beast! Take heed, brother—do not listen to the suggestions of the devil. The Evil Spirit, furious that you have consecrated yourself forever to the Lord, is prowling around you like a ravening wolf and making a last effort to obtain possession of you. Instead of allowing yourself to be conquered, my dear Romuald, make to yourself a cuirass of prayers, a buckler of mortifications, and combat the enemy like a valiant man; you will then assuredly overcome him. Virtue must be proved by temptation, and gold comes forth purer from the hands of the assayer. Fear not. Never allow yourself to become discouraged. The most watchful and steadfast souls are at moments liable to such temptation. Pray, fast, meditate, and the Evil Spirit will depart from you."

The words of the Abbé Sérapion restored me to myself, and I became a little more calm.

"I came," he continued, "to tell you that you have been appointed to the curacy of C———. The priest who had charge of it has just died, and Monsignor the Bishop has ordered me to have you installed there at once. Be ready, therefore, to start tomorrow."

I responded with an inclination of the head, and the Abbé retired. I opened my missal and commenced reading some prayers, but the letters became confused and blurred under my eyes, the thread of the ideas entangled itself hopelessly in my brain, and the volume at last fell from my hands without my being aware of it.

To leave tomorrow without having been able to see her again, to add yet another barrier to the many already interposed between us, to lose forever all hope of being able to meet her, except, indeed, through a miracle! Even to write to her, alas! would be impossible, for by whom could I dispatch my letter? With my sacred character of priest, to whom could I dare unbosom myself, in whom could I confide? I became a prey to the bitterest anxiety.

Then suddenly recurred to me the words of the Abbé Sérapion regarding the artifices of the devil; and the strange character of the adventure, the supernatural beauty of Clarimonde, the phosphoric light of her eyes, the burning imprint of her hand, the agony into which she had thrown me, the sudden change wrought within me when all my piety vanished in a single instant—these and other things clearly testified to the work of the Evil One, and perhaps that satiny hand was but the glove which concealed his claws. Filled with terror at these fancies, I again picked up the missal which had slipped from my knees and fallen upon the floor, and once more gave myself up to prayer.

Next morning Sérapion came to take me away. Two mules freighted with our miserable valises awaited us at the gate. He mounted one, and I the other as well as I knew how.

As we passed along the streets of the city, I gazed attentively at all the windows and balconies in the hope of seeing Clarimonde, but it was yet early in the morning, and the city had hardly opened its eyes. Mine sought to penetrate the blinds and window-curtains of all the palaces before which we were passing. Sérapion doubtless attributed this curiosity to my admiration of the architecture, for he slackened the pace of his animal in order to give me time to look around me. At last we passed the city gates and commenced to mount the hill beyond. When we arrived at its summit I turned to take a last look at the place where Clarimonde dwelt. The shadow of a great cloud hung over all the city; the contrasting colors of its blue and red roofs were lost in the uniform half-tint, through which here and there floated upward, like white flakes of foam, the smoke of freshly kindled fires. By a singular optical effect one edifice, which surpassed in height all the neighboring buildings that were still dimly veiled by the vapors, towered up, fair and lustrous with the gilding of a solitary beam of sunlight—although actually more than a league away it seemed quite near. The smallest details of its architecture were plainly distinguishable—the turrets, the platforms, the window-casements, and even the swallow-tailed weather-vanes.

"What is that palace I see over there, all lighted up by the sun?" I asked Sérapion. He shaded his eyes with his hand, and having looked in the direction indicated, replied: "It is the ancient palace which the Prince Concini has given to the courtesan Clarimonde. Awful things are done there!"

At that instant, I know not yet whether it was a reality or an illusion, I fancied I saw gliding along the terrace a shapely white figure, which gleamed for a moment in passing and as quickly vanished. It was Clarimonde.

Oh, did she know that at that very hour, all feverish and restless—from the height of the rugged road which separated me from her, and which, alas! I could never more descend—I was directing my eyes upon the palace where she dwelt, and which a mocking beam of sunlight seemed to bring nigh to me, as though inviting me to enter therein as its lord? Undoubtedly she must have known it, for her soul was too sympathetically united with mine not to have felt its least emotional thrill, and that subtle sympathy it must have been which prompted her to climb—although clad only in her nightdress—to the summit of the terrace, amid the icy dews of the morning.

The shadow gained the palace, and the scene became to the eye only a motionless ocean of roofs and gables, amid which one mountainous undulation was distinctly visible. Sérapion urged his mule forward, my own at once followed at the same gait, and a sharp angle in the road at last hid the city of S—— forever from my eyes, as I was destined never to return thither. At the close of a weary three-days' journey through dismal country fields, we caught sight of the cock upon the steeple of the church which I was to take charge of, peeping above the trees, and after having followed some winding roads fringed with thatched cottages and little gardens, we found ourselves in front of the façade, which certainly possessed few features of magnificence. A porch ornamented with some moldings, and two or three pillars rudely hewn from sandstone; a tiled roof with counterforts of the same sandstone as the pillars—that was all. To the left lay the cemetery, overgrown with high weeds, and having a great iron cross rising up in its centre; to the right stood the presbytery under the shadow of the church. It was a house of the most extreme simplicity and frigid cleanliness. We entered the enclosure. A few chickens were picking up some oats scattered upon the ground; accustomed, seemingly, to the black habit of ecclesiastics, they showed no fear of our presence and scarcely troubled themselves to get out of our way. A hoarse, wheezy barking fell upon our ears, and we saw an aged dog running toward us.

It was my predecessor's dog. He had dull bleared eyes, grizzled hair, and every mark of the greatest age to which a dog can possibly attain. I patted him gently, and he proceeded at once to march along beside me with an air of satisfaction unspeakable. A very old woman, who had been the housekeeper of the former curé, also came to meet us, and after having invited me into a little back parlor, asked whether I intended to retain her. I replied that I would take care of her, and the dog, and the chickens, and all the furniture her master had bequeathed her at his death. At this she became fairly transported with joy, and the Abbé Sérapion at once paid her the price which she asked for her little property.

As soon as my installation was over, the Abbé Sérapion returned to the seminary. I was, therefore, left alone, with no one but myself to look to for aid or counsel. The thought of Clarimonde again began to haunt me, and in spite of all my endeavors to banish it, I always found it present in my meditations. One evening, while promenading in my little garden along the walks bordered with box-plants, I fancied that I saw through the elm-trees the figure of a woman, who followed my every movement, and that I beheld two sea-green eyes gleaming through the foliage; but it was only an illusion, and on going round to the other side of the garden, I could find nothing except a footprint on the sanded walk—a footprint so small that it seemed to have been made by the foot of a child. The garden was enclosed by very high walls. I searched every nook and corner of it, but could discover no one there. I have never succeeded in fully accounting for this circumstance, which, after all, was nothing compared with the strange things which happened to me afterward.

For a whole year I lived thus, filling all the duties of my calling with the most scrupulous exactitude, praying and fasting, exhorting and lending ghostly aid to the sick, and bestowing alms even to the extent of frequently depriving myself of the very necessaries of life. But I felt a great aridness within me, and the sources of grace seemed closed against me. I never found that happiness which should spring from the fulfillment of a holy mission; my thoughts were far away, and the words of Clarimonde were ever upon my lips like an involuntary refrain.

Oh, brother, meditate well on this! Through having but once lifted my eyes to look upon a woman, through one fault apparently so venial, I have for years remained a victim to the most miserable agonies, and the happiness of my life has been destroyed forever.

I will not longer dwell upon those defeats, or on those inward victories invariably followed by yet more terrible falls, but will at once proceed to the facts of my story. One night my doorbell was long and violently rung. The aged housekeeper arose and opened to the stranger, and the figure of a man, whose complexion was deeply bronzed, and who was richly clad in a foreign costume, with a poniard at his girdle, appeared under the rays of Barbara's lantern. Her first impulse was one of terror, but the stranger reassured her, and stated that he desired to see me at once on matters relating to my holy calling. Barbara invited him upstairs, where I was on the point of retiring.

The stranger told me that his mistress, a very noble lady, was lying at the point of death, and desired to see a priest. I replied that I was prepared to follow him, took with me the sacred articles necessary for extreme unction, and descended in all haste. Two horses black as the night itself stood without the gate, pawing the ground with impatience, and veiling their chests with long streams of smoky vapor exhaled from their nostrils. He held the stirrup and aided me to mount upon one; then, merely laying his hand upon the pommel of the saddle, he vaulted on the other, pressed the animal's sides with his knees, and loosened rein. The horse bounded forward with the velocity of an arrow. Mine, of which the stranger held the bridle, also started off at a swift gallop, keeping up with his companion.

We devoured the road. The ground flowed backward beneath us in a long streaked line of pale gray, and the black silhouettes of the trees seemed fleeing by us on either side like an army in rout. We passed through a forest so profoundly gloomy that I felt my flesh creep in the chill darkness with superstitious fear. The showers of bright sparks which flew from the stony road under the iron-shod feet of our horses remained glowing in our wake like a fiery trail; and had anyone at that hour of the night beheld us both—my guide and myself—he must have taken us for two specters riding upon nightmares. Witch-fires ever and anon flitted across the road before us, and the night-birds shrieked fearsomely in the depth of the woods beyond, where we beheld at intervals glow the phosphorescent eyes of wild cats. The manes of the horses became more and more disheveled, the sweat streamed over their flanks, and their breath came through their nostrils hard and fast. But when he found them slacking pace, the guide reanimated them by uttering a strange, guttural, unearthly cry, and the gallop recommenced with fury.

At last the whirlwind race ceased; a huge black mass pierced through with many bright points of light suddenly rose before us, the hoofs of our horses echoed louder upon a strong wooden drawbridge, and we rode under a great vaulted archway which darkly yawned between two enormous towers. Some great excitement evidently reigned in the castle. Servants with torches were crossing the courtyard in every direction, and above lights were ascending and descending from landing to landing. I obtained a confused glimpse of vast masses of architecture—columns, arcades, flights of steps, stairways—a royal voluptuousness and elfin magnificence of construction worthy of fairyland. A servant—the same who had before brought me the tablet from Clarimonde, and whom I instantly recognized—approached to aid me in dismounting, and the major-domo, attired in black velvet with a gold chain about his neck, advanced to meet me, supporting himself upon an ivory cane. Large tears were falling from his eyes and streaming over his cheeks and white beard.

"Too late!" he cried, sorrowfully shaking his venerable head. "Too late, sir priest! But if you have not been able to save the soul, come at least to watch by the poor body."

He took my arm and conducted me to the death-chamber. I wept not less bitterly than he, for I had learned that the dead one was none other than that Clarimonde whom I had so deeply and so wildly loved. A *prie-dieu* stood at the foot of the bed; a bluish flame flickering in a bronze patera filled all the room with a wan, deceptive light, here and there bringing out in the darkness at intervals some projection of furniture or cornice. In a chiseled urn upon the table there was a faded white rose, whose leaves—excepting one that still held—had all fallen, like odorous tears, to the foot of the vase. A broken black mask, a fan, and disguises of every variety, which were lying on the armchairs, bore witness that death had entered suddenly and unannounced into that sumptuous dwelling.

Without daring to cast my eyes upon the bed, I knelt down and commenced to repeat the Psalms for the Dead, with exceeding fervor, thanking God that He had placed the tomb between me and the memory of this woman, so that I might thereafter be able to utter her name in my prayers as a name forever sanctified by death. But my fervor gradually weakened, and I fell insensibly into a reverie. That chamber bore no semblance to a chamber of death. In lieu of the fetid and cadaverous odors which I had been accustomed to breathe during such funereal vigils, a languorous vapor of Oriental perfume—I know not what amorous odor of woman—softly floated through the tepid air. That pale light seemed rather a twilight gloom contrived for voluptuous pleasure, than a substitute for the yellow-flickering watch-tapers which shine by the side of corpses. I thought upon the strange destiny which enabled me to meet Clarimonde again at the very moment when she was lost to me forever, and a sigh of regretful anguish escaped from my breast. Then it seemed to me that someone behind me had also sighed, and I turned round to look. It was only an echo. But in that moment my eyes fell upon the bed of death which they had till then avoided.

The red damask curtains, decorated with large flowers worked in embroidery and looped up with gold bullion, permitted me to behold the fair dead, lying at full length, with hands joined upon her bosom. She was covered with a linen wrapping of dazzling whiteness, which formed a strong contrast with the gloomy purple of the hangings, and was of so fine a texture that it concealed nothing of her body's charming form, and allowed the eye to follow those beautiful outlines—undulating like the neck of a swan—which even death had not robbed of their supple grace. She seemed an alabaster statue executed by some skillful sculptor to place upon the tomb of a queen, or rather, perhaps, like a slumbering maiden over whom the silent snow had woven a spotless veil.

I could no longer maintain my constrained attitude of prayer. The air of the alcove intoxicated me, that febrile perfume of half-faded roses penetrated my very brain, and I commenced to pace restlessly up and down the chamber, pausing at each turn before the bier to contemplate the graceful corpse lying beneath the transparency of its shroud. Wild fancies came thronging to my brain. I thought to myself that she might not, perhaps, be really dead; that she might only have feigned death for the purpose of bringing me to her castle, and then declaring her love. At one time I even thought I saw her foot move under the whiteness of the coverings, and slightly disarrange the long straight folds of the winding-sheet.

And then I asked myself, "Is this indeed Clarimonde? What proof have I that it is she? Might not that servant have passed into the service of some other lady? Surely, I must be going mad to torture and afflict myself thus!" But my heart answered with a fierce throbbing: "It is she; it is she indeed!"

I approached the bed again, and fixed my eyes with redoubled attention upon the object of my incertitude. Ah, must I confess it? That exquisite perfection of bodily form, although purified and made sacred by the shadow of death, affected me more voluptuously than it should have done; and that repose so closely resembled slumber that one might well have mistaken it for such.

I forgot that I had come there to perform a funeral ceremony; I fancied myself a young bridegroom entering the chamber of the bride, who all modestly hides her fair face, and through coyness seeks to keep herself wholly veiled.

Heartbroken with grief, yet wild with hope, shuddering at once with fear and pleasure, I bent over her and grasped the corner of the sheet. I lifted it back, holding my breath all the while through fear of waking her. My arteries throbbed with such violence that I felt them hiss through my temples, and the sweat poured from my forehead in streams, as though I had lifted a mighty slab of marble.

There, indeed, lay Clarimonde, even as I had seen her at the church on the day of my ordination. She was not less charming than then. With her, death seemed but a last coquetry. The pallor of her cheeks, the less brilliant carnation of her lips, her long eyelashes lowered and relieving their dark fringe against that white skin, lent her an unspeakably seductive aspect of melancholy chastity and mental suffering; her long loose hair, still intertwined with some little blue flowers, made a shining pillow for her head, and veiled the nudity of her shoulders with its thick ringlets; her beautiful hands, purer, more diaphanous, than the Host, were crossed on her bosom in an attitude of pious rest and silent prayer, which served to counteract all that might have proven otherwise too alluring—even after death—in the exquisite roundness and ivory polish of her bare arms from which the pearl bracelets had not yet been removed.

I remained long in mute contemplation, and the more I gazed, the less could I persuade myself that life had really abandoned that beautiful body forever. I do not know whether it was an illusion or a reflection of the lamplight, but it seemed to me that the blood was again commencing to circulate under that lifeless pallor, although she remained all motionless. I laid my hand lightly on her arm; it was cold, but not colder than her hand on the day when it touched mine at the portals of the church. I resumed my position, bending my face above her, and bathing her cheek with the warm dew of my tears. Ah, what bitter feelings of despair and helplessness, what agonies unutterable did I endure in that long watch!

Vainly did I wish that I could have gathered all my life into one mass that I might give it all to her, and breathe into her chill remains the flame which devoured me. The night advanced, and feeling the moment of eternal separation approach, I could not deny myself the last sad sweet pleasure of imprinting a kiss upon the dead lips of her who had been my only love. . . .

Oh, miracle! A faint breath mingled itself with my breath, and the mouth of Clarimonde responded to the passionate pressure of mine. Her eyes unclosed, and lighted up with something of their former brilliancy; she uttered a long sigh, and uncrossing her arms, passed them around my neck with a look of ineffable delight.

"Ah, it is thou, Romuald!" she murmured in a voice languishingly sweet as the last vibrations of a harp. "What ailed thee, dearest? I waited so long for thee that I am dead; but we are now betrothed: I can see thee and visit thee. Adieu, Romuald, adieu! I love thee. That is all I wished to tell thee, and I give thee back the life which thy kiss for a moment recalled. We shall soon meet again."

Her head fell back, but her arms yet encircled me, as though to retain me still. A furious whirlwind suddenly burst in the window and entered the chamber. The last remaining leaf of the white rose for a moment palpitated at the extremity of the stalk like a butterfly's wing, then it detached itself and flew forth through the open casement, bearing with it the soul of Clarimonde. The lamp was extinguished and I fell insensible upon the bosom of the beautiful dead.

When I came to myself again I was lying on the bed in my little room at the presbytery, and the old dog of the former curé was licking my hand, which had been hanging down outside of the covers. Barbara, all trembling with age and anxiety, was busying herself about the room, opening and shutting drawers, and emptying powders into glasses.

On seeing me open my eyes, the old woman uttered a cry of joy, the dog yelped and wagged his tail, but I was still so weak that I could not speak a single word or make the slightest motion.

Afterward I learned that I had lain thus for three days, giving no evidence of life beyond the faintest respiration. Those three days do not reckon in my life, nor could I ever imagine whither my spirit had departed during those three days; I have no recollection of aught relating to them. Barbara told me that the same coppery-complexioned man who came to seek me on the night of my departure from the presbytery had brought me back the next morning in a close litter, and departed immediately afterward.

When I became able to collect my scattered thoughts, I reviewed within my mind all the circumstances of that fateful night. At first I thought I had been the victim of some magical illusion, but ere long the recollection of other circumstances, real and palpable in themselves, came to forbid that supposition. I could not believe that I had been dreaming, since Barbara as well as myself had seen the strange man with his two black horses, and described with exactness every detail of his figure and apparel. Nevertheless it appeared that none knew of any castle in the neighborhood answering to the description of that in which I had again found Clarimonde.

One morning I found the Abbé Sérapion in my room. Barbara had advised him that I was ill, and he had come with all speed to see me. Although this haste on his part testified to an affectionate interest in me, yet his visit did not cause me the pleasure which it should have done. The Abbé Sérapion had something penetrating and inquisitorial in his gaze which made me feel very ill at ease. His presence filled me with embarrassment and a sense of guilt. At the first glance he divined my interior trouble, and I hated him for his clairvoyance.

While he inquired after my health in hypocritically honeyed accents, he constantly kept his two great yellow lion-eyes fixed upon me, and plunged his look into my soul like a sounding-lead. Then he asked me how I directed my parish, if I was happy in it, how I passed the leisure hours allowed me in the intervals of pastoral duty, whether I had become acquainted with many of the inhabitants of the place, what was my favorite reading, and a thousand other such questions. I answered these inquiries as briefly as possible, and he, without ever waiting for my answers, passed rapidly from one subject of query to another. That conversation had evidently no connection with what he actually wished to say. At last, without any premonition, but as though repeating a piece of news which he had recalled on the instant, and feared might otherwise be forgotten subsequently, he suddenly said, in a clear vibrant voice, which rang in my ears like the trumpets of the Last Judgment:

"The great courtesan Clarimonde died a few days ago, at the close of an orgy which lasted eight days and eight nights. It was something infernally splendid. The abominations of the banquets of Belshazzar and Cleopatra were re-enacted there. Good God, what age are we living in? The guests were served by swarthy slaves who spoke an unknown tongue, and who seemed to me to be veritable demons. The livery of the very least among them would have served for the gala-dress of an emperor. There have always been very strange stories told of this Clarimonde, and all her lovers came to a violent or miserable end. They used to say that she was a ghoul, a female vampire; but I believe she was none other than Beelzebub himself."

He ceased to speak, and commenced to regard me more attentively than ever, as though to observe the effect of his words on me. I could not refrain from starting when I heard him utter the name of Clarimonde, and this news of her death, in addition to the pain it caused me by reason of its coincidence with the nocturnal scenes I had witnessed, filled me with an agony and terror which my face betrayed, despite my utmost endeavors to appear composed. Sérapion fixed an anxious and severe look upon me, and then observed, "My son, I must warn you that you are standing with foot raised upon the brink of an abyss; take heed lest you fall therein. Satan's claws are long, and tombs are not always true to their trust. The tombstone of Clarimonde should be sealed down with a triple seal, for, if report be true, it is not the first time she has died. May God watch over you, Romuald!"

And with these words the Abbé walked slowly to the door. I did not see him again at that time, for he left for S——— almost immediately.

I became completely restored to health and resumed my accustomed duties. The memory of Clarimonde and the words of the old Abbé were constantly in my mind; nevertheless no extraordinary event had occurred to verify the funereal predictions of Sérapion, and I had commenced to believe that his fears and my own terrors were over-exaggerated, when one night I had a strange dream. I had hardly fallen asleep when I heard my bed-curtains drawn apart, as their rings slid back upon the curtain rod with a sharp sound.

I rose up quickly upon my elbow, and beheld the shadow of a woman standing erect before me. I recognized Clarimonde immediately. She bore in her hand a little lamp, shaped like those which are placed in tombs, and its light lent her fingers a rosy transparency, which extended itself by lessening degrees even to the opaque and milky whiteness of her bare arm. Her only garment was the linen winding-sheet which had shrouded her when lying upon the bed of death. She sought to gather its folds over her bosom as though ashamed of being so scantily clad, but her little hand was not equal to the task. She was so white that the color of the drapery blended with that of her flesh under the pallid rays of the lamp. Enveloped with this subtle tissue which betrayed all the contour of her body, she seemed rather the marble statue of some fair antique bather than a woman endowed with life.

But dead or living, statue or woman, shadow or body, her beauty was still the same, only that the green light of her eyes was less brilliant, and her mouth, once so warmly crimson, was only tinted with a faint tender rosiness, like that of her cheeks. The little blue flowers which I had noticed entwined in her hair were withered and dry, and had lost nearly all their leaves, but this did not prevent her from being charming—so charming that, notwithstanding the strange character of the adventure, and the unexplainable manner in which she had entered my room, I felt not even for a moment the least fear.

She placed the lamp on the table and seated herself at the foot of my bed; then bending toward me, she said, in that voice at once silvery clear and yet velvety in its sweet softness, such as I never heard from any lips save hers:

"I have kept thee long in waiting, dear Romuald, and it must have seemed to thee that I had forgotten thee. But I come from afar off, very far off, and from a land whence no other has ever yet returned. There is neither sun nor moon in that land whence I come: all is but space and shadow; there is neither road nor pathway: no earth for the foot, no air for the wing; and nevertheless behold me here, for Love is stronger than Death and must conquer him in the end.

"Oh what sad faces and fearful things I have seen on my way hither! What difficulty my soul, returned to earth through the power of will alone, has had in finding its body and reinstating itself therein! What terrible efforts I had to make ere I could lift the ponderous slab with which they had covered me! See, the palms of my poor hands are all bruised! Kiss them, sweet love, that they may be healed!"

She laid the cold palms of her hands upon my mouth, one after the other. I kissed them, indeed, many times, and she the while watched me with a smile of ineffable affection.

I confess to my shame that I had entirely forgotten the advice of the Abbé Sérapion and the sacred office wherewith I had been invested. I had fallen without resistance, and at the first assault. I had not even made the least effort to repel the tempter. The fresh coolness of Clarimonde's skin penetrated my own, and I felt voluptuous tremors pass over my whole body. Poor child! in spite of all I saw afterward, I can hardly yet believe she was a demon; at least she had no appearance of being such, and never did Satan so skillfully conceal his claws and horns. She had drawn her feet up beneath her, and squatted down on the edge of the couch in an attitude full of negligent coquetry. From time to time she passed her little hand through my hair and twisted it into curls, as though trying how a new style of wearing it would become my face. I abandoned myself to her hands with the most guilty pleasure, while she accompanied her gentle play with the prettiest prattle. The most remarkable fact was that I felt no astonishment whatever at so extraordinary an adventure, and as in dreams one finds no difficulty in accepting the most fantastic events as simple facts, so all these circumstances seemed to me perfectly natural in themselves.

"I loved thee long ere I saw thee, dear Romuald, and sought thee everywhere. Thou wast my dream, and I first saw thee in the church at the fatal moment. I said at once, 'It is he!' I gave thee a look into which I threw all the love I ever had, all the love I now have, all the love I shall ever have for thee—a look that would have damned a cardinal or brought a king to his knees at my feet in view of all his court. Thou remainedst unmoved, preferring thy God to me!

"Ah, how jealous I am of that God whom thou didst love and still lovest more than me!

"Woe is me, unhappy one that I am! I can never have thy heart all to myself, I whom thou didst recall to life with a kiss—dead Clarimonde, who for thy sake bursts asunder the gates of the tomb, and comes to consecrate to thee a life which she has resumed only to make thee happy!"

All her words were accompanied with the most impassioned caresses, which bewildered my sense and my reason to such an extent, that I did not fear to utter a frightful blasphemy for the sake of consoling her, and to declare that I loved her as much as God.

Her eyes rekindled and shone like chrysoprases. "In truth?—in very truth?—as much as God!" she cried, flinging her beautiful arms around me. "Since it is so, thou wilt come with me; thou wilt follow me whithersoever I desire. Thou wilt cast away thy ugly black habit. Thou shalt be the proudest and most envied of cavaliers; thou shalt be my lover! To be the acknowledged lover of Clarimonde, who has refused even a Pope! That will be something to feel proud of. Ah, the fair, unspeakably happy existence, the beautiful golden life we shall live together! And when shall we depart, my fair sir?"

"Tomorrow! Tomorrow!" I cried in my delirium.

"Tomorrow, then, so let it be!" she answered. "In the meanwhile I shall have opportunity to change my clothes, for this is a little too light and in nowise suited for a voyage. I must also forthwith notify all my friends who believe me dead, and mourn for me as deeply as they are capable of doing. The money, the dresses, the carriages—all will be ready. I shall call for thee at this same hour. Adieu, dear heart!"

And she lightly touched my forehead with her lips. The lamp went out, the curtains closed again, and all became dark; a leaden, dreamless sleep fell on me and held me unconscious until the morning following.

I awoke later than usual, and the recollection of this singular adventure troubled me during the whole day. I finally persuaded myself that it was a mere vapor of my heated imagination. Nevertheless its sensations had been so vivid that it was difficult to persuade myself that they were not real, and it was not without some presentiment of what was going to happen that I got into bed at last, after having prayed God to drive far from me all thoughts of evil, and to protect the chastity of my slumber.

I soon fell into a deep sleep, and my dream was continued. The curtains again parted, and I beheld Clarimonde, not as on the former occasion, pale in her pale winding-sheet, with the violets of death upon her cheeks, but gay, sprightly, jaunty, in a superb traveling-dress of green velvet, trimmed with gold lace, and looped up on either side to allow a glimpse of satin petticoat. Her blonde hair escaped in thick ringlets from beneath a broad black felt hat, decorated with white feathers whimsically twisted into various shapes. In one hand she held a little riding-whip terminated by a golden whistle. She tapped me lightly with it, and exclaimed, "Well, my fine sleeper, is this the way you make your preparations? I thought I would find you up and dressed. Arise quickly, we have no time to lose."

I leaped out of bed at once.

"Come, dress yourself, and let us go," she continued, pointing to a little package she had brought with her. "The horses are becoming impatient of delay and champing their bits at the door. We ought to have been by this time at least ten leagues distant from here."

I dressed myself hurriedly, and she handed me the articles of apparel herself one by one, bursting into laughter from time to time at my awkwardness, as she explained to me the use of a garment when I had made a mistake. She hurriedly arranged my hair, and this done, held up before me a little pocket-mirror of Venetian crystal, rimmed with silver filigree-work, and playfully asked, "How dost find thyself now? Wilt engage me for thy valet de chamber?"

I was no longer the same person, and I could not even recognize myself. I resembled my former self no more than a finished statue resembles a block of stone. My old face seemed but a coarse daub of the one reflected in the mirror. I was handsome, and my vanity was sensibly tickled by the metamorphosis. That elegant apparel, that richly embroidered vest had made of me a totally different personage, and I marveled at the power of transformation owned by a few yards of cloth cut after a certain pattern. The spirit of my costume penetrated my very skin and within ten minutes more I had become something of a coxcomb.

In order to feel more at ease in my new attire, I took several turns up and down the room. Clarimonde watched me with an air of maternal pleasure, and appeared well satisfied with her work.

"Come, enough of this child's play! Let us start, Romuald, dear. We have far to go, and we may not get there in time."

She took my hand and led me forth. All the doors opened before her at a touch, and we passed by the dog without awaking him.

At the gate we found Margheritone waiting, the same swarthy groom who had once before been my escort. He held the bridles of three horses, all black like those which bore us to the castle—one for me, one for him, one for Clarimonde. Those horses must have been Spanish genets born of mares fecundated by a zephyr, for they were fleet as the wind itself, and the moon, which had just risen at our departure to light us on the way, rolled over the sky like a wheel detached from her own chariot. We beheld her on the right leaping from tree to tree, and putting herself out of breath in the effort to keep up with us.

Soon we came upon a level plain where, hard by a clump of trees, a carriage with four vigorous horses awaited us. We entered it, and the postillions urged their animals into a mad gallop. I had one arm around Clarimonde's waist, and one of her hands clasped in mine; her head leaned upon my shoulder, and I felt her bosom, half bare, lightly pressing against my arm. I had never known such intense happiness. In that hour I had forgotten everything, and I no more remembered having ever been a priest than I remembered what I had been doing in my mother's womb, so great was the fascination which the evil spirit exerted upon me.

From that night my nature seemed in some sort to have become halved, and there were two men within me, neither of whom knew the other. At one moment I believed myself a priest who dreamed nightly that he was a gentleman, at another that I was a gentleman who dreamed he was a priest. I could no longer distinguish the dream from the reality, nor could I discover where the reality began or where ended the dream. The exquisite young lord and libertine railed at the priest, the priest loathed the dissolute habits of the young lord. Two spirals entangled and confounded the one with the other, yet never touching, would afford a fair representation of this bicephalic life which I lived.

Despite the strange character of my condition, I do not believe that I ever inclined, even for a moment, to madness. I always retained with extreme vividness all the perceptions of my two lives. Only there was one absurd fact which I could not explain to myself—namely, that the consciousness of the same individuality existed in two men so opposite in character. It was an anomaly for which I could not account—whether I believed myself to be the curé of the little village of C———, or *Il Signor Romualdo*, the titled lover of Clarimonde.

Be that as it may, I lived, at least I believed that I lived, in Venice. I have never been able to discover rightly how much of illusion and how much of reality there was in this fantastic adventure. We dwelt in a great palace on the Canaleio, filled with frescoes and statues, and containing two Titians in the noblest style of the great master, which were hung in Clarimonde's chamber. It was a palace well worthy of a king. We had each our gondola, our *barcarolli* in family livery, our music hall, and our special poet. Clarimonde always lived upon a magnificent scale; there was something of Cleopatra in her nature.

As for me, I had the retinue of a prince's son, and I was regarded with as much reverential respect as though I had been of the family of one of the twelve Apostles or the four Evangelists of the Most Serene Republic. I would not have turned aside to allow even the Doge to pass, and I do not believe that since Satan fell from heaven, any creature was ever prouder or more insolent than I. I went to the Ridotto, and played with a luck which seemed absolutely infernal. I received the best of all society—the sons of ruined families, women of the theatre, shrewd knaves, parasites, hectoring swashbucklers.

But notwithstanding the dissipation of such a life, I always remained faithful to Clarimonde. I loved her wildly. She would have excited satiety itself, and chained inconstancy. To have Clarimonde was to have twenty mistresses; ay, to possess all women: so mobile, so varied of aspect, so fresh in new charms was she all in herself—a very chameleon of a woman, in sooth. She made you commit with her the infidelity you would have committed with another, by donning to perfection the character, the attraction, the style of beauty of the woman who appeared to please you.

She returned my love a hundred-fold, and it was in vain that the young patricians and even the Ancients of the Council of Ten made her the most magnificent proposals. A Foscari even went so far as to offer to espouse her. She rejected all his overtures. Of gold she had enough. She wished no longer for anything but love—a love youthful, pure, evoked by herself, and which should be a first and last passion.

I would have been perfectly happy but for a cursed nightmare which recurred every night, and in which I believed myself to be a poor village curé, practicing mortification and penance for my excesses during the day. Reassured by my constant association with her, I never thought further of the strange manner in which I had become acquainted with Clarimonde. But the words of the Abbé Sérapion concerning her recurred often to my memory, and never ceased to cause me uneasiness.

For some time the health of Clarimonde had not been so good as usual; her complexion grew paler day by day. The physicians who were summoned could not comprehend the nature of her malady and knew not how to treat it. They all prescribed some insignificant remedies, and never called a second time. Her paleness, nevertheless, visibly increased, and she became colder and colder, until she seemed almost as white and dead as upon that memorable night in the unknown castle. I grieved with anguish unspeakable to behold her thus slowly perishing; and she, touched by my agony, smiled upon me sweetly and sadly with the fateful smile of those who feel that they must die.

One morning I was seated at her bedside, and breakfasting from a little table placed close at hand, so that I might not be obliged to leave her for a single instant. In the act of cutting some fruit I accidentally inflicted rather a deep gash on my finger. The blood immediately gushed forth in a little purple jet, and a few drops spurted upon Clarimonde. Her eyes flashed, her face suddenly assumed an expression of savage and ferocious joy such as I had never before observed in her. She leaped out of her bed with animal agility—the agility, as it were, of an ape or a cat—and sprang upon my wound, which she commenced to suck with an air of unutterable pleasure. She swallowed the blood in little mouthfuls, slowly and carefully, like a connoisseur tasting a wine from Xeres or Syracuse. Gradually her eyelids half closed, and the pupils of her green eyes became oblong instead of round. From time to time she paused in order to kiss my hand, then she would recommence to press her lips to the lips of the wound in order to coax forth a few more ruddy drops. When she found that the blood would no longer come, she arose with eyes liquid and brilliant, rosier than a May dawn; her face full and fresh, her hand warm and moist—in fine, more beautiful than ever, and in the most perfect health.

"I shall not die! I shall not die!" she cried, clinging to my neck, half mad with joy. "I can love thee yet for a long time. My life is thine, and all that is of me comes from thee. A few drops of thy rich and noble blood, more precious and more potent than all the elixirs of the earth, have given me back life."

This scene long haunted my memory, and inspired me with strange doubts in regard to Clarimonde; and the same evening, when slumber had transported me to my presbytery, I beheld the Abbé Sérapion, graver and more anxious of aspect than ever. He gazed attentively at me, and sorrowfully exclaimed, "Not content with losing your soul, you now desire also to lose your body. Wretched young man, into how terrible a plight have you fallen!"

The tone in which he uttered these words powerfully affected me, but in spite of its vividness even that impression was soon dissipated, and a thousand other cares erased it from my mind. At last one evening, while looking into a mirror whose traitorous position she had not taken into account, I saw Clarimonde in the act of emptying a powder into the cup of spiced wine which she had long been in the habit of preparing after our repasts. I took the cup, feigned to carry it to my lips, and then placed it on the nearest article of furniture as though intending to finish it at my leisure. Taking advantage of a moment when the fair one's back was turned, I threw the contents under the table, after which I retired to my chamber and went to bed, fully resolved not to sleep, but to watch and discover what should come of all this mystery. I did not have to wait long, Clarimonde entered in her nightdress, and having removed her apparel, crept into bed and lay down beside me. When she felt assured that I was asleep, she bared my arm, and drawing a gold pin from her hair, commenced to murmur in a low voice:

"One drop, only one drop! One ruby at the end of my needle. . . . Since thou lovest me yet, I must not die! . . . Ah, poor love! His beautiful blood, so brightly purple, I must drink it. Sleep, my only treasure! Sleep, my god, my child! I will do thee no harm; I will only take of thy life what I must to keep my own from being forever extinguished. But that I love thee so much, I could well resolve to have other lovers whose veins I could drain; but since I have known thee all other men have become hateful to me. . . . Ah, the beautiful arm! How round it is! How white it is! How shall I ever dare to prick this pretty blue vein!"

And while thus murmuring to herself she wept, and I felt her tears raining on my arm as she clasped it with her hands. At last she took the resolve, slightly punctured me with her pin, and commenced to suck up the blood which oozed from the place. Although she swallowed only a few drops, the fear of weakening me soon seized her, and she carefully tied a little band around my arm, afterward rubbing the wound with an unguent which immediately cicatrised it.

Further doubts were impossible. The Abbé Sérapion was right. Notwithstanding this positive knowledge, however, I could not cease to love Clarimonde, and I would gladly of my own accord have given her all the blood she required to sustain her factitious life. Moreover, I felt but little fear of her. The woman seemed to plead with me for the vampire, and what I had already heard and seen sufficed to reassure me completely. In those days I had plenteous veins, which would not have been so easily exhausted as at present; and I would not have thought of bargaining for my blood, drop by drop. I would rather have opened myself the veins of my arm and said to her, "Drink, and may my love infiltrate itself throughout thy body together with my blood!"

I carefully avoided ever making the least reference to the narcotic drink she had prepared for me, or to the incident of the pin, and we lived in the most perfect harmony.

Yet my priestly scruples commenced to torment me more than ever, and I was at a loss to imagine what new penance I could invent in order to mortify and subdue my flesh. Although these visions were involuntary, and though I did not actually participate in anything relating to them, I could not dare to touch the body of Christ with hands so impure and a mind defiled by such debauches whether real or imaginary.

In the effort to avoid falling under the influence of these wearisome hallucinations, I strove to prevent myself from being overcome by sleep. I held my eyelids open with my fingers, and stood for hours together leaning upright against the wall, fighting sleep with all my might; but the dust of drowsiness invariably gathered upon my eyes at last, and finding all resistance useless, I would have to let my arms fall in the extremity of despairing weariness, and the current of slumber would again bear me away to the perfidious shores. Sérapion addressed me with the most vehement exhortations, severely reproaching me for my softness and want of fervor.

Finally, one day when I was more wretched than usual, he said to me, "There is but one way by which you can obtain relief from this continual torment, and though it is an extreme measure it must be made use of; violent diseases require violent remedies. I know where Clarimonde is buried. It is necessary that we shall disinter her remains, and that you shall behold in how pitiable a state the object of your love is. Then you will no longer be tempted to lose your soul for the sake of an unclean corpse devoured by worms and ready to crumble into dust. That will assuredly restore you to yourself."

For my part, I was so tired of this double life that I at once consented, desiring to ascertain beyond a doubt whether a priest or a gentleman had been the victim of delusion. I had become fully resolved either to kill one of the two men within me for the benefit of the other, or else to kill both, for so terrible an existence could not last long and be endured. The Abbé Sérapion provided himself with a mattock, a lever, and a lantern, and at midnight we wended our way to the cemetery of ———, the location and place of which were perfectly familiar to him.

After having directed the rays of the dark lantern upon the inscriptions of several tombs, we came at last upon a great slab, half concealed by huge weeds and devoured by mosses and parasitic plants, whereupon we deciphered the opening lines of the epitaph:

> *Here lies Clarimonde*
> *Who was famed in her lifetime*
> *As the fairest of women.*

"It is here without a doubt," muttered Sérapion, and placing his lantern on the ground, he forced the point of the lever under the edge of the stone and commenced to raise it. The stone yielded, and he proceeded to work with the mattock. Darker and more silent than the night itself, I stood by and watched him do it, while he, bending over his dismal toil, streamed with sweat, panted, and his hard-coming breath seemed to have the harsh tone of a death rattle.

It was a weird scene, and had any persons from without beheld us, they would assuredly have taken us rather for profane wretches and shroud-stealers than for priests of God. There was something grim and fierce in Sérapion's zeal which lent him the air of a demon rather than of an apostle or an angel, and his great aquiline face, with all its stern features, brought out in strong relief by the lantern-light, had something fearsome in it which enhanced the unpleasant fancy.

I felt an icy sweat come out upon my forehead in huge beads, and my hair stood up with a hideous fear. Within the depths of my own heart I felt that the act of the austere Sérapion was an abominable sacrilege; and I could have prayed that a triangle of fire would issue from the entrails of the dark clouds, heavily rolling above us, to reduce him to cinders.

The owls which had been nestling in the cypress-trees, startled by the gleam of the lantern, flew against it from time to time, striking their dusty wings against its panes, and uttering plaintive cries of lamentation; wild foxes yelped in the far darkness, and a thousand sinister noises detached themselves from the silence.

At last Sérapion's mattock struck the coffin itself, making its planks re-echo with a deep sonorous sound, with that terrible sound nothingness utters when stricken. He wrenched apart and tore up the lid, and I beheld Clarimonde, pallid as a figure of marble, with hands joined; her white winding-sheet made but one fold from her head to her feet. A little crimson drop sparkled like a speck of dew at one corner of her colorless mouth.

Sérapion, at this spectacle, burst into fury: "Ah, thou art here, demon! Impure courtesan! Drinker of blood and gold!" And he flung holy water upon the corpse and the coffin, over which he traced the sign of the cross with his sprinkler. Poor Clarimonde had no sooner been touched by the blessed spray than her beautiful body crumbled into dust, and became only a shapeless and frightful mass of cinders and half-calcined bones.

"Behold your mistress, my Lord Romuald!" cried the inexorable priest, as he pointed to these sad remains. "Will you be easily tempted after this to promenade on the Lido or at Fusina with your beauty?"

I covered my face with my hands, a vast ruin had taken place within me. I returned to my presbytery, and the noble Lord Romuald, the lover of Clarimonde, separated himself from the poor priest with whom he had kept such strange company so long.

But once only, the following night, I saw Clarimonde. She said to me, as she had said the first time at the portals of the church, "Unhappy man! Unhappy man! What hast thou done? Wherefore have hearkened to that imbecile priest? Wert thou not happy? And what harm had I ever done thee that thou shouldst violate my poor tomb, and lay bare the miseries of my nothingness? All communication between our souls and our bodies is henceforth forever broken. Adieu! Thou wilt yet regret me!"

She vanished in air as smoke, and I never saw her more.

Alas! she spoke truly indeed. I have regretted her more than once, and I regret her still. My soul's peace has been very dearly bought. The love of God was not too much to replace such a love as hers. And this, brother, is the story of my youth. Never gaze upon a woman, and walk abroad only with eyes ever fixed upon the ground; for however chaste and watchful one may be, the error of a single moment is enough to make one lose eternity.

THE METAMORPHOSES OF A VAMPIRE

Charles Baudelaire

Charles Baudelaire's life was miserable, marked by poverty and disease. He contracted syphilis when young, and the intense pain forced him to resort to alcohol and opium for relief. Baudelaire was a French poet, critic, and short story writer. During his lifetime he was best known for translating Edgar Allan Poe's works into French, and his own works show Poe's influence. It wasn't until after his death that his poetry received recognition. The *Encyclopedia Americana* called Baudelaire "the most influential of all the modern poets."

"Les Métamorphoses du Vampire" ("The Metamorphoses of a Vampire") was originally included in Charles Baudelaire's 1857 masterpiece, *Les Fleurs du Mal* (*Flowers of Evil*). This collection of poetry was deemed too offensive for publication and the French courts confiscated the first edition of the book. Baudelaire was convicted of obscenity and fined. They allowed the book to be published after six poems were removed. The excised poems were later published in the 1866 edition. This was one of those banned poems.

◆　◆　◆

Meanwhile, the woman's strawberry lips
Undulated like a snake on smoldering embers—
Her bust struggling against the restraining bodice—
Released these words with scented musk:
"My mouth is moist and I have the expertise
To dissolve prudishness in the depths of a bed.
Sorrows vanish on my exuberant breasts,
Making mature men gleefully laugh like infants.
For the man who sees me naked,
I'll replace the moon, sun, sky and the stars!
I'm so skilled, my champion, in the voluptuous arts of pleasure,
When I wrap a man in my deadly arms
Or abandon my breasts to his bites—
Shy and lustful, and sensitive and rugged—
On my two soft cushions swooning with emotion.
Impotent angels would damn their souls for me!"

After she had sucked the marrow from my bones,
I turned to her languidly
To return her amorous kiss, and I saw her
As a swollen slimy wineskin, bulging with pus!
I shut my eyes in frigid terror,
And when I opened them in the clear daylight,
At my side, in place of that putrescent figure
That seemed fully gorged on my blood,
Lie vaguely quivering skeletal debris
Creaking shrilly like a weathercock
Or a rusty sign dangling from an iron rod
Swinging in the wind on a chill winter night.

FRANKENSTEIN

(Abbreviated)

Mary Shelley

Mary Shelley was the wife of poet Percy Bysshe Shelley, although she may be better known as the author of the gothic novel *Frankenstein, or The Modern Prometheus*—which is presented here in an abridged form, making it much easier to read. This is one of the great tales from the Romantic Movement. Mary began writing this classic tale when she was eighteen and it was published when she was twenty-one. She was sixteen when she ran away with Percy to France and Switzerland. They married four years later, after his pregnant first wife committed suicide by drowning.

Mary's life was full of tragedy. Her mother died after giving birth to her. Her half sister committed suicide. Her thirteen-day-old premature baby daughter, her year-old daughter, and her three-year-old son all died. She almost died herself from hemorrhaging after a dangerous miscarriage and two weeks later Percy drowned, causing her to have a nervous breakdown and leaving her penniless. She was twenty-four, with a two-year-old son. Shunned by much of English society, she spent the rest of her life struggling to provide for her son and her father. She became an invalid at age forty-nine and died from a brain tumor four years later.

Mary appears to have modeled Victor Frankenstein to some extent on Percy, who, growing up, had a strong interest in alchemy and chemistry. While Frankenstein's explorations involved the living and the dead, Percy was more interested in making explosives.

The idea for *Frankenstein* came to Mary in a nightmare where she saw "the hideous phantasm of a man stretched out, and then, on the working of some powerful engine, show signs of life, and stir with an uneasy, half vital motion." This probably stemmed from listening to discussions Percy had with Lord Byron on galvanism, in which electricity was applied to the faces of convicts to cause involuntary grimaces or to the legs of dead frogs to cause them to make jumping movements as if they were still alive.

◆　◆　◆

August 5th, 17—

To Mrs. Saville, England

So strange an accident has happened to us that I cannot forbear recording it, although it is very probable that you will see me before these papers can come into your possession.

Last Monday (July 31st) we were nearly surrounded by ice, which closed in the ship on all sides, scarcely leaving her the sea-room in which she floated. Our situation was somewhat dangerous, especially as we were compassed round by a very thick fog. We accordingly lay to, hoping that some change would take place in the atmosphere and weather.

About two o'clock the mist cleared away, and we beheld, stretched out in every direction, vast and irregular plains of ice, which seemed to have no end. Some of my comrades groaned, and my own mind began to grow watchful with anxious thoughts, when a strange sight suddenly attracted our attention and diverted our solicitude from our own situation.

We perceived a low carriage, fixed on a sledge and drawn by dogs, pass on towards the north, at the distance of half a mile; a being which had the shape of a man, but apparently of gigantic stature, sat in the sledge and guided the dogs. We watched the rapid progress of the traveler with our telescopes until he was lost among the distant inequalities of the ice. This appearance excited our unqualified wonder. We were, as we believed, many hundred miles from any land; but this apparition seemed to denote that it was not, in reality, so distant as we had supposed. Shut in, however, by ice, it was impossible to follow his track, which we had observed with the greatest attention.

About two hours after this occurrence we heard the ground sea, and before night the ice broke and freed our ship. We, however, lay to until the morning, fearing to encounter in the dark those large loose masses which float about after the breaking up of the ice. I profited of this time to rest for a few hours.

In the morning, however, as soon as it was light, I went upon deck and found all the sailors busy on one side of the vessel, apparently talking to someone in the sea. It was, in fact, a sledge, like that we had seen before, which had drifted towards us in the night on a large fragment of ice. Only one dog remained alive; but there was a human being within it whom the sailors were persuading to enter the vessel. He was not, as the other traveler seemed to be, a savage inhabitant of some undiscovered island, but a European. When I appeared on deck the master said, "Here is our captain, and he will not allow you to perish on the open sea."

On perceiving me, the stranger addressed me in English, although with a foreign accent.

"Before I come on board your vessel," said he, "will you have the kindness to inform me whither you are bound?"

You may conceive my astonishment on hearing such a question addressed to me from a man on the brink of destruction and to whom I should have supposed that my vessel would have been a resource which he would not have exchanged for the most precious wealth the earth can afford. I replied, however, that we were on a voyage of discovery towards the northern pole.

Upon hearing this he appeared satisfied and consented to come on board. Good God! Margaret, if you had seen the man who thus capitulated for his safety, your surprise would have been boundless. His limbs were nearly frozen, and his body dreadfully emaciated by fatigue and suffering. I never saw a man in so wretched a condition. We attempted to carry him into the cabin, but as soon as he had quitted the fresh air he fainted. When my guest was a little recovered I had great trouble to keep off the men, who wished to ask him a thousand questions; but I would not allow him to be tormented by their idle curiosity, in a state of body and mind whose restoration evidently depended upon entire repose. Once, however, the lieutenant asked why he had come so far upon the ice in so strange a vehicle.

His countenance instantly assumed an aspect of the deepest gloom, and he replied, "To seek one who fled from me."

"And did the man whom you pursued travel in the same fashion?"

"Yes."

"Then I fancy we have seen him, for the day before we picked you up we saw some dogs drawing a sledge, with a man in it, across the ice."

This aroused the stranger's attention, and he asked a multitude of questions concerning the route which the demon, as he called him, had pursued.

August 13th, 17—

He is now much recovered from his illness and is continually on the deck, apparently watching for the sledge that preceded his own. Yet, although unhappy, he is not so utterly occupied by his own misery but that he interests himself deeply in the projects of others.

August 19, 17—

Yesterday the stranger said to me, "You may easily perceive, Captain Walton, that I have suffered great and unparalleled misfortunes. I had determined at one time that the memory of these evils should die with me, but you have won me to alter my determination."

He then told me that he would commence his narrative the next day when I should be at leisure. This promise drew from me the warmest thanks. I have resolved every night, when I am not imperatively occupied by my duties, to record, as nearly as possible in his own words, what he has related during the day.

Strange and harrowing must be his story, frightful the storm which embraced the gallant vessel on its course and wrecked it—thus!

I am by birth a Genevese, and my family is one of the most distinguished of that republic. My ancestors had been for many years counselors and syndics, and my father had filled several public situations with honor and reputation. There was a considerable difference between the ages of my parents, but this circumstance seemed to unite them only closer in bonds of devoted affection. During the two years that had elapsed previous to their marriage my father had gradually relinquished all his public functions; and immediately after their union they sought the pleasant climate of Italy.

I, their eldest child, was born at Naples, and as an infant accompanied them in their rambles. I remained for several years their only child. Much as they were attached to each other, they seemed to draw inexhaustible stores of affection from a very mine of love to bestow them upon me. For a long time I was their only care. My mother had much desired to have a daughter, but I continued their single offspring.

One day, when my father had gone by himself to Milan, my mother found a peasant and his wife, hard working, bent down by care and labor, distributing a scanty meal to five hungry babes. Among these there was one which attracted my mother far above all the rest. Her hair was the brightest living gold, and despite the poverty of her clothing, seemed to set a crown of distinction on her head. Her brow was clear and ample, her blue eyes cloudless, and her lips and the molding of her face so expressive of sensibility and sweetness that none could behold her without looking on her as of a distinct species, a being heaven-sent, and bearing a celestial stamp in all her features.

The peasant woman, perceiving that my mother fixed eyes of wonder and admiration on this lovely girl, eagerly communicated her history. She was not her child, but the daughter of a Milanese nobleman. Her mother was a German and had died on giving her birth. The infant had been placed with these good people to nurse: they were better off then. Whether the father had died or still lingered in the dungeons of Austria was not known. His property was confiscated; his child became an orphan and a beggar.

When my father returned from Milan, he found playing with me in the hall of our villa a child fairer than a pictured cherub. The apparition was soon explained. With his permission my mother prevailed on her rustic guardians to yield their charge to her.

Everyone loved Elizabeth. The passionate and almost reverential attachment with which all regarded her became, while I shared it, my pride and my delight. We called each other familiarly by the name of cousin. We were brought up together; there was not quite a year difference in our ages. Elizabeth was of a calmer and more concentrated disposition; but, with all my ardor, I was capable of a more intense application and was more deeply smitten with the thirst for knowledge.

On the birth of a second son, my junior by seven years, my parents gave up entirely their wandering life and fixed themselves in their native country. We possessed a house in Geneva, and a campagne on Belrive, the eastern shore of the lake, at the distance of rather more than a league from the city. We resided principally in the latter, and the lives of my parents were passed in considerable seclusion.

It was my temper to avoid a crowd and to attach myself fervently to a few. I was indifferent, therefore, to my school-fellows in general; but I united myself in the bonds of the closest friendship to one among them. Henry Clerval was the son of a merchant of Geneva. He was a boy of singular talent and fancy. He loved enterprise, hardship, and even danger for its own sake.

No human being could have passed a happier childhood than myself. My parents were possessed by the very spirit of kindness and indulgence. When I mingled with other families I distinctly discerned how peculiarly fortunate my lot was, and gratitude assisted the development of filial love.

My temper was sometimes violent, and my passions vehement; but they were turned to an eager desire to learn, and not to learn all things indiscriminately. I confess that neither the structure of languages, nor the code of governments, nor the politics of various states possessed attractions for me. It was the secrets of heaven and earth that I desired to learn; and whether it was the outward substance of things or the inner spirit of nature and the mysterious soul of man that occupied me, still my inquiries were directed to the metaphysical, or in its highest sense, the physical secrets of the world.

Meanwhile Clerval occupied himself, so to speak, with the moral relations of things. The virtues of heroes and the actions of men were his theme. The saintly soul of Elizabeth shone like a shrine-dedicated lamp in our peaceful home. Her sympathy was ours; her smile, her soft voice were ever there to bless and animate us. She was the living spirit of love to soften and attract.

When I was thirteen years of age we all went on a party of pleasure to the baths near Thonon; the inclemency of the weather obliged us to remain a day confined to the inn. In this house I chanced to find a volume of the works of Cornelius Agrippa. A new light seemed to dawn upon my mind. When I returned home my first care was to procure the whole works of this author, and afterwards of Paracelsus and Albertus Magnus. I read and studied the wild fancies of these writers with delight; they appeared to me treasures known to few besides myself. My father was not scientific, and I was left to struggle with a child's blindness, added to a student's thirst for knowledge. Under the guidance of my new preceptors I entered with the greatest diligence into the search of the philosopher's stone and the elixir of life; but the latter soon obtained my undivided attention. Wealth was an inferior object, but what glory would attend the discovery if I could banish disease from the human frame and render man invulnerable to any but a violent death!

Nor were these my only visions. The raising of ghosts or devils was a promise liberally accorded by my favorite authors, the fulfillment of which I most eagerly sought; and if my incantations were always unsuccessful, I attributed the failure rather to my own inexperience and mistake than to a want of skill or fidelity in my instructors.

When I had attained the age of seventeen my parents resolved that I should become a student at the university of Ingolstadt. I had hitherto attended the schools of Geneva, but my father thought it necessary for the completion of my education that I should be made acquainted with other customs than those of my native country.

My departure was therefore fixed at an early date, but before the day resolved upon could arrive, the first misfortune of my life occurred—an omen, as it were, of my future misery. Elizabeth had caught the scarlet fever; her illness was severe, and she was in the greatest danger. During her illness many arguments had been urged to persuade my mother to refrain from attending upon her, but she attended her sickbed; her watchful attentions triumphed over the malignity of the distemper—Elizabeth was saved, but the consequences of this imprudence were fatal to her preserver. On the third day my mother sickened; her fever was accompanied by the most alarming symptoms. On her deathbed the fortitude and benignity of this best of women did not desert her. She joined the hands of Elizabeth and myself.

"My children," she said, "my firmest hopes of future happiness were placed on the prospect of your union. This expectation will now be the consolation of your father.

"Elizabeth, my love, you must supply my place to my younger children. Alas! I regret that I am taken from you; I will endeavor to resign myself cheerfully to death and will indulge a hope of meeting you in another world."

She died calmly, and her countenance expressed affection even in death. I need not describe the feelings of those whose dearest ties are rent by that most irreparable evil, the void that presents itself to the soul, and the despair that is exhibited on the countenance. It is so long before the mind can persuade itself that she whom we saw every day and whose very existence appeared a part of our own can have departed forever—that the brightness of a beloved eye can have been extinguished and the sound of a voice so familiar and dear to the ear can be hushed, never more to be heard. These are the reflections of the first days; but when the lapse of time proves the reality of the evil, then the actual bitterness of grief commences. Yet from whom has not that rude hand rent away some dear connection? And why should I describe a sorrow which all have felt, and must feel?

The day of my departure at length arrived. Clerval spent the last evening with us. He had endeavored to persuade his father to permit him to accompany me and to become my fellow student, but in vain. His father was a narrow-minded trader and saw idleness and ruin in the aspirations and ambition of his son.

My journey to Ingolstadt was long and fatiguing. The next morning I delivered my letters of introduction and paid a visit to some of the principal professors.

Partly from curiosity and partly from idleness, I went into the lecturing room, which M. Waldman entered shortly after. He appeared about fifty years of age, but with an aspect expressive of the greatest benevolence; a few grey hairs covered his temples, but those at the back of his head were nearly black. His person was short but remarkably erect and his voice the sweetest I had ever heard.

He began his lecture by a recapitulation of the history of chemistry and the various improvements made by different men of learning, pronouncing with fervor the names of the most distinguished discoverers. He then took a cursory view of the present state of the science and explained many of its elementary terms.

After having made a few preparatory experiments, he concluded with a panegyric upon modern chemistry, the terms of which I shall never forget:

"The ancient teachers of this science," said he, "promised impossibilities and performed nothing. The modern masters promise very little; they know that metals cannot be transmuted and that the elixir of life is a chimera but these philosophers, whose hands seem only made to dabble in dirt, and their eyes to pore over the microscope or crucible, have indeed performed miracles. They penetrate into the recesses of nature and show how she works in her hiding-places. They ascend into the heavens; they have discovered how the blood circulates, and the nature of the air we breathe. They have acquired new and almost un-limited powers; they can command the thunders of heaven, mimic the earthquake, and even mock the invisible world with its own shadows."

Such were the professor's words—rather let me say such the words of the fate—enounced to destroy me. So much has been done, ex-claimed the soul of Frankenstein—more, far more, will I achieve; tread-ing in the steps already marked, I will pioneer a new way, explore unknown powers, and unfold to the world the deepest mysteries of creation.

From this day natural philosophy, and particularly chemistry, in the most comprehensive sense of the term, became nearly my sole occupa-tion. My application was at first fluctuating and uncertain; it gained strength as I proceeded and soon became so ardent and eager that the stars often disappeared in the light of morning whilst I was yet engaged in my laboratory.

One of the phenomena which had peculiarly attracted my attention was the structure of the human frame, and, indeed, any animal endued with life. To examine the causes of life, we must first have recourse to death. I became acquainted with the science of anatomy, but this was not sufficient; I must also observe the natural decay and corruption of the human body.

In my education my father had taken the greatest precautions that my mind should be impressed with no supernatural horrors. I do not ever remember to have trembled at a tale of superstition or to have feared the apparition of a spirit. Darkness had no effect upon my fancy, and a churchyard was to me merely the receptacle of bodies deprived of life, which, from being the seat of beauty and strength, had become food for the worm.

Now I was led to examine the cause and progress of this decay and forced to spend days and nights in vaults and charnel-houses. My attention was fixed upon every object the most insupportable to the delicacy of the human feelings. I saw how the fine form of man was degraded and wasted; I beheld the corruption of death succeed to the blooming cheek of life; I saw how the worm inherited the wonders of the eye and brain. I paused, examining and analyzing all the minutiae of causation, as exemplified in the change from life to death, and death to life, until from the midst of this darkness a sudden light broke in upon me—a light so brilliant and wondrous, yet so simple, that while I became dizzy with the immensity of the prospect which it illustrated, I was surprised that among so many men of genius who had directed their inquiries towards the same science, that I alone should be reserved to discover so astonishing a secret.

Remember, I am not recording the vision of a madman. After days and nights of incredible labor and fatigue, I succeeded in discovering the cause of generation and life; nay, more, I became myself capable of bestowing animation upon lifeless matter.

The astonishment which I had at first experienced on this discovery soon gave place to delight and rapture. I was like the Arabian who had been buried with the dead and found a passage to life, aided only by one glimmering and seemingly ineffectual light.

When I found so astonishing a power placed within my hands, I hesitated a long time concerning the manner in which I should employ it. Although I possessed the capacity of bestowing animation, yet to prepare a frame for the reception of it, with all its intricacies of fibers, muscles, and veins, still remained a work of inconceivable difficulty and labor.

I doubted at first whether I should attempt the creation of a being like myself, or one of simpler organization; but my imagination was too much exalted by my first success to permit me to doubt of my ability to give life to an animal as complex and wonderful as man. The materials at present within my command hardly appeared adequate to so arduous an undertaking, but I doubted not that I should ultimately succeed.

I prepared myself for a multitude of reverses; my operations might be incessantly baffled, and at last my work be imperfect, yet when I considered the improvement which every day takes place in science and mechanics, I was encouraged to hope my present attempts would at least lay the foundations of future success.

Nor could I consider the magnitude and complexity of my plan as any argument of its impracticability. It was with these feelings that I began the creation of a human being. As the minuteness of the parts formed a great hindrance to my speed, I resolved, contrary to my first intention, to make the being of a gigantic stature, that is to say, about eight feet in height, and proportionably large. After having formed this determination and having spent some months in successfully collecting and arranging my materials, I began.

No one can conceive the variety of feelings which bore me onwards, like a hurricane, in the first enthusiasm of success. Life and death appeared to me ideal bounds, which I should first break through, and pour a torrent of light into our dark world. A new species would bless me as its creator and source; many happy and excellent natures would owe their being to me. No father could claim the gratitude of his child so completely as I should deserve theirs.

Pursuing these reflections, I thought that if I could bestow animation upon lifeless matter, I might in process of time—although I now found it impossible—renew life where death had apparently devoted the body to corruption.

One secret which I alone possessed was the hope to which I had dedicated myself; and the moon gazed on my midnight labors, while, with unrelaxed and breathless eagerness, I pursued nature to her hiding-places.

Who shall conceive the horrors of my secret toil as I dabbled among the unhallowed damps of the grave or tortured the living animal to animate the lifeless clay? My limbs now tremble, and my eyes swim with the remembrance; but then a resistless and almost frantic impulse urged me forward; I seemed to have lost all soul or sensation but for this one pursuit. I collected bones from charnel-houses and disturbed, with profane fingers, the tremendous secrets of the human frame.

In a solitary chamber, or rather cell, at the top of the house, and separated from all the other apartments by a gallery and staircase, I kept my workshop of filthy creation; my eyeballs were starting from their sockets in attending to the details of my employment. The dissecting room and the slaughter-house furnished many of my materials; and often did my human nature turn with loathing from my occupation, whilst, still urged on by an eagerness which perpetually increased, I brought my work near to a conclusion.

The summer months passed while I was thus engaged, heart and soul, in one pursuit. It was a most beautiful season; never did the fields bestow a more plentiful harvest or the vines yield a more luxuriant vintage, but my eyes were insensible to the charms of nature.

The leaves of that year had withered before my work drew near to a close, and now every day showed me more plainly how well I had succeeded. It was on a dreary night of November that I beheld the accomplishment of my toils. With an anxiety that almost amounted to agony, I collected the instruments of life around me, that I might infuse a spark of being into the lifeless thing that lay at my feet.

It was already one in the morning; the rain pattered dismally against the panes, and my candle was nearly burnt out, when, by the glimmer of the half-extinguished light, I saw the dull yellow eye of the creature open; it breathed hard, and a convulsive motion agitated its limbs.

How can I describe my emotions at this catastrophe, or how delineate the wretch whom with such infinite pains and care I had endeavored to form? His limbs were in proportion, and I had selected his features as beautiful. Beautiful! Great God! His yellow skin scarcely covered the work of muscles and arteries beneath; his hair was of a lustrous black, and flowing; his teeth of a pearly whiteness; but these luxuriances only formed a more horrid contrast with his watery eyes, that seemed almost of the same color as the dun-white sockets in which they were set, his shriveled complexion and straight black lips.

The different accidents of life are not so changeable as the feelings of human nature. I had worked hard for nearly two years, for the sole purpose of infusing life into an inanimate body. For this I had deprived myself of rest and health. I had desired it with an ardor that far exceeded moderation; but now that I had finished, the beauty of the dream vanished, and breathless horror and disgust filled my heart. Unable to endure the aspect of the being I had created, I rushed out of the room and continued a long time traversing my bed-chamber, unable to compose my mind to sleep.

At length lassitude succeeded to the tumult I had before endured, and I threw myself on the bed in my clothes, endeavoring to seek a few moments of forgetfulness. But it was in vain; I slept, indeed, but I was disturbed by the wildest dreams. I thought I saw Elizabeth, in the bloom of health, walking in the streets of Ingolstadt. Delighted and surprised, I embraced her, but as I imprinted the first kiss on her lips, they became livid with the hue of death; her features appeared to change, and I thought that I held the corpse of my dead mother in my arms; a shroud enveloped her form, and I saw the grave-worms crawling in the folds of the flannel.

I started from my sleep with horror; a cold dew covered my forehead, my teeth chattered, and every limb became convulsed; when, by the dim and yellow light of the moon, as it forced its way through the window shutters, I beheld the wretch—the miserable monster whom I had created. He held up the curtain of the bed; and his eyes, if eyes they may be called, were fixed on me. His jaws opened, and he muttered some inarticulate sounds, while a grin wrinkled his cheeks. He might have spoken, but I did not hear; one hand was stretched out, seemingly to detain me, but I escaped and rushed downstairs.

I took refuge in the courtyard belonging to the house which I inhabited, where I remained during the rest of the night, walking up and down in the greatest agitation, listening attentively, catching and fearing each sound as if it were to announce the approach of the demoniacal corpse to which I had so miserably given life.

Oh! No mortal could support the horror of that countenance. A mummy again endued with animation could not be so hideous as that wretch. I had gazed on him while unfinished; he was ugly then, but when those muscles and joints were rendered capable of motion, it became a thing such as even Dante could not have conceived.

Morning, dismal and wet, at length dawned and discovered to my sleepless and aching eyes the church of Ingolstadt, its white steeple and clock, which indicated the sixth hour. The porter opened the gates of the court, which had that night been my asylum, and I issued into the streets, pacing them with quick steps, as if I sought to avoid the wretch whom I feared every turning of the street would present to my view. I did not dare return to the apartment which I inhabited, but felt impelled to hurry on, although drenched by the rain which poured from a black and comfortless sky.

I came at length opposite to the inn at which the various diligences and carriages usually stopped. Here I paused, I knew not why; but I remained some minutes with my eyes fixed on a coach that was coming towards me from the other end of the street. As it drew nearer I observed that it was the Swiss diligence; it stopped just where I was standing, and on the door being opened, I perceived Henry Clerval, who, on seeing me, instantly sprung out.

"My dear Frankenstein," exclaimed he, "how glad I am to see you! How fortunate that you should be here at the very moment of my alighting!"

Nothing could equal my delight on seeing Clerval; his presence brought back to my thoughts my father, Elizabeth, and all those scenes of home so dear to my recollection. I grasped his hand, and in a moment forgot my horror and misfortune; I felt suddenly, and for the first time during many months, calm and serene joy. I welcomed my friend, therefore, in the most cordial manner, and we walked towards my college.

"You may easily believe," said he, "how great was the difficulty to persuade my father that all necessary knowledge was not comprised in the noble art of bookkeeping, but his affection for me at length overcame his dislike of learning and he has permitted me to undertake a voyage of discovery to the land of knowledge."

"It gives me the greatest delight to see you; but tell me how you left my father, brothers, and Elizabeth."

"Very well, and very happy, only a little uneasy that they hear from you so seldom. By the by, I mean to lecture you a little upon their account myself. But, my dear Frankenstein," continued he, stopping short and gazing full in my face, "I did not before remark how very ill you appear; so thin and pale; you look as if you had been watching for several nights."

"You have guessed right; I have lately been so deeply engaged in one occupation that I have not allowed myself sufficient rest, as you see; but I hope, I sincerely hope, that all these employments are now at an end and that I am at length free."

I trembled excessively; I could not endure to think of, and far less to allude to, the occurrences of the preceding night. I walked with a quick pace, and we soon arrived at my college. I then reflected, and the thought made me shiver, that the creature whom I had left in my apartment might still be there, alive and walking about. I dreaded to behold this monster, but I feared still more that Henry should see him.

Entreating him, therefore, to remain a few minutes at the bottom of the stairs, I darted up towards my own room. My hand was already on the lock of the door before I recollected myself. I then paused, and a cold shivering came over me. I threw the door forcibly open, as children are accustomed to do when they expect a specter to stand in waiting for them on the other side; but nothing appeared. I stepped fearfully in: the apartment was empty, and my bedroom was also freed from its hideous guest. I could hardly believe that so great a good fortune could have befallen me, but when I became assured that my enemy had indeed fled, I clapped my hands for joy and ran down to Clerval.

We ascended into my room, and the servant presently brought breakfast; but I was unable to contain myself. It was not joy only that possessed me; I felt my flesh tingle with excess of sensitiveness, and my pulse beat rapidly. I was unable to remain for a single instant in the same place; I jumped over the chairs, clapped my hands, and laughed aloud. Clerval at first attributed my unusual spirits to joy on his arrival, but when he observed me more attentively, he saw a wildness in my eyes for which he could not account, and my loud, unrestrained, heartless laughter frightened and astonished him.

"My dear Victor," cried he, "what, for God's sake, is the matter? Do not laugh in that manner. How ill you are! What is the cause of all this?"

"Do not ask me," cried I, putting my hands before my eyes, for I thought I saw the dreaded specter glide into the room; "*He* can tell. Oh, save me! Save me!"

I imagined that the monster seized me; I struggled furiously and fell down in a fit.

Poor Clerval! What must have been his feelings? A meeting, which he anticipated with such joy, so strangely turned to bitterness. But I was not the witness of his grief, for I was lifeless and did not recover my senses for a long, long time.

This was the commencement of a nervous fever which confined me for several months. During all that time Henry was my only nurse. I was in reality very ill. The form of the monster on whom I had bestowed existence was forever before my eyes, and I raved incessantly concerning him. By very slow degrees, and with frequent relapses that alarmed and grieved my friend, I recovered.

Clerval had never sympathized in my tastes for natural science; and his literary pursuits differed wholly from those which had occupied me. He came to the university with the design of making himself complete master of the oriental languages, and thus he should open a field for the plan of life he had marked out for himself. The Persian, Arabic, and Sanskrit languages engaged his attention, and I was easily induced to enter on the same studies. Idleness had ever been irksome to me, and now that I wished to fly from reflection and hated my former studies, I felt great relief in being the fellow-pupil with my friend, and found not only instruction but consolation in the works of the orientalists.

Summer passed away in these occupations, and my return to Geneva was fixed for the latter end of autumn; but being delayed by several accidents, winter and snow arrived, the roads were deemed impassable, and my journey was retarded until the ensuing spring. I felt this delay very bitterly; for I longed to see my native town and my beloved friends.

The month of May had already commenced, and I expected the letter daily which was to fix the date of my departure, when Henry proposed a pedestrian tour in the environs of Ingolstadt, that I might bid a personal farewell to the country I had so long inhabited. I acceded with pleasure to this proposition: I was fond of exercise, and Clerval had always been my favorite companion in the ramble of this nature that I had taken among the scenes of my native country.

I became the same happy creature who, a few years ago, loved and beloved by all, had no sorrow or care. When happy, inanimate nature had the power of bestowing on me the most delightful sensations. A serene sky and verdant fields filled me with ecstasy. The present season was indeed divine; the flowers of spring bloomed in the hedges, while those of summer were already in bud. We returned to our college on a Sunday afternoon: the peasants were dancing, and everyone we met appeared gay and happy. My own spirits were high, and I bounded along with feelings of unbridled joy and hilarity.

On my return, I found the following letter from my father:

My dear Victor,
You have probably waited impatiently for a letter to fix the date of your
return to us; and I was at first tempted to write only a few lines, merely

mentioning the day on which I should expect you. But that would be a cruel kindness, and I dare not do it. I wish to prepare you for the woeful news, but I know it is impossible; even now your eye skims over the page to seek the words which are to convey to you the horrible tidings.

William is dead!—that sweet child, whose smiles delighted and warmed my heart, who was so gentle, yet so gay! Victor, he is murdered!

I will not attempt to console you; but will simply relate the circumstances of the transaction. Last Thursday (May 7th), I, my niece, and your two brothers, went to walk in Plainpalais. The evening was warm and serene, and we prolonged our walk farther than usual. Presently Ernest came, and enquired if we had seen his brother; he said, that he had been playing with him, that William had run away to hide himself, and that he vainly sought for him, and afterwards waited for a long time, but that he did not return.

This account rather alarmed us, and we continued to search for him until night fell, when Elizabeth conjectured that he might have returned to the house. He was not there. We returned again, with torches; for I could not rest, when I thought that my sweet boy had lost himself, and was exposed to all the damps and dews of night; Elizabeth also suffered extreme anguish. About five in the morning I discovered my lovely boy, whom the night before I had seen blooming and active in health, stretched on the grass livid and motionless; the print of the murderer's finger was on his neck.

He was conveyed home, and the anguish that was visible in my countenance betrayed the secret to Elizabeth. She was very earnest to see the corpse. At first I attempted to prevent her but she persisted, and entering the room where it lay, hastily examined the neck of the victim, and clasping her hands exclaimed, 'O God! I have murdered my darling child!'

She fainted, and was restored with extreme difficulty. When she again lived, it was only to weep and sigh. She told me, that that same evening William had teased her to let him wear a very valuable miniature that she possessed of your mother. This picture is gone, and was *doubtless the temptation which urged the murderer to the deed. We have no trace of him at present, although our exertions to discover him are unremitted; but they will not restore my beloved William!*

Come, dearest Victor; you alone can console Elizabeth. She weeps continually, and accuses herself unjustly as the cause of his death; her words pierce my heart. We are all unhappy; but will not that be an additional motive for you, my son, to return and be our comforter? Your dear mother! Alas, Victor! I now say, Thank God she did not live to witness the cruel, miserable death of her youngest darling!

Your affectionate and afflicted father,
Alphonse Frankenstein
Geneva, May 12th, 17—

Clerval, who had watched my countenance as I read this letter, was surprised to observe the despair that succeeded the joy I at first expressed on receiving news from my friends. I threw the letter on the table, and covered my face with my hands.

"My dear Frankenstein," exclaimed Henry, when he perceived me weep with bitterness, "what has happened?"

I motioned him to take up the letter, while I walked up and down the room in the extremest agitation. Tears also gushed from the eyes of Clerval, as he read the account of my misfortune.

"I can offer you no consolation, my friend," said he; "your disaster is irreparable. What do you intend to do?"

"To go instantly to Geneva: come with me, Henry, to order the horses."

My journey was very melancholy. At first I wished to hurry on, for I longed to console and sympathize with my loved and sorrowing friends; but when I drew near my native town, I slackened my progress. It was completely dark when I arrived in the environs of Geneva; the gates of the town were already shut; and I was obliged to pass the night at Secheron, a village at the distance of half a league from the city.

The sky was serene; and, as I was unable to rest, I resolved to visit the spot where my poor William had been murdered. As I could not pass through the town, I was obliged to cross the lake in a boat to arrive at Plainpalais. During this short voyage I saw the lightning playing on the summit of Mont Blanc in the most beautiful figures. The storm appeared to approach rapidly.

I quitted my seat, and walked on, although the darkness and storm increased every minute, and the thunder burst with a terrific crash over my head. It was echoed from Saleve, the Juras, and the Alps of Savoy; vivid flashes of lightning dazzled my eyes, illuminating the lake, making it appear like a vast sheet of fire; then for an instant everything seemed of a pitchy darkness, until the eye recovered itself from the preceding flash.

While I watched the tempest, so beautiful yet terrific, I wandered on with a hasty step. This noble war in the sky elevated my spirits; I clasped my hands, and exclaimed aloud, "William, dear angel! this is thy funeral, this thy dirge!"

As I said these words, I perceived in the gloom a figure which stole from behind a clump of trees near me; I stood fixed, gazing intently: I could not be mistaken. A flash of lightning illuminated the object, and discovered its shape plainly to me; its gigantic stature, and the deformity of its aspect more hideous than belongs to humanity, instantly informed me that it was the wretch, the filthy demon, to whom I had given life.

What did he there? Could he be the murderer of my brother? No sooner did that idea cross my imagination, than I became convinced of its truth; my teeth chattered, and I was forced to lean against a tree for support. The figure passed me quickly and I lost it in the gloom.

Nothing in human shape could have destroyed the fair child. *He* was the murderer! I thought of pursuing the devil; but it would have been in vain, for another flash discovered him to me hanging among the rocks of the nearly perpendicular ascent of Mont Salève, a hill that bounds Plainpalais on the south. He soon reached the summit and disappeared.

I remained motionless. The thunder ceased; but the rain still continued, and the scene was enveloped in an impenetrable darkness. I revolved in my mind the events which I had until now sought to forget: the whole train of my progress towards the creation. Two years had now nearly elapsed since the night on which he first received life; and was this his first crime? Alas! I had turned loose into the world a depraved wretch, whose delight was in carnage and misery.

No one can conceive the anguish I suffered during the remainder of the night, which I spent, cold and wet, in the open air. But I did not feel the inconvenience of the weather; my imagination was busy in scenes of evil and despair. I considered the being whom I had cast among mankind, and endowed with the will and power to effect purposes of horror, such as the deed which he had now done, nearly in the light of my own vampire, my own spirit let loose from the grave, and forced to destroy all that was dear to me.

Day dawned; and I directed my steps towards the town. The gates were open and I hastened to my father's house. My first thought was to discover what I knew of the murderer and cause instant pursuit to be made, but I paused when I reflected on the story that I had to tell. A being whom I myself had formed and endued with life, had met me at midnight among the precipices of an inaccessible mountain.

I remembered also the nervous fever with which I had been seized just at the time that I dated my creation, and which would give an air of delirium to a tale otherwise so utterly improbable. I well knew that if any other had communicated such a relation to me, I should have looked upon it as the ravings of insanity.

Besides, the strange nature of the animal would elude all pursuit, even if I were so far credited as to persuade my relatives to commence it. And then of what use would be pursuit? Who could arrest a creature capable of scaling the overhanging sides of Mont Salève? These reflections determined me, and I resolved to remain silent.

It was about five in the morning when I entered my father's house. I told the servants not to disturb the family and went into the library to attend their usual hour of rising.

Six years had elapsed, passed in a dream but for one indelible trace, and I stood in the same place where I had last embraced my father before my departure for Ingolstadt. Beloved and venerable parent! he still remained to me. I gazed on the picture of my mother, which stood over the mantel-piece. It was an historical subject, painted at my father's desire, and represented her in an agony of despair, kneeling by the coffin of her dead father. Her garb was rustic, and her cheek pale; but there was an air of dignity and beauty, that hardly permitted the sentiment of pity. Below this picture was a miniature of William; and my tears flowed when I looked upon it.

While I was thus engaged, Ernest entered: he had heard me arrive, and hastened to welcome me:

"Welcome, my dearest Victor," said he. "Ah! I wish you had come three months ago, and then you would have found us all joyous and delighted. You come to us now to share a misery which nothing can alleviate; yet your presence will, I hope, revive our father, who seems sinking under his misfortune; and your persuasions will induce poor Elizabeth to cease her vain and tormenting self-accusations. She most of all requires consolation; she accused herself of having caused the death of my brother, and that made her very wretched. But since the murderer has been discovered—"

"The murderer discovered! Good God! how can that be? who could attempt to pursue him? It is impossible; one might as well try to overtake the winds, or confine a mountain-stream with a straw. I saw him too; he was free last night!"

"I do not know what you mean," replied my brother, in accents of wonder, "but to us the discovery we have made completes our misery. No one would believe it at first; and even now Elizabeth will not be convinced, notwithstanding all the evidence. Indeed, who would credit that Justine Moritz, who was so amiable and fond of all the family, could suddenly become so capable of so frightful, so appalling a crime?"

"Justine Moritz! Poor, poor girl, is she the accused? But it is wrongfully; everyone knows that; no one believes it, surely, Ernest?"

"No one did at first; but several circumstances came out, that have almost forced conviction upon us; and her own behavior has been so confused, as to add to the evidence of facts a weight that, I fear, leaves no hope for doubt. But she will be tried today, and you will then hear all."

He then related that, the morning on which the murder of poor William had been discovered, Justine had been taken ill, and confined to her bed for several days. During this interval, one of the servants, happening to examine the apparel she had worn on the night of the murder, had discovered in her pocket the picture of my mother, which had been judged to be the temptation of the murderer. The servant instantly showed it to one of the others, who, without saying a word to any of the family, went to a magistrate; and, upon their deposition, Justine was apprehended. On being charged with the fact, the poor girl confirmed the suspicion in a great measure by her extreme confusion of manner.

This was a strange tale, but it did not shake my faith; and I replied earnestly, "You are all mistaken; I know the murderer. Justine, poor, good Justine, is innocent."

At that instant my father entered. I saw unhappiness deeply impressed on his countenance, but he endeavored to welcome me cheerfully; and, after we had exchanged our mournful greeting, would have introduced some other topic than that of our disaster, had not Ernest exclaimed, "Good God, papa! Victor says that he knows who was the murderer of poor William."

"We do also, unfortunately," replied my father, "for indeed I had rather have been forever ignorant than have discovered so much depravity and ingratitude in one I valued so highly."

"My dear father, you are mistaken; Justine is innocent."

"If she is, God forbid that she should suffer as guilty. She is to be tried today, and I hope, I sincerely hope, that she will be acquitted."

This speech calmed me. I was firmly convinced in my own mind that Justine, and indeed every human being, was guiltless of this murder. I had no fear, therefore, that any circumstantial evidence could be brought forward strong enough to convict her. My tale was not one to announce publicly; its astounding horror would be looked upon as madness by the vulgar. Did anyone indeed exist, except I, the creator, who would believe, unless his senses convinced him, in the existence of the living monument of presumption and rash ignorance which I had let loose upon the world?

We were soon joined by Elizabeth. Time had altered her since I last beheld her; it had endowed her with loveliness surpassing the beauty of her childish years. There was the same candor, the same vivacity, but it was allied to an expression more full of sensibility and intellect. She welcomed me with the greatest affection.

"Your arrival, my dear cousin," said she, "fills me with hope. You perhaps will find some means to justify my poor guiltless Justine. I rely on her innocence as certainly as I do upon my own. Our misfortune is doubly hard to us; we have not only lost that lovely darling boy, but this poor girl, whom I sincerely love, is to be torn away by even a worse fate."

"She is innocent, my Elizabeth," said I, "and that shall be proved; fear nothing, but let your spirits be cheered by the assurance of her acquittal."

"How kind and generous you are! Everyone else believes in her guilt, and that made me wretched, for I knew that it was impossible: and to see everyone else prejudiced in so deadly a manner rendered me hopeless and despairing."

She wept.

"Dearest niece," said my father, "dry your tears. If she is, as you believe, innocent, rely on the justice of our laws, and the activity with which I shall prevent the slightest shadow of partiality."

We passed a few sad hours until eleven o'clock, when the trial was to commence. My father and the rest of the family being obliged to attend as witnesses, I accompanied them to the court.

During the whole of this wretched mockery of justice I suffered living torture. A thousand times rather would I have confessed myself guilty of the crime ascribed to Justine, but I was absent when it was committed, and such a declaration would have been considered as the ravings of a madman and would not have exculpated her who suffered through me.

The appearance of Justine was calm. She was dressed in mourning, and her countenance, always engaging, was rendered, by the solemnity of her feelings, exquisitely beautiful. Yet she appeared confident in innocence and did not tremble, although gazed on and execrated by thousands, for all the kindness which her beauty might otherwise have excited was obliterated in the minds of the spectators by the imagination of the enormity she was supposed to have committed.

The trial began, and after the advocate against her had stated the charge, several witnesses were called. Several strange facts combined against her. She had been out the whole of the night on which the murder had been committed and towards morning had been perceived by a market-woman not far from the spot where the body of the murdered child had been afterwards found. The woman asked her what she did there, but she looked very strangely and only returned a confused and unintelligible answer.

She returned to the house about eight o'clock, and when one inquired where she had passed the night, she replied that she had been looking for the child and demanded earnestly if anything had been heard concerning him. When shown the body, she fell into violent hysterics and kept her bed for several days. The picture was then produced which the servant had found in her pocket; and when Elizabeth, in a faltering voice, proved that it was the same which, an hour before the child had been missed, she had placed round his neck, a murmur of horror and indignation filled the court.

Justine was called on for her defense. As the trial had proceeded, her countenance had altered. Surprise, horror, and misery were strongly expressed. Sometimes she struggled with her tears, but when she was desired to plead, she collected her powers and spoke in an audible although variable voice.

"God knows," she said, "how entirely I am innocent."

She then related that, by the permission of Elizabeth, she had passed the evening of the night on which the murder had been committed at the house of an aunt at Chene, a village situated at about a league from Geneva. On her return, at about nine o'clock, she met a man who asked her if she had seen anything of the child who was lost. She was alarmed by this account and passed several hours in looking for him, when the gates of Geneva were shut, and she was forced to remain several hours of the night in a barn belonging to a cottage, being unwilling to call up the inhabitants, to whom she was well known.

Most of the night she spent here watching; towards morning she believed that she slept for a few minutes; some steps disturbed her and she awoke. It was dawn and she quitted her asylum, that she might again endeavor to find my brother. If she had gone near the spot where his body lay, it was without her knowledge. That she had been bewildered when questioned by the market-woman was not surprising, since she had passed a sleepless night and the fate of poor William was yet uncertain. Concerning the picture she could give no account.

"I know," continued the unhappy victim, "how heavily and fatally this one circumstance weighs against me, but I have no power of explaining it; and when I have expressed my utter ignorance, I am only left to conjecture concerning the probabilities by which it might have been placed in my pocket. But here also I am checked. I believe that I have no enemy on earth, and none surely would have been so wicked as to destroy me wantonly. Did the murderer place it there? I know of no opportunity afforded him for so doing; or, if I had, why should he have stolen the jewel, to part with it again so soon?

"I commit my cause to the justice of my judges, yet I see no room for hope. I beg permission to have a few witnesses examined concerning my character."

Several witnesses were called who had known her for many years; but fear and hatred of the crime of which they supposed her guilty rendered them timorous and unwilling to come forward. Elizabeth saw even this last resource, her excellent dispositions and irreproachable conduct, about to fail the accused, when, although violently agitated, she desired permission to address the court.

"I am," said she, "the cousin of the unhappy child who was murdered, or rather his sister, for I was educated by and have lived with his parents ever since and even long before his birth. It may therefore be judged indecent in me to come forward on this occasion, but when I see a fellow creature about to perish through the cowardice of her pretended friends, I wish to be allowed to speak, that I may say what I know of her character.

"I am well acquainted with the accused. I have lived in the same house with her, at one time for five and at another for nearly two years. During all that period she appeared to me the most amiable and benevolent of human creatures. She nursed Madame Frankenstein, my aunt, in her last illness, with the greatest affection and care and afterwards attended her own mother during a tedious illness, in a manner that excited the admiration of all who knew her, after which she again lived in my uncle's house, where she was beloved by all the family.

"She was warmly attached to the child who is now dead and acted towards him like a most affectionate mother. I do not hesitate to say that, notwithstanding all the evidence produced against her, I believe and rely on her perfect innocence. She had no temptation for such an action; as to the bauble on which the chief proof rests, if she had earnestly desired it, I should have willingly given it to her, so much do I esteem and value her."

A murmur of approbation followed Elizabeth's simple and powerful appeal, but it was excited by her generous interference, and not in favor of poor Justine, on whom the public indignation was turned with renewed violence, charging her with the blackest ingratitude.

I passed a night of unmingled wretchedness. In the morning I went to the court; my lips and throat were parched. I dared not ask the fatal question, but I was known, and the officer guessed the cause of my visit. The ballots had been thrown; they were all black, and Justine was condemned.

I cannot pretend to describe what I then felt. I had before experienced sensations of horror, and I have endeavored to bestow upon them adequate expressions, but words cannot convey an idea of the heart-sickening despair that I then endured. The person to whom I addressed myself added that Justine had already confessed her guilt.

This was strange and unexpected intelligence; what could it mean? Had my eyes deceived me? And was I really as mad as the whole world would believe me to be if I disclosed the object of my suspicions? I hastened to return home, and Elizabeth eagerly demanded the result.

"My cousin," replied I, "it is decided as you may have expected; all judges had rather that ten innocent should suffer than that one guilty should escape. But she has confessed."

This was a dire blow to poor Elizabeth, who had relied with firmness upon Justine's innocence.

"Alas!" said she. "How shall I ever again believe in human goodness? Justine, whom I loved and esteemed as my sister, how could she put on those smiles of innocence only to betray? Her mild eyes seemed incapable of any severity or guile, and yet she has committed a murder."

Soon after we heard that the poor victim had expressed a desire to see my cousin. The idea of this visit was torture to me, yet I could not refuse. We entered the gloomy prison chamber and beheld Justine sitting on some straw at the farther end; her hands were manacled, and her head rested on her knees. She rose on seeing us enter, and when we were left alone with her, she threw herself at the feet of Elizabeth, weeping bitterly. My cousin wept also.

"Oh, Justine!" said she. "Why did you rob me of my last consolation? I relied on your innocence, and although I was then very wretched, I was not so miserable as I am now."

"I did confess, but I confessed a lie." Her voice was suffocated with sobs. "I confessed, that I might obtain absolution; but now that falsehood lies heavier at my heart than all my other sins. The God of heaven forgive me!

"Ever since I was condemned, my confessor has besieged me; he threatened and menaced, until I almost began to think that I was the monster that he said I was. He threatened excommunication and hell fire in my last moments if I continued obdurate. Dear lady, I had none to support me; all looked on me as a wretch doomed to ignominy and perdition. What could I do? In an evil hour I subscribed to a lie; and now only am I truly miserable."

"Oh, Justine! Forgive me for having for one moment distrusted you. Do not fear. I will proclaim, I will prove your innocence. You, my playfellow, my companion, my sister, perish on the scaffold! No! No!"

Justine shook her head mournfully. "I do not fear to die," she said; "that pang is past. God raises my weakness and gives me courage to endure the worst. I leave a sad and bitter world; and if you remember me and think of me as of one unjustly condemned, I am resigned to the fate awaiting me. Learn from me, dear lady, to submit in patience to the will of heaven!"

During this conversation I had retired to a corner of the prison room, where I could conceal the horrid anguish that possessed me. The poor victim, who on the morrow was to pass the awful boundary between life and death, felt not, as I did, such deep and bitter agony. I, the true murderer, felt the never-dying worm alive in my bosom, which allowed of no hope or consolation.

We stayed several hours with Justine, and it was with great difficulty that Elizabeth could tear herself away. And on the morrow Justine died. Elizabeth's heart-rending eloquence failed to move the judges from their settled conviction in the criminality of the saintly sufferer. My passionate and indignant appeals were lost upon them. She perished on the scaffold as a murderess!

Torn by remorse, horror, and despair, I beheld those I loved spend vain sorrow upon the graves of William and Justine, the first hapless victims to my unhallowed arts.

Sleep fled from my eyes; I wandered like an evil spirit, for I had committed deeds of mischief beyond description horrible. Yet my heart overflowed with kindness and the love of virtue. I had begun life with benevolent intentions and thirsted for the moment when I should put them in practice and make myself useful to my fellow beings. Now all was blasted; instead of that serenity of conscience which allowed me to look back upon the past with self-satisfaction, and from thence to gather promise of new hopes, I was seized by remorse and the sense of guilt, which hurried me away to a hell of intense tortures such as no language can describe.

I lived in daily fear lest the monster whom I had created should perpetrate some new wickedness. I had an obscure feeling that all was not over and that he would still commit some signal crime, which by its enormity should almost efface the recollection of the past. My abhorrence of this fiend cannot be conceived. When I thought of him I gnashed my teeth, my eyes became inflamed, and I ardently wished to extinguish that life which I had so thoughtlessly bestowed. When I reflected on his crimes and malice, my hatred and revenge burst all bounds of moderation. I wished to see him again, that I might wreak the utmost extent of abhorrence on his head and avenge the deaths of William and Justine.

Our house was the house of mourning. My father's health was deeply shaken by the horror of the recent events. Elizabeth was sad and desponding; she no longer took delight in her ordinary occupations; all pleasure seemed to her sacrilege towards the dead; eternal woe and tears she then thought was the just tribute she should pay to innocence so blasted and destroyed. Sometimes I could cope with the sullen despair that overwhelmed me, but sometimes the whirlwind passions of my soul drove me to seek, by bodily exercise and by change of place, some relief from my intolerable sensations.

It was during an access of this kind that I suddenly left my home, and bending my steps towards the near Alpine valleys, sought in the magnificence, the eternity of such scenes to forget myself and my sorrows. I performed the first part of my journey on horseback. I afterwards hired a mule, as the more sure-footed and least liable to receive injury on these rugged roads. The weather was fine; it was about the middle of the month of August, nearly two months after the death of Justine.

The immense mountains and precipices that overhung me on every side, the sound of the river raging among the rocks, and the dashing of the waterfalls around spoke of a power mighty as Omnipotence—and I ceased to fear or to bend before any being less almighty than that which had created and ruled the elements, here displayed in their most terrific guise. Still, as I ascended higher, the valley assumed a more magnificent and astonishing character. Ruined castles hanging on the precipices of piney mountains, the impetuous Arve, and cottages every here and there peeping forth from among the trees formed a scene of singular beauty. But it was augmented and rendered sublime by the mighty Alps, whose white and shining pyramids and domes towered above all, as belonging to another earth, the habitations of another race of beings.

My mule was brought and I resolved to ascend to the summit of Montanvert. I remembered the effect that the view of the tremendous and ever-moving glacier had produced upon my mind when I first saw it. It had then filled me with a sublime ecstasy that gave wings to the soul and allowed it to soar from the obscure world to light and joy.

The ascent is precipitous, but the path is cut into continual and short windings, which enable you to surmount the perpendicularity of the mountain. The path, as you ascend higher, is intersected by ravines of snow, down which stones continually roll from above; one of them is particularly dangerous, as the slightest sound, such as even speaking in a loud voice, produces a concussion of air sufficient to draw destruction upon the head of the speaker.

I looked on the valley beneath; vast mists were rising from the rivers which ran through it and curling in thick wreaths around the opposite mountains, whose summits were hid in the uniform clouds, while rain poured from the dark sky and added to the melancholy impression I received from the objects around me.

It was nearly noon when I arrived at the top of the ascent. For some time I sat upon the rock that overlooks the sea of ice. A mist covered both that and the surrounding mountains. I remained in a recess of the rock, gazing on this wonderful and stupendous scene. The sea, or rather the vast river of ice, wound among its dependent mountains, whose aerial summits hung over its recesses. Their icy and glittering peaks shone in the sunlight over the clouds. My heart, which was before sorrowful, now swelled with something like joy; I exclaimed, "Wandering spirits, if indeed ye wander, and do not rest in your narrow beds, allow me this faint happiness, or take me, as your companion, away from the joys of life."

As I said this I suddenly beheld the figure of a man, at some distance, advancing towards me with superhuman speed. He bounded over the crevices in the ice, among which I had walked with caution; his stature, also, as he approached, seemed to exceed that of man. I was troubled; a mist came over my eyes, and I felt a faintness seize me, but I was quickly restored by the cold gale of the mountains. I perceived, as the shape came nearer, that it was the wretch whom I had created. I trembled with rage and horror, resolving to wait his approach and then close with him in mortal combat.

He approached; his countenance bespoke bitter anguish, combined with disdain and malignity, while its unearthly ugliness rendered it almost too horrible for human eyes. But I scarcely observed this; rage and hatred had at first deprived me of utterance, and I recovered only to overwhelm him with words expressive of furious detestation and contempt.

"Devil," I exclaimed, "do you dare approach me? Begone, vile insect! Or rather, stay, that I may trample you to dust! And, oh! That I could, with the extinction of your miserable existence, restore those victims whom you have so diabolically murdered!"

"I expected this reception," said the demon. "All men hate the wretched; how, then, must I be hated, who am miserable beyond all living things! Yet you, my creator, detest and spurn me, thy creature, to whom thou art bound by ties only dissoluble by the annihilation of one of us. You purpose to kill me. How dare you sport thus with life? Do your duty towards me, and I will do mine towards you and the rest of mankind. If you will comply with my conditions, I will leave them and you at peace; but if you refuse, I will glut the maw of death, until it be satiated with the blood of your remaining friends."

"The tortures of hell are too mild a vengeance for thy crimes. Wretched devil! You reproach me with your creation, come on, then, that I may extinguish the spark which I so negligently bestowed."

My rage was without bounds; I sprang on him, impelled by all the feelings which can arm one being against the existence of another.

He easily eluded me and said, "Be calm! I entreat you to hear me before you give vent to your hatred on my devoted head. Have I not suffered enough, that you seek to increase my misery? Life, although it may only be an accumulation of anguish, is dear to me, and I will defend it. Remember, thou hast made me more powerful than thyself; my height is superior to thine, my joints more supple. But I will not be tempted to set myself in opposition to thee. I am thy creature, and I will be even mild and docile to my natural lord and king if thou wilt also perform thy part, that which thou owest me. Oh, Frankenstein, be not equitable to every other and trample upon me alone, to whom thy justice, and even thy clemency and affection, is most due.

"Remember that I am thy creature; I ought to be thy Adam, but I am rather the fallen angel, whom thou drivest from joy for no misdeed. Everywhere I see bliss, from which I alone am irrevocably excluded. I was benevolent and good; misery made me a fiend. Make me happy, and I shall again be virtuous."

"Begone! I will not hear you. There can be no community between you and me; we are enemies. Begone, or let us try our strength in a fight, in which one must fall."

"How can I move thee? Will no entreaties cause thee to turn a favorable eye upon thy creature, who implores thy goodness and compassion? Believe me, Frankenstein, I was benevolent; my soul glowed with love and humanity; but am I not alone, miserably alone? You, my creator, abhor me; what hope can I gather from your fellow creatures, who owe me nothing? They spurn and hate me. The desert mountains and dreary glaciers are my refuge. I have wandered here many days; the caves of ice, which I only do not fear, are a dwelling to me, and the only one which man does not grudge. These bleak skies I hail, for they are kinder to me than your fellow beings. Yet it is in your power to recompense me. I ask you not to spare me; listen to me, and then, if you can, and if you will, destroy the work of your hands.

"On you it rests, whether I quit forever the neighborhood of man and lead a harmless life, or become the scourge of your fellow creatures and the author of your own speedy ruin."

I was partly urged by curiosity, and compassion confirmed my resolution. I had hitherto supposed him to be the murderer of my brother, and I eagerly sought a confirmation or denial of this opinion. I consented to listen and he thus began his tale.

"It is with considerable difficulty that I remember the original era of my being; all the events of that period appear confused and indistinct. A strange multiplicity of sensations seized me, and I saw, felt, heard, and smelt at the same time; and it was, indeed, a long time before I learned to distinguish between the operations of my various senses. The light became more and more oppressive to me, and the heat wearying me as I walked, I sought a place where I could receive shade. This was the forest near Ingolstadt. I felt cold and half frightened finding myself so desolate. I was a poor, helpless, miserable wretch; I knew, and could distinguish, nothing; but feeling pain invade me on all sides, I sat down and wept.

"Several changes of day and night passed, and the orb of night had greatly lessened, when I began to distinguish my sensations from each other. I gradually saw plainly the clear stream that supplied me with drink and the trees that shaded me with their foliage. I found some of the offals that the travelers had left had been roasted, and tasted much more savory than the berries I gathered from the trees. I tried, therefore, to dress my food in the same manner, placing it on the live embers. I found that the berries were spoiled by this operation, and the nuts and roots much improved. Food, however, became scarce, and I struck across the wood towards the setting sun.

"I passed three days in these rambles and at length discovered the open country. I proceeded across the fields for several hours, until at sunset I arrived at a village. How miraculous did this appear! The huts, the neater cottages, and stately houses engaged my admiration by turns. The vegetables in the gardens, the milk and cheese that I saw placed at the windows of some of the cottages, allured my appetite.

"One of the best of these I entered, but I had hardly placed my foot within the door before the children shrieked, and one of the women fainted. The whole village was roused; some fled, some attacked me, until, grievously bruised by stones and many other kinds of missile weapons, I escaped to the open country and fearfully took refuge in a low hovel, quite bare, and making a wretched appearance after the palaces I had beheld in the village. This hovel, however, joined a cottage of a neat and pleasant appearance, but after my late dearly bought experience, I dared not enter it.

"On examining my dwelling, I found that one of the windows of the cottage had formerly occupied a part of it, but the panes had been filled up with wood. In one of these was a small and almost imperceptible chink through which the eye could just penetrate. Through this crevice a small room was visible, whitewashed and clean but very bare of furniture. In one corner near a small fire sat an old man, leaning his head on his hands in a disconsolate attitude. The young girl was occupied in arranging the cottage. Soon after this the young man returned, bearing on his shoulders a load of wood.

"By great application, and after having remained during the space of several revolutions of the moon in my hovel, I discovered the names that were given to some of the most familiar objects of discourse; I learned and applied the words, 'fire,' 'milk,' 'bread,' and 'wood.' I learned also the names of the cottagers themselves.

"I had admired the perfect forms of my cottagers—their grace, beauty, and delicate complexions; but how was I terrified when I viewed myself in a transparent pool! I became fully convinced that I was in reality the monster that I am, I was filled with the bitterest sensations of despondence and mortification. Alas! I did not yet entirely know the fatal effects of this miserable deformity.

"Of my creation and creator I was absolutely ignorant, but I knew that I possessed no money, no friends, no kind of property. I was not even of the same nature as man. I was more agile than they and could subsist upon coarser diet; I bore the extremes of heat and cold with less injury to my frame; my stature far exceeded theirs. When I looked around I saw and heard of none like me. Was I, then, a monster, a blot upon the earth, from which all men fled and whom all men disowned?

"One night during my accustomed visit to the neighboring wood where I collected my own food and brought home firing for my protectors, I found on the ground a leathern portmanteau containing several articles of dress and some books. The possession of these treasures gave me extreme delight; I now continually studied and exercised my mind upon these, whilst my friends were employed in their ordinary occupations.

"Soon after my arrival in the hovel I discovered some papers in the pocket of the dress which I had taken from your laboratory. At first I had neglected them, but now that I was able to decipher the characters in which they were written, I began to study them with diligence. It was your journal of the four months that preceded my creation. Everything is related in them which bears reference to my accursed origin; the whole detail of that series of disgusting circumstances which produced it is set in view; the minutest description of my odious and loathsome person is given, in language which painted your own horrors and rendered mine indelible. I sickened as I read. 'Hateful day when I received life!' I exclaimed in agony. 'Accursed creator! Why did you form a monster so hideous that even *you* turned from me in disgust?' You had mentioned Geneva as the name of your native town, and towards this place I resolved to proceed.

"I continued to wind among the paths of the wood, until I came to its boundary, which was skirted by a deep and rapid river, into which many of the trees bent their branches, now budding with the fresh spring. Here I paused, not exactly knowing what path to pursue, when I heard the sound of voices, that induced me to conceal myself under the shade of a cypress. I was scarcely hid when a young girl came running towards the spot where I was concealed, laughing, as if she ran from someone in sport.

"She continued her course along the precipitous sides of the river, when suddenly her foot slipped, and she fell into the rapid stream. I rushed from my hiding-place and with extreme labor, from the force of the current, saved her and dragged her to shore. She was senseless, and I endeavored by every means in my power to restore animation, when I was suddenly interrupted by the approach of a rustic, who was probably the person from whom she had playfully fled.

"On seeing me, he darted towards me, and tearing the girl from my arms, hastened towards the deeper parts of the wood. I followed speedily, I hardly knew why; but when the man saw me draw near, he aimed a gun, which he carried, at my body and fired. I sank to the ground, and my injurer, with increased swiftness, escaped into the wood.

"'This was then the reward of my benevolence! I had saved a human being from destruction, and as a recompense I now writhed under the miserable pain of a wound which shattered the flesh and bone. The feelings of kindness and gentleness which I had entertained but a few moments before gave place to hellish rage and gnashing of teeth. Inflamed by pain, I vowed eternal hatred and vengeance to all mankind. But the agony of my wound overcame me; my pulses paused, and I fainted.

"For some weeks I led a miserable life in the woods, endeavoring to cure the wound which I had received. The ball had entered my shoulder, and I knew not whether it had remained there or passed through; at any rate I had no means of extracting it.

"But my toils now drew near a close, and in two months from this time I reached the environs of Geneva. At this time a slight sleep relieved me from the pain of reflection, which was disturbed by the approach of a beautiful child, who came running into the recess I had chosen, with all the sportiveness of infancy. Suddenly, as I gazed on him, an idea seized me that this little creature was unprejudiced and had lived too short a time to have imbibed a horror of deformity. If, therefore, I could seize him and educate him as my companion and friend, I should not be so desolate in this peopled earth.

"Urged by this impulse, I seized on the boy as he passed and drew him towards me. As soon as he beheld my form, he placed his hands before his eyes and uttered a shrill scream; I drew his hand forcibly from his face and said, 'Child, what is the meaning of this? I do not intend to hurt you; listen to me.'

"He struggled violently. 'Let me go,' he cried; 'monster! Ugly wretch! You wish to eat me and tear me to pieces. You are an ogre. Let me go, or I will tell my papa.'

"'Boy, you will never see your father again; you must come with me.'

"'Hideous monster! Let me go. My papa is a syndic—he is M. Frankenstein—he will punish you. You dare not keep me.'

"'Frankenstein! you belong then to my enemy—to him towards whom I have sworn eternal revenge; you shall be my first victim.'

"The child still struggled and loaded me with epithets which carried despair to my heart; I grasped his throat to silence him, and in a moment he lay dead at my feet.

"I gazed on my victim, and my heart swelled with exultation and hellish triumph; clapping my hands, I exclaimed, 'I too can create desolation; my enemy is not invulnerable; this death will carry despair to him, and a thousand other miseries shall torment and destroy him.'

"As I fixed my eyes on the child, I saw something glittering on his breast. I took it; it was a portrait of a most lovely woman. While I was overcome by these feelings, I left the spot where I had committed the murder, and seeking a more secluded hiding-place, I entered a barn which had appeared to me to be empty. A woman was sleeping on some straw. Here, I thought, is one of those whose joy-imparting smiles are bestowed on all but me.

"The sleeper stirred; a thrill of terror ran through me. Should she indeed awake, and see me, and curse me, and denounce the murderer? Thus would she assuredly act if her darkened eyes opened and she beheld me. The thought was madness; it stirred the fiend within me—not I, but she, shall suffer; the murder I have committed because I am forever robbed of all that she could give me, she shall atone. I bent over her and placed the portrait securely in one of the folds of her dress. She moved again and I fled.

"At length I wandered towards these mountains, and have ranged through their immense recesses, consumed by a burning passion which you alone can gratify. We may not part until you have promised to comply with my requisition. I am alone and miserable; man will not associate with me; but one as deformed and horrible as myself would not deny herself to me. My companion must be of the same species and have the same defects. This being you must create. You must create a female for me with whom I can live in the interchange of those sympathies necessary for my being. This you alone can do, and I demand it of you as a right which you must not refuse to concede."

"I do refuse it," I replied; "and no torture shall ever extort a consent from me. Shall I create another like yourself, whose joint wickedness might desolate the world? Begone!"

"You are in the wrong," replied the fiend; "and instead of threatening, I am content to reason with you. I am malicious because I am miserable. I will revenge my injuries; if I cannot inspire love, I will cause fear, and chiefly towards you my arch-enemy. Have a care; I will work at your destruction so that you shall curse the hour of your birth."

A fiendish rage animated him as he said this; his face was wrinkled into contortions too horrible for human eyes to behold; but presently he calmed himself and proceeded—

"I intended to reason. This passion is detrimental to me, for you do not reflect that *you* are the cause of its excess. What I ask of you is reasonable and moderate, and it shall content me. It is true, we shall be monsters, cut off from all the world; but on that account we shall be more attached to one another. Oh! My creator, make me happy; let me feel gratitude towards you for one benefit! Let me see that I excite the sympathy of some existing thing; do not deny me my request!"

I was moved. I shuddered when I thought of the possible consequences of my consent, but I felt that there was some justice in his argument. His tale and the feelings he now expressed proved him to be a creature of fine sensations, and did I not as his maker owe him all the portion of happiness that it was in my power to bestow?

He saw my change of feeling and continued, "If you consent, neither you nor any other human being shall ever see us again; I will go to the vast wilds of South America. My food is not that of man; I do not destroy the lamb and the kid to glut my appetite; acorns and berries afford me sufficient nourishment. My companion will be of the same nature as myself and will be content with the same fare. We shall make our bed of dried leaves; the sun will shine on us as on man and will ripen our food. My life will flow quietly away, and in my dying moments I shall not curse my maker. The picture I present to you is peaceful and human, and you must feel that you could deny it only in the wantonness of power and cruelty."

His words had a strange effect upon me. I compassionated him and sometimes felt a wish to console him, but when I looked upon him, when I saw the filthy mass that moved and talked, my heart sickened and my feelings were altered to those of horror and hatred. I tried to stifle these sensations; I thought that as I could not sympathize with him, I had no right to withhold from him the small portion of happiness which was yet in my power to bestow.

I paused some time to reflect on all he had related and the various arguments which he had employed. After a long pause of reflection I concluded that the justice due both to him and my fellow creatures demanded of me that I should comply with his request.

Turning to him, therefore, I said, "I consent to your demand, on your solemn oath to quit Europe forever, and every other place in the neighborhood of man, as soon as I shall deliver into your hands a female who will accompany you in your exile."

"I swear," he cried. "Depart to your home and commence your labors; I shall watch their progress with unutterable anxiety; and fear not but that when you are ready I shall appear."

Saying this, he suddenly quitted me, fearful, perhaps, of any change in my sentiments. I saw him descend the mountain with greater speed than the flight of an eagle, and quickly lost among the undulations of the sea of ice.

Day after day, week after week, passed away on my return to Geneva; and I could not collect the courage to recommence my work. I feared the vengeance of the disappointed fiend, yet I was unable to overcome my repugnance to the task which was enjoined me. I found that I could not compose a female without again devoting several months to profound study and laborious disquisition. I clung to every pretence of delay and shrank from taking the first step in an undertaking whose immediate necessity began to appear less absolute to me.

A change indeed had taken place in me; my health, which had hitherto declined, was now much restored; and my spirits, when unchecked by the memory of my unhappy promise, rose proportionably. I passed whole days on the lake alone in a little boat, watching the clouds and listening to the rippling of the waves, silent and listless.

It was after my return from one of these rambles that my father, calling me aside, thus addressed me, "I am happy to remark, my dear son, that you have resumed your former pleasures and seem to be returning to yourself. And yet you are still unhappy and still avoid our society. I confess, my son, that I have always looked forward to your marriage with our dear Elizabeth as the tie of our domestic comfort and the stay of my declining years. You, perhaps, regard her as your sister, without any wish that she might become your wife. Nay, you may have met with another whom you may love; and considering yourself as bound in honor to Elizabeth, this struggle may occasion the poignant misery which you appear to feel."

"My dear father, reassure yourself. I love my cousin tenderly and sincerely. I never saw any woman who excited, as Elizabeth does, my warmest admiration and affection. My future hopes and prospects are entirely bound up in the expectation of our union."

"The expression of your sentiments of this subject, my dear Victor, gives me more pleasure than I have for some time experienced. Tell me, therefore, whether you object to an immediate solemnization of the marriage."

I listened to my father in silence and remained for some time incapable of offering any reply. Alas! To me the idea of an immediate union with my Elizabeth was one of horror and dismay. Could I enter into a festival with this deadly weight yet hanging round my neck and bowing me to the ground? I must perform my engagement and let the monster depart with his mate before I allowed myself to enjoy the delight of a union from which I expected peace.

I had an insurmountable aversion to the idea of engaging myself in my loathsome task in my father's house while in habits of familiar intercourse with those I loved. I knew that a thousand fearful accidents might occur, the slightest of which would disclose a tale to thrill all connected with me with horror. I was aware also that I should often lose all self-command, all capacity of hiding the harrowing sensations that would possess me during the progress of my unearthly occupation. I must absent myself from all I loved while thus employed. Once commenced, it would quickly be achieved, and I might be restored to my family in peace and happiness. My promise fulfilled, the monster would depart forever. Or—so my fond fancy imaged—some accident might meanwhile occur to destroy him and put an end to my slavery forever.

The duration of my absence was left to my own choice; a few months, or at most a year, was the period contemplated. One paternal kind precaution he had taken to ensure my having a companion. Without previously communicating with me, he had, in concert with Elizabeth, arranged that Clerval should join me at Strasbourg. This interfered with the solitude I coveted for the prosecution of my task; yet at the commencement of my journey the presence of my friend could in no way be an impediment, and truly I rejoiced that thus I should be saved many hours of lonely, maddening reflection. Nay, Henry might stand between me and the intrusion of my foe. For myself, there was one reward I promised myself from my detested toils—one consolation for my unparalleled sufferings; it was the prospect of that day when I might claim Elizabeth and forget the past in my union with her.

It was in the latter end of September that I again quitted my native country. Sometimes I thought that the fiend followed me and might expedite my remissness by murdering my companion. When these thoughts possessed me, I would not quit Henry for a moment, but followed him as his shadow, to protect him from the fancied rage of his destroyer. I was impatient to arrive at the termination of my journey and accordingly I told Clerval that I wished to make the tour of Scotland alone. Henry wished to dissuade me, but seeing me bent on this plan, ceased to remonstrate.

Having parted from my friend, I determined to visit some remote spot of Scotland and finish my work in solitude. I did not doubt but that the monster followed me and would discover himself to me when I should have finished, that he might receive his companion. With this resolution I traversed the northern highlands and fixed on one of the remotest of the Orkneys as the scene of my labors. It was a place fitted for such a work, being hardly more than a rock whose high sides were continually beaten upon by the waves.

On the whole island there were but three miserable huts, and one of these was vacant when I arrived. This I hired. In this retreat I devoted the morning to labor; but in the evening, when the weather permitted, I walked on the stony beach of the sea to listen to the waves as they roared and dashed at my feet.

Sometimes I could not prevail on myself to enter my laboratory for several days, and at other times I toiled day and night in order to complete my work. It was, indeed, a filthy process in which I was engaged. During my first experiment, a kind of enthusiastic frenzy had blinded me to the horror of my employment; my mind was intently fixed on the consummation of my labor, and my eyes were shut to the horror of my proceedings. But now I went to it in cold blood, and my heart often sickened at the work of my hands. I looked towards its completion with a tremulous and eager hope, which I dared not trust myself to question but which was intermixed with obscure forebodings of evil that made my heart sicken in my bosom.

I sat one evening in my laboratory; the sun had set, and the moon was just rising from the sea; I had not sufficient light for my employment, and I remained idle, in a pause of consideration of whether I should leave my labor for the night or hasten its conclusion by an unremitting attention to it. As I sat, a train of reflection occurred to me which led me to consider the effects of what I was now doing.

Three years before, I was engaged in the same manner and had created a fiend whose unparalleled barbarity had desolated my heart and filled it forever with the bitterest remorse. I was now about to form another being of whose dispositions I was alike ignorant; she might become ten thousand times more malignant than her mate and delight, for its own sake, in murder and wretchedness. He had sworn to quit the neighborhood of man and hide himself in deserts, but she had not; and she, who in all probability was to become a thinking and reasoning animal, might refuse to comply with a compact made before her creation. They might even hate each other; the creature who already lived loathed his own deformity, and might he not conceive a greater abhorrence for it when it came before his eyes in the female form? She also might turn with disgust from him to the superior beauty of man; she might quit him, and he be again alone, exasperated by the fresh provocation of being deserted by one of his own species.

Even if they were to leave Europe and inhabit the deserts of the new world, yet one of the first results of those sympathies for which the demon thirsted would be children, and a race of devils would be propagated upon the earth who might make the very existence of the species of man a condition precarious and full of terror. Had I right, for my own benefit, to inflict this curse upon everlasting generations? I had before been moved by the sophisms of the being I had created; I had been struck senseless by his fiendish threats; but now, for the first time, the wickedness of my promise burst upon me; I shuddered to think that future ages might curse me as their pest, whose selfishness had not hesitated to buy its own peace at the price, perhaps, of the existence of the whole human race.

I trembled and my heart failed within me, when, on looking up, I saw by the light of the moon the demon at the casement. A ghastly grin wrinkled his lips as he gazed on me, where I sat fulfilling the task which he had allotted to me. Yes, he had followed me in my travels; he had loitered in forests, hid himself in caves, or taken refuge in wide and desert heaths; and he now came to mark my progress and claim the fulfillment of my promise.

As I looked on him, his countenance expressed the utmost extent of malice and treachery. I thought with a sensation of madness on my promise of creating another like to him, and trembling with passion, tore to pieces the thing on which I was engaged. The wretch saw me destroy the creature on whose future existence he depended for happiness, and with a howl of devilish despair and revenge, withdrew.

I left the room, and locking the door, made a solemn vow in my own heart never to resume my labors; and then, with trembling steps, I sought my own apartment.

Several hours passed, and I remained near my window gazing on the sea; it was almost motionless, for the winds were hushed, and all nature reposed under the eye of the quiet moon. A few fishing vessels alone specked the water, and now and then the gentle breeze wafted the sound of voices as the fishermen called to one another. I felt the silence, although I was hardly conscious of its extreme profundity, until my ear was suddenly arrested by the paddling of oars near the shore, and a person landed close to my house.

In a few minutes after, I heard the creaking of my door, as if someone endeavored to open it softly. I trembled from head to foot; but I was overcome by the sensation of helplessness, so often felt in frightful dreams, when you in vain endeavor to fly from an impending danger, and was rooted to the spot. Presently I heard the sound of footsteps along the passage; the door opened, and the wretch whom I dreaded appeared.

Shutting the door, he approached me and said in a smothered voice, "You have destroyed the work which you began; what is it that you intend? Do you dare to break your promise?"

"Begone! I do break my promise; never will I create another like yourself, equal in deformity and wickedness."

"Slave, I before reasoned with you, but you have proved yourself unworthy of my condescension. Remember that I have power; you believe yourself miserable, but I can make you so wretched that the light of day will be hateful to you. You are my creator, but I am your master; obey!"

"The hour of my irresolution is past," I replied, "and the period of your power is arrived. Your threats cannot move me to do an act of wickedness; but they confirm me in a determination of not creating you a companion in vice. Shall I, in cool blood, set loose upon the earth a demon whose delight is in death and wretchedness? Begone! I am firm, and your words will only exasperate my rage."

The monster saw my determination in my face and gnashed his teeth in the impotence of anger.

"Shall each man," cried he, "find a wife for his bosom, and each beast have his mate, and I be alone? I had feelings of affection, and they were requited by detestation and scorn. Man! You may hate, but beware! Your hours will pass in dread and misery, and soon the bolt will fall which must ravish from you your happiness forever. I will watch with the wiliness of a snake, that I may sting with its venom. I go; but remember, I shall be with you on your wedding night."

I started forward and exclaimed, "Villain! Before you sign my death-warrant, be sure that you are yourself safe."

I would have seized him, but he eluded me and quitted the house with precipitation. In a few moments I saw him in his boat, which shot across the waters with an arrowy swiftness and was soon lost amidst the waves.

I burnt with rage to pursue the murderer of my peace and precipitate him into the ocean. I walked up and down my room hastily and perturbed, while my imagination conjured up a thousand images to torment and sting me. I thought again of his words—"*I will be with you on your wedding night.*" That, then, was the period fixed for the fulfillment of my destiny. In that hour I should die and at once satisfy and extinguish his malice. The prospect did not move me to fear; yet when I thought of my beloved Elizabeth, of her tears and endless sorrow, when she should find her lover so barbarously snatched from her, tears, the first I had shed for many months, streamed from my eyes, and I resolved not to fall before my enemy without a bitter struggle.

I desired that I might pass my life on that barren rock, wearily, it is true, but uninterrupted by any sudden shock of misery. If I returned, it was to be sacrificed or to see those whom I most loved die under the grasp of a demon whom I had myself created.

I walked about the isle like a restless specter, separated from all it loved and miserable in the separation. I determined to quit my island at the expiration of two days. Yet, before I departed, there was a task to perform, on which I shuddered to reflect; I must pack up my chemical instruments, and for that purpose I must enter the room which had been the scene of my odious work, and I must handle those utensils the sight of which was sickening to me.

The next morning, at daybreak, I summoned sufficient courage and unlocked the door of my laboratory. The remains of the half-finished creature, whom I had destroyed, lay scattered on the floor, and I almost felt as if I had mangled the living flesh of a human being. I paused to collect myself and then entered the chamber. With trembling hand I conveyed the instruments out of the room, but I reflected that I ought not to leave the relics of my work to excite the horror and suspicion of the peasants; and I accordingly put them into a basket, with a great quantity of stones, and laying them up, determined to throw them into the sea that very night; and in the meantime I sat upon the beach, employed in cleaning and arranging my chemical apparatus.

Between two and three in the morning the moon rose; and I then, putting my basket aboard a little skiff, sailed out about four miles from the shore. The scene was perfectly solitary; a few boats were returning towards land, but I sailed away from them. I felt as if I was about the commission of a dreadful crime and avoided with shuddering anxiety any encounter with my fellow creatures.

At one time the moon, which had before been clear, was suddenly overspread by a thick cloud, and I took advantage of the moment of darkness and cast my basket into the sea; I listened to the gurgling sound as it sank and then sailed away from the spot. The sky became clouded, but the air was pure, although chilled by the northeast breeze that was then rising. But it refreshed me and filled me with such agreeable sensations that I resolved to prolong my stay on the water, and fixing the rudder in a direct position, stretched myself at the bottom of the boat. Clouds hid the moon, everything was obscure, and I heard only the sound of the boat as its keel cut through the waves; the murmur lulled me, and in a short time I slept soundly.

I do not know how long I remained in this situation, but when I awoke I found that the sun had already mounted considerably. The wind was high, and the waves continually threatened the safety of my little skiff. I endeavored to change my course but quickly found that if I again made the attempt the boat would be instantly filled with water. Thus situated, my only resource was to drive before the wind. I confess that I felt a few sensations of terror. I had no compass with me and was so slenderly acquainted with the geography of this part of the world that the sun was of little benefit to me. I looked on the heavens, which were covered by clouds that flew before the wind, only to be replaced by others; I looked upon the sea; it was to be my grave.

Some hours passed thus; but by degrees, as the sun declined towards the horizon, the wind died away into a gentle breeze and the sea became free from breakers, when suddenly I saw a line of high land towards the south. I carefully traced the windings of the land and hailed a steeple which I at length saw issuing from behind a small promontory. As I turned the promontory I perceived a small neat town and a good harbor, which I entered, my heart bounding with joy at my unexpected escape.

As I was occupied in fixing the boat and arranging the sails, several people crowded towards the spot. They seemed much surprised at my appearance, but instead of offering me any assistance, whispered together with gestures that at any other time might have produced in me a slight sensation of alarm.

"My good friends," said I, "will you be so kind as to tell me the name of this town and inform me where I am?"

"You will know that soon enough," replied a man with a hoarse voice. "Maybe you are come to a place that will not prove much to your taste, but you will not be consulted as to your quarters, I promise you."

I was exceedingly surprised on receiving so rude an answer from a stranger. I perceived the crowd rapidly increase. Their faces expressed a mixture of curiosity and anger, which annoyed and in some degree alarmed me. I then moved forward, and a murmuring sound arose from the crowd as they followed and surrounded me, when an ill-looking man approaching tapped me on the shoulder and said, "Come, sir, you must follow me to Mr. Kirwin's to give an account of yourself."

"Who is Mr. Kirwin? Why am I to give an account of myself?"

"Mr. Kirwin is a magistrate, and you are to give an account of the death of a gentleman who was found murdered here last night."

This answer startled me, but I presently recovered myself. I was innocent; that could easily be proved. I was soon introduced into the presence of the magistrate, an old benevolent man with calm and mild manners. He looked upon me, however, with some degree of severity, and then, turning towards my conductors, he asked who appeared as witnesses on this occasion.

About half a dozen men came forward; and, one being selected by the magistrate, he deposed that he had been out fishing the night before with his son and brother-in-law, Daniel Nugent, when, about ten o'clock, they observed a strong northerly blast rising, and they accordingly put in for port. It was a very dark night, as the moon had not yet risen. As he was proceeding along the sands, he struck his foot against something and fell at his length on the ground. His companions came up to assist him, and by the light of their lantern they found that he had fallen on the body of a man. It appeared to be a handsome young man, about five and twenty years of age. He had apparently been strangled, for there was no sign of any violence except the black mark of fingers on his neck.

The first part of this deposition did not in the least interest me, but when the mark of the fingers was mentioned I remembered the murder of my brother and felt myself extremely agitated; my limbs trembled, and a mist came over my eyes, which obliged me to lean on a chair for support. The magistrate observed me with a keen eye and of course drew an unfavorable augury from my manner.

The son confirmed his father's account, but when Daniel Nugent was called he swore positively that just before the fall of his companion, he saw a boat, with a single man in it, at a short distance from the shore; and as far as he could judge by the light of a few stars, it was the same boat in which I had just landed. A woman deposed that she lived near the beach and was standing at the door of her cottage, waiting for the return of the fishermen, about an hour before she heard of the discovery of the body, when she saw a boat with only one man in it push off from that part of the shore where the corpse was afterwards found.

Several other men were examined concerning my landing, and they agreed that, with the strong north wind that had arisen during the night, it was very probable that I had beaten about for many hours and had been obliged to return nearly to the same spot from which I had departed. I might have put into the harbor ignorant of the distance of the town from the place where I had deposited the corpse.

Mr. Kirwin, on hearing this evidence, desired that I should be taken into the room where the body lay for interment, that it might be observed what effect the sight of it would produce upon me. I was accordingly conducted, by the magistrate and several other persons, to the inn. I could not help being struck by the strange coincidences that had taken place during this eventful night; but, knowing that I had been conversing with several persons in the island I had inhabited about the time that the body had been found, I was perfectly tranquil as to the consequences of the affair.

I entered the room where the corpse lay and was led up to the coffin. How can I describe my sensations on beholding it? I feel yet parched with horror, nor can I reflect on that terrible moment without shuddering and agony. The examination, the presence of the magistrate and witnesses, passed like a dream from my memory when I saw the lifeless form of Henry Clerval stretched before me. I gasped for breath, and throwing myself on the body, I exclaimed, "Have my machinations deprived you also, my dearest Henry, of life?"

I was carried out of the room in strong convulsions. A fever succeeded to this. I lay for two months on the point of death; my ravings, as I afterwards heard, were frightful; I called myself the murderer of William, of Justine, and of Clerval. Sometimes I entreated my attendants to assist me in the destruction of the fiend by whom I was tormented; and at others I felt the fingers of the monster already grasping my neck, and screamed aloud with agony and terror. Why did I not die? Death snatches away many blooming children, the only hopes of their doting parents; how many brides and youthful lovers have been one day in the bloom of health and hope, and the next a prey for worms and the decay of the tomb! But I was doomed to live and in two months found myself as awaking from a dream, in a prison, stretched on a wretched bed, surrounded by jailers, turnkeys, bolts, and all the miserable apparatus of a dungeon.

The whole series of my life appeared to me as a dream; I sometimes doubted if indeed it were all true, for it never presented itself to my mind with the force of reality.

I was overcome by gloom and misery and often reflected I had better seek death than desire to remain in a world which to me was replete with wretchedness. At one time I considered whether I should not declare myself guilty and suffer the penalty of the law, less innocent than poor Justine had been. Such were my thoughts when the door of my apartment was opened and Mr. Kirwin entered.

"Immediately upon your being taken ill, all the papers that were on your person were brought me, and I examined them that I might discover some trace by which I could send to your relations an account of your misfortune and illness. Your family is perfectly well," said Mr. Kirwin with gentleness; "and your father has come to visit you."

"My father!" cried I, while every feature and every muscle was relaxed from anguish to pleasure. "Is my father indeed come? How kind, how very kind! But where is he?"

He rose and quitted the room with my nurse, and in a moment my father entered it.

Nothing, at this moment, could have given me greater pleasure than the arrival of my father. I stretched out my hand to him and cried, "Are you, then, safe—and Elizabeth—and Ernest?" My father calmed me with assurances of their welfare and endeavored to raise my desponding spirits.

We were not allowed to converse for any length of time, for the precarious state of my health rendered every precaution necessary that could ensure tranquility. Mr. Kirwin came in and insisted that my strength should not be exhausted by too much exertion. But the appearance of my father was to me like that of my good angel, and I gradually recovered my health.

I had already been three months in prison, and although I was still weak and in continual danger of a relapse, I was obliged to travel nearly a hundred miles to the country town where the court was held. The grand jury rejected the bill, on its being proved that I was on the Orkney Islands at the hour the body of my friend was found; and a fortnight after my removal I was liberated from prison.

My father was enraptured on finding me freed from the vexations of a criminal charge, that I was again allowed to breathe the fresh atmosphere and permitted to return to my native country. I did not participate in these feelings, for to me the cup of life was poisoned forever, and although the sun shone upon me, I saw around me nothing but a dense and frightful darkness, penetrated by no light but the glimmer of two eyes that glared upon me.

Yet one duty remained to me. It was necessary that I should return without delay to Geneva, there to watch over the lives of those I so fondly loved and to lie in wait for the murderer, that if any chance led me to the place of his concealment, or if he dared again to blast me by his presence, I might, with unfailing aim, put an end to the existence of the monstrous image which I had endued with the mockery of a soul still more monstrous.

My father still desired to delay our departure, fearful that I could not sustain the fatigues of a journey, for I was a shattered wreck—the shadow of a human being. My strength was gone. I was a mere skeleton, and fever night and day preyed upon my wasted frame. Still, as I urged our leaving with such inquietude and impatience, my father thought it best to yield. A few days before we left, I received the following letter from Elizabeth:

My dear Friend,

My poor cousin, how much you must have suffered! This winter has been passed most miserably, tortured as I have been by anxious suspense; yet I hope to find that your heart is not totally void of comfort and tranquility.

Yet I fear that the same feelings now exist that made you so miserable a year ago, even perhaps augmented by time. You well know, Victor, that our union had been the favorite plan of your parents ever since our infancy. But as brother and sister often entertain a lively affection towards each other without desiring a more intimate union, may not such also be our case? Tell me, dearest Victor. Answer me, I conjure you by our mutual happiness, with simple truth—Do you not love another?

I confess to you, my friend, that when I saw you last autumn so unhappy, flying to solitude from the society of every creature, I could not help supposing that you might regret our connection and believe yourself bound in honor to fulfill the wishes of your parents. I confess to you, my friend, that I love you and that in my airy dreams of futurity you have been my constant friend and companion. But it is your happiness I desire as well as my own when I declare to you that our marriage would render me eternally miserable unless it were the dictate of your own free choice. Ah! Victor, be assured that your cousin and playmate has too sincere a love for you not to be made miserable by this supposition.

Elizabeth Lavenza
Geneva, May 18th, 17—

This letter revived in my memory what I had before forgotten, the threat of the fiend—"*I will be with you on your wedding night!*" Such was my sentence, and on that night would the demon employ every art to destroy me and tear me from the glimpse of happiness which promised partly to console my sufferings. On that night he had determined to consummate his crimes by my death. Well, be it so; a deadly struggle would then assuredly take place, in which if he were victorious I should be at peace and his power over me be at an end. If he were vanquished, I should be a free man.

In this state of mind I wrote to Elizabeth. My letter was calm and affectionate.

"I fear, my beloved girl," I said, "little happiness remains for us on earth; yet all that I may one day enjoy is centered in you. Chase away your idle fears; to you alone do I consecrate my life and my endeavors for contentment. I have one secret, Elizabeth, a dreadful one; when revealed to you, it will chill your frame with horror, and then, far from being surprised at my misery, you will only wonder that I survive what I have endured. I will confide this tale of misery and terror to you the day after our marriage shall take place, for, my sweet cousin, there must be perfect confidence between us. But until then, I conjure you, do not mention or allude to it. This I most earnestly entreat, and I know you will comply."

In about a week after the arrival of Elizabeth's letter we returned to Geneva. The sweet girl welcomed me with warm affection, yet tears were in her eyes as she beheld my emaciated frame and feverish cheeks.

I saw a change in her also. She was thinner and had lost much of that heavenly vivacity that had before charmed me; but her gentleness and soft looks of compassion made her a more fit companion for one blasted and miserable as I was.

The tranquility which I now enjoyed did not endure. Memory brought madness with it, and when I thought of what had passed, a real insanity possessed me; sometimes I was furious and burnt with rage, sometimes low and despondent.

Great God! If for one instant I had thought what might be the hellish intention of my fiendish adversary, I would rather have banished myself forever from my native country and wandered a friendless outcast over the earth than have consented to this miserable marriage. But, as if possessed of magic powers, the monster had blinded me to his real intentions; and when I thought that I had prepared only my own death, I hastened that of a far dearer victim.

As the period fixed for our marriage drew nearer, whether from cowardice or a prophetic feeling, I felt my heart sink within me. But I concealed my feelings by an appearance of hilarity that brought smiles and joy to the countenance of my father, but hardly deceived the ever-watchful and nicer eye of Elizabeth. She looked forward to our union with placid contentment, not unmingled with a little fear that what now appeared certain and tangible happiness might soon dissipate into an airy dream.

Through my father's exertions a part of the inheritance of Elizabeth had been restored to her by the Austrian government. A small possession on the shores of Como belonged to her. It was agreed that, immediately after our union, we should proceed to Villa Lavenza and spend our first days of happiness beside the beautiful lake near which it stood.

In the meantime I took every precaution to defend my person in case the fiend should openly attack me. I carried pistols and a dagger constantly about me. Indeed, as the period approached, the threat appeared more as a delusion, while the happiness I hoped for in my marriage wore a greater appearance of certainty as the day fixed drew nearer.

After the ceremony was performed a large party assembled at my father's, but it was agreed that Elizabeth and I should commence our journey by water, sleeping that night at Evian and continuing our voyage on the following day. The day was fair, the wind favorable; all smiled on our nuptial embarkation.

I took the hand of Elizabeth. "You are sorrowful, my love. Ah! If you knew what I have suffered and what I may yet endure, you would endeavor to let me taste the quiet and freedom from despair that this one day at least permits me to enjoy."

"Be happy, my dear Victor," replied Elizabeth; "there is, I hope, nothing to distress you; and be assured that if a lively joy is not painted in my face, my heart is contented. Observe how fast we move along and how the clouds, which sometimes obscure and sometimes rise above the dome of Mont Blanc, render this scene of beauty still more interesting. Look also at the innumerable fish that are swimming in the clear waters, where we can distinguish every pebble that lies at the bottom. What a divine day! How happy and serene all nature appears!"

Thus Elizabeth endeavored to divert her thoughts and mine from all reflection upon melancholy subjects.

The wind, which had hitherto carried us along with amazing rapidity, sank at sunset to a light breeze; the soft air just ruffled the water and caused a pleasant motion among the trees as we approached the shore, from which it wafted the most delightful scent of flowers and hay. The sun sank beneath the horizon as we landed, and as I touched the shore I felt those cares and fears revive which soon were to clasp me and cling to me forever.

It was eight o'clock when we landed; we walked for a short time on the shore, enjoying the transitory light, and then retired to the inn and contemplated the lovely scene of waters, woods, and mountains, obscured in darkness, yet still displaying their black outlines.

The wind, which had fallen in the south, now rose with great violence in the west. Suddenly a heavy storm of rain descended.

I had been calm during the day, but so soon as night obscured the
shapes of objects, a thousand fears arose in my mind. I was anxious and
watchful, while my right hand grasped a pistol which was hidden in my
bosom; every sound terrified me, but I resolved that I would sell my life
dearly and not shrink from the conflict until my own life or that of my
adversary was extinguished. Elizabeth observed my agitation for some
time in timid and fearful silence, but there was something in my glance
which communicated terror to her, and trembling, she asked, "What is
it that agitates you, my dear Victor? What is it you fear?"

"Oh! Peace, peace, my love," replied I; "this night, and all will be safe;
but this night is dreadful, very dreadful."

I passed an hour in this state of mind, when suddenly I reflected
how fearful the combat which I momentarily expected would be to my
wife, and I earnestly entreated her to retire, resolving not to join her
until I had obtained some knowledge as to the situation of my enemy.

She left me, and I continued some time walking up and down the
passages of the house and inspecting every corner that might afford a
retreat to my adversary. But I discovered no trace of him and was beginning to conjecture that some fortunate chance had intervened to prevent the execution of his menaces when suddenly I heard a shrill and
dreadful scream. It came from the room into which Elizabeth had retired. As I heard it, the whole truth rushed into my mind. The scream
was repeated and I rushed into the room.

She was there, lifeless and inanimate, thrown across the bed, her
head hanging down and her pale and distorted features half covered by
her hair. Everywhere I turn I see the same figure—her bloodless arms
and relaxed form flung by the murderer on its bridal bier. Could I behold this and live? Alas! Life is obstinate and clings closest where it is
most hated.

I rushed towards her and embraced her with ardor, but the deadly
languor and coldness of the limbs told me that what I now held in my

arms had ceased to be the Elizabeth whom I had loved and cherished. The murderous mark of the fiend's grasp was on her neck, and the breath had ceased to issue from her lips.

While I still hung over her in the agony of despair, I happened to look up. The windows of the room had before been darkened, and I felt a kind of panic on seeing the pale yellow light of the moon illuminate the chamber. The shutters had been thrown back, and with a sensation of horror not to be described, I saw at the open window a figure the most hideous and abhorred. A grin was on the face of the monster; he seemed to jeer, as with his fiendish finger he pointed towards the corpse of my wife. I rushed towards the window, and drawing a pistol from my bosom, fired; but he eluded me, leaped from his station, and running with the swiftness of lightning, plunged into the lake.

The report of the pistol brought a crowd into the room. I pointed to the spot where he had disappeared, and we followed the track with boats; nets were cast, but in vain. After passing several hours, we returned hopeless, most of my companions believing it to have been a form conjured up by my fancy. After having landed, they proceeded to search the country, parties going in different directions among the woods and vines.

I attempted to accompany them and proceeded a short distance from the house, but my head whirled round, my steps were like those of a drunken man, I fell at last in a state of utter exhaustion; a film covered my eyes, and my skin was parched with the heat of fever. In this state I was carried back and placed on a bed, hardly conscious of what had happened; my eyes wandered round the room as if to seek something that I had lost.

After an interval I arose, and as if by instinct, crawled into the room where the corpse of my beloved lay. I was bewildered, in a cloud of wonder and horror. The death of William, the execution of Justine, the murder of Clerval, and lastly of my wife; even at that moment I knew not that my only remaining friends were safe from the malignity of the fiend; my father even now might be writhing under his grasp, and

Ernest might be dead at his feet. This idea made me shudder and recalled me to action. I started up and resolved to return to Geneva with all possible speed.

Mine has been a tale of horrors; I have reached their acme, and what I must now relate can but be tedious to you. I arrived at Geneva. My father and Ernest yet lived, but the former sunk under the tidings that I bore. I see him now, excellent and venerable old man! His eyes wandered in vacancy, for they had lost their charm and their delight. He could not live under the horrors that were accumulated around him; the springs of existence suddenly gave way; he was unable to rise from his bed, and in a few days he died in my arms.

What then became of me? I know not; I lost sensation, and chains and darkness were the only objects that pressed upon me. Sometimes, indeed, I dreamt that I wandered in flowery meadows and pleasant vales with the friends of my youth, but I awoke and found myself in a dungeon. Melancholy followed, but by degrees I gained a clear conception of my miseries and situation and was then released from my prison. For they had called me mad, and during many months, as I understood, a solitary cell had been my habitation.

As the memory of past misfortunes pressed upon me, I began to reflect on their cause—the monster whom I had created, the miserable demon whom I had sent abroad into the world for my destruction. I was possessed by a maddening rage when I thought of him, and desired and ardently prayed that I might have him within my grasp to wreak a great and signal revenge on his cursed head. I had formed in my heart a resolution to pursue my destroyer to death, and this purpose quieted my agony and for an interval reconciled me to life.

My first resolution was to quit Geneva forever; my country, which now, in my adversity, became hateful. I provided myself with a sum of money, together with a few jewels which had belonged to my mother, and departed. And now my wanderings began which are to cease but with life. I have traversed a vast portion of the earth and have endured all the hardships which travelers in deserts and barbarous countries are wont to meet. But revenge kept me alive; I dared not die and leave my adversary in being.

When I quitted Geneva my first labor was to gain some clue by which I might trace the steps of my fiendish enemy. But my plan was unsettled, and I wandered many hours round the confines of the town, uncertain what path I should pursue. As night approached I found myself at the entrance of the cemetery where William, Elizabeth, and my father reposed. I entered it and approached the tomb which marked their graves. Everything was silent except the leaves of the trees, which were gently agitated by the wind; the night was nearly dark, and the scene would have been solemn and affecting even to an uninterested observer. The spirits of the departed seemed to flit around and to cast a shadow, which was felt but not seen, around the head of the mourner.

The deep grief which this scene had at first excited quickly gave way to rage and despair. I knelt on the grass and kissed the earth and with quivering lips exclaimed, "By the shades that wander near me, I swear to pursue the demon who caused this misery, until he or I shall perish in mortal conflict. And I call on you, spirits of the dead, and on you, wandering ministers of vengeance, to aid and conduct me in my work. Let the cursed and hellish monster drink deep of agony; let him feel the despair that now torments me."

I had begun my adjuration with solemnity and an awe which almost assured me that the shades of my murdered friends heard and approved my devotion. I was answered through the stillness of night by a loud and fiendish laugh. It rang on my ears long and heavily; the mountains re-echoed it, and I felt as if all hell surrounded me with mockery and laughter. The laughter died away, when a well-known and abhorred voice, apparently close to my ear, addressed me in an audible whisper, "I am satisfied, miserable wretch! You have determined to live, and I am satisfied."

I darted towards the spot from which the sound proceeded, but the devil eluded my grasp. Suddenly the broad disk of the moon arose and shone full upon his ghastly and distorted shape as he fled with more than mortal speed.

I pursued him, and for many months this has been my task. Guided by a slight clue, I followed the windings of the Rhone, but vainly. The blue Mediterranean appeared, and by a strange chance, I saw the fiend enter by night and hide himself in a vessel bound for the Black Sea. I took my passage in the same ship, but he escaped, I know not how.

Amidst the wilds of Tartary and Russia, although he still evaded me, I have ever followed in his track. Sometimes the peasants, scared by this horrid apparition, informed me of his path; sometimes he himself, who feared that if I lost all trace of him I should despair and die, left some mark to guide me. The snows descended on my head, and I saw the print of his huge step on the white plain. Sometimes, when nature, overcome by hunger, sank under the exhaustion, a repast was prepared for me in the desert that restored and inspirited me. The fare was, indeed, coarse, such as the peasants of the country ate, but I will not doubt that it was set there by the spirits that I had invoked to aid me. Often, when all was dry, the heavens cloudless, and I was parched by thirst, a slight cloud would bedim the sky, shed the few drops that revived me, and vanish.

I followed, when I could, the courses of the rivers; but the demon generally avoided these, as it was here that the population of the country chiefly collected. In other places human beings were seldom seen, and I generally subsisted on the wild animals that crossed my path. I had money with me and gained the friendship of the villagers by distributing it; or I brought with me some food that I had killed, which, after taking a small part, I always presented to those who had provided me with fire and utensils for cooking.

Sometimes, indeed, he left marks in writing on the barks of the trees or cut in stone that guided me and instigated my fury.

"My reign is not yet over"—these words were legible in one of these inscriptions—"you live, and my power is complete. Follow me; I seek the everlasting ices of the north, where you will feel the misery of cold and frost, to which I am impassive. You will find near this place, if you follow not too tardily, a dead hare; eat and be refreshed. Come on, my enemy; we have yet to wrestle for our lives, but many hard and miserable hours must you endure until that period shall arrive."

I had procured a sledge and dogs and thus traversed the snows with inconceivable speed. I found that, as before I had daily lost ground in the pursuit, I now gained on him, so much so that when I first saw the ocean he was but one day's journey in advance, and I hoped to intercept him before he should reach the beach. With new courage, therefore, I pressed on, and in two days arrived at a wretched hamlet on the seashore.

I inquired of the inhabitants concerning the fiend and gained accurate information. A gigantic monster, they said, had arrived the night before, armed with a gun and many pistols, putting to flight the inhabitants of a solitary cottage through fear of his terrific appearance. He had carried off their store of winter food, and placing it in a sledge, to draw which he had seized on a numerous drove of trained dogs, he had harnessed them, and the same night, to the joy of the horror-struck villagers, had pursued his journey across the sea in a direction that led to no land; and they conjectured that he must speedily be destroyed by the breaking of the ice or frozen by the eternal frosts.

He had escaped me, and I must commence a destructive and almost endless journey across the mountainous ices of the ocean, amidst cold that few of the inhabitants could long endure and which I, the native of a genial and sunny climate, could not hope to survive. After a slight repose, during which the spirits of the dead hovered round and instigated me to toil and revenge, I prepared for my journey. I exchanged my land-sledge for one fashioned for the inequalities of the frozen ocean, and purchasing a plentiful stock of provisions, I departed from land.

I cannot guess how many days have passed since then. Immense and rugged mountains of ice often barred up my passage, and I often heard the thunder of the ground sea, which threatened my destruction. But again the frost came and made the paths of the sea secure.

By the quantity of provision which I had consumed, I should guess that I had passed three weeks in this journey. Once, after the poor animals that conveyed me had with incredible toil gained the summit of a sloping ice mountain, and one, sinking under his fatigue, died, I viewed the expanse before me with anguish, when suddenly my eye caught a dark speck upon the dusky plain. I disencumbered the dogs of their dead companion, gave them a plentiful portion of food, and after an hour's rest, which was absolutely necessary, and yet which was bitterly irksome to me, I continued my route. The sledge was still visible, nor did I again lose sight of it except at the moments when for a short time some ice-rock concealed it with its intervening crags. I indeed perceptibly gained on it, and when, after nearly two days' journey, I beheld my enemy at no more than a mile distant, my heart bounded within me.

But now, when I appeared almost within grasp of my foe, my hopes were suddenly extinguished, and I lost all trace of him more utterly than I had ever done before. I pressed on, but in vain. The wind arose; the sea roared; and, as with the mighty shock of an earthquake, it split and cracked with a tremendous and overwhelming sound. The work was soon finished; in a few minutes a tumultuous sea rolled between me and my enemy, and I was left drifting on a scattered piece of ice that was continually lessening and thus preparing for me a hideous death.

In this manner many appalling hours passed; several of my dogs died, and I myself was about to sink under the accumulation of distress when I saw your vessel riding at anchor and holding forth to me hopes of succor and life. I had no conception that vessels ever came so far north and was astounded at the sight.

I quickly destroyed part of my sledge to construct oars, and by these means was enabled, with infinite fatigue, to move my ice raft in the direction of your ship. I had determined, if you were going southwards, still to trust myself to the mercy of the seas rather than abandon my purpose. I hoped to induce you to grant me a boat with which I could pursue my enemy. But your direction was northwards. You took me on board when my vigor was exhausted, and I should soon have sunk under my multiplied hardships into a death which I still dread, for my task is unfulfilled.

Yet, when I am dead, if he should appear, if the ministers of vengeance should conduct him to you, swear that he shall not live—swear that he shall not triumph over my accumulated woes and survive to add to the list of his dark crimes. Thrust your sword into his heart. I will hover near and direct the steel aright.

Captain Walton, in continuation.

August 26th, 17—
You have read this strange and terrific story, Margaret; and do you not feel your blood congeal with horror, like that which even now curdles mine? His tale is connected and told with an appearance of the simplest truth, yet I own to you that the monster seen from our ship, brought to me a greater conviction of the truth of his narrative than his asseverations, however earnest and connected. Such a monster has, then, really existence! I cannot doubt it, yet I am lost in surprise and admiration. Sometimes I endeavored to gain from Frankenstein the particulars of his creature's formation, but on this point he was impenetrable.

"Are you mad, my friend?" said he. "Or whither does your senseless curiosity lead you? Would you also create for yourself and the world a demoniacal enemy? Peace, peace! Learn my miseries and do not seek to increase your own."

Frankenstein discovered that I made notes concerning his history; he asked to see them and then himself corrected and augmented them in many places, but principally in giving the life and spirit to the conversations he held with his enemy.

"When younger," said he, "I believed myself destined for some great enterprise. My feelings are profound, but I possessed a coolness of judgment that fitted me for illustrious achievements. When I reflected on the work I had completed, no less a one than the creation of a sensitive and rational animal, I could not rank myself with the herd of common projectors. My imagination was vivid, yet my powers of analysis and application were intense; by the union of these qualities I conceived the idea and executed the creation of a man."

September 2nd

My beloved Sister,

I write to you, encompassed by peril and ignorant whether I am ever doomed to see again dear England and the dearer friends that inhabit it. I am surrounded by mountains of ice which admit of no escape and threaten every moment to crush my vessel. The brave fellows whom I have persuaded to be my companions look towards me for aid, but I have none to bestow. There is something terribly appalling in our situation, yet my courage and hopes do not desert me. Yet it is terrible to reflect that the lives of all these men are endangered through me. If we are lost, my mad schemes are the cause.

And what, Margaret, will be the state of your mind? You will not hear of my destruction, and you will anxiously await my return. Years will pass, and you will have visitings of despair and yet be tortured by hope.

My unfortunate guest regards me with the tenderest compassion. He endeavors to fill me with hope and talks as if life were a possession which he valued. He reminds me how often the same accidents have happened to other navigators who have attempted this sea, and in spite of myself, he fills me with cheerful auguries. Even the sailors feel the power of his eloquence; when he speaks, they no longer despair.

September 12th

It is past; I am returning to England. I have lost my hopes of utility and glory; I have lost my friend. But I will endeavor to detail these bitter circumstances to you, my dear sister; and while I am wafted towards England and towards you, I will not despond.

September 9th, the ice began to move, and roarings like thunder were heard at a distance as the islands split and cracked in every direction. We were in the most imminent peril, but as we could only remain passive, my chief attention was occupied by my unfortunate guest whose illness increased in such a degree that he was entirely confined to his bed. The ice cracked behind us and was driven with force towards the north; a breeze sprang from the west, and on the 11th the passage towards the south became perfectly free. When the sailors saw this and that their return to their native country was apparently assured, a shout of tumultuous joy broke from them, loud and long-continued. Frankenstein, who was dozing, awoke and asked the cause of the tumult.

"They shout," I said, "because they will soon return to England."

"Do you, then, really return?"

"Alas! Yes; I cannot withstand their demands. I cannot lead them unwillingly to danger, and I must return."

"Do so, if you will; but I will not. You may give up your purpose, but mine is assigned to me by heaven, and I dare not. I am weak, but surely the spirits who assist my vengeance will endow me with sufficient strength."

Saying this, he endeavored to spring from the bed, but the exertion was too great for him; he fell back and fainted.

I sat by his bed, watching him; his eyes were closed, and I thought he slept; but presently he called to me in a feeble voice, and bidding me come near, said, "Alas! The strength I relied on is gone; I feel that I shall soon die. In a fit of enthusiastic madness I created a rational creature and was bound towards him to assure, as far as was in my power, his happiness and well-being.

"This was my duty, but there was another still paramount to that. My duties towards the beings of my own species had greater claims to my attention because they included a greater proportion of happiness or misery. Urged by this view, I refused, and I did right in refusing, to create a companion for the first creature. He showed unparalleled malignity and selfishness in evil; he destroyed my friends; he devoted to destruction beings who possessed exquisite sensations, happiness, and wisdom; nor do I know where this thirst for vengeance may end. The task of his destruction was mine, but I have failed.

"That he should live to be an instrument of mischief disturbs me; in other respects, this hour, when I momentarily expect my release, is the only happy one which I have enjoyed for several years. The forms of the beloved dead flit before me, and I hasten to their arms. Farewell, Walton! Seek happiness in tranquility and avoid ambition, even if it be only the apparently innocent one of distinguishing yourself in science and discoveries."

His voice became fainter as he spoke, and at length, exhausted by his effort, he sank into silence. About half an hour afterwards he attempted again to speak but was unable; he pressed my hand feebly, and his eyes closed forever, while the irradiation of a gentle smile passed away from his lips.

Margaret, what comment can I make on the untimely extinction of this glorious spirit? But I journey towards England, and I may there find consolation.

Great God! what a scene has just taken place! I am yet dizzy with the remembrance of it. I hardly know whether I shall have the power to detail it; yet the tale which I have recorded would be incomplete without this final and wonderful catastrophe. I entered the cabin where lay the remains of my ill-fated and admirable friend. Over him hung a form which I cannot find words to describe—gigantic in stature, yet uncouth and distorted in its proportions.

As he hung over the coffin, his face was concealed by long locks of ragged hair; but one vast hand was extended, in color and apparent texture like that of a mummy. When he heard the sound of my approach, he ceased to utter exclamations of grief and horror and sprung towards the window. Never did I behold a vision so horrible as his face, of such loathsome yet appalling hideousness. I shut my eyes involuntarily and endeavored to recollect what were my duties with regard to this destroyer. I called on him to stay.

He paused, looking on me with wonder, and again turning towards the lifeless form of his creator, he seemed to forget my presence, and every feature and gesture seemed instigated by the wildest rage of some uncontrollable passion.

"That is also my victim!" he exclaimed. "In his murder my crimes are consummated; the miserable series of my being is wound to its close! Oh, Frankenstein! Generous and self-devoted being! What does it avail that I now ask thee to pardon me? I, who irretrievably destroyed thee by destroying all thou lovedst. Alas! He is cold, he cannot answer me."

His voice seemed suffocated, and my first impulses, which had suggested to me the duty of obeying the dying request of my friend in destroying his enemy, were now suspended by a mixture of curiosity and compassion. I approached this tremendous being; I dared not again raise my eyes to his face, there was something so scaring and unearthly in his ugliness. At length I gathered resolution to address him in a pause of the tempest of his passion.

"Your repentance," I said, "is now superfluous. If you had listened to the voice of conscience and heeded the stings of remorse before you had urged your diabolical vengeance to this extremity, Frankenstein would yet have lived."

"And do you dream?" said the demon. "Do you think that I was then dead to agony and remorse? He," he continued, pointing to the corpse, "he suffered not in the consummation of the deed. Oh! Not the ten-thousandth portion of the anguish that was mine during the lingering detail of its execution. A frightful selfishness hurried me on, while my heart was poisoned with remorse. Think you that the groans of Clerval were music to my ears? My heart was fashioned to be susceptible of love and sympathy, and when wrenched by misery to vice and hatred, it did not endure the violence of the change without torture such as you cannot even imagine.

"After the murder of Clerval I returned to Switzerland, heart-broken and overcome. I pitied Frankenstein; my pity amounted to horror; I abhorred myself. But when I discovered that he, the author at once of my existence and of its unspeakable torments, dared to hope for happiness, that while he accumulated wretchedness and despair upon me he sought his own enjoyment in feelings and passions from the indulgence of which I was forever barred, then impotent envy and bitter indignation filled me with an insatiable thirst for vengeance. I recollected my threat and resolved that it should be accomplished. And now it is ended; there is my last victim!"

"Wretch!" I said. "It is well that you come here to whine over the desolation that you have made. You throw a torch into a pile of buildings, and when they are consumed, you sit among the ruins and lament the fall. Hypocritical fiend! If he whom you mourn still lived, again would he become the prey of your accursed vengeance. It is not pity that you feel; you lament only because the victim of your malignity is withdrawn from your power."

"Oh, it is not thus—not thus," interrupted the being. "Yet such must be the impression conveyed to you by what appears to be the purport of my actions. Yet I seek not a fellow feeling in my misery. No sympathy may I ever find. Once my fancy was soothed with dreams of virtue, of fame, and of enjoyment. Once I falsely hoped to meet with beings who, pardoning my outward form, would love me for the excellent qualities which I was capable of unfolding. I was nourished with high thoughts of honor and devotion. But now crime has degraded me beneath the meanest animal. No guilt, no mischief, no malignity, no misery, can be found comparable to mine. When I run over the frightful catalogue of my sins, I cannot believe that I am the same creature whose thoughts were once filled with sublime and transcendent visions of the beauty and the majesty of goodness. But it is even so; the fallen angel becomes a malignant devil. Yet even that enemy of God and man had friends and associates in his desolation; I am alone.

"You, who call Frankenstein your friend, seem to have a knowledge of my crimes and his misfortunes. Am I to be thought the only criminal, when all humankind sinned against me? Why do you not execrate the rustic who sought to destroy the savior of his child? I, the miserable and the abandoned, am an abortion, to be spurned at, and kicked, and trampled on. Even now my blood boils at the recollection of this injustice.

"But it is true that I am a wretch. I have murdered the lovely and the helpless; I have strangled the innocent as they slept and grasped to death his throat who never injured me or any other living thing. I have devoted my creator, the select specimen of all that is worthy of love and admiration among men, to misery; I have pursued him even to that irremediable ruin.

"There he lies, white and cold in death. You hate me, but your abhorrence cannot equal that with which I regard myself. Fear not that I shall be the instrument of future mischief. My work is nearly complete. Neither yours nor any man's death is needed to consummate the series of my being and accomplish that which must be done, but it requires my own. Do not think that I shall be slow to perform this sacrifice. I shall quit your vessel on the ice raft which brought me thither and shall seek the most northern extremity of the globe; I shall collect my funeral pile and consume to ashes this miserable frame, that its remains may afford no light to any curious and unhallowed wretch who would create such another as I have been. He is dead who called me into being; and when I shall be no more, the very remembrance of us both will speedily vanish. I shall no longer see the sun or stars or feel the winds play on my cheeks. I shall ascend my funeral pile triumphantly and exult in the agony of the torturing flames. The light of that conflagration will fade away; my ashes will be swept into the sea by the winds."

He sprang from the cabin window as he said this, upon the ice raft which lay close to the vessel. He was soon borne away by the waves and lost in darkness and distance.

THE GHOUL

Sir Hugh Clifford

Sir Hugh Clifford served as the British governor of North Borneo, the Gold Coast, Nigeria, and Ceylon and as the British high commissioner in Malaya. He also wrote books, including a number of stories and novels about Malayan life.

◆　◆　◆

We had been sitting late upon the veranda of my bungalow at Kuâla Lîpis, which, from the top of a low hill covered with coarse grass, overlooked the long, narrow reach formed by the combined waters of the Lîpis and the Jĕlai. The moon had risen some hours earlier, and the river ran white between the black masses of forest, which seemed to shut it in on all sides, giving to it the appearance of an isolated tarn. The roughly cleared compound, with the tennis ground which had never got beyond the stage of being dug over and weeded, and the rank growths beyond the bamboo fence, were flooded by the soft light, every tattered detail of their ugliness standing revealed as relentlessly as though it were noon. The night was very still, but the heavy, scented air was cool after the fierce heat of the day.

I had been holding forth to the handful of men who had been dining with me on the subject of Malay superstitions, while they manfully stifled their yawns. When a man has a working knowledge of anything which is not commonly known to his neighbors, he is apt to presuppose their interest in it when a chance to descant upon it occurs, and in those days it was only at long intervals that I had an opportunity of forgathering with other foreigners. Therefore, I had made the most of it, and looking back, I fear that I had occupied the rostrum during the greater part of that evening. I had told my audience of the *pĕnanggal*—the "Undone One"—that horrible wraith of a woman who has died in childbirth, who comes to torment and prey upon small children in the guise of a ghastly face and bust, with a comet's tail of blood-stained entrails flying in her wake; of the *mâti-ânak*, the weird little white animal which makes beast noises round the graves of children, and is supposed to have absorbed their souls; and of the *pôlong*, or familiar spirits, which men bind to their service by raising them up from the corpses of babies that have been stillborn, the tips of whose tongues they bite off and swallow after the infant has been brought to life by magic agencies.

It was at this point that young Middleton began to pluck up his ears; and I, finding that one of my hearers was at last showing signs of being interested, launched out with renewed vigor, until my sorely tried companions, one by one, went off to bed, each to his own quarters.

Middleton was staying with me at the time, and he and I sat for a while in silence, after the others had gone, looking at the moonlight on the river. Middleton was the first to speak.

"That was a curious myth you were telling us about the *pôlong*," he said. "There is an incident connected with it which I have never spoken of before, and have always sworn that I would keep to myself; but I have a good mind to tell you about it, because you are the only man I know who will not write me down a liar if I do."

"That's all right. Fire away," I said.

"Well," said Middleton. "It was like this. You remember Juggins, of course? He was a naturalist, you know, dead nuts upon becoming an F. R. S. and all that sort of thing, and he came to stay with me during the close season last year. [The close season being when the rivers on the eastern seaboard of the Malay Peninsula are closed to traffic because of the North East Monsoon.] He was hunting for bugs and orchids and things, and spoke of himself as an anthropologist and a botanist and a zoologist, and Heaven knows what besides; and he used to fill his bedroom with all sorts of creeping, crawling things, kept in very indifferent custody, and my veranda with all kinds of trash and rotting green trade that he brought in from the jungle.

"He stopped with me for about ten days, and when he heard that duty was taking me upriver into the Sâkai country, he asked me to let him come, too. I was rather bored, for the tribesmen are mighty shy of strangers and were only just getting used to me; but he was awfully keen, and a decent beggar enough, in spite of his dirty ways, so I couldn't very well say 'No.' When we had poled upstream for about a week, and had got well up into the Sâkai country, we had to leave our boats behind at the foot of the big rapids, and leg it for the rest of the time. It was very rough going, wading up and down streams when one wasn't clambering up a hillside or sliding down the opposite slope—you know the sort of thing—and the leeches were worse than I have ever seen them—thousands of them, swarming up your back, and fastening in clusters on to your neck, even when you had defeated those which made a frontal attack.

"I had not enough men with me to do more than hump the camp-kit and a few clothes, so we had to live on the country, which doesn't yield much up among the Sâkai except yams and tapioca roots and a little Indian corn, and soft stuff of that sort. It was all new to Juggins, and gave him fits; but he stuck to it like a man.

"Well, one evening when the night was shutting down pretty fast and rain was beginning to fall, Juggins and I struck a fairly large Sâkai camp in the middle of a clearing. As soon as we came out of the jungle, and began tightroping along the felled timber, the Sâkai sighted us and bolted for cover *en masse*. By the time we reached the huts it was pelting in earnest, and as my men were pretty well tired out, I decided to spend the night in the camp, and not to make them put up temporary shelters for us. Sâkai huts are uncleanly places at best, and any port has to do in a storm.

"We went into the largest of the hovels, and there we found a woman lying by the side of her dead child. She had apparently felt too sick to bolt with the rest of her tribe. The kid was as stiff as Herod, and had not been born many hours, I should say. The mother seemed pretty bad, and I went to her, thinking I might be able to do something for her; but she did not seem to see it, and bit and snarled at me like a wounded animal, clutching at the dead child the while, as though she feared I should take it from her. I therefore left her alone; and Juggins and I took up our quarters in a smaller hut nearby, which was fairly new and not so filthy dirty as most Sâkai lairs.

"Presently, when the beggars who had run away found out that I was the intruder, they began to come back again. You know their way. First a couple of men came and peeped at us, and vanished as soon as they saw they were observed. Then they came a trifle nearer, bobbed up suddenly, and peeped at us again. I called to them in Sĕ-noi, which always reassures them, and when they at last summoned up courage to approach, gave them each a handful of tobacco. Then they went back into the jungle and fetched the others, and very soon the place was crawling with Sâkai of both sexes and all ages.

"We got a meal of sorts, and settled down for the night as best we could; but it wasn't a restful business. Juggins swore with eloquence at the uneven flooring, made of very roughly trimmed boughs, which is an infernally uncomfortable thing to lie down upon, and makes one's bones ache as though they were coming out at the joints, and the Sâkai are abominably restless bedfellows as you know. They are naturally nocturnal.

"Anyway, they never sleep for long at a stretch, though from time to time they snuggle down and snore among the piles of warm wood ashes round the central fireplace, and whenever you wake, you will always see half a dozen of them squatting near the blazing logs, half hidden by the smoke, and jabbering like monkeys. It is a marvel to me what they find to yarn about: food, or rather the patent impossibility of ever getting enough to eat, and the stony-heartedness of Providence and of the neighboring Malays must furnish the principal topics, I should fancy, with an occasional respectful mention of beasts of prey and forest demons.

"That night they were more than ordinarily restless. The dead baby was enough to make them uneasy, and besides, they had got wet while hiding in the jungle after our arrival, and that always sets the skin disease, with which all Sâkai are smothered, itching like mad. Whenever I woke I could hear their nails going on their hides; but I had had a hard day and was used to my hosts' little ways, so I contrived to sleep fairly sound.

"Juggins told me next morning that he had had *une nuit blanche* and he nearly caused another stampede among the Sâkai by trying to get a specimen of the fungus or bacillus, or whatever it is, that occasions the skin disease. I do not know whether he succeeded. For my own part, I think it is probably due to chronic anemia—the poor devils have never had more than a very occasional full meal for hundreds of generations. I have seen little brats, hardly able to stand, white with it, the skin peeling off in flakes, and I used to frighten Juggins out of his senses by telling him he had contracted it when his nose was flayed by the sun.

"Next morning I woke just in time to see the still-born baby put into a hole in the ground. They fitted its body into a piece of bark, and stuck it in the grave they had dug for it at the edge of the clearing. They buried a flint and steel and a woodknife and some food, and a few other things with it, though no living baby could have had any use for most of them, let alone a dead one. Then the old medicine man of the tribe recited the ritual over the grave. I took the trouble to translate it once. It goes something like this:

"'O Thou, who hast gone forth from among those who dwell upon the surface of the earth, and hast taken for thy dwelling-place the land which is beneath the earth, flint and steel have we given thee to kindle thy fire, raiment to clothe thy nakedness, food to fill thy belly, and a woodknife to clear thy path. Go, then, and make unto thyself friends among those who dwell beneath the earth, and come back no more to trouble or molest those who dwell upon the surface of the earth.'

"It was short and to the point; and then they trampled down the soil, while the mother, who had got upon her feet by now, whimpered about the place like a cat that had lost its kittens. A mangy, half-starved dog came and smelt hungrily about the grave, until it was sent howling away by kicks from every human animal that could reach it; and a poor little brat, who chanced to set up a piping song a few minutes later, was kicked and cuffed and knocked about by all who could conveniently get at him with foot, hand, or missile.

"Abstinence from song and dance for a period of nine days is the Sâkai way of mourning the dead, and any breach of this is held to give great offence to the spirit of the departed and to bring bad luck upon the tribe. It was considered necessary, therefore, to give the urchin who had done the wrong a fairly bad time of it in order to propitiate the implacable dead baby.

"Next the Sâkai set to work to pack all their household goods—not a very laborious business; and in about half an hour the last of the laden women, who was carrying so many cooking-pots, and babies and rattan bags and carved bamboo-boxes and things, that she looked like the outside of a gipsy's cart at home, had filed out of the clearing and disappeared in the forest. The Sâkai always shift camp, like that, when a death occurs, because they think the ghost of the dead haunts the place where the body died. When an epidemic breaks out among them they are so busy changing quarters, building new huts, and planting fresh catch crops that they have no time to procure proper food, and half those who are not used up by the disease die of semi-starvation. They are a queer lot.

"Well, Juggins and I were left alone, but my men needed a rest, so I decided to trek no farther that day, and Juggins and I spent our time trying to get a shot at a *sêlâdang* [a wild buffalo], but though we came upon great ploughed-up runs, which the herds had made going down to water, we saw neither hoof nor horn, and returned at night to the deserted Sâkai camp, two of my Malays fairly staggering under the piles of rubbish which Juggins called his botanical specimens. The men we had left behind had contrived to catch some fish, and with that and yams we got a pretty decent meal, and I was lying on my mat reading by the aid of a *dâmar* torch, and thinking how lucky it was that the Sâkai had cleared out, when suddenly old Juggins sat up, with his eyes fairly snapping at me through his gig-lamps in his excitement.

"'I say,' he said. 'I must have that baby. It would make a unique and invaluable ethnological specimen.'

"'Rot,' I said. 'Go to sleep, old man. I want to read.'

"'No, but I'm serious,' said Juggins. 'You do not realize the unprecedented character of the opportunity. The Sâkai have gone away, so their susceptibilities would not be outraged. The potential gain to science is immense—simply immense. It would be criminal to neglect such a chance. I regard the thing in the light of a duty which I owe to human knowledge. I tell you straight, I mean to have that baby whether you like it or not, and that is flat.'

"Juggins was forever talking about human knowledge, as though he and it were partners in a business firm.

"'It is not only the Sâkai one has to consider,' I said. 'My Malays are sensitive about body snatching, too. One has to think about the effect upon them.'

"'I can't help that,' said Juggins resolutely. 'I am going out to dig it up now.'

"He had already put his boots on, and was sorting out his botanical tools in search of a trowel. I saw that there was no holding him.

"'Juggins,' I said sharply. 'Sit down. You are a lunatic, of course, but I was another when I allowed you to come up here with me, knowing as I did that you are the particular species of crank you are. However, I've done you as well as circumstances permitted, and as a mere matter of gratitude and decency, I think you might do what I wish.'

"'I am sorry,' said Juggins stiffly. 'I am extremely sorry not to be able to oblige you. My duty as a man of science, however, compels me to avail myself of this god-sent opportunity of enlarging our ethnological knowledge of a little-known people.'

"'I thought you did not believe in God,' I said sourly; for Juggins added a militant agnosticism to his other attractive qualities.

"'I believe in my duty to human knowledge,' he replied sententiously. 'And if you will not help me to perform it, I must discharge it unaided.'

"He had found his trowel, and again rose to his feet.

"'Don't be an ass, Juggins,' I said. 'Listen to me. I have forgotten more about the people and the country here than you will ever learn. If you go and dig up that dead baby, and my Malays see you, there will be the devil to pay. They do not hold with exhumed corpses, and have no liking for or sympathy with people who go fooling about with such things. They have not yet been educated up to the pitch of interest in the secrets of science which has made of you a potential criminal, and if they could understand our talk, they would be convinced that you needed the kid's body for some devilry or witchcraft business, and ten to one they would clear out and leave us in the lurch. Then who would carry your precious botanical specimens back to the boats for you, and just think how the loss of them would knock the bottom out of human knowledge for good and all.'

"'The skeleton of the child is more valuable still,' replied Juggins. 'It is well that you should understand that in this matter—which for me is a question of my duty—I am not to be moved from my purpose either by arguments or threats.'

"He was as obstinate as a mule, and I was pretty sick with him; but I saw that if I left him to himself he would do the thing so clumsily that my fellows would get wind of it, and if that happened I was afraid that they might desert us. The tracks in that Sâkai country are abominably confusing, and quite apart from the fear of losing all our camp-kit, which we could not hump for ourselves, I was by no means certain that I could find my own way back to civilization unaided. Making a virtue of necessity, therefore, I decided that I would let Juggins have his beastly specimen, provided that he would consent to be guided entirely by me in all details connected with the exhumation.

"'You are a rotter of the first water,' I said frankly. 'And if I ever get you back to my station, I'll have nothing more to do with you as long as I live. All the same, I am to blame for having brought you up here, and I suppose I must see you through.'

"'You're a brick,' said Juggins, quite unmoved by my insults. 'Come on.'

"'Wait,' I replied repressively. 'This thing cannot be done until my people are all asleep. Lie down on your mat and keep quiet. When it is safe, I'll give you the word.'

"Juggins groaned, and tried to persuade me to let him go at once; but I swore that nothing would induce me to move before midnight, and with that I rolled over on my side and lay reading and smoking, while Juggins fumed and fretted as he watched the slow hands of his watch creeping round the dial.

"I always take books with me into the jungle, and the more completely incongruous they are to my immediate surroundings the more refreshing I find them. That evening, I remember, I happened to be rereading Miss Florence Montgomery's *Misunderstood* with the tears running down my nose; and by the time my Malays were all asleep, this incidental wallowing in sentimentality had made me more sick with Juggins and his disgusting project than ever.

"I never felt so like a criminal as I did that night, as Juggins and I gingerly picked our way out of the hut across the prostrate forms of my sleeping Malays; nor had I realized before what a difficult job it is to walk without noise on an openwork flooring of uneven boughs. We got out of the place and down the crazy stair-ladder at last, without waking

any of my fellows, and we then began to creep along the edge of the
jungle that hedged the clearing about. Why did we think it necessary to
creep? I don't know. Partly we did not want to be seen by the Malays, if
any of them happened to wake; but besides that, the long wait and the
uncanny sort of work we were after had set our nerves going a bit, I
expect.

"The night was as still as most nights are in real, *pukka* jungle. That
is to say, that it was as full of noises—little, quiet, half-heard beast and
tree noises—as an egg is full of meat; and every occasional louder sound
made me jump almost out of my skin. There was not a breath astir in
the clearing, but miles up above our heads the clouds were racing across
the moon, which looked as though it were scudding through them
in the opposite direction at a tremendous rate, like a great white fire
balloon. It was pitch dark along the edge of the clearing, for the jungle
threw a heavy shadow; and Juggins kept knocking those great clumsy
feet of his against the stumps, and swearing softly under his breath.

"Just as we were getting near the child's grave the clouds obscuring
the moon became a trifle thinner, and the slightly increased light showed
me something that caused me to clutch Juggins by the arm.

"'Hold hard!' I whispered, squatting down instinctively in the
shadow, and dragging him after me. 'What's that on the grave?'

"Juggins hauled out his six-shooter with a tug, and looking at his
face, I saw that he was as pale as death and more than a little shaky. He
was pressing up against me, too, as he squatted, a bit closer, I fancied,
than he would have thought necessary at any other time, and it seemed
to me that he was trembling. I whispered to him, telling him not to
shoot; and we sat there for nearly a minute, I should think, peering
through the uncertain light, and trying to make out what the creature
might be which was crouching above the grave and making a strange
scratching noise.

"Then the moon came out suddenly into a patch of open sky, and we
could see clearly at last, and what it revealed did not make me, for one,

feel any better. The thing we had been looking at was kneeling on the grave, facing us. It, or rather she, was an old, old Sâkai hag. She was stark naked, and in the brilliant light of the moon I could see her long, pendulous breasts swaying about like an ox's dewlap, and the creases and wrinkles with which her withered hide was criss-crossed, and the discolored patches of foul skin disease. Her hair hung about her face in great matted locks, falling forward as she bent above the grave, and her eyes glinted through the tangle like those of some unclean and shaggy animal. Her long fingers, which had nails like claws, were tearing at the dirt of the grave, and her body was drenched with sweat, so that it glistened in the moonlight.

"'It looks as though someone else wanted your precious baby for a specimen, Juggins,' I whispered; and a spirit of emulation set him floundering on to his feet, till I pulled him back. 'Keep still, man,' I added. 'Let us see what the old hag is up to. It isn't the brat's mother, is it?'

"'No,' panted Juggins. 'This is a much older woman. Great God! What a ghoul it is!'

"Then we were silent again. Where we squatted we were hidden from the hag by a few tufts of rank *lâlang* grass, and the shadow of the jungle also covered us. Even if we had been in the open, however, I question whether the old woman would have seen us, she was so eagerly intent upon her work. For full five minutes, as near as I can guess, we squatted there watching her scrape and tear and scratch at the earth of the grave, with a sort of frenzy of energy; and all the while her lips kept going like a shivering man's teeth, though no sound that I could hear came from them.

"At length she got down to the corpse, and I saw her lift the bark wrapper out of the grave, and draw the baby's body from it. Then she sat back upon her heels, threw up her head, just like a dog, and bayed at the moon. She did this three times, and I do not know what there was about those long-drawn howls that jangled up one's nerves, but each time the sound became more insistent and intolerable, and as I listened, my hair fairly lifted. Then, very carefully, she laid the child's body down in a position that seemed to have some connection with the points of the compass, for she took a long time, and consulted the moon and the shadows repeatedly before she was satisfied with the orientation of the thing's head and feet.

"Then she got up, and began very slowly to dance round and round the grave. It was not a reassuring sight, out there in the awful loneliness of the night, miles away from every one and everything, to watch that abominable old beldam capering uncleanly in the moonlight, while those restless lips of hers called noiselessly upon all the devils in hell, with words that we could not hear.

"Juggins pressed up against me harder than ever, and his hand on my arm gripped tighter and tighter. He was shaking like a leaf, and I do not fancy that I was much steadier. It does not sound very terrible, as I tell it to you here in comparatively civilized surroundings; but at the time, the sight of that obscure figure dancing silently in the moonlight with its ungainly shadow scared me badly.

"She capered like that for some minutes, setting to the dead baby as though she were inviting it to join her, and the intent purposefulness of her made me feel sick. If anybody had told me that morning that I was capable of being frightened out of my wits by an old woman, I should have laughed; but I saw nothing outlandish in the idea while that grotesque dancing lasted.

"Her movements, which had been very slow at first, became gradually faster and faster, till every atom of her was in violent motion, and her body and limbs were swaying this way and that, like the boughs of a tree in a tornado. Then, all of a sudden, she collapsed on the ground, with her back toward us, and seized the baby's body. She seemed to nurse it, as a mother might nurse her child; and as she swayed from side to side, I could see first the curve of the creature's head, resting on her thin left arm, and then its feet near the crook of her right elbow. And now she was crooning to it in a cracked falsetto chant that might have been a lullaby or perhaps some incantation.

"She rocked the child slowly at first, but very rapidly the pace quickened, until her body was swaying to and fro from the hips, and from side to side, at such a rate that, to me, she looked as though she were falling all ways at once. And simultaneously her shrill chanting became faster and faster, and every instant more nerve-sawing.

"Next she suddenly changed the motion. She gripped the thing she was nursing by its arms, and began to dance it up and down, still moving with incredible agility, and crooning more damnably than ever. I could see the small, puckered face of the thing above her head every time she danced it up, and then, as she brought it down again, I lost sight of it for a second, until she danced it up once more. I kept my eyes fixed upon the thing's face every time it came into view, and I swear it was not an optical illusion—*it began to be alive*. Its eyes were open and moving, and its mouth was working, like that of a child which tries to laugh but is too young to do it properly. Its face ceased to be like that of a new-born baby at all. It was distorted by a horrible animation. It was the most unearthly sight.

"Juggins saw it, too, for I could hear him drawing his breath harder and shorter than a healthy man should.

"Then, all in a moment, the hag did something. I did not see clearly precisely what it was; but it looked to me as though she bent forward and kissed it; and at that very instant a cry went up like the wail of a lost soul. It may have been something in the jungle, but I know my Malayan forests pretty thoroughly, and I have never heard any cry like it before nor since.

"The next thing we knew was that the old hag had thrown the body back into the grave, and was dumping down the earth and jumping on it, while that strange cry grew fainter and fainter. It all happened so quickly that I had not had time to think or move before I was startled back into full consciousness by the sharp crack of Juggins's revolver fired close to my ear.

"'She's burying it alive!' he cried.

"It was a queer thing for a man to say, who had seen the child lying stark and dead more than thirty hours earlier; but the same thought was in my mind, too, as we both started forward at a run. The hag had vanished into the jungle as silently as a shadow. Juggins had missed her, of course. He was always a rotten bad shot. However, we had no thought for her. We just flung ourselves upon the grave, and dug at the earth with our hands, until the baby lay in my arms. It was cold and stiff, and putrefaction had already begun its work. I forced open its mouth, and saw something that I had expected. The tip of its tongue was missing. It looked as though it had been bitten off by a set of shocking bad teeth, for the edge left behind was like a saw.

"'The thing's quite dead,' I said to Juggins.

"'But it cried—it cried!' whimpered Juggins. 'I can hear it now. To think that we let that horrible creature murder it.'

"He sat down with his head in his hands. He was utterly unmanned.

"Now that the fright was over, I was beginning to be quite brave again. It is a way I have.

"'Rot,' I said. 'The thing's been dead for hours, and anyway, here's your precious specimen if you want it.'

"I had put it down, and now pointed at it from a distance. Its proximity was not pleasant. Juggins, however, only shuddered.

"'Bury it, in Heaven's name,' he said, his voice broken by sobs. 'I would not have it for the world. Besides, it *was* alive. I saw and heard it.'

"Well, I put it back in its grave, and next day we left the Sâkai country. Juggins had a whacking dose of fever, and anyway we had had about enough of the Sâkai and of all their engaging habits to last us for a bit.

"We swore one another to secrecy as Juggins, when he got his nerve back, said that the accuracy of our observations was not susceptible of scientific proof, which, I understand, was the rock his religion had gone to pieces on; and I did not fancy being told that I was drunk or that I was lying. You, however, know something of the uncanny things of the East, so tonight I have broken our vow. Now I'm going to turn in. Don't give me away."

Young Middleton died of fever and dysentery, somewhere upcountry, a year or two later. His name was not Middleton, of course; so I am not really "giving him away," as he called it, even now. As for his companion, though when I last heard of him he was still alive and a shining light in the scientific world, I have named him Juggins, and as the family is a large one, he will run no great risk of being identified.

THE FACTS OF M. VALDEMAR'S CASE

Edgar Allan Poe

Edgar Allan Poe was born in Boston, but was soon orphaned and subsequently raised by a foster family, which he did not get along well with. While his foster family lived in England for five years, he went to a private school near London. When he returned to the United States, he entered the University of Virginia. He took to gambling to support himself, but his drinking and mounting debts forced him to leave college.

Poe spent two years in the army and rose to the rank of sergeant major. Shortly after he received an honorable discharge, he entered West Point in an effort to please his foster father. When he realized he would never receive an inheritance, he got himself thrown out of the academy. After being refused by the Polish army, he focused more on his writing and began working as a magazine editor.

When he was twenty-seven, he married his fourteen-year-old cousin. It was during this period that he wrote his great horror stories, including "The Tell-Tale Heart," "The Pit and the Pendulum," "The Fall of the House of Usher," and "The Murders in the Rue Morgue," and his classic poem "The Raven." He is also credited with having invented the detective story.

His drinking increased throughout his wife's long illness and eventual death from tuberculosis. Poe was on the way to his second wedding, this time to his childhood sweetheart, when he disappeared; he was found unconscious several days later. He never regained consciousness and the cause of his death at the age of forty remains a mystery.

Poe's complete works fill seventeen volumes, with only one novel—which is actually more of a novella. Although he was just beginning to be recognized when he died, Poe is now considered to be one of America's greatest writers and poets.

This story was later retitled "The Facts in the Case of M. Valdemar."

✦   ✦   ✦

Of course I shall not pretend to consider it any matter for wonder, that the extraordinary case of M. Valdemar has excited discussion. It would have been a miracle had it not—especially under the circumstances. Through the desire of all parties concerned to keep the affair from the public, at least for the present, or until we had farther opportunities for investigation—through our endeavors to effect this—a garbled or exaggerated account made its way into society, and became the source of many unpleasant misrepresentations, and, very naturally, of a great deal of disbelief.

It is now rendered necessary that I give the *facts*—as far as I comprehend them myself. They are, succinctly, these:

My attention, for the last three years, had been repeatedly drawn to the subject of Mesmerism; and, about nine months ago it occurred to me, quite suddenly, that in the series of experiments made hitherto, there had been a very remarkable and most unaccountable omission:—no person had as yet been mesmerized *in articulo mortis*. It remained to be seen, first, whether, in such condition, there existed in the patient any susceptibility to the magnetic influence; secondly, whether, if any existed, it was impaired or increased by the condition; thirdly, to what extent, or for how long a period, the encroachments of Death might be arrested by the process. There were other points to be ascertained, but these most excited my curiosity—the last in especial, from the immensely important character of its consequences.

In looking around me for some subject by whose means I might test these particulars, I was brought to think of my friend, M. Ernest Valdemar, the well-known compiler of the *Bibliotheca Forensica*, and author (under the *nom de plume* of Issachar Marx) of the Polish versions of *Wallenstein* and *Gargantua*.

M. Valdemar, who has resided principally at Harlaem, N. Y., since the year 1839, is (or was) particularly noticeable for the extreme spareness of his person—his lower limbs much resembling those of John Randolph; and, also, for the whiteness of his whiskers, in violent contrast to the blackness of his hair—the latter, in consequence, being very generally mistaken for a wig.

His temperament was markedly nervous, and rendered him a good subject for mesmeric experiment. On two or three occasions I had put him to sleep with little difficulty, but was disappointed in other results which his peculiar constitution had naturally led me to anticipate. His will was at no period positively, or thoroughly, under my control, and in regard to *clairvoyance*, I could accomplish with him nothing to be relied upon. I always attributed my failure at these points to the disordered state of his health. For some months previous to my becoming acquainted with him, his physicians had declared him in a confirmed phthisis. It was his custom, indeed, to speak calmly of his approaching dissolution, as of a matter neither to be avoided nor regretted.

When the ideas to which I have alluded first occurred to me, it was of course very natural that I should think of M. Valdemar. I knew the steady philosophy of the man too well to apprehend any scruples from *him*; and he had no relatives in America who would be likely to interfere. I spoke to him frankly upon the subject; and, to my surprise, his interest seemed vividly excited. I say to my surprise, for, although he had always yielded his person freely to my experiments, he had never before given me any tokens of sympathy with what I did. His disease was of that character which would admit of exact calculation in respect to the epoch of its termination in death; and it was finally arranged between us that he would send for me about twenty-four hours before the period announced by his physicians as that of his decease.

It is now rather more than seven months since I received, from M. Valdemar himself, the subjoined note:

MY DEAR P——,
You may as well come now. D—— and F—— are agreed that I cannot hold out beyond tomorrow midnight; and I think they have hit the time very nearly.

VALDEMAR

I received this note within half an hour after it was written, and in fifteen minutes more I was in the dying man's chamber. I had not seen him for ten days, and was appalled by the fearful alteration which the brief interval had wrought in him. His face wore a leaden hue; the eyes were utterly lustreless; and the emaciation was so extreme that the skin had been broken through by the cheekbones. His expectoration was excessive. The pulse was barely perceptible. He retained, nevertheless, in a very remarkable manner, both his mental power and a certain degree of physical strength. He spoke with distinctness—took some palliative medicines without aid—and, when I entered the room, was occupied in penciling memoranda in a pocket-book. He was propped up in the bed by pillows. Doctors D—— and F—— were in attendance.

After pressing Valdemar's hand, I took these gentlemen aside, and obtained from them a minute account of the patient's condition. The left lung had been for eighteen months in a semi-osseous or cartilaginous state, and was, of course, entirely useless for all purposes of vitality. The right, in its upper portion, was also partially, if not thoroughly, ossified, while the lower region was merely a mass of purulent tubercles, running one into another. Several extensive perforations existed; and, at one point, permanent adhesion to the ribs had taken place. These appearances in the right lobe were of comparatively recent date. The ossification had proceeded with very unusual rapidity; no sign of it had discovered a month before, and the adhesion had only been observed during the three previous days. Independently of the phthisis, the patient was suspected of aneurism of the aorta; but on this point the osseous symptoms rendered an exact diagnosis impossible. It was the opinion of both physicians that M. Valdemar would die about midnight on the morrow (Sunday). It was then seven o'clock on Saturday evening.

On quitting the invalid's bedside to hold conversation with myself, Doctors D—— and F—— had bidden him a final farewell. It had not been their intention to return; but, at my request, they agreed to look in upon the patient about ten the next night.

When they had gone, I spoke freely with M. Valdemar on the subject of his approaching dissolution, as well as, more particularly, of the experiment proposed. He still professed himself quite willing and even anxious to have it made, and urged me to commence it at once. A male and a female nurse were in attendance; but I did not feel myself altogether at liberty to engage in a task of this character with no more reliable witnesses than these people, in case of sudden accident, might prove. I therefore postponed operations until about eight the next night, when the arrival of a medical student with whom I had some acquaintance, (Mr. Theodore L——l,) relieved me from farther embarrassment. It had been my design, originally, to wait for the physicians; but I was induced to proceed, first, by the urgent entreaties of M. Valdemar, and secondly, by my conviction that I had not a moment to lose, as he was evidently sinking fast.

Mr. L——l was so kind as to accede to my desire that he would take notes of all that occurred, and it is from his memoranda that what I now have to relate is, for the most part, either condensed or copied *verbatim*.

It wanted about five minutes of eight when, taking the patient's hand, I begged him to state, as distinctly as he could, to Mr. L——l, whether he (M. Valdemar) was entirely willing that I should make the experiment of mesmerizing him in his then condition.

He replied feebly, yet quite audibly, "Yes, I wish to be mesmerized"— adding immediately afterwards, "I fear you have deferred it too long."

While he spoke thus, I commenced the passes which I had already found most effectual in subduing him. He was evidently influenced with the first lateral stroke of my hand across his forehead; but although I exerted all my powers, no farther perceptible effect was induced until some minutes after ten o'clock, when Doctors D—— and F—— called, according to appointment. I explained to them, in a few words, what I designed, and as they opposed no objection, saying that the patient was already in the death agony, I proceeded without hesitation— exchanging, however, the lateral passes for downward ones, and direct- ing my gaze entirely into the right eye of the sufferer.

By this time his pulse was imperceptible and his breathing was ster- torous, and at intervals of half a minute.

This condition was nearly unaltered for a quarter of an hour. At the expiration of this period, however, a natural although a very deep sigh escaped the bosom of the dying man, and the stertorous breathing ceased—that is to say, its stertorousness was no longer apparent; the intervals were undiminished. The patient's extremities were of an icy coldness.

At five minutes before eleven I perceived unequivocal signs of the mesmeric influence. The glassy roll of the eye was changed for that ex- pression of uneasy inward examination which is never seen except in cases of sleep-waking, and which it is quite impossible to mistake. With a few rapid lateral passes I made the lids quiver, as in incipient sleep, and with a few more I closed them altogether. I was not satisfied, how- ever, with this, but continued the manipulations vigorously, and with the fullest exertion of the will, until I had completely stiffened the limbs of the slumberer, after placing them in a seemingly easy position. The legs were at full length; the arms were nearly so, and reposed on the bed at a moderate distance from the loins. The head was very slightly elevated.

When I had accomplished this, it was fully midnight, and I requested the gentlemen present to examine M. Valdemar's condition. After a few experiments, they admitted him to be in an unusually perfect state of mesmeric trance. The curiosity of both the physicians was greatly excited. Dr. D—— resolved at once to remain with the patient all night, while Dr. F—— took leave with a promise to return at daybreak. Mr. L——l and the nurses remained.

We left M. Valdemar entirely undisturbed until about three o'clock in the morning, when I approached him and found him in precisely the same condition as when Dr. F—— went away—that is to say, he lay in the same position; the pulse was imperceptible; the breathing was gentle (scarcely noticeable, unless through the application of a mirror to the lips); the eyes were closed naturally; and the limbs were as rigid and as cold as marble. Still, the general appearance was certainly not that of death.

As I approached M. Valdemar I made a kind of half effort to influence his right arm into pursuit of my own, as I passed the latter gently to and fro above his person. In such experiments with this patient I had never perfectly succeeded before, and assuredly I had little thought of succeeding now; but to my astonishment, his arm very readily, although feebly, followed every direction I assigned it with mine. I determined to hazard a few words of conversation.

"M. Valdemar," I said, "are you asleep?" He made no answer, but I perceived a tremor about the lips, and was thus induced to repeat the question, again and again. At its third repetition, his whole frame was agitated by a very slight shivering; the eyelids unclosed themselves so far as to display a white line of the ball; the lips moved sluggishly, and from between them, in a barely audible whisper, issued the words, "Yes—asleep now. Do not wake me!—let me die so!"

I here felt the limbs and found them as rigid as ever. The right arm, as before, obeyed the direction of my hand. I questioned the sleep-waker again:

"Do you still feel pain in the breast, M. Valdemar?"

The answer now was immediate, but even less audible than before: "No pain—I am dying."

I did not think it advisable to disturb him farther just then, and nothing more was said or done until the arrival of Dr. F——, who came a little before sunrise, and expressed unbounded astonishment at finding the patient still alive. After feeling the pulse and applying a mirror to the lips, he requested me to speak to the sleep-waker again. I did so, saying, "M. Valdemar, do you still sleep?"

As before, some minutes elapsed ere a reply was made; and during the interval the dying man seemed to be collecting his energies to speak. At my fourth repetition of the question, he said very faintly, almost inaudibly, "Yes; still asleep—dying."

It was now the opinion, or rather the wish, of the physicians, that M. Valdemar should be suffered to remain undisturbed in his present apparently tranquil condition, until death should supervene—and this, it was generally agreed, must now take place within a few minutes. I concluded, however, to speak to him once more, and merely repeated my previous question.

While I spoke, there came a marked change over the countenance of the sleep-waker. The eyes rolled themselves slowly open, the pupils disappearing upwardly; the skin generally assumed a cadaverous hue, resembling not so much parchment as white paper; and the circular hectic spots which, hitherto, had been strongly defined in the centre of each cheek, *went out* at once. I use this expression, because the suddenness of their departure put me in mind of nothing so much as the extinguishment of a candle by a puff of the breath. The upper lip, at the same time, writhed itself away from the teeth, which it had previously covered completely; while the lower jaw fell with an audible jerk, leaving the mouth widely extended, and disclosing in full view the swollen and blackened tongue. I presume that no member of the party then present had been unaccustomed to death-bed horrors; but so hideous beyond conception was the appearance of M. Valdemar at this moment, that there was a general shrinking back from the region of the bed.

I now feel that I have reached a point of this narrative at which every reader will be startled into positive disbelief. It is my business, however, simply to proceed.

There was no longer the faintest sign of vitality in M. Valdemar; and concluding him to be dead, we were consigning him to the charge of the nurses, when a strong vibratory motion was observable in the tongue. This continued for perhaps a minute. At the expiration of this period, there issued from the distended and motionless jaws a voice—such as it would be madness in me to attempt describing. There are, indeed, two or three epithets which might be considered as applicable to it in part; I might say, for example, that the sound was harsh, and broken and hollow; but the hideous whole is indescribable, for the simple reason that no similar sounds have ever jarred upon the ear of humanity. There were two particulars, nevertheless, which I thought then, and still think, might fairly be stated as characteristic of the intonation—as well adapted to convey some idea of its unearthly peculiarity. In the first place, the voice seemed to reach our ears—at least mine—from a vast distance, or from some deep cavern within the earth. In the second place, it impressed me (I fear, indeed, that it will be impossible to make myself comprehended) as gelatinous or glutinous matters impress the sense of touch.

I have spoken both of "sound" and of "voice." I mean to say that the sound was one of distinct—of even wonderfully, thrillingly distinct— syllabification. M. Valdemar *spoke*—obviously in reply to the question I had propounded to him a few minutes before. I had asked him, it will be remembered, if he still slept.

He now said, "Yes—no—I *have been* sleeping—and now—now—*I am dead*."

No person present even affected to deny, or attempted to repress, the unutterable, shuddering horror which these few words, thus uttered, were so well calculated to convey. Mr. L——l (the student) swooned. The nurses immediately left the chamber, and could not be induced to return. My own impressions I would not pretend to render intelligible to the reader. For nearly an hour, we busied ourselves, silently—without the utterance of a word—in endeavors to revive Mr. L——l. When he came to himself, we addressed ourselves again to an investigation of M. Valdemar's condition.

It remained in all respects as I have last described it, with the exception that the mirror no longer afforded evidence of respiration. An attempt to draw blood from the arm failed. I should mention, too, that this limb was no farther subject to my will. I endeavored in vain to make it follow the direction of my hand. The only real indication, indeed, of the mesmeric influence, was now found in the vibratory movement of the tongue, whenever I addressed M. Valdemar a question. He seemed to be making an effort to reply, but had no longer sufficient volition. To queries put to him by any other person than myself he seemed utterly insensible—although I endeavored to place each member of the company in mesmeric *rapport* with him. I believe that I have now related all that is necessary to an understanding of the sleep-waker's state at this epoch. Other nurses were procured; and at ten o'clock I left the house in company with the two physicians and Mr. L——l.

In the afternoon we all called again to see the patient. His condition remained precisely the same. We had now some discussion as to the propriety and feasibility of awakening him; but we had little difficulty in agreeing that no good purpose would be served by so doing. It was evident that, so far, death (or what is usually termed death) had been arrested by the mesmeric process. It seemed clear to us all that to awaken M. Valdemar would be merely to insure his instant, or at least his speedy dissolution.

From this period until the close of last week—*an interval of nearly seven months*—we continued to make daily calls at M. Valdemar's house, accompanied, now and then, by medical and other friends. All this time the sleeper-waker remained exactly as I have last described him. The nurses' attentions were continual.

It was on Friday last that we finally resolved to make the experiment of awakening or attempting to awaken him; and it is the (perhaps) unfortunate result of this latter experiment which has given rise to so much discussion in private circles—to so much of what I cannot help thinking unwarranted popular feeling.

For the purpose of relieving M. Valdemar from the mesmeric trance, I made use of the customary passes. These, for a time, were unsuccessful. The first indication of revival was afforded by a partial descent of the iris. It was observed, as especially remarkable, that this lowering of the pupil was accompanied by the profuse out-flowing of a yellowish ichor (from beneath the lids) of a pungent and highly offensive odor.

It was now suggested that I should attempt to influence the patient's arm, as heretofore. I made the attempt and failed. Dr. F—— then intimated a desire to have me put a question. I did so, as follows:

"M. Valdemar, can you explain to us what are your feelings or wishes now?"

There was an instant return of the hectic circles on the cheeks; the tongue quivered, or rather rolled violently in the mouth (although the jaws and lips remained rigid as before); and at length the same hideous voice which I have already described, broke forth:

"For God's sake!—quick!—quick!—put me to sleep—or, quick!—waken me!—quick!—*I say to you that I am dead!*"

I was thoroughly unnerved, and for an instant remained undecided what to do. At first I made an endeavor to re-compose the patient; but, failing in this through total abeyance of the will, I retraced my steps and as earnestly struggled to awaken him. In this attempt I soon saw that I should be successful—or at least I soon fancied that my success would be complete—and I am sure that all in the room were prepared to see the patient awaken.

For what really occurred, however, it is quite impossible that any human being could have been prepared.

As I rapidly made the mesmeric passes, amid ejaculations of "dead! dead!" absolutely *bursting* from the tongue and not from the lips of the sufferer, his whole frame at once—within the space of a single minute, or even less, shrunk—crumbled—absolutely *rotted* away beneath my hands. Upon the bed, before that whole company, there lay a nearly liquid mass of loathsome—of detestable putrescence.

THE CORPSE THAT RAN AWAY

from *The Evening Telegram*

This article is from the August 14, 1888, edition of the St. John's, New-foundland, *Evening Telegram*. Its subheadline read, "Henry Graham's Great Act in Running Away After Having Been Hanged."

◆ ◆ ◆

That the bodies of the dead, even a long time after the moment of death, do perform actions which have all the appearance of volition, are instances familiar to every student of medical literature. Physicians, it is true, assure us that in these movements volition does not enter; and they have given to this muscular movement the name of "reflex action," and this, apparently, we are expected to accept as a perfectly lucid explanation of a phenomenon which without the name would be obscure. Enlightened by the term "reflex action" it must be discontented and exacting curiosity that would not rest and be thankful.

At Hawley's Bar, a mining camp near Virginia City, M.T. [Montana Territory], a gambler named Henry Graham, but commonly known as "Gray Hank," met a miner named Dreyfuss one day with whom he had had a dispute the previous night about a pack of cards, and asked him into a barroom to have a drink. The unfortunate miner taking this as an overture of peace gladly consented. They stood at the counter, and while Dreyfuss was in the act of drinking, Graham shot him dead. This was in 1865. Within an hour after the murder Graham was in the hands of the vigilantes, and that evening at sunset, after a fair, informal trial, he was hanged to the limb of a tree which grew upon a little eminence within sight of the whole camp.

The original intention had been to "string him up," as is customary in such affairs, and with a view to that operation the long rope had been thrown over the limb, while a dozen pairs of hands were ready to hoist away. For some reason the plan was abandoned, the rope was given a single turn about the limb at a suitable distance from the noose, the free end fast to a bush and the victim compelled to stand on a horse, which at the cut of a whip sprang from under him, leaving him swinging. When steadied his feet were about eighteen inches from the earth.

The body remained suspended for exactly half an hour, the greater part of the crowd remaining about it. Then the "judge" ordered it taken down. The rope was untied from the bush, and two men stood by to lower away. The moment the feet came squarely upon the ground the men engaged in lowering, thinking, doubtless, that those standing about the body had hold of it to support it, let go the rope. The body at once ran quickly forward toward the main part of the crowd, the rope paying out as it went. The head rolled from side to side, the eyes and tongue protruding. With cries of horror the crowd ran hither and thither, scrambling, rolling over one another, cursing. In and out among them, over the fallen, coming in collision with others, his direction governed by blind caprice, the horrible dead man "pranced," his feet lifted so high at each step that his knees struck his breast. The deepening twilight added its terror to the uncanny scene, and brave men fled from the spot, not daring to look behind.

Straight into this confusion from the outskirts of the crowd walked with rapid steps the tall figure of a man whom all recognized as a master spirit. This was Dr. Arnold Spier, who, with two other physicians, had pronounced the man dead, and had been retiring from the camp. He moved as directly toward the dead man as the now somewhat less rapid and erratic movements of the latter would permit, and seized him in his arms. Encouraged by this, a score of men sprang shouting to the free end of the rope, which had been drawn entirely over the limb, and laid hold of it, intending to make a finish of their work. They ran with it toward the bush to which it had been fastened, but there was no resistance; the physician had cut it from the dead murderer's neck. In a moment the body was lying on its back, with composed limbs and face upturned to the kindling stars in the motionless rigidity appropriate to death. The hanging had been done well enough; the neck had been broken by the drop. Dr. Spier knew that a corpse which, placed upon its feet, would walk and run, would lie still when placed upon its back. The dead are creatures of habit.

◆   ◆   ◆

This newspaper article gives new meaning to the phrase, "running around like a headless chicken."

THE HAND

Guy de Maupassant

Henri René Albert Guy de Maupassant is considered the greatest of all French short story writers. He was trained in writing fiction by Gustave Flaubert (author of *Madame Bovary*) and wrote seventeen volumes of short stories in thirteen years, plus additional novels, plays, and travelogues. Unfortunately the ravages of syphilis drove him to a Paris insane asylum, where he eventually died.

This story was inspired by a mummified hand that English poet Algernon Swinburne showed him when he was a teenager.

✦ ✦ ✦

They made a circle around Judge Bermutier, who was giving his opinion of the mysterious affair that had happened at Saint-Cloud. For a month Paris had doted on this inexplicable crime. No one could understand it at all.

M. Bermutier, standing with his back to the chimney, talked about it, discussed the divers opinions, but came to no conclusions.

Many women had risen and come nearer, remaining standing, with eyes fixed upon the shaven mouth of the magistrate, whence issued these grave words. They shivered and vibrated, crisp through their curious fear, through that eager, insatiable need of terror which haunts their soul, torturing them like a hunger.

One of them, paler than the others, after a silence, said, "It is frightful. It touches the supernatural. We shall never know anything about it."

The magistrate turned toward her, saying, "Yes, Madame, it is probable that we never shall know anything about it. As for the word 'supernatural,' when you come to use that, it has no place here. We are in the presence of a crime skillfully conceived, very skillfully executed, and so well enveloped in mystery that we cannot separate the impenetrable circumstances which surround it. But, once in my life, I had to follow an affair which seemed truly to be mixed up with something very unusual. However, it was necessary to give it up, as there was no means of explaining it."

Many of the ladies called out at the same time, so quickly that their voices sounded as one, "Oh! tell us about it."

M. Bermutier smiled gravely, as judges should, and replied, "You must not suppose, for an instant, that I, at least, believed there was anything superhuman in the adventure. I believe only in normal causes. And, if in place of using the word 'supernatural' to express what we cannot comprehend we should simply use the word 'inexplicable,' it would be much better. In any case, the surrounding circumstances in the affair I am going to relate to you, as well as the preparatory circumstances, have affected me much. Here are the facts:

"I was then judge of Instruction at Ajaccio, a little white town lying on the border of an admirable gulf that was surrounded on all sides by high mountains.

"What I particularly had to look after there was the affairs of vendetta. Some of them were superb; as dramatic as possible, ferocious, and heroic. We find there the most beautiful subjects of vengeance that one could dream of, hatred a century old, appeased for a moment but never extinguished, abominable plots, assassinations becoming massacres and almost glorious battles. For two years I heard of nothing but the price of blood, of the terribly prejudiced Corsican who is bound to avenge all injury upon the person of him who is the cause of it, or upon his nearest descendants. I saw old men and infants, cousins, with their throats cut, and my head was full of these stories.

"One day we learned that an Englishman had rented for some years a little villa at the end of the Gulf. He had brought with him a French domestic, picked up at Marseilles on the way.

"Soon everybody was occupied with this singular person, who lived alone in his house, only going out to hunt and fish. He spoke to no one, never came to the town, and, every morning, practiced shooting with a pistol and a rifle for an hour or two.

"Some legends about him were abroad. They pretended that he was a high personage fled from his own country for political reasons; then they affirmed that he was concealing himself after having committed a frightful crime. They even cited some of the particularly horrible details.

"In my capacity of judge, I wished to get some information about this man. But it was impossible to learn anything. He called himself Sir John Rowell.

"I contented myself with watching him closely; although, in reality, there seemed nothing to suspect regarding him.

"Nevertheless, as rumors on his account continued, grew, and became general, I resolved to try and see this stranger myself, and for this purpose began to hunt regularly in the neighborhood of his property.

"I waited long for an occasion. It finally came in the form of a partridge which I shot and killed before the very nose of the Englishman. My dog brought it to me; but, immediately taking it I went and begged Sir John Rowell to accept the dead bird, excusing myself for intrusion.

"He was a tall man with red hair and red beard, very large, a sort of placid, polite Hercules. He had none of the so-called British haughtiness, and heartily thanked me for the delicacy in French, with a beyond-the-Channel accent. At the end of a month we had chatted together five or six times.

"Finally, one evening, as I was passing by his door, I perceived him astride a chair in the garden, smoking his pipe. I saluted him and he asked me in to have a glass of beer. It was not necessary for him to repeat before I accepted.

"He received me with the fastidious courtesy of the English, spoke in praise of France and of Corsica, and declared that he loved that country and that shore.

"Then, with great precaution in the form of a lively interest, I put some questions to him about his life and his projects. He responded without embarrassment, told me that he had traveled much, in Africa, in the Indies, and in America. He added, laughing, 'I have had many adventures, oh! yes.'

"I began to talk about hunting, and he gave me many curious details of hunting the hippopotamus, the tiger, the elephant, and even of hunting the gorilla.

"I said, 'All these animals are very formidable.'

"He laughed, 'Oh! no. The worst animal is man.' Then he began to laugh, with the hearty laugh of a big contented Englishman. He continued, 'I have often hunted man, also.'

"He spoke of weapons and asked me to go into his house to see his guns of various makes and kinds.

"His drawing-room was hung in black, in black silk embroidered with gold. There were great yellow flowers running over the somber stuff, shining like fire.

"'It is Japanese cloth,' he said.

"But in the middle of a large panel, a strange thing attracted my eye. Upon a square of red velvet, a black object was attached. I approached and found it was a hand, the hand of a man. Not a skeleton hand, white and characteristic, but a black, desiccated hand, with yellow joints with the muscles bare and on them traces of old blood, of blood that seemed like a scale, over the bones sharply cut off at about the middle of the fore-arm, as with a blow of a hatchet. About the wrist was an enormous iron chain, riveted, soldered to this unclean member, attaching it to the wall by a ring sufficiently strong to hold an elephant.

"I asked: 'What is that?'

"The Englishman responded tranquilly:

"'It belonged to my worst enemy. It came from America. It was broken with a saber, cut off with a sharp stone, and dried in the sun for eight days. Oh, very good for me, that was!'

"I touched the human relic, which must have belonged to a colossus. The fingers were immoderately long and attached by enormous tendons that held the straps of skin in place. This dried hand was frightful to see, making one think, naturally, of the vengeance of a savage.

"I said, 'This man must have been very strong.'

"With gentleness the Englishman answered, 'Oh! yes; but I was stronger than he. I put this chain on him to hold him.'

"I thought he spoke in jest and replied, 'The chain is useless now that the hand cannot escape.'

"Sir John Rowell replied gravely, 'It always wishes to escape. The chain is necessary.'

"With a rapid, questioning glance, I asked myself, 'Is he mad, or is that an unpleasant joke?'

"But the face remained impenetrable, tranquil, and friendly. I spoke of other things and admired the guns.

"Nevertheless, I noticed three loaded revolvers on the pieces of furniture, as if this man lived in constant fear of attack.

"I went there many times after that; then for some time I did not go. We had become accustomed to his presence; he had become indifferent to us.

"A whole year slipped away. Then, one morning, toward the end of November, my domestic awoke me with the announcement that Sir John Rowell had been assassinated in the night.

"A half hour later, I entered the Englishman's house with the central Commissary and the Captain of Police. The servant, lost in despair, was weeping at the door. I suspected him at first, but afterward found that he was innocent.

"The guilty one could never be found.

"Upon entering Sir John's drawing-room, I perceived his dead body stretched out upon its back, in the middle of the room. His waistcoat was torn, a sleeve was hanging, and it was evident that a terrible struggle had taken place.

"The Englishman had been strangled! His frightfully black and swollen face seemed to express an abominable fear; he held something between his set teeth; and his neck, pierced with five holes apparently done with a pointed iron, was covered with blood.

"A doctor joined us. He examined closely the prints of fingers in the flesh and pronounced these strange words, 'One would think he had been strangled by a skeleton.'

"A shiver ran down my back and I cast my eyes to the place on the wall where I had seen the horrible, torn-off hand. It was no longer there. The chain was broken and hanging.

"Then I bent over the dead man and found in his mouth a piece of one of the fingers of the missing hand, cut off, or rather sawed off by the teeth exactly at the second joint.

"Then they tried to collect evidence. They could find nothing. No door had been forced, no window opened, or piece of furniture moved. The two watchdogs on the premises had not been aroused.

"Here, in a few words, is the deposition of the servant:

"For a month, his master had seemed agitated. He had received many letters which he had burned immediately. Often, taking a whip, in anger which seemed like dementia, he had struck in fury, this dried hand, fastened to the wall and taken, one knew not how, at the moment of a crime.

"He had retired late and shut himself in with care. He always carried arms. Often in the night he talked out loud, as if he were quarreling with someone. On that night, however, there had been no noise, and it was only on coming to open the windows that the servant had found Sir John assassinated. He suspected no one.

"I communicated what I knew of the death to the magistrates and public officers, and they made minute inquiries upon the whole island. They discovered nothing.

"One night, three months after the crime, I had a frightful nightmare. It seemed to me that I saw that hand, that horrible hand, running like a scorpion or a spider along my curtains and my walls. Three times I awoke, three times I fell asleep and again saw that hideous relic galloping about my room, moving its fingers like paws.

"The next day they brought it to me, found in the cemetery upon the tomb where Sir John Rowell was interred—for they had not been able to find his family. The index finger was missing.

"This, ladies, is my story. I know no more about it."

The ladies were terrified, pale, and shivering. One of them cried, "But that is not the end, for there was no explanation! We cannot sleep if you do not tell us what was your idea of the reason of it all."

The magistrate smiled with severity, and answered, "Oh! certainly, ladies, but it will spoil all your terrible dreams. I simply think that the legitimate proprietor of the hand was not dead and that he came for it with the one that remained to him. But I was never able to find out how he did it. It was one kind of revenge."

One of the women murmured, "No, it could not be thus."

And the Judge of Information, smiling still, concluded, "I told you in the beginning that my explanation would not satisfy you."

HERBERT WEST: REANIMATOR

H. P. Lovecraft

The works of Howard Phillips Lovecraft originally appeared in pulp magazines and through amateur presses, and he remained virtually unknown until well after his death. It was through the persistent efforts of his friends and admirers that he finally received a wider (and ever-growing) audience. Two fellow writers tried to convince publishers to reprint posthumous collections of Lovecraft's work. When their efforts failed, they formed their own publishing company and published the books themselves. Soon the major publishers began coming out with collections of his stories. He is now one of the best-known authors of horror and supernatural fiction.

Lovecraft created the Cthulhu Mythos, a series of stories that other authors have widely imitated and supplemented. His most famous stories are "The Call of Cthulhu" and "The Dunwich Horror." Much of his work has been made into movies, and even some fantasy role-playing and computer games are based on his work. His stories are now continually in print and he's considered to be one of the great masters of the macabre and the father of modern horror. His best stories are a blend of science fiction and horror, of which this is an excellent example.

✦ ✦ ✦

FROM THE DARK

Of Herbert West, who was my friend in college and in after life, I can speak only with extreme terror. This terror is not due altogether to the sinister manner of his recent disappearance, but was engendered by the whole nature of his life-work, and first gained its acute form more than seventeen years ago, when we were in the third year of our course at the Miskatonic University Medical School in Arkham. While he was with me, the wonder and diabolism of his experiments fascinated me utterly, and I was his closest companion. Now that he is gone and the spell is broken, the actual fear is greater. Memories and possibilities are ever more hideous than realities.

The first horrible incident of our acquaintance was the greatest shock I ever experienced, and it is only with reluctance that I repeat it. As I have said, it happened when we were in the medical school where West had already made himself notorious through his wild theories on the nature of death and the possibility of overcoming it artificially. His views, which were widely ridiculed by the faculty and by his fellow-students, hinged on the essentially mechanistic nature of life; and concerned means for operating the organic machinery of mankind by calculated chemical action after the failure of natural processes. In his experiments with various animating solutions, he had killed and treated immense numbers of rabbits, guinea-pigs, cats, dogs, and monkeys, till he had become the prime nuisance of the college. Several times he had actually obtained signs of life in animals supposedly dead; in many cases violent signs; but he soon saw that the perfection of his process, if indeed possible, would necessarily involve a lifetime of research. It likewise became clear that, since the same solution never worked alike on different organic species, he would require human subjects for further and more specialized progress. It was here that he first came into conflict with the college authorities, and was debarred from future experiments by no less a dignitary than the dean of the medical school himself—the learned and benevolent Dr. Allan Halsey, whose work in behalf of the stricken is recalled by every old resident of Arkham.

I had always been exceptionally tolerant of West's pursuits, and we frequently discussed his theories, whose ramifications and corollaries were almost infinite. Holding with Haeckel that all life is a chemical and physical process, and that the so-called "soul" is a myth, my friend believed that artificial reanimation of the dead can depend only on the condition of the tissues; and that unless actual decomposition has set in, a corpse fully equipped with organs may with suitable measures be set going again in the peculiar fashion known as life. That the psychic or intellectual life might be impaired by the slight deterioration of sensitive brain-cells which even a short period of death would be apt to cause, West fully realized. It had at first been his hope to find a reagent which would restore vitality before the actual advent of death, and only repeated failures on animals had shewn him that the natural and artificial life-motions were incompatible. He then sought extreme freshness in his specimens, injecting his solutions into the blood immediately after the extinction of life. It was this circumstance which made the professors so carelessly skeptical, for they felt that true death had not occurred in any case. They did not stop to view the matter closely and reasoningly.

It was not long after the faculty had interdicted his work that West confided to me his resolution to get fresh human bodies in some manner, and continue in secret the experiments he could no longer perform openly. To hear him discussing ways and means was rather ghastly, for at the college we had never procured anatomical specimens ourselves. Whenever the morgue proved inadequate, two local men attended to this matter, and they were seldom questioned. West was then a small, slender, spectacled youth with delicate features, yellow hair, pale blue eyes, and a soft voice, and it was uncanny to hear him dwelling on the relative merits of Christchurch Cemetery and the potter's field. We finally decided on the potter's field, because practically every body in

Christchurch was embalmed; a thing of course ruinous to West's researches.

I was by this time his active and enthralled assistant, and helped him make all his decisions, not only concerning the source of bodies but concerning a suitable place for our loathsome work. It was I who thought of the deserted Chapman farmhouse beyond Meadow Hill, where we fitted up on the ground floor an operating room and a laboratory, each with dark curtains to conceal our midnight doings. The place was far from any road, and in sight of no other house, yet precautions were none the less necessary; since rumors of strange lights, started by chance nocturnal roamers, would soon bring disaster on our enterprise. It was agreed to call the whole thing a chemical laboratory if discovery should occur. Gradually we equipped our sinister haunt of science with materials either purchased in Boston or quietly borrowed from the college—materials carefully made unrecognizable save to expert eyes—and provided spades and picks for the many burials we should have to make in the cellar. At the college we used an incinerator, but the apparatus was too costly for our unauthorized laboratory. Bodies were always a nuisance—even the small guinea-pig bodies from the slight clandestine experiments in West's room at the boarding-house.

We followed the local death-notices like ghouls, for our specimens demanded particular qualities. What we wanted were corpses interred soon after death and without artificial preservation; preferably free from malforming disease, and certainly with all organs present. Accident victims were our best hope. Not for many weeks did we hear of anything suitable; though we talked with morgue and hospital authorities, ostensibly in the college's interest, as often as we could without exciting suspicion. We found that the college had first choice in every case, so that it might be necessary to remain in Arkham during the summer, when only the limited summer-school classes were held. In the end, though, luck favored us; for one day we heard of an almost ideal case in the potter's field; a brawny young workman drowned only the morning before in Summer's Pond, and buried at the town's expense without delay or embalming. That afternoon we found the new grave, and determined to begin work soon after midnight.

It was a repulsive task that we undertook in the black small hours, even though we lacked at that time the special horror of graveyards which later experiences brought to us. We carried spades and oil dark lanterns, for although electric torches were then manufactured, they were not as satisfactory as the tungsten contrivances of today. The process of unearthing was slow and sordid—it might have been gruesomely poetical if we had been artists instead of scientists—and we were glad when our spades struck wood. When the pine box was fully uncovered, West scrambled down and removed the lid, dragging out and propping up the contents. I reached down and hauled the contents out of the grave, and then both toiled hard to restore the spot to its former appearance. The affair made us rather nervous, especially the stiff form and vacant face of our first trophy, but we managed to remove all traces of our visit. When we had patted down the last shovelful of earth, we put the specimen in a canvas sack and set out for the old Chapman place beyond Meadow Hill.

On an improvised dissecting-table in the old farmhouse, by the light of a powerful acetylene lamp, the specimen was not very spectral looking. It had been a sturdy and apparently unimaginative youth of wholesome plebeian type—large-framed, grey-eyed, and brown-haired—a sound animal without psychological subtleties, and probably having vital processes of the simplest and healthiest sort. Now, with the eyes closed, it looked more asleep than dead; though the expert test of my friend soon left no doubt on that score. We had at last what West had always longed for—a real dead man of the ideal kind, ready for the solution as prepared according to the most careful calculations and theories for human use. The tension on our part became very great. We knew that there was scarcely a chance for anything like complete success, and could not avoid hideous fears at possible grotesque results of partial animation. Especially were we apprehensive concerning the mind and impulses of the creature, since in the space following death some of the more delicate cerebral cells might well have suffered deterioration. I, myself, still held some curious notions about the traditional "soul" of man, and felt an awe at the secrets that might be told by one returning from the dead. I wondered what sights this placid youth might have seen in inaccessible spheres, and what he could relate if fully restored to life. But my wonder was not overwhelming, since for the most part I shared the materialism of my friend. He was calmer than I as he forced a large quantity of his fluid into a vein of the body's arm, immediately binding the incision securely.

The waiting was gruesome, but West never faltered. Every now and then he applied his stethoscope to the specimen, and bore the negative results philosophically. After about three-quarters of an hour without the least sign of life he disappointedly pronounced the solution inadequate, but determined to make the most of his opportunity and try one change in the formula before disposing of his ghastly prize. We had that afternoon dug a grave in the cellar, and would have to fill it by dawn—for although we had fixed a lock on the house, we wished to shun even the remotest risk of a ghoulish discovery. Besides, the body would not be even approximately fresh the next night. So taking the solitary acetylene lamp into the adjacent laboratory, we left our silent guest on the slab in the dark, and bent every energy to the mixing of a new solution; the weighing and measuring supervised by West with an almost fanatical care.

The awful event was very sudden, and wholly unexpected. I was pouring something from one test-tube to another, and West was busy over the alcohol blast-lamp which had to answer for a Bunsen burner in this gasless edifice, when from the pitch-black room we had left there burst the most appalling and daemoniac succession of cries that either of us had ever heard. Not more unutterable could have been the chaos of hellish sound if the pit itself had opened to release the agony of the damned, for in one inconceivable cacophony was centered all the supernal terror and unnatural despair of animate nature. Human it could not have been—it is not in man to make such sounds—and without a thought of our late employment or its possible discovery, both West and I leaped to the nearest window like stricken animals; overturning tubes, lamp, and retorts, and vaulting madly into the starred abyss of the rural night. I think we screamed ourselves as we stumbled frantically toward the town, though as we reached the outskirts we put on a semblance of restraint—just enough to seem like belated revelers staggering home from a debauch.

We did not separate, but managed to get to West's room, where we whispered with the gas up until dawn. By then we had calmed ourselves a little with rational theories and plans for investigation, so that we could sleep through the day—classes being disregarded. But that evening two items in the paper, wholly unrelated, made it again impossible for us to sleep. The old deserted Chapman house had inexplicably burned to an amorphous heap of ashes; that we could understand because of the upset lamp. Also, an attempt had been made to disturb a new grave in the potter's field, as if by futile and spadeless clawing at the earth. That we could not understand, for we had patted down the mould very carefully.

And for seventeen years after that West would look frequently over his shoulder, and complain of fancied footsteps behind him. Now he has disappeared.

THE PLAGUE-DAEMON

I shall never forget that hideous summer sixteen years ago, when like a noxious afrite from the halls of Eblis typhoid stalked leeringly through Arkham. It is by that satanic scourge that most recall the year, for truly terror brooded with bat-wings over the piles of coffins in the tombs of Christchurch Cemetery; yet for me there is a greater horror in that time—a horror known to me alone now that Herbert West has disappeared.

West and I were doing post-graduate work in summer classes at the

medical school of Miskatonic University, and my friend had attained a
wide notoriety because of his experiments leading toward the revivifica-
tion of the dead. After the scientific slaughter of uncounted small animals the freakish work had ostensibly stopped by order of our skeptical
dean, Dr. Allan Halsey; though West had continued to perform certain
secret tests in his dingy boarding-house room, and had on one terrible
and unforgettable occasion taken a human body from its grave in the
potter's field to a deserted farmhouse beyond Meadow Hill.

I was with him on that odious occasion, and saw him inject into the
still veins the elixir which he thought would to some extent restore life's
chemical and physical processes. It had ended horribly—in a delirium
of fear which we gradually came to attribute to our own overwrought
nerves—and West had never afterward been able to shake off a maddening sensation of being haunted and hunted. The body had not been
quite fresh enough; it is obvious that to restore normal mental attri-
butes a body must be very fresh indeed; and the burning of the old
house had prevented us from burying the thing. It would have been
better if we could have known it was underground.

After that experience West had dropped his researches for some
time; but as the zeal of the born scientist slowly returned, he again became importunate with the college faculty, pleading for the use of the
dissecting-room and of fresh human specimens for the work he regarded
as so overwhelmingly important. His pleas, however, were wholly in
vain; for the decision of Dr. Halsey was inflexible, and the other professors all endorsed the verdict of their leader. In the radical theory of
reanimation they saw nothing but the immature vagaries of a youthful
enthusiast whose slight form, yellow hair, spectacled blue eyes, and soft
voice gave no hint of the supernormal—almost diabolical—power of
the cold brain within. I can see him now as he was then—and I shiver.
He grew sterner of face, but never elderly. And now Sefton Asylum has
had the mishap and West has vanished.

West clashed disagreeably with Dr. Halsey near the end of our last
undergraduate term in a wordy dispute that did less credit to him than

to the kindly dean in point of courtesy. He felt that he was needlessly and irrationally retarded in a supremely great work; a work which he could of course conduct to suit himself in later years, but which he wished to begin while still possessed of the exceptional facilities of the university. That the tradition-bound elders should ignore his singular results on animals, and persist in their denial of the possibility of reanimation, was inexpressibly disgusting and almost incomprehensible to a youth of West's logical temperament. Only greater maturity could help him understand the chronic mental limitations of the "professor-doctor" type—the product of generations of pathetic Puritanism; kindly, conscientious, and sometimes gentle and amiable, yet always narrow, intolerant, custom-ridden, and lacking in perspective. Age has more charity for these incomplete yet high-souled characters, whose worst real vice is timidity, and who are ultimately punished by general ridicule for their intellectual sins—sins like Ptolemaism, Calvinism, anti-Darwinism, anti-Nietzscheism, and every sort of Sabbatarianism and sumptuary legislation. West, young despite his marvelous scientific acquirements, had scant patience with good Dr. Halsey and his erudite colleagues; and nursed an increasing resentment, coupled with a desire to prove his theories to these obtuse worthies in some striking and dramatic fashion. Like most youths, he indulged in elaborate daydreams of revenge, triumph, and final magnanimous forgiveness.

And then had come the scourge, grinning and lethal, from the nightmare caverns of Tartarus. West and I had graduated about the time of its beginning, but had remained for additional work at the summer school, so that we were in Arkham when it broke with full daemoniac fury upon the town. Though not as yet licensed physicians, we now had our degrees, and were pressed frantically into public service as the numbers of the stricken grew. The situation was almost past management, and deaths ensued too frequently for the local undertakers fully to handle. Burials without embalming were made in rapid succession, and even the Christchurch Cemetery receiving tomb was crammed with coffins of the unembalmed dead. This circumstance was not without effect on West, who thought often of the irony of the situation—so many fresh specimens, yet none for his persecuted researches! We were frightfully overworked, and the terrific mental and nervous strain made my friend brood morbidly.

But West's gentle enemies were no less harassed with prostrating duties. College had all but closed, and every doctor of the medical faculty was helping to fight the typhoid plague. Dr. Halsey in particular had distinguished himself in sacrificing service, applying his extreme skill with whole-hearted energy to cases which many others shunned because of danger or apparent hopelessness. Before a month was over the fearless dean had become a popular hero, though he seemed unconscious of his fame as he struggled to keep from collapsing with physical fatigue and nervous exhaustion. West could not withhold admiration for the fortitude of his foe, but because of this was even more determined to prove to him the truth of his amazing doctrines. Taking advantage of the disorganization of both college work and municipal health regulations, he managed to get a recently deceased body smuggled into the university dissecting-room one night, and in my presence injected a new modification of his solution. The thing actually opened its eyes, but only stared at the ceiling with a look of soul-petrifying horror before collapsing into an inertness from which nothing could rouse it. West said it was not fresh enough—the hot summer air does not favor corpses. That time we were almost caught before we incinerated the thing, and West doubted the advisability of repeating his daring misuse of the college laboratory.

The peak of the epidemic was reached in August. West and I were almost dead, and Dr. Halsey did die on the 14th. The students all attended the hasty funeral on the 15th, and bought an impressive wreath, though the latter was quite overshadowed by the tributes sent by wealthy Arkham citizens and by the municipality itself. It was almost a public affair, for the dean had surely been a public benefactor. After the entombment we were all somewhat depressed, and spent the afternoon at the bar of the Commercial House; where West, though shaken by the death of his chief opponent, chilled the rest of us with references to his notorious theories. Most of the students went home, or to various duties, as the evening advanced; but West persuaded me to aid him in "making a night of it." West's landlady saw us arrive at his room about two in the morning, with a third man between us; and told her husband that we had all evidently dined and wined rather well.

Apparently this acidulous matron was right; for about 3 a.m. the whole house was aroused by cries coming from West's room, where when they broke down the door, they found the two of us unconscious on the blood-stained carpet, beaten, scratched, and mauled, and with the broken remnants of West's bottles and instruments around us. Only an open window told what had become of our assailant, and many wondered how he himself had fared after the terrific leap from the second story to the lawn which he must have made. There were some strange garments in the room, but West upon regaining consciousness said they did not belong to the stranger, but were specimens collected for bacteriological analysis in the course of investigations on the transmission of germ diseases. He ordered them burned as soon as possible in the capacious fireplace. To the police we both declared ignorance of our late companion's identity. He was, West nervously said, a congenial stranger whom we had met at some downtown bar of uncertain location. We had all been rather jovial, and West and I did not wish to have our pugnacious companion hunted down.

That same night saw the beginning of the second Arkham horror—the horror that to me eclipsed the plague itself. Christchurch Cemetery was the scene of a terrible killing; a watchman having been clawed to death in a manner not only too hideous for description, but raising a doubt as to the human agency of the deed. The victim had been seen alive considerably after midnight—the dawn revealed the unutterable thing. The manager of a circus at the neighboring town of Bolton was questioned, but he swore that no beast had at any time escaped from its cage. Those who found the body noted a trail of blood leading to the receiving tomb, where a small pool of red lay on the concrete just outside the gate. A fainter trail led away toward the woods, but it soon gave out.

The next night devils danced on the roofs of Arkham, and unnatural madness howled in the wind. Through the fevered town had crept a curse which some said was greater than the plague, and which some whispered was the embodied daemon-soul of the plague itself. Eight houses were entered by a nameless thing which strewed red death in its wake—in all, seventeen maimed and shapeless remnants of bodies were left behind by the voiceless, sadistic monster that crept abroad. A few persons had half seen it in the dark, and said it was white and like a malformed ape or anthropomorphic fiend. It had not left behind quite all that it had attacked, for sometimes it had been hungry. The number it had killed was fourteen; three of the bodies had been in stricken homes and had not been alive.

On the third night frantic bands of searchers, led by the police, captured it in a house on Crane Street near the Miskatonic campus. They had organized the quest with care, keeping in touch by means of volunteer telephone stations, and when someone in the college district had reported hearing a scratching at a shuttered window, the net was quickly spread. On account of the general alarm and precautions, there were only two more victims, and the capture was effected without major casualties. The thing was finally stopped by a bullet, though not a fatal one, and was rushed to the local hospital amidst universal excitement and loathing.

For it had been a man. This much was clear despite the nauseous eyes, the voiceless simianism, and the daemoniac savagery. They dressed its wound and carted it to the asylum at Sefton, where it beat its head against the walls of a padded cell for sixteen years—until the recent mishap, when it escaped under circumstances that few like to mention. What had most disgusted the searchers of Arkham was the thing they noticed when the monster's face was cleaned—the mocking, unbelievable resemblance to a learned and self-sacrificing martyr who had been entombed but three days before—the late Dr. Allan Halsey, public benefactor and dean of the medical school of Miskatonic University.

To the vanished Herbert West and to me the disgust and horror were supreme. I shudder tonight as I think of it; shudder even more than I did that morning when West muttered through his bandages, "Damn it, it wasn't quite fresh enough!"

SIX SHOTS BY MOONLIGHT

It is uncommon to fire all six shots of a revolver with great suddenness when one would probably be sufficient, but many things in the life of Herbert West were uncommon. It is, for instance, not often that a young physician leaving college is obliged to conceal the principles which guide his selection of a home and office, yet that was the case with Herbert West. When he and I obtained our degrees at the medical school of Miskatonic University, and sought to relieve our poverty by setting up as general practitioners, we took great care not to say that we chose our house because it was fairly well isolated, and as near as possible to the potter's field.

Reticence such as this is seldom without a cause, nor indeed was ours; for our requirements were those resulting from a life-work distinctly unpopular. Outwardly we were doctors only, but beneath the surface were aims of far greater and more terrible moment—for the essence of Herbert West's existence was a quest amid black and forbidden realms of the unknown, in which he hoped to uncover the secret of life and restore to perpetual animation the graveyard's cold clay. Such a quest demands strange materials, among them fresh human bodies; and in order to keep supplied with these indispensable things one must live quietly and not far from a place of informal interment.

West and I had met in college, and I had been the only one to sympathize with his hideous experiments. Gradually I had come to be his inseparable assistant, and now that we were out of college we had to keep together. It was not easy to find a good opening for two doctors in company, but finally the influence of the university secured us a practice in Bolton—a factory town near Arkham, the seat of the college. The Bolton Worsted Mills are the largest in the Miskatonic Valley, and their polyglot employees are never popular as patients with the local physicians. We chose our house with the greatest care, seizing at last on a rather run-down cottage near the end of Pond Street; five numbers from the closest neighbor, and separated from the local potter's field by only a stretch of meadow land, bisected by a narrow neck of the rather dense forest which lies to the north. The distance was greater than we wished, but we could get no nearer house without going on the other side of the field, wholly out of the factory district. We were not much displeased, however, since there were no people between us and our sinister source of supplies. The walk was a trifle long, but we could haul our silent specimens undisturbed.

Our practice was surprisingly large from the very first—large enough to please most young doctors, and large enough to prove a bore and a burden to students whose real interest lay elsewhere. The mill-hands were of somewhat turbulent inclinations; and besides their many natural needs, their frequent clashes and stabbing affrays gave us plenty to do. But what actually absorbed our minds was the secret laboratory we had fitted up in the cellar—the laboratory with the long table under the electric lights, where in the small hours of the morning we often injected West's various solutions into the veins of the things we dragged from the potter's field. West was experimenting madly to find something which would start man's vital motions anew after they had been stopped by the thing we call death, but had encountered the most ghastly obstacles. The solution had to be differently compounded for different types—what would serve for guinea-pigs would not serve for human beings, and different human specimens required large modifications.

The bodies had to be exceedingly fresh, or the slight decomposition of brain tissue would render perfect reanimation impossible. Indeed, the greatest problem was to get them fresh enough—West had had horrible experiences during his secret college researches with corpses of doubtful vintage. The results of partial or imperfect animation were much more hideous than were the total failures, and we both held fearsome recollections of such things. Ever since our first daemoniac session in the deserted farmhouse on Meadow Hill in Arkham, we had felt a brooding menace; and West, though a calm, blond, blue-eyed scientific automaton in most respects, often confessed to a shuddering sensation of stealthy pursuit. He half felt that he was followed—a psychological delusion of shaken nerves, enhanced by the undeniably disturbing fact that at least one of our reanimated specimens was still alive—a frightful carnivorous thing in a padded cell at Sefton. Then there was another—our first—whose exact fate we had never learned.

We had fair luck with specimens in Bolton—much better than in Arkham. We had not been settled a week before we got an accident victim on the very night of burial, and made it open its eyes with an amazingly rational expression before the solution failed. It had lost an arm—if it had been a perfect body we might have succeeded better. Between then and the next January we secured three more; one total failure, one case of marked muscular motion, and one rather shivery thing—it rose of itself and uttered a sound. Then came a period when luck was poor; interments fell off, and those that did occur were of specimens either too diseased or too maimed for use. We kept track of all the deaths and their circumstances with systematic care.

One March night, however, we unexpectedly obtained a specimen which did not come from the potter's field. In Bolton the prevailing spirit of Puritanism had outlawed the sport of boxing—with the usual result. Surreptitious and ill-conducted bouts among the mill-workers were common, and occasionally professional talent of low grade was imported. This late winter night there had been such a match; evidently with disastrous results, since two timorous Poles had come to us with incoherently whispered entreaties to attend to a very secret and desperate case. We followed them to an abandoned barn, where the remnants of a crowd of frightened foreigners were watching a silent form on the floor.

The match had been between Kid O'Brien—a lubberly and now quaking youth with a most un-Hibernian hooked nose—and Buck Robinson, "The Harlem Smoke." The fighter had been knocked out, and a moment's examination showed us that he would permanently remain so. He was a loathsome, gorilla-like thing, with abnormally long arms which I could not help calling fore legs, and a face that conjured up thoughts of unspeakable Congo secrets and tom-tom poundings under an eerie moon. The body must have looked even worse in life—but the world holds many ugly things. Fear was upon the whole pitiful crowd, for they did not know what the law would exact of them if the affair were not hushed up; and they were grateful when West, in spite of my involuntary shudders, offered to get rid of the thing quietly—for a purpose I knew too well.

There was bright moonlight over the snowless landscape, but we dressed the thing and carried it home between us through the deserted streets and meadows, as we had carried a similar thing one horrible night in Arkham. We approached the house from the field in the rear, took the specimen in the back door and down the cellar stairs, and prepared it for the usual experiment. Our fear of the police was absurdly great, though we had timed our trip to avoid the solitary patrolman of that section.

The result was wearily anticlimactic. Ghastly as our prize appeared, it was wholly unresponsive to every solution we injected in its arm; solutions prepared from experience with white specimens only. So as the hour grew dangerously near to dawn, we did as we had done with the others—dragged the thing across the meadows to the neck of the woods near the potter's field, and buried it there in the best sort of grave the frozen ground would furnish. The grave was not very deep, but fully as good as that of the previous specimen—the thing which had risen of itself and uttered a sound. In the light of our dark lanterns we carefully covered it with leaves and dead vines, fairly certain that the police would never find it in a forest so dim and dense.

The next day I was increasingly apprehensive about the police, for a patient brought rumors of a suspected fight and death. West had still another source of worry, for he had been called in the afternoon to a case which ended very threateningly. An Italian woman had become hysterical over her missing child—a lad of five who had strayed off early in the morning and failed to appear for dinner—and had developed symptoms highly alarming in view of an always weak heart. It was a very foolish hysteria, for the boy had often run away before; but Italian peasants are exceedingly superstitious, and this woman seemed as much harassed by omens as by facts. About seven o'clock in the evening she had died, and her frantic husband had made a frightful scene in his efforts to kill West, whom he wildly blamed for not saving her life. Friends had held him when he drew a stiletto, but West departed amidst his inhuman shrieks, curses and oaths of vengeance. In his latest affliction the fellow seemed to have forgotten his child, who was still missing as the night advanced. There was some talk of searching the woods, but most of the family's friends were busy with the dead woman and the screaming man. Altogether, the nervous strain upon West must have been tremendous. Thoughts of the police and of the mad Italian both weighed heavily.

We retired about eleven, but I did not sleep well. Bolton had a surprisingly good police force for so small a town, and I could not help fearing the mess which would ensue if the affair of the night before were ever tracked down. It might mean the end of all our local work—and perhaps prison for both West and me. I did not like those rumors of a fight which were floating about. After the clock had struck three the moon shone in my eyes, but I turned over without rising to pull down the shade. Then came the steady rattling at the back door.

I lay still and somewhat dazed, but before long heard West's rap on my door. He was clad in dressing gown and slippers, and had in his hands a revolver and an electric flashlight. From the revolver I knew that he was thinking more of the crazed Italian than of the police.

"We'd better both go," he whispered. "It wouldn't do not to answer it anyway, and it may be a patient—it would be like one of those fools to try the back door."

So we both went down the stairs on tiptoe, with a fear partly justified and partly that which comes only from the soul of the weird small hours. The rattling continued, growing somewhat louder. When we reached the door I cautiously unbolted it and threw it open, and as the moon streamed revealingly down on the form silhouetted there, West did a peculiar thing. Despite the obvious danger of attracting notice and bringing down on our heads the dreaded police investigation—a thing which after all was mercifully averted by the relative isolation of our cottage—my friend suddenly, excitedly, and unnecessarily emptied all six chambers of his revolver into the nocturnal visitor.

For that visitor was neither Italian nor policeman. Looming hideously against the spectral moon was a gigantic misshapen thing not to be imagined save in nightmares—a glassy-eyed apparition nearly on all fours, covered with bits of mould, leaves, and vines, foul with caked blood, and having between its glistening teeth a snow-white, terrible, cylindrical object terminating in a tiny hand.

THE SCREAM OF THE DEAD

The scream of a dead man gave to me that acute and added horror of Dr. Herbert West which harassed the latter years of our companionship. It is natural that such a thing as a dead man's scream should give horror, for it is obviously, not a pleasing or ordinary occurrence; but I was used to similar experiences, hence suffered on this occasion only because of a particular circumstance. And, as I have implied, it was not of the dead man himself that I became afraid.

Herbert West, whose associate and assistant I was, possessed scientific interests far beyond the usual routine of a village physician. That was why, when establishing his practice in Bolton, he had chosen an isolated house near the potter's field. Briefly and brutally stated, West's sole absorbing interest was a secret study of the phenomena of life and its cessation, leading toward the reanimation of the dead through injections of an excitant solution. For this ghastly experimenting it was necessary to have a constant supply of very fresh human bodies; very fresh because even the least decay hopelessly damaged the brain structure, and human because we found that the solution had to be compounded differently for different types of organisms. Scores of rabbits and guinea-pigs had been killed and treated, but their trail was a blind one. West had never fully succeeded because he had never been able to secure a corpse sufficiently fresh. What he wanted were bodies from which vitality had only just departed; bodies with every cell intact and capable of receiving again the impulse toward that mode of motion called life. There was hope that this second and artificial life might be made perpetual by repetitions of the injection, but we had learned that an ordinary natural life would not respond to the action. To establish the artificial motion, natural life must be extinct—the specimens must be very fresh, but genuinely dead.

The awesome quest had begun when West and I were students at the Miskatonic University Medical School in Arkham, vividly conscious for the first time of the thoroughly mechanical nature of life. That was seven years before, but West looked scarcely a day older now—he was small, blond, clean-shaven, soft-voiced, and spectacled, with only an occasional flash of a cold blue eye to tell of the hardening and growing fanaticism of his character under the pressure of his terrible investigations. Our experiences had often been hideous in the extreme; the results of defective reanimation, when lumps of graveyard clay had been galvanized into morbid, unnatural, and brainless motion by various modifications of the vital solution.

One thing had uttered a nerve-shattering scream; another had risen violently, beaten us both to unconsciousness, and run amuck in a shocking way before it could be placed behind asylum bars; still another, a loathsome African monstrosity, had clawed out of its shallow grave and done a deed—West had had to shoot that object. We could not get bodies fresh enough to show any trace of reason when reanimated, so had perforce created nameless horrors. It was disturbing to think that one, perhaps two, of our monsters still lived—that thought haunted us shadowingly, till finally West disappeared under frightful circumstances. But at the time of the scream in the cellar laboratory of the isolated Bolton cottage, our fears were subordinate to our anxiety for extremely fresh specimens. West was more avid than I, so that it almost seemed to me that he looked half-covetously at any very healthy living physique.

It was in July, 1910, that the bad luck regarding specimens began to turn. I had been on a long visit to my parents in Illinois, and upon my return found West in a state of singular elation. He had, he told me excitedly, in all likelihood solved the problem of freshness through an approach from an entirely new angle—that of artificial preservation. I had known that he was working on a new and highly unusual embalming compound, and was not surprised that it had turned out well; but until he explained the details I was rather puzzled as to how such a compound could help in our work, since the objectionable staleness of the specimens was largely due to delay occurring before we secured them. This, I now saw, West had clearly recognized; creating his embalming compound for future rather than immediate use, and trusting to fate to supply again some very recent and unburied corpse, as it had years before when we obtained the boxer killed in the Bolton prizefight. At last fate had been kind, so that on this occasion there lay in the secret cellar laboratory a corpse whose decay could not by any possibility have begun. What would happen on reanimation, and whether we could hope for a revival of mind and reason, West did not venture to predict. The experiment would be a landmark in our studies, and he had saved the new body for my return, so that both might share the spectacle in accustomed fashion.

West told me how he had obtained the specimen. It had been a

vigorous man; a well-dressed stranger just off the train on his way
to transact some business with the Bolton Worsted Mills. The walk
through the town had been long, and by the time the traveler paused
at our cottage to ask the way to the factories, his heart had become
greatly overtaxed. He had refused a stimulant, and had suddenly
dropped dead only a moment later. The body, as might be expected,
seemed to West a heaven-sent gift. In his brief conversation the stranger
had made it clear that he was unknown in Bolton, and a search of his
pockets subsequently revealed him to be one Robert Leavitt of St.
Louis, apparently without a family to make instant inquiries about his
disappearance. If this man could not be restored to life, no one would
know of our experiment. We buried our materials in a dense strip of
woods between the house and the potter's field. If, on the other hand,
he could be restored, our fame would be brilliantly and perpetually established. So without delay West had injected into the body's wrist the
compound which would hold it fresh for use after my arrival. The matter of the presumably weak heart, which to my mind imperiled the success of our experiment, did not appear to trouble West extensively. He
hoped at last to obtain what he had never obtained before—a rekindled
spark of reason and perhaps a normal, living creature.

So on the night of July 18, 1910, Herbert West and I stood in the
cellar laboratory and gazed at a white, silent figure beneath the dazzling
arc-light. The embalming compound had worked uncannily well, for as
I stared fascinatedly at the sturdy frame which had lain two weeks without stiffening, I was moved to seek West's assurance that the thing was
really dead. This assurance he gave readily enough; reminding me that
the reanimating solution was never used without careful tests as to life,
since it could have no effect if any of the original vitality were present.
As West proceeded to take preliminary steps, I was impressed by the
vast intricacy of the new experiment; an intricacy so vast that he could
trust no hand less delicate than his own. Forbidding me to touch the
body, he first injected a drug in the wrist just beside the place his needle
had punctured when injecting the embalming compound. This, he said,

was to neutralize the compound and release the system to a normal relaxation so that the reanimating solution might freely work when injected. Slightly later, when a change and a gentle tremor seemed to affect the dead limbs; West stuffed a pillow-like object violently over the twitching face, not withdrawing it until the corpse appeared quiet and ready for our attempt at reanimation. The pale enthusiast now applied some last perfunctory tests for absolute lifelessness, withdrew satisfied, and finally injected into the left arm an accurately measured amount of the vital elixir, prepared during the afternoon with a greater care than we had used since college days, when our feats were new and groping. I cannot express the wild, breathless suspense with which we waited for results on this first really fresh specimen—the first we could reasonably expect to open its lips in rational speech, perhaps to tell of what it had seen beyond the unfathomable abyss.

West was a materialist, believing in no soul and attributing all the working of consciousness to bodily phenomena; consequently he looked for no revelation of hideous secrets from gulfs and caverns beyond death's barrier. I did not wholly disagree with him theoretically, yet held vague instinctive remnants of the primitive faith of my forefathers; so that I could not help eyeing the corpse with a certain amount of awe and terrible expectation. Besides—I could not extract from my memory that hideous, inhuman shriek we heard on the night we tried our first experiment in the deserted farmhouse at Arkham.

Very little time had elapsed before I saw the attempt was not to be a total failure. A touch of color came to cheeks hitherto chalk-white, and spread out under the curiously ample stubble of sandy beard. West, who had his hand on the pulse of the left wrist, suddenly nodded significantly; and almost simultaneously a mist appeared on the mirror inclined above the body's mouth. There followed a few spasmodic muscular motions, and then an audible breathing and visible motion of the chest. I looked at the closed eyelids, and thought I detected a quivering. Then the lids opened, showing eyes which were grey, calm, and alive, but still unintelligent and not even curious.

In a moment of fantastic whim I whispered questions to the reddening ears; questions of other worlds of which the memory might still be present. Subsequent terror drove them from my mind, but I think the last one, which I repeated, was: "Where have you been?" I do not yet know whether I was answered or not, for no sound came from the well-shaped mouth; but I do know that at that moment I firmly thought the thin lips moved silently, forming syllables which I would have vocalized as "only now" if that phrase had possessed any sense or relevancy. At that moment, as I say, I was elated with the conviction that the one great goal had been attained; and that for the first time a reanimated corpse had uttered distinct words impelled by actual reason. In the next moment there was no doubt about the triumph; no doubt that the solution had truly accomplished, at least temporarily, its full mission of restoring rational and articulate life to the dead. But in that triumph there came to me the greatest of all horrors—not horror of the thing that spoke, but of the deed that I had witnessed and of the man with whom my professional fortunes were joined.

For that very fresh body, at last writhing into full and terrifying consciousness with eyes dilated at the memory of its last scene on earth, threw out its frantic hands in a life and death struggle with the air, and suddenly collapsing into a second and final dissolution from which there could be no return, screamed out the cry that will ring eternally in my aching brain:

"Help! Keep off, you cursed little tow-head fiend—keep that damned needle away from me!"

THE HORROR FROM THE SHADOWS

Many men have related hideous things, not mentioned in print, which happened on the battlefields of the Great War. Some of these things have made me faint, others have convulsed me with devastating nausea, while still others have made me tremble and look behind me in the dark; yet despite the worst of them I believe I can myself relate the most hideous thing of all—the shocking, the unnatural, the unbelievable horror from the shadows.

In 1915 I was a physician with the rank of First Lieutenant in a Canadian regiment in Flanders, one of many Americans to precede the government itself into the gigantic struggle. I had not entered the army on my own initiative, but rather as a natural result of the enlistment of the man whose indispensable assistant I was—the celebrated Boston surgical specialist, Dr. Herbert West. Dr. West had been avid for a chance to serve as surgeon in a great war, and when the chance had come, he carried me with him almost against my will. There were reasons why I could have been glad to let the war separate us; reasons why I found the practice of medicine and the companionship of West more and more irritating; but when he had gone to Ottawa and through a colleague's influence secured a medical commission as Major, I could not resist the imperious persuasion of one determined that I should accompany him in my usual capacity.

When I say that Dr. West was avid to serve in battle, I do not mean to imply that he was either naturally warlike or anxious for the safety of civilization. Always an ice-cold intellectual machine; slight, blond, blue-eyed, and spectacled; I think he secretly sneered at my occasional martial enthusiasms and censures of supine neutrality. There was, however, something he wanted in embattled Flanders; and in order to secure it had had to assume a military exterior. What he wanted was not a thing which many persons want, but something connected with the peculiar branch of medical science which he had chosen quite clandestinely to follow, and in which he had achieved amazing and occasionally hideous results. It was, in fact, nothing more or less than an abundant supply of freshly killed men in every stage of dismemberment.

Herbert West needed fresh bodies because his life-work was the reanimation of the dead. This work was not known to the fashionable clientele who had so swiftly built up his fame after his arrival in Boston; but was only too well known to me, who had been his closest friend and sole assistant since the old days in Miskatonic University Medical School at Arkham. It was in those college days that he had begun his terrible experiments, first on small animals and then on human bodies shockingly obtained. There was a solution which he injected into the veins of dead things, and if they were fresh enough they responded in strange ways. He had had much trouble in discovering the proper formula, for each type of organism was found to need a stimulus especially adapted to it. Terror stalked him when he reflected on his partial failures; nameless things resulting from imperfect solutions or from bodies insufficiently fresh. A certain number of these failures had remained alive—one was in an asylum while others had vanished—and as he thought of conceivable yet virtually impossible eventualities he often shivered beneath his usual stolidity.

West had soon learned that absolute freshness was the prime requisite for useful specimens, and had accordingly resorted to frightful and unnatural expedients in body-snatching. In college, and during our early practice together in the factory town of Bolton, my attitude toward him had been largely one of fascinated admiration; but as his boldness in methods grew, I began to develop a gnawing fear. I did not like the way he looked at healthy living bodies; and then there came a nightmarish session in the cellar laboratory when I learned that a certain specimen had been a living body when he secured it. That was the first time he had ever been able to revive the quality of rational thought in a corpse; and his success, obtained at such a loathsome cost, had completely hardened him.

Of his methods in the intervening five years I dare not speak. I was held to him by sheer force of fear, and witnessed sights that no human tongue could repeat. Gradually I came to find Herbert West himself more horrible than anything he did—that was when it dawned on me that his once normal scientific zeal for prolonging life had subtly degenerated into a mere morbid and ghoulish curiosity and secret sense of charnel picturesqueness. His interest became a hellish and perverse addiction to the repellently and fiendishly abnormal; he gloated calmly over artificial monstrosities which would make most healthy men drop dead from fright and disgust; he became, behind his pallid intellectuality, a fastidious Baudelaire of physical experiment—a languid Elagabalus of the tombs.

Dangers he met unflinchingly; crimes he committed unmoved. I think the climax came when he had proved his point that rational life can be restored, and had sought new worlds to conquer by experimenting on the reanimation of detached parts of bodies. He had wild and original ideas on the independent vital properties of organic cells and nerve-tissue separated from natural physiological systems; and achieved some hideous preliminary results in the form of never-dying, artificially nourished tissue obtained from the nearly hatched eggs of an indescribable tropical reptile. Two biological points he was exceedingly anxious to settle—first, whether any amount of consciousness and rational action be possible without the brain, proceeding from the spinal cord and various nerve-centers; and second, whether any kind of ethereal, intangible relation distinct from the material cells may exist to link the surgically separated parts of what has previously been a single living organism. All this research work required a prodigious supply of freshly slaughtered human flesh—and that was why Herbert West had entered the Great War.

The phantasmal, unmentionable thing occurred one midnight late in March, 1915, in a field hospital behind the lines of St. Eloi. I wonder even now if it could have been other than a daemoniac dream of delirium. West had a private laboratory in an east room of the barn-like temporary edifice, assigned him on his plea that he was devising new and radical methods for the treatment of hitherto hopeless cases of maiming. There he worked like a butcher in the midst of his gory wares—I could never get used to the levity with which he handled and classified certain things. At times he actually did perform marvels of surgery for the soldiers; but his chief delights were of a less public and philanthropic kind, requiring many explanations of sounds which

seemed peculiar even amidst that babel of the damned. Among these
sounds were frequent revolver-shots—surely not uncommon on a battlefield, but distinctly uncommon in a hospital. Dr. West's reanimated
specimens were not meant for long existence or a large audience. Besides human tissue, West employed much of the reptile embryo tissue
which he had cultivated with such singular results. It was better than
human material for maintaining life in organless fragments, and that
was now my friend's chief activity. In a dark corner of the laboratory,
over a queer incubating burner, he kept a large covered vat full of this
reptilian cell-matter; which multiplied and grew puffily and hideously.

On the night of which I speak we had a splendid new specimen—a
man at once physically powerful and of such high mentality that a sensitive nervous system was assured. It was rather ironic, for he was the officer who had helped West to his commission, and who was now to have
been our associate. Moreover, he had in the past secretly studied the
theory of reanimation to some extent under West. Major Sir Eric
Moreland Clapham-Lee, D.S.O., was the greatest surgeon in our division, and had been hastily assigned to the St. Eloi sector when news of
the heavy fighting reached headquarters. He had come in an airplane
piloted by the intrepid Lieut. Ronald Hill, only to be shot down when
directly over his destination. The fall had been spectacular and awful;
Hill was unrecognizable afterward, but the wreck yielded up the great
surgeon in a nearly decapitated but otherwise intact condition. West had
greedily seized the lifeless thing which had once been his friend and
fellow-scholar; and I shuddered when he finished severing the head,
placed it in his hellish vat of pulpy reptile-tissue to preserve it for future
experiments, and proceeded to treat the decapitated body on the operating table. He injected new blood, joined certain veins, arteries, and nerves
at the headless neck, and closed the ghastly aperture with engrafted skin
from an unidentified specimen which had borne an officer's uniform. I
knew what he wanted—to see if this highly organized body could exhibit, without its head, any of the signs of mental life which had distin-

guished Sir Eric Moreland Clapham-Lee. Once a student of reanimation, this silent trunk was now gruesomely called upon to exemplify it.

I can still see Herbert West under the sinister electric light as he injected his reanimating solution into the arm of the headless body. The scene I cannot describe—I should faint if I tried it, for there is madness in a room full of classified charnel things, with blood and lesser human debris almost ankle-deep on the slimy floor, and with hideous reptilian abnormalities sprouting, bubbling, and baking over a winking bluish-green specter of dim flame in a far corner of black shadows.

The specimen, as West repeatedly observed, had a splendid nervous system. Much was expected of it; and as a few twitching motions began to appear, I could see the feverish interest on West's face. He was ready, I think, to see proof of his increasingly strong opinion that conscious-ness, reason, and personality can exist independently of the brain—that man has no central connective spirit, but is merely a machine of nervous matter, each section more or less complete in itself. In one triumphant demonstration West was about to relegate the mystery of life to the category of myth. The body now twitched more vigorously, and beneath our avid eyes commenced to heave in a frightful way. The arms stirred disquietingly, the legs drew up, and various muscles contracted in a re-pulsive kind of writhing. Then the headless thing threw out its arms in a gesture which was unmistakably one of desperation—an intelligent desperation apparently sufficient to prove every theory of Herbert West. Certainly, the nerves were recalling the man's last act in life; the struggle to get free of the falling airplane.

What followed, I shall never positively know. It may have been wholly a hallucination from the shock caused at that instant by the sud-den and complete destruction of the building in a cataclysm of German shell-fire—who can gainsay it, since West and I were the only proved survivors? West liked to think that before his recent disappearance, but there were times when he could not; for it was queer that we both had the same hallucination. The hideous occurrence itself was very simple, notable only for what it implied.

The body on the table had risen with a blind and terrible groping, and we had heard a sound. I should not call that sound a voice, for it was too awful. And yet its timbre was not the most awful thing about it. Neither was its message—it had merely screamed, "Jump, Ronald, for God's sake, jump!" The awful thing was its source.

For it had come from the large covered vat in that ghoulish corner of crawling black shadows.

THE TOMB-LEGIONS

When Dr. Herbert West disappeared a year ago, the Boston police questioned me closely. They suspected that I was holding something back, and perhaps suspected graver things; but I could not tell them the truth because they would not have believed it. They knew, indeed, that West had been connected with activities beyond the credence of ordinary men; for his hideous experiments in the reanimation of dead bodies had long been too extensive to admit of perfect secrecy; but the final soul-shattering catastrophe held elements of daemoniac phantasy which make even me doubt the reality of what I saw.

I was West's closest friend and only confidential assistant. We had met years before, in medical school, and from the first I had shared his terrible researches. He had slowly tried to perfect a solution which, injected into the veins of the newly deceased, would restore life; a labor demanding an abundance of fresh corpses and therefore involving the most unnatural actions. Still more shocking were the products of some of the experiments—grisly masses of flesh that had been dead, but that West waked to a blind, brainless, nauseous animation. These were the usual results, for in order to reawaken the mind it was necessary to have specimens so absolutely fresh that no decay could possibly affect the delicate brain-cells.

This need for very fresh corpses had been West's moral undoing. They were hard to get, and one awful day he had secured his specimen while it was still alive and vigorous. A struggle, a needle, and a powerful alkaloid had transformed it to a very fresh corpse, and the experiment had succeeded for a brief and memorable moment; but West had emerged with a soul calloused and seared, and a hardened eye which sometimes glanced with a kind of hideous and calculating appraisal at men of especially sensitive brain and especially vigorous physique. Toward the last I became acutely afraid of West, for he began to look at me that way. People did not seem to notice his glances, but they noticed my fear; and after his disappearance used that as a basis for some absurd suspicions.

West, in reality, was more afraid than I; for his abominable pursuits entailed a life of furtiveness and dread of every shadow. Partly it was the police he feared; but sometimes his nervousness was deeper and more nebulous, touching on certain indescribable things into which he had injected a morbid life, and from which he had not seen that life depart. He usually finished his experiments with a revolver, but a few times he had not been quick enough. There was that first specimen on whose rifled grave marks of clawing were later seen. There was also that Arkham professor's body which had done cannibal things before it had been captured and thrust unidentified into a madhouse cell at Sefton, where it beat the walls for sixteen years. Most of the other possibly surviving results were things less easy to speak of—for in later years West's scientific zeal had degenerated to an unhealthy and fantastic mania, and he had spent his chief skill in vitalizing not entire human bodies but isolated parts of bodies, or parts joined to organic matter other than human. It had become fiendishly disgusting by the time he disappeared; many of the experiments could not even be hinted at in print. The Great War, through which both of us served as surgeons, had intensified this side of West.

In saying that West's fear of his specimens was nebulous, I have in mind particularly its complex nature. Part of it came merely from knowing of the existence of such nameless monsters, while another part arose from apprehension of the bodily harm they might under certain circumstances do him. Their disappearance added horror to the situation—of them all, West knew the whereabouts of only one, the pitiful asylum thing. Then there was a more subtle fear—a very fantastic sensation resulting from a curious experiment in the Canadian army in 1915. West, in the midst of a severe battle, had reanimated Major Sir Eric Moreland Clapham-Lee, D.S.O., a fellow-physician who knew about his experiments and could have duplicated them. The head had been removed, so that the possibilities of quasi-intelligent life in the trunk might be investigated. Just as the building was wiped out by a German shell, there had been a success. The trunk had moved intelligently; and, unbelievable to relate, we were both sickeningly sure that articulate sounds had come from the detached head as it lay in a shadowy corner of the laboratory. The shell had been merciful, in a way—but West could never feel as certain as he wished, that we two were the only survivors. He used to make shuddering conjectures about the possible actions of a headless physician with the power of reanimating the dead.

West's last quarters were in a venerable house of much elegance, overlooking one of the oldest burying grounds in Boston. He had chosen the place for purely symbolic and fantastically aesthetic reasons, since most of the interments were of the colonial period and therefore of little use to a scientist seeking very fresh bodies. The laboratory was in a sub-cellar secretly constructed by imported workmen, and contained a huge incinerator for the quiet and complete disposal of such bodies, or fragments and synthetic mockeries of bodies, as might remain from the morbid experiments and unhallowed amusements of the owner. During the excavation of this cellar the workmen had struck some exceedingly ancient masonry; undoubtedly connected with the old burying-ground, yet far too deep to correspond with any known sepulcher therein. After a number of calculations West decided that it represented some secret chamber beneath the tomb of the Averills, where the last interment had been made in 1768. I was with him when he studied the nitrous, dripping walls laid bare by the spades and mattocks of the men, and was prepared for the gruesome thrill which would attend the uncovering of centuried grave-secrets; but for the first time West's new timidity conquered his natural curiosity, and he betrayed his degenerating fiber by ordering the masonry left intact and plastered over. Thus it remained till that final hellish night; part of the walls of the secret laboratory. I speak of West's decadence, but must add that it was a purely mental and intangible thing. Outwardly he was the same to the last—calm, cold, slight, and yellow-haired, with spectacled blue eyes and a general aspect of youth which years and fears seemed never to change. He seemed calm even when he thought of that clawed grave and looked over his shoulder; even when he thought of the carnivorous thing that gnawed and pawed at Sefton bars.

The end of Herbert West began one evening in our joint study when he was dividing his curious glance between the newspaper and me. A strange headline item had struck at him from the crumpled pages, and a nameless titan claw had seemed to reach down through sixteen years. Something fearsome and incredible had happened at Sefton Asylum fifty miles away, stunning the neighborhood and baffling the police. In the small hours of the morning a body of silent men had entered the grounds, and their leader had aroused the attendants. He was a menacing military figure who talked without moving his lips and whose voice seemed almost ventriloquially connected with an immense black case he carried. His expressionless face was handsome to the point of radiant beauty, but had shocked the superintendent when the hall light fell on it—for it was a wax face with eyes of painted glass. Some nameless accident had befallen this man. A larger man guided his steps; a repellent hulk whose bluish face seemed half eaten away by some unknown malady. The speaker had asked for the custody of the cannibal monster committed from Arkham sixteen years before; and upon being refused, gave a signal which precipitated a shocking riot. The fiends had beaten, trampled, and bitten every attendant who did not flee; killing four and finally succeeding in the liberation of the monster. Those victims who could recall the event without hysteria swore that the creatures had acted less like men than like unthinkable automata guided by the wax-faced leader. By the time help could be summoned, every trace of the men and of their mad charge had vanished.

From the hour of reading this item until midnight, West sat almost paralyzed. At midnight the doorbell rang, startling him fearfully. All the servants were asleep in the attic, so I answered the bell. As I have told the police, there was no wagon in the street, but only a group of strange-looking figures bearing a large square box which they deposited in the hallway after one of them had grunted in a highly unnatural voice, "Express—prepaid." They filed out of the house with a jerky tread, and as I watched them go I had an odd idea that they were turning toward the ancient cemetery on which the back of the house abutted. When I slammed the door after them West came downstairs and looked at the box. It was about two feet square, and bore West's correct name and present address. It also bore the inscription, "From Eric Moreland Clapham-Lee, St. Eloi, Flanders." Six years before, in Flanders, a shelled hospital had fallen upon the headless reanimated trunk of Dr. Clapham-Lee, and upon the detached head which—perhaps—had uttered articulate sounds.

West was not even excited now. His condition was more ghastly. Quickly he said, "It's the finish—but let's incinerate—this." We carried the thing down to the laboratory—listening. I do not remember many particulars—you can imagine my state of mind—but it is a vicious lie to say it was Herbert West's body which I put into the incinerator. We both inserted the whole unopened wooden box, closed the door, and started the electricity. Nor did any sound come from the box, after all.

It was West who first noticed the falling plaster on that part of the wall where the ancient tomb masonry had been covered up. I was going to run, but he stopped me. Then I saw a small black aperture, felt a ghoulish wind of ice, and smelled the charnel bowels of a putrescent earth. There was no sound, but just then the electric lights went out and I saw outlined against some phosphorescence of the nether world a horde of silent toiling things which only insanity—or worse—could create. Their outlines were human, semi-human, fractionally human, and not human at all—the horde was grotesquely heterogeneous. They were removing the stones quietly, one by one, from the centuried wall. And then, as the breach became large enough, they came out into the laboratory in single file; led by a talking thing with a beautiful head made of wax. A sort of mad-eyed monstrosity behind the leader seized on Herbert West. West did not resist or utter a sound. Then they all sprang at him and tore him to pieces before my eyes, bearing the fragments away into that subterranean vault of fabulous abominations. West's head was carried off by the wax-headed leader, who wore a Canadian officer's uniform. As it disappeared I saw that the blue eyes behind the spectacles were hideously blazing with their first touch of frantic, visible emotion.

Servants found me unconscious in the morning. West was gone. The incinerator contained only unidentifiable ashes. Detectives have questioned me, but what can I say? The Sefton tragedy they will not connect with West; not that, nor the men with the box, whose existence they deny. I told them of the vault, and they pointed to the unbroken plaster wall and laughed. So I told them no more. They imply that I am either a madman or a murderer—probably I am mad. But I might not be mad if those accursed tomb-legions had not been so silent.

THE HOLLOW MAN

Thomas Burke

Just as Christianity has its dark side in Satanism, so the religions of Africa have their dark side—and the sorcerer cults are considered the evilest of the evil. Followers will do just about anything to enhance their powers. West Africa's Leopard Men, for example, believe their supernatural powers are derived from a gris-gris—or luck bag—called a *borfima*. It's said the contents of this bag come primarily from the victims of human sacrifice. A *borfima* might contain the white of a hen's egg, a few grains of rice, human intestines, and other parts from the corpses of the victims. The bag must regularly be anointed with human fat and blood, so people must continually be sacrificed. Practitioners believe this talisman brings them riches, makes them invincible, and enables them to transform themselves into leopards.

For their ceremonies, they dress in leopard skins and attach steel claws or knives to their hands and slash their human sacrifices to death, whereupon they promptly eat the victims' flesh and drink the blood. At least, that's what has been reported. It's said their primary victims are young women.

The following story briefly alludes to the Leopard Men and a murder that took place many years before. But in tales involving magic, the repercussions usually catch up with you eventually . . . and not always in the way you would expect.

✦ ✦ ✦

He came up one of the narrow streets which lead from the docks, and turned into a road whose farther end was bright with the light of London. At the end of this road he went deep into the lights of London, and sometimes into its shadows, farther and farther away from the river, and did not pause until he reached a poor quarter near the centre.

He was a tall, spare figure, wearing a black macintosh. Below this could be seen brown dungaree trousers. A peaked cap hid most of his face; the little that was exposed was white and sharp. In the autumn mist that filled the lighted streets as well as the dark he seemed a wraith, and some of those who passed him looked again, not sure whether they had indeed seen a living man. One or two of them moved their shoulders, as though shrinking from something.

His legs were long, but he walked with the short, deliberate steps of a blind man, though he was not blind. His eyes were open, and he stared straight ahead; but he seemed to see nothing and hear nothing.

Neither the mournful hooting of sirens across the black water of the river, nor the genial windows of the shops in the big streets near the centre drew his head to right or left. He walked as though he had no destination in mind, yet constantly, at this corner or that, he turned. It seemed that an unseen hand was guiding him to a given point of whose location he was himself ignorant.

He was searching for a friend of fifteen years ago, and the unseen hand, or some dog-instinct, had led him from Africa to London, and was now leading him, along the last mile of his search, to a certain little eating-house. He did not know that he was going to the eating-house of his friend Nameless, but he did know, from the time he left Africa, that he was journeying towards Nameless, and he now knew that he was very near to Nameless.

Nameless didn't know that his old friend was anywhere near *him*, though, had he observed conditions that evening, he might have wondered why he was sitting up an hour later than usual. He was seated in one of the pews of his prosperous little workmen's dining-rooms—a little goldmine his wife's relations called it—and he was smoking and looking at nothing.

He had added up the till and written the copies of the bill of fare for next day, and there was nothing to keep him out of bed after his fifteen hours' attention to business. Had he been asked why he was sitting up later than usual, he would first have answered that he didn't know that he was, and would then have explained, in default of any other explanation, that it was for the purpose of having a last pipe. He was quite unaware that he was sitting up and keeping the door unlatched because a long-parted friend from Africa was seeking him and slowly approaching him, and needed his services.

He was quite unaware that he had left the door unlatched at that late hour—half-past eleven—to admit pain and woe. But even as many bells sent dolefully across the night from their steeples their disagreement as to the point of half-past eleven, pain and woe were but two streets away from him. The macintosh and dungarees and the sharp white face were coming nearer every moment.

There was silence in the house and in the streets; a heavy silence, broken, or sometimes stressed, by the occasional night-noises—motor horns, back-firing of lorries, shunting at a distant terminus. That silence seemed to envelop the house, but he did not notice it. He did not notice the bells, and he did not even notice the lagging step that approached his shop, and passed—and returned—and passed again—and halted. He was aware of nothing save that he was smoking a last pipe, and he was sitting in that state of hazy reverie which he called thinking, deaf and blind to anything not in his immediate neighborhood.

But when a hand was laid on the latch, and the latch was lifted, he did hear that, and he looked up. And he saw the door open, and got up and went to it. And there, just within the door, he came face to face with the thin figure of pain and woe.

———

To kill a fellow-creature is a frightful thing. At the time the act is committed the murderer may have sound and convincing reasons (to him) for his act. But time and reflection may bring regret; even remorse; and this may live with him for many years. Examined in wakeful hours of the night or early morning, the reasons for the act may shed their cold logic, and may cease to be reasons and become mere excuses.

And these naked excuses may strip the murderer and show him to himself as he is. They begin to hunt his soul, and to run into every little corner of his mind and every little nerve, in search of it.

And if to kill a fellow-creature and to suffer the recurrent regret for an act of heated blood is a frightful thing, it is still more frightful to kill a fellow-creature and bury his body deep in an African jungle, and then, fifteen years later, at about midnight, to see the latch of your door lifted by the hand you had stilled and to see the man, looking much as he did fifteen years ago, walk into your home and claim your hospitality.

When the man in macintosh and dungarees walked into the dining-rooms, Nameless stood still; stared; staggered against a table; supported himself by a hand, and said, "Oh!"

The other man said, "Nameless!"

Then they looked at each other; Nameless with head thrust forward, mouth dropped, eyes wide; the visitor with a dull, glazed expression. If Nameless had not been the man he was—thick, bovine and costive—he would have flung up his arms and screamed. At that moment he felt the need of some such outlet, but he did not know how to find it. The only dramatic expression he gave to the situation was to whisper instead of speak.

Twenty emotions came to life in his head and spine, and wrestled there. But they showed themselves only in his staring eyes and his whisper. His first thought, or rather, spasm, was Ghosts-Indigestion-Nervous-Breakdown. His second, when he saw that the figure was substantial and real, was Impersonation. But a slight movement on the part of the visitor dismissed that.

It was a little habitual movement which belonged only to that man; an unconscious twitching of the third finger of the left hand. He knew then that it was Gopak. Gopak, a little changed, but still, miraculously, thirty-two. Gopak, alive, breathing and real. No ghost. No phantom of the stomach. He was as certain of that as he was that fifteen years ago he had killed Gopak stone-dead and buried him.

The blackness of the moment was lightened by Gopak. In thin, flat tones he asked, "May I sit down? I'm tired." He sat down, and said, "So tired. So tired."

Nameless still held the table. He whispered, "Gopak . . . Gopak . . . But I—I *killed* you. I killed you in the jungle. You were dead. I know you were."

Gopak passed his hand across his face. He seemed about to cry. "I know you did. I know. That's all I can remember about this earth. You killed me." The voice became thinner and flatter. "And I was so comfortable. So comfortable. It was—such a rest. Such a rest as you don't know. And then they came and—disturbed me. They woke me up. And brought me back." He sat with shoulders sagged, arms drooping, hands hanging between his knees. After the first recognition he did not look at Nameless; he looked at the floor.

"Came and disturbed you?" Nameless leaned forward and whispered the words. "Woke you up? Who?"

"The Leopard Men."

"The what?"

"The Leopard Men." The watery voice said it as casually as if it were saying "the night watchman."

"The Leopard Men?" Nameless stared, and his fat face crinkled in an effort to take in the situation of a midnight visitation from a dead man, and the dead man talking nonsense. He felt his blood moving out of its course. He looked at his own hand to see if it was his own hand. He looked at the table to see if it was his table. The hand and the table were facts, and if the dead man was a fact—and he was—his story might be a fact! It seemed anyway as sensible as the dead man's presence. He gave a heavy sigh from the stomach. "A-ah . . . The Leopard Men . . . Yes, I heard about them out there. Tales!"

Gopak slowly wagged his head. "Not tales. They're real. If they weren't real—I wouldn't be here. Would I? I'd be at rest."

Nameless had to admit this. He had heard many tales "out there" about the Leopard Men, and had dismissed them as jungle yarns. But now, it seemed, jungle yarns had become commonplace fact in a little London shop.

The watery voice went on. "They do it. I saw them. I came back in the middle of a circle of them. They killed a native to put his life into me. They wanted a foreigner—for their farm. So they brought me back. You may not believe it. You wouldn't want to believe it. You wouldn't want to—see or know anything like them. And I wouldn't want any man to. But it's true. That's how I'm here."

"But I left you absolutely dead. I made every test. It was three days before I buried you. And buried you deep."

"I know. But that wouldn't make any difference to them. It was a long time after when they came and brought me back. And I'm still dead, you know. It's only my body they brought back." The voice trailed into a thread. "And I'm so tired. So tired. I want to go back—to rest."

Sitting in his prosperous eating-house, Nameless was in the presence of an achieved miracle, but the everyday, solid appointments of the eating-house wouldn't let him fully comprehend it. Foolishly, as he realised when he had spoken, he asked Gopak to explain what had happened. Asked a man who couldn't really be alive to explain how he came to be alive. It was like asking Nothing to explain Everything.

Constantly, as he talked, he felt his grasp on his own mind slipping. The surprise of a sudden visitor at a late hour; the shock of the arrival of a long-dead man; and the realisation that this long-dead man was not a wraith, were too much for him.

During the next half-hour he found himself talking to Gopak as to the Gopak he had known seventeen years ago when they were partners. Then he would be halted by the freezing knowledge that he was talking to a dead man, and that a dead man was faintly answering him. He felt that the thing couldn't really have happened, but in the interchange of talk he kept forgetting the improbable side of it, and accepting it. With each recollection of the truth, his mind would clear and settle in one thought—"I've got to get rid of him. How am I going to get rid of him?"

"But how did you get here?"

"I escaped." The words came slowly and thinly, and out of the body rather than the mouth.

"How?"

"I don't—know. I don't remember anything—except our quarrel. And being at rest."

"But why come all the way here? Why didn't you stay on the coast?"

"I don't—know. But you're the only man I know. The only man I can remember."

"But how did you find me?"

"I don't know. But I had to—find you. You're the only man—who can help me."

"But how can I help you?"

The head turned weakly from side to side. "I don't—know. But nobody else—can."

Nameless stared through the window, looking on to the lamplit street and seeing nothing of it. The everyday being which had been his half an hour ago had been annihilated; the everyday beliefs and disbeliefs shattered and mixed together. But some shred of his old sense and his old standard remained. He must handle this situation. "Well—what do you want to do? What are you going to do? I don't see how I can help you. And you can't stay here, obviously." A demon of perversity sent a facetious notion into his head—introducing Gopak to his wife—"This is my dead friend."

But on his last spoken remark Gopak made the effort of raising his head and staring with the glazed eyes at Nameless. "But I must stay here. There's nowhere else I can stay. I must stay here. That's why I came. You got to help me."

"But you can't stay here. I got no room. All occupied. Nowhere for you to sleep."

The wan voice said, "That doesn't matter. I don't sleep."

"Eh?"

"I *don't* sleep. I haven't slept since they brought me back. I can sit here—till you can think of some way of helping me."

"But how *can* I?"

He again forgot the background of the situation, and began to get angry at the vision of a dead man sitting about the place waiting for him to think of something. "How can I if you don't tell me how?"

"I don't—know. But you got to. You killed me. And I was dead—and comfortable. As it all came from you—killing me—you're responsible for me being—like this. So, you got to—help me. That's why I—came to you."

"But what do you want me to do?"

"I don't—know. I can't—think. But nobody but you can help me. I had to come to you. Something brought me—straight to you. That means that you're the one—that can help me. Now I'm with you, something will—happen to help me. I feel it will. In time you'll—think of something."

Nameless found his legs suddenly weak. He sat down and stared with a sick scowl at the hideous and the incomprehensible. Here was a dead man in his house—a man he had murdered in a moment of black temper—and he knew in his heart that he couldn't turn the man out. For one thing, he would have been afraid to touch him; he couldn't see himself touching him. For another, faced with the miracle of the presence of a fifteen-years-dead man, he doubted whether physical force or any material agency would be effectual in moving the man.

His soul shivered, as all men's souls shiver at the demonstration of forces outside their mental or spiritual horizon. He had murdered this man, and often, in fifteen years, he had repented the act. If the man's appalling story were true, then he had some sort of right to turn to Nameless. Nameless recognised that, and knew that whatever happened he couldn't turn him out. His hot-tempered sin had literally come home to him.

The wan voice broke into his nightmare. "You go to rest, Nameless. I'll sit here. You go to rest." He put his face down to his hands and uttered a little moan. "Oh, why can't I rest? Why can't I go back to my beautiful rest?"

Nameless came down early next morning with a half-hope that Gopak would not be there. But he was there, seated where Nameless had left him last night. Nameless made some tea, and showed him where he might wash. He washed listlessly, and crawled back to his seat, and listlessly drank the tea which Nameless brought to him.

To his wife and the kitchen helpers Nameless mentioned him as an old friend who had had a bit of a shock. "Shipwrecked and knocked on the head. But quite harmless, and he won't be staying long. He's waiting for admission to a home. A good pal to me in the past, and it's the least I can do to let him stay here a few days. Suffers from sleeplessness and prefers to sit up at night. Quite harmless."

But Gopak stayed more than a few days. He outstayed everybody. Even when the customers had gone Gopak was still there.

On the first morning of his visit when the regular customers came in at mid-day, they looked at the odd, white figure sitting vacantly in the first pew, then stared, then moved away.

All avoided the pew in which he sat. Nameless explained him to them, but his explanation did not seem to relieve the slight tension which settled on the dining-room. The atmosphere was not so brisk and chatty as usual. Even those who had their backs to the stranger seemed to be affected by his presence.

At the end of the first day Nameless, noticing this, told him that he had arranged a nice corner of the front room upstairs, where he could sit by the window and took his arm to take him upstairs. But Gopak feebly shook the hand away, and sat where he was. "No. I don't want to go. I'll stay here. I'll stay here. I don't want to move."

And he wouldn't move. After a few more pleadings Nameless realised with dismay that his refusal was definite; that it would be futile to press him or force him; that he was going to sit in that dining-room forever. He was as weak as a child and as firm as a rock.

He continued to sit in that first pew, and the customers continued to avoid it, and to give odd glances at it. It seemed that they half-recognised that he was something more than a fellow who had had a shock.

During the second week of his stay three of the regular customers were missing, and more than one of those that remained made acidly facetious suggestions to Nameless that he park his lively friend somewhere else. He made things too exciting for them; all that whoopee took them off their work, and interfered with digestion. Nameless told them he would be staying only a day or so longer, but they found that this was untrue, and at the end of the second week eight of the regulars had found another place.

Each day, when the dinner-hour came, Nameless tried to get him to take a little walk, but always he refused.

He would go out only at night, and then never more than two hundred yards from the shop. For the rest, he sat in his pew, sometimes dozing in the afternoon, at other times staring at the floor. He took his food abstractedly, and never knew whether he had had food or not. He spoke only when questioned, and the burden of his talk was "I'm so tired. So tired."

One thing only seemed to arouse any light of interest in him; one thing only drew his eyes from the floor. That was the seventeen-year-old daughter of his host, who was known as Bubbles, and who helped with the waiting. And Bubbles seemed to be the only member of the shop and its customers who did not shrink from him.

She knew nothing of the truth about him, but she seemed to understand him, and the only response he ever gave to anything was to her childish sympathy. She sat and chatted foolish chatter to him—"bringing him out of himself" she called it—and sometimes he would be brought out to the extent of a watery smile. He came to recognise her step and would look up before she entered the room. Once or twice in the evening, when the shop was empty, and Nameless was sitting miserably with him, he would ask, without lifting his eyes, "Where's Bubbles?" and would be told that Bubbles had gone to the pictures or was out at a dance, and would relapse into deeper vacancy.

Nameless didn't like this. He was already visited by a curse which, in four weeks, had destroyed most of his business. Regular customers had dropped off two by two, and no new customers came to take their place. Strangers who dropped in once for a meal did not come again; they could not keep their eyes or their minds off the forbidding, white-faced figure sitting motionless in the first pew. At mid-day, when the place had been crowded and latecomers had to wait for a seat, it was now two-thirds empty; only a few of the most thick-skinned remained faithful.

And on top of this there was the interest of the dead man in his daughter, an interest which seemed to be having an unpleasant effect. Nameless hadn't noticed it, but his wife had. "Bubbles don't seem as bright and lively as she was. You noticed it lately? She's getting quiet—and a bit slack. Sits about a lot. Paler than she used to be."

"Her age, perhaps."

"No. She's not one of these thin dark sort. No—it's something else. Just the last week or two I've noticed it. Off her food. Sits about doing nothing. No interest. May be nothing; just out of sorts, perhaps . . . How much longer's that horrible friend of yours going to stay?"

The horrible friend stayed some weeks longer—ten weeks in all—while Nameless watched his business drop to nothing and his daughter get pale and peevish. He knew the cause of it. There was no home in all England like his: no home that had a dead man sitting in it for ten weeks. A dead man brought, after a long time, from the grave, to sit and disturb his customers and take the vitality from his daughter. He couldn't tell this to anybody. Nobody would believe such nonsense.

But he *knew* that he was entertaining a dead man, and, knowing that a long-dead man was walking the earth, he could believe in any result of that fact. He could believe almost anything that he would have derided ten weeks ago. His customers had abandoned his shop, not because of the presence of a silent, white-faced man, but because of the presence of a dead-living man.

Their minds might not know it, but their blood knew it. And, as his business had been destroyed, so, he believed, would his daughter be destroyed. Her blood was not warming her; her blood told her only that this was a long ago friend of her father's, and she was drawn to him.

It was at this point that Nameless, having no work to do, began to drink. And it was well that he did so. For out of the drink came an idea, and with that idea he freed himself from the curse upon him and his house.

The shop now served scarcely half a dozen customers at mid-day. It had become ill-kempt and dusty, and the service and the food were bad. Nameless took no trouble to be civil to his few customers. Often, when he was notably under drink, he went to the trouble of being very rude to them. They talked about this. They talked about the decline of his business and the dustiness of the shop and the bad food. They talked about his drinking, and, of course, exaggerated it.

And they talked about the strange fellow who sat there day after day and gave everybody the creeps. A few outsiders, hearing the gossip, came to the dining-rooms to see the unusual fellow and the always-tight proprietor; but they did not come again, and there were not enough of the curious to keep the place busy. It went down until it served scarcely two customers a day. And Nameless went down with it into drink.

Then, one evening, out of the drink he fished an inspiration.

He took it downstairs to Gopak, who was sitting in his usual seat, hands hanging, eyes on the floor. "Gopak—listen. You came here because I was the only man who could help you in your trouble. You listening?"

A faint "Yes" was his answer.

"Well, now. You told me I'd got to think of something. I've thought of something. . . . Listen. You say I'm responsible for your condition and got to get you out of it, because I killed you. I did. We had a row. You made me wild. You dared me. And what with that sun and the jungle and the insects, I wasn't meself. I killed you. The moment it was done I could a-cut me hand off. Because you and me were pals. I could a-cut me right hand off."

"I know. I felt that directly it was over. I knew you were suffering."

"Ah! . . . I have suffered. And I'm suffering now. Well, this is what I've thought. All your present trouble comes from me killing you in that jungle and burying you. An idea came to me. Do you think it would help you—do you think it would put you back to rest if I—if I—if I—killed you again?"

For some seconds Gopak continued to stare at the floor. Then his shoulders moved. Then, while Nameless watched every little response to his idea, the watery voice began. "Yes. Yes. That's it. That's what I was waiting for. That's why I came here. I can see now. That's why I had to get here. Nobody else could kill me. Only you. I've got to be killed again. Yes, I see. But nobody else would be able to kill me. Only the man who first killed me. . . . Yes, you've found—what we're both—waiting for. Anybody else could shoot me—stab me—hang me—but they couldn't kill me. Only you. That's why I managed to get here and find you."

The watery voice rose to a thin strength. "That's it. And you must do it. Do it now. You don't want to, I know. But you must. You *must*."

His head drooped and he stared at the floor. Nameless, too, stared at the floor. He was seeing things. He had murdered a man and had escaped all punishment save that of his own mind, which had been terrible enough. But now he was going to murder him again—not in a jungle but in a city; and he saw the slow points of the result.

He saw the arrest. He saw the first hearing. He saw the trial. He saw the cell. He saw the rope. He shuddered. Then he saw the alternative—the breakdown of his life—a ruined business, poverty, the poorhouse, a daughter robbed of her health and perhaps dying, and always the curse of the dead-living man, who might follow him to the poorhouse. Better to end it all, he thought. Rid himself of the curse which Gopak had brought upon him and his family, and then rid his family of himself with a revolver. Better to follow up his idea.

He got stiffly to his feet. The hour was late evening—half-past ten—and the streets were quiet. He had pulled down the shop-blinds and locked the door. The room was lit by one light at the further end. He moved about uncertainly and looked at Gopak. "Er—how would you—how shall I—"

Gopak said, "You did it with a knife. Just under the heart. You must do it that way again."

Nameless stood and looked at him for some seconds. Then, with an air of resolve, he shook himself. He walked quickly to the kitchen.

Three minutes later his wife and daughter heard a crash, as though a table had been overturned. They called but got no answer. When they came down they found him sitting in one of the pews, wiping sweat from his forehead. He was white and shaking, and appeared to be recovering from a faint.

"Whatever's the matter? You all right?"

He waved them away. "Yes, I'm all right. Touch of giddiness. Smoking too much, I think."

"Mmmm. Or drinking. . . . Where's your friend? Out for a walk?"

"No. He's gone off. Said he wouldn't impose any longer, had to go and find an infirmary." He spoke weakly and found trouble in picking words. "Didn't you hear that bang—when he shut the door?"

"I thought that was you fell down."

"No. It was him when he went. I couldn't stop him."

"Mmmm. Just as well, I think." She looked about her. "Things seem to a-gone wrong since he's been here."

There was a general air of dustiness about the place. The tablecloths were dirty, not from use but from disuse. The windows were dim. A long knife, very dusty, was lying on the table under the window. In a corner by the door leading to the kitchen, unseen by her, lay a dusty macintosh and dungarees, which appeared to have been tossed there. But it was over by the main door, near the first pew, that the dust was thickest—a long trail of it—grayish-white dust.

"Reely, this place gets more and more slapdash. Why can't you attend to business? You didn't use to be like this. No wonder it's gone down, letting the place get into this state. Why don't you pull yourself together. Just look at that dust by the door. Looks as though somebody's been spilling ashes all over the place."

Nameless looked at it, and his hands shook a little. But he answered, more firmly than before, "Yes, I know. I'll have a proper clean-up tomorrow. I'll put it all to rights tomorrow. I been getting a bit slack."

For the first time in ten weeks he smiled at them; a thin, haggard smile, but a smile.

WAKE NOT THE DEAD

John H. Knox

Although John H. Knox was a prolific pulp fiction writer, little is known of him other than he lived in Abilene, Texas, and was the son of a preacher. Still, he is one of the most popular pulp writers.

✦ ✦ ✦

The service was proceeding smoothly, reverently, quietly. Our small and decorous Gothic chapel was dimly beautiful. The light filtering through the rose window beyond the chancel threw a warm glow over the high altar, over the minister intoning the stately service, and over the gray stone catafalque with its banked flowers beneath which lay Porter Bruton in his coffin.

Personally, I liked this solemn warmth of rite and ritual. As half-owner of the Sun Hill Crematorium, I was proud of the skill with which we helped to veil the raw harshness of death. But today, curiously, it did not seem enough. As I watched the pallid faces of that congregation of college students, teachers, and commonplace suburbanites, I was beginning to sense something of what my partner, Tom Carlin, had meant when he had said, "Watch them, Willis. With things as they are in Oakvale now, you can't trust people around funerals any more."

It had sounded absurd, far-fetched. For Oakvale had been an ordinary enough college suburb when the need for a serious operation had taken me away three months ago. Of course, I knew that during my absence the community had been somewhat upset by the suicide of Professor Grenfel, which followed the man's mad attempt to snatch at the dark secrets of life and death.

It was rather weird that only yesterday, on the very day of my return, Grenfel's young successor to the chair of biochemistry had followed his former chief in self-inflicted death. But was that enough to account for Tom's ominous hysterical and rather cryptic warning?

Bits of jumbled talk he had let fall came back to me now. Hints at body-snatching and some weird mania smoldering among the under-graduates at Oakvale. Dark references to Major Dennis Macklin and the two natives he had brought back with him from Africa. And this had seemed to connect in some way with a change that had come over Faustine Grenfel, the dead professor's daughter, who had been openly in love with the young assistant who now lay there under the banked flowers.

I looked at Faustine Grenfel now. She had always been eccentric, something of a poser, I thought. But she did possess an eerie and rather disturbing sort of beauty, a supple fluidity of slender limbs and serpentine white arms which, enhanced by her pallid and over-rouged face under the tight-clustered gold curls, gave her an unearthly, even a death-like air.

What shocked and repelled me now was the fact that instead of the black she should have worn on this occasion she was dressed in a scarlet gown of daring cut—as if she had come, not to a funeral, but to a rendezvous! Moreover, the avid fixity with which she regarded the coffin, leaning forward with delicate nostrils dilated and scarlet lips moving faintly as if in some unholy communion with the corpse of the man on whom she had lavished an unwelcome love, had rather more than a little of the horrible enveloping it.

For it was known that Porter Bruton had spurned her, had loved, hopelessly in his turn, Lilly Langburn, the daughter of the president of Oakvale College—the girl who had promised to become my wife.

It was with relief that I turned toward Lilly now, rejoicing that her lovely face, with its large brown eyes and tender lips, though sad, was as radiantly serene as the flower whose name she bore. Thank God, nothing of this stupid hysteria had touched her, not even though Major Macklin was her father's cousin, Faustine was her friend, and the dead man himself had been a suitor for her love. But then, nothing like that could touch Lilly!

Perhaps it was all exaggerated, anyhow. The service was nearly ended and nothing had happened yet. Even Faustine, sitting there with that awful look of expecting the dead man to rise at any moment, might manage to refrain from causing a scene.

"Earth to earth, ashes to ashes, dust to dust—"

There, it was almost over. Tom Carlin was solemnly sprinkling the dust and ashes over the coffin. With a deep breath of relief, I pressed the button and watched the casket sink slowly below the floor to leave only the flowers visible. Then, while the audience slowly rose, I turned and hurried down into the receiving room.

My partner followed me. We found old Dr. Bruton, the dead young teacher's father, waiting there with our superintendent, Sam Fleagle. Tom put a gentle hand on the old man's shoulder.

"You still insist on—staying?" he asked.

The aged doctor lifted his stricken but tearless face.

"Certainly," he said. "I watched him die, and I prepared his body for the last rites. I shall see him through to the last. It isn't in the trappings of funerals that we show our love for our dead, but in the ministering of hands."

It was a relief to see one Spartan at least in a crazed community. Tom sprang to help the old man as he raised his gaunt frame and moved toward the coffin from which Sam Fleagle was removing the lid. I turned to close the door, but stopped. Standing there, a scarlet apparition against the dimness, was Faustine Grenfel.

It was a tense instant. I could still hear feet moving upstairs and I dreaded the thought of the scene she might cause. For though her face was as immobile as a death mask, garish with paint, her greenish eyes glowed with a febrile threat that I could not misinterpret.

"Faustine," I began soothingly, "you mustn't—"

I broke off as she moved forward and I suddenly rushed her. But like a streaking flame she slithered past me and darted toward the coffin.

"Stop!" she shrilled. "You shall not burn him! You shall not destroy that splendid body!"

The others whirled and stood speechless as the girl flung herself upon the coffin, pressing her breast against it as she clawed and tugged to drag it to the floor.

"They shan't burn you, Porter!" she sobbed madly. "I'll tear the coffin apart! I'll press my body to you, and life will come into you again!"

It was ghastly, revolting. In another instant she would have dragged coffin and corpse crashing to the floor, but Tom came to his senses and grabbed her. I sprang to his aid and we pulled her away by main force. We shoved her, fighting and screaming, toward the door.

People were crowding down the steps, but I yelled at them to go back. We began pushing her up the stairs, while she continued to scream.

"You want to burn him, Willis Payne! You want to burn him to keep him from getting Lilly. But the dead aren't as dead as you think! He'll come back—"

I flung a hand over her mouth and the next moment we had her in the chapel. Dr. Pelham, who had run to his car for a hypo, had jabbed the needle into her arm, and that part of the nightmare was over.

We went back down and found old Dr. Bruton on the verge of a collapse. This had been too much even for him, and when Tom offered to take him home, he consented weakly.

Left alone with Sam Fleagle, I locked the door and set about helping him get the coffin into the crematorium oven. Then I left him to seal the chamber and close the gilded doors, and went back and sat down to get my breath.

Thank God it was over now, anyhow! How could a girl allow her nerves to make such a fool of her, I asked myself. And then I gave a start. It was only the first whine of the motor, the preliminary roar of the flames in the bowels of the masonry, but it sent a queer tremor through me. What was wrong? Was I letting that mad girl's words upset me?

The dead aren't as dead as you think!

Rot! I sat up and stared at the furnace. A sudden booming had begun as the oil burner in the combustion chamber warmed up. It rose to a roar as the flames spurted into the oven to embrace the casket. Suppose Porter Bruton was not really dead? Suppose—

Damn it, was I getting morbid like the others? Angrily I got up, walked over and stood at the peephole at the back of the oven where Sam Fleagle was watching the color of the flames.

"A corpse is just so much matter," I told myself steadily, "not a person at all."

Inside there the fire roared like hell. I saw a dark line creep down the center of the flame-enshrouded casket. It widened. The casket split like an eggshell and black smoke blasted angrily against the peephole.

"Porter Bruton's entity is not in there," I said, "just the lifeless husk of him."

Why were my palms so sweaty?

A tremor rumbled like an earthquake through the masonry and Fleagle snatched at the air valves to reduce the flame. Then soot on the peephole thinned and I saw the thing inside, melting as it were, in the white oxidation of the fire, shrinking, twisting. . . .

I started to turn away. It had never affected me like this before. But I seemed unable to withdraw my eyes from the shape that moved uneasily between the obscuring flashes of fire. It made me dizzy for an instant and it was then that I experienced the queer hallucination. For suddenly, rising above the flame's roar, wild and windy and remote as an echo thrown up from the abyss, there came a shriek, "Lilly, Lilly, I'm not dead! They're burning me alive! Save me, Lilly!"

Despite the great heat, a sheath of ice froze round my limbs, and as my brain spun like something whirled on the end of a string, it came again—a distillation of intolerable agony, black despair and immortal hate that would have chilled a devil's blood, "God curse you, Willis Payne! I'll come back!"

Then there was only the flames' roar, and with limbs atremble I turned to Sam Fleagle who was just straightening up.

"Did you hear something, Sam?"

He grinned. "Hear? Sure. Them flames makes all sorts of noises. Sometimes they seem to scream, sometimes to laugh."

"I guess so," I managed. "Well, I think I'll go now."

I staggered up the steps, through the chapel and out into the late afternoon sunlight, my brain still in a daze. Over and over I told myself it was all imagination. But I knew better; I had heard! And he had called, not Faustine's name, but Lilly's!

Now I wasn't quite a fool, even in my terror. I couldn't believe that a voice from the blazing coffin had come through the thick masonry of the oven. But I did know that telepathy is a proven phenomenon, that in the intensity of death's agony, the dying have been known to project not only thoughts, but actual apparitions that stand before the eyes of the living—and speak!

I got into the roadster, fumbled with the ignition key, finally got the engine started, and drove to the apartment which Tom Carlin and I called home. Tom was seated in the living room, morose and haggard, with a drink in his hand.

"Well, Willis," he said, without looking up, "a little more of this and we're finished. People won't bring their dead out from the city to a place with the atmosphere of a chamber of horrors. And it's my fault for dragging you into the business, too. I sometimes feel that I ought to offer to buy you out—"

He looked up, grinning wryly, and saw my face. "What's wrong? You look like you'd seen—"

"A ghost?" I asked. I looked him straight in the eyes. "Tell me the truth, Tom, do you know that Porter Bruton was dead? Do you know that the poison he took actually killed him?"

"What do you mean?" he exclaimed. But something evasive in his face told me he knew well enough. "Of course he was dead. Dr. Bruton saw him die, signed the death certificate, dressed the body. You're not suggesting that the old man could have connived at his own son's murder?"

I poured myself a drink, sat down to gulp it, and then told Tom exactly what had happened. Once he tried to interrupt me with some weak protest about the state of my nerves, but I silenced him and went on.

"You've been holding back on me, Tom, probably because you think I'm still too sick to stand the shock. But you may as well open up. I want to know what in hell is wrong here in Oakvale," I concluded.

He chewed that over a moment. Then:

"I wish I knew," he said. "Some sort of weird traffic with the dead must be going on, for bodies have been stolen. As to who's behind it, I have only a guess. I may be wrong. Let's start at the first and see what you think."

"Start with Grenfel's death, you mean?"

"With the things that led up to it," Tom said. "First, the argument with Major Dennis Macklin. You've probably heard of their argument, of how Grenfel boasted that science would soon know how to bring the dead back to life, and of how Macklin, in his role of cynical, wealthy explorer, sneered, said the secret would never come from a test tube and that if he wanted to know it he would go to the savages who had guarded the forbidden secret for ages.

"Well, the argument got hot and resulted in a wager that sent Macklin chasing off to Africa, to the regions west of the Ruwenzori, where a tribe called 'The People-Who-Dance-with-the-Dead' are said to live. And Grenfel set up a secret laboratory and set feverishly to work."

He paused and drew a breath.

"It created a lot of excitement and talk. All day and night in the upper halls of the science building you could hear the hissing of those glass retorts of Grenfel's, in which hearts and other organs throbbed with an eerie, unnatural life. And Grenfel got leaner and wilder, until a day came when a crowd gathered under his third-story window to hear some promised, startling announcement.

"But what they saw was a white-haired, emaciated madman appear suddenly against the darkness of the room, wave his arms wildly and then plunge down with a scream to smash his brains out on the pavement below. And when they rushed to his laboratory they found his terrified assistant reading a brief document which Grenfel had left and which read:

"'I have found it. A mere detail added to the usual artificial respiration and arterial injections of defibrinated blood, physiological salts and epinephrine, will do the trick. The horrible truth is that not half of our dead are really dead, until we kill them in graves, in ovens, or under the embalmers' knives. But to bring back the *thing* that comes back from death is a crime against God. No man who knows what I know can let death take him unawares.'"

I shuddered. "And that started the panic? Yet Porter Bruton insisted on going on with the experiments?"

Tom nodded. "He was like a madman himself, wild to get at what Grenfel had discovered. And he made no secret of his reason." He paused to look at me uncertainly. "He wanted Lilly, believed that the fame and fortune that discovery would bring would enable him to take her away from you."

I swallowed uncomfortably and wished that Tom hadn't brought that up.

"But the madness got him, just as it did Grenfel?" I asked.

"I wonder," Tom mused. "I think what got him was Dennis Macklin."

"Macklin?"

"Yes. He came rushing back from Africa by plane, bringing those witch-men with him. That was when the ugly rumors started about Faustine Grenfel and those crazy college kids who call themselves

'Thrill-hunters.' It was said that Macklin and his voodoo men were teaching them some devilish things that can be done with dead bodies. And bodies were stolen, Grenfel's among them."

"Grenfel's! And his own daughter—"

"I couldn't swear to anything except that I found his coffin in the mausoleum empty," Tom said. "Also another body is missing from a pauper's grave. I got suspicious of it and had it dug into before dawn this morning. The body had been taken out and the coffin re-buried. But what's worrying me now, since you told me what you thought you heard there by the oven, is a scene I saw in the graveyard last night. I'm almost afraid to tell you."

"Go on," I urged.

Tom poured himself another drink and swallowed it neat; there was a bead of fine sweat on his forehead.

"I'd been prowling about to see if I could catch any body-snatchers," he said, "when I heard voices and stole up behind a cypress to watch a strange scene. What I saw was Porter Bruton seated on a low tombstone with Macklin standing in front of him and two African witchmen behind. And Bruton was pleading.

"'For God's sake, Dennis,' I heard him say, 'don't do that to me. Have mercy.'

"'You have your choice,' Macklin replied coldly.

"Then Bruton got up and went stumbling off, and presently Macklin and his witch-men marched off, too."

"Good God!" I gulped. It sounded exactly like descriptions I had read of death-curses in the jungle. "And right after that Porter Bruton went home and killed himself with poison—or did he?"

Tom grimaced.

"His father says he did," he said.

"But if Macklin put a witch-spell on him—" I choked it off.

"In that case," Tom said hollowly, "we'd better get drunk, because we've just burned a man alive."

I got up and took another drink, but it didn't seem to do me any good. Half of me was cold and the other half was hot and my palms were oozing a clammy sweat.

"I'm glad I didn't hear him scream," Tom said, "especially that about coming back."

"Oh, shut up!" I growled. But instinctively I glanced at the window. The sun was down and the blue dusk had flattened itself against the pane like some blind amorphous monster pressing for entry. "I can't stand any more of this. I'm going to find Macklin and have it out with him!"

"Better go easy," Tom cautioned. "He might put a spell on you. I'd hate to have to burn you, too. Anyhow, I believe I'd be thinking of Lilly. If Bruton did come back he'd come back for her."

"Go to hell!" I said. But I turned and stalked to the phone.

I called Lilly's house to see if she was there and also to ask about Macklin, who was a guest of her father's. It was Macklin himself who answered the phone, and he said that Lilly had gone out.

"Where is she?" I blurted.

"She left about an hour ago," his suave voice answered, "with Willy Richmond and Faustine Grenfel. I think they were headed for the Clover Club."

"Willy Richmond and Faustine Grenfel!" I exclaimed, and hung up.

Tom stared at me. "She went out with those two? Good God, Willis, they're the ring leaders of those corpse-snatchers!"

I started toward him, fists doubled. "Don't you intimate anything about Lilly," I growled, "or I'll—"

The change that had come over his face caused me to pause. I couldn't believe I had scared him that badly, but his jaw had dropped down and his eyes were suddenly bulging from his head. Then I realized that he was not looking at me but at the window behind me. I whirled.

But the window was a murky square of blackness.

I turned back. "What the hell did you see?"

He had tottered upright and his blood-drained face still wore its look of imbecile terror as he passed a shaking hand across his eyes.

"So help me God, Willis, it was him—Porter Bruton. It was his burned corpse standing there and—and"—his agonized eyes sought my face—"he had something flung over one shoulder—something that looked like a body!"

I spun about and raced for the door. Outside it was almost dark except for a sickly yellowish glow still lingering in the sky. I rounded the corner and sprinted for the window. I almost stumbled on the thing before I saw it.

Shakily I went down on hands and knees and struck a match. It lay sprawled, face up, the body of a thin, sallow-faced youth. The bugged-out eyeballs, suffused with blood, the purple, swollen tongue protruding between the teeth, the livid marks on the throat all pointed to strangulation.

I bent nearer, staring at those marks. My nostrils caught an odor, and I turned sick. It was a smell of fire and death, of burned flesh, and over those discolorations left by clawed, strangling fingers there was a smear of slime, pustular and clouded with a char of black ashes.

The corpse was that of Willy Richmond, the youth with whom Lilly and Faustine had gone out only an hour or two ago!

Weakly I staggered upright, staring idiotically about into the silent dark which was vibrant with the muted voices of insects, pulsing, it seemed, in dirges for their own small dead. Tom's voice called from the front.

"Willis, what is it?"

That jarred me back to my senses. I turned and started running for my car.

Passing Tom, I panted, "Go and see for yourself," and ran on.

He could call the police or do what he pleased; the only thought in my mind was to find Lilly. I sprang into my car and stomped the engine into life.

The Clover Club was a small night spot not far from the campus. There had never been anything sinister about the place. At least I had never noticed it until tonight when I staggered in, waved a waiter aside and stood blinking while my eyes probed the dimness for a loved and familiar face. But now it was plain some sort of soul-rot had crept in here where once innocent gaiety had prevailed.

It was in the air, in the hectic faces that shone corpselike under the blue lights; something that glowed lewd and secretive in fevered eyes, that breathed obscenely in hot whispers from drunken lips. It was in the music, in the weird, mysterious, jerky notes that crept in above the muted crooning of the brasses. It was in the movements of the dancers who hugged close and slithered like zombies, smoothly, subtly, but with a slight roll, like the unsteady gait of things that slouch blindly through darkness.

But I could not see either Lilly or Faustine.

I swung toward a table where a thin, horse-faced youth was leaning drunkenly toward his painted girl companion. When I asked if they had seen either of the girls the youth laughed, raised his glass and drank sloppily.

"They were here," he said, "but they left about an hour ago." He rolled his drunken eyes. "I wouldn't follow them, though. A simple undertaker might get shocked."

I resisted an impulse to smash his teeth back into his throat, whirled and went back out, a cackle of drunken laughter following me. I got back into my car and drove to the cottage where Faustine had lived alone since the death of her father.

The place was dark, but I didn't let that stop me. When I found the door locked I slammed my shoulder against it and crashed it in. Then, snapping on lights as I went, I made a tour of the whole house.

But no one was there; the place was neat and in order. I paused in the kitchen, wondering if I was making a fool of myself. Certainly there was a killer at large, but that didn't prove that Faustine and her silly followers had any connection with him. Faustine was a nervous wreck, and probably Lilly had taken her home to look after her. Willy Richmond might have left them long ago.

I started to turn back, but noticed the steps leading down into the basement and thought I might as well search there before I left. I stumbled down into a furnace room and struck a match. The place was empty, but my eye was attracted to a small door on which there was a formidable-looking padlock. Why such a padlock as that? I had already smashed one door, so another wouldn't matter. I dropped the match, picked up a lawnmower I had spotted and slammed it like a battering ram into the door.

The thin panels crashed under the blows, and I pushed myself through the splintered aperture. Then I straightened up in the darkness and my blood began a slow process of curdling. It was nothing I saw or felt, it was a smell—the smell of formaldehyde!

I struck another match, and as it blazed against the smothering darkness I saw the coffin, a new one, against one wall. A horrible premonition laid strangling fingers on my throat then, but I forced myself forward and flung the casket open. The full impact of the horror smote me then and my last doubts and reservations crumbled away in my instinctive revulsion.

Stretched out in that casket lay the body of Professor Grenfel. That wasn't all. The clothing had been cut away, the torso and abdomen laid bare, and a gaping gash yawned from his sternum down, its horrible discolored lips curling over an empty cavity from which his vital organs had been removed!

I had to turn away then because I was physically sick. But as I staggered back through the door, the sickness in my brain made the mere physical reaction inconsequential. I had read enough of savage practices to know what sort of grisly traffic the evisceration of a dead body might mean. And this mad girl had butchered the body of her own father! And she had my fiancée with her—if Lilly had not already been delivered into the hands of a lust-mad killer.

I staggered back to my car and stood leaning on the door. Anger had mounted to bloodlust in me and I swore a terrible vow.

"If I find her, I'll strangle her. She's not human, she's got no right to live!"

But a second thought sobered me. Faustine must be insane. It was the fiend behind her madness, behind all the rest of this horror that I should think of. And who was that fiend but Macklin? He was the cancer, the seat of all the vile corruption that had poisoned the community and led finally to ghastly murder. He was the one I must deal with!

Now that I had a definite purpose, it steadied me a little. I reached the tall, ivy-covered Langburn house with a somewhat better grip on my nerves. The only light I saw was downstairs in the library. I was ushered in by one of Macklin's servants. I found the explorer seated under a reading lamp with a book on his knees.

He was a small, compact, wiry man with a tanned, lean face, close-clipped black mustache and dark eyes that seemed to sparkle always with some sly, inner mockery. He rose and greeted me politely, then sat down again.

"Anything I can do for you, Payne?"

"You can tell me where Lilly is," I growled.

"But I told you that she left with Faustine Grenfel."

"But where are they now?"

He shrugged. "How should I know?"

Something was boiling up dangerously in my throat; I held it back as best I could, but my voice quavered when I answered.

"Because you're the devil at the bottom of all this madness, this vile, unnatural death-obsession, this—"

His laughter interrupted me. "My dear young man, a preoccupation with the dead is the most natural thing in human nature. In Africa, for instance, the natives bring their dead back to life and mingle with them familiarly—even dance with them."

"And that's the sort of rot you've been poisoning these students' minds with?" I grated. "Well, you went too far when you carried things to the point of murder!"

"Murder?" His eyebrows lifted. "Whose murder?"

"Porter Bruton's, for one," I said. "You didn't know it, but you were seen there in the graveyard last night when you put some sort of hypnotic spell on him. And he went into the oven today—alive!"

That jarred him for a moment. He paled slightly, but quickly recovered his composure and laughed.

"What an idea! However, if he did go into the flames alive, he's unquestionably dead now."

"He screamed," I said, "when the flames hit him, screamed that he would come back."

"Really? I'm sorry I didn't hear it."

His words stunned me. There was a curtained alcove behind his chair, and the light striking the plum-colored drapes, glanced off on his bony cheeks, giving them a cadaverous hue. Was this man human who had no human feelings? It seemed that God would strike a man dead for less than this, and so deep was that conviction, that when the curtains behind him stirred as to a faint breeze, I gave a violent start.

"Why do you jump?" The mocking smile was still on his lips.

"The curtain behind you moved," I whispered.

"The ghost of Porter Bruton probably," he jeered. "But no, though the dead return, the bodies of those who burn don't walk—"

His words broke off. He didn't jump or start, he simply went cautiously still. At the same instant it reached my nostrils, too—an odor in which burned cloth was mingled with scorched flesh and hair—and my eyes riveted to the gap where the curtain failed to meet.

I didn't believe what I saw at first. It was so strangely still, so like what a fevered brain might build out of air and terror. For the thing in the darkness there had Porter Bruton's face, though now it was livid and blackened, with puffed greenish lips peeled back from grinning teeth and an ooze of some blood-streaked substance rolling down from raw eye sockets over flame-blasted cheeks. It had a body, too, a shrunken frame from which hung the charred remnants of a black suit. The flesh that shone through was like the face, and a clawed hand was like a blackened root dragged from a fire.

Macklin's face was drained of blood now, and as he watched the horror mirrored in mine, he seemed too paralyzed to move. At the same instant it seemed to dawn on my dazed senses that the thing was real, but before I could move, or even scream, the blackened hand shot out to the light cord, and the smothering dark came down as the horror, shining with a greenish glow in the blackness, leaped. From Macklin burst a scream.

What I might have done, if left to my own inclinations, I don't know. But at that moment the door behind me opened and a witch-man—summoned by Macklin's scream—came pounding in. I was the first object with which he collided, and taking me for the attacker, he flung his massive arms around me. I fought, pummeling his face and body as I tried to wriggle free. But in my weakened condition I was like a child in a boa's coils, and suddenly, with Macklin's screams still blasting in my ears, I felt myself lifted bodily and hurled.

I struck the glass of a window, and its crash echoed about me as the ground slammed up to smash consciousness from my brain.

I came to my senses, feeling like something that has crawled out from under a steam roller, and sat up. I was a mass of cuts and aching bruises, but my mind was beginning to clear. My first thought was to wonder if this was another stage trick of Macklin's, a ruse to divert suspicion from himself.

I got up, and with joints creaking, stumbled toward the shattered window through which faint light was again shining. I stared in and my senses reeled. In the circular pool of yellow light cast by the lamp, Major Dennis Macklin lay asprawl. Dead? He was worse than dead. His face, his hands, the whole upper part of his torso, from which it seemed invisible flames had eaten the clothing away, was a raw, blistered, viscous mass of cooked skin and tissue, which, while I looked seemed still to boil and crawl as with a living corruption.

"Burned alive," I muttered hoarsely. "Burned alive, like Porter Bruton, but not by any earthly fire."

There was no one else in the room, but the air reeked with an acrid smell like brimstone.

Turning, I ran toward my car. Whatever that revenant shape had been, I knew now that the African's entrance was all that had saved me from Macklin's fate, knew what grisly doom awaited me when next I faced that apparition out of hell. Yet my mind did not dwell on that. The need to find Lilly swallowed up all other considerations.

But where to go, where to look for her? Instinctively I piloted my car back toward Faustine Grenfel's house, and this time, a block away, I saw a light. Pulling into the curb, I parked and sneaked up the rest of the way on foot. There was a light in the front and one in the back, and I stole up behind a trellis and peered into the living room.

A swift wave of relief swept over me, for Lilly was there, unharmed, seated on a divan under a bridge lamp. But the next instant a chill of apprehension crept into my blood. It was the queer look on her face, as leaning forward, with the light falling softly on her brown hair and creamy skin, she was staring at something in her lap, staring with a weird absorption at what I now saw was a photograph of Porter Bruton!

I turned and made for the front door, rushing straight in without knocking. Lilly sprang to her feet with a gasp, and I saw her drop the photograph with a furtive movement at the end of the divan. Then with a quick and patently false smile, she came toward me.

"Why, Willis, you startled me—"

I reached out, gripped her shoulders, and I didn't smile back.

"What are you doing here?" I demanded.

"Why," she stammered, "just waiting for Faustine to come in."

Why this fear of me, this evasiveness? Suddenly I noticed that one of her small hands was crushing tightly something which she seemed to be trying to conceal.

"What's that?" I rasped, and grabbing her hand, I loosened the tight-clenched fingers and pulled out a ball of wadded paper.

"Willis, please!" She tried to snatch it back.

But I swung toward the light, smoothed it out and felt the scalp crawl on my neck as I read:

Faustine:
If I appear to die, know that I will not be dead. But do not let them cremate me. If they attempt that, you must come to the service, and if by the time it is over I have not revived, prevent their burning me at all cost. Keep my secret and do not fail me.

Porter

I whirled back on Lilly, who had sunk down weakly on the divan. "Where did you get this?"

Terror was in her eyes and her voice came faint and hoarse from her throat.

"He mailed it to Faustine—last night before he took the poison. And oh, Willis, he did come back! I saw him. I've been looking at his picture and I know it was he—his face, there at the window at the Clover Club. And Willy Richmond went out to see, and he didn't come back—" Her voice broke on a sob and her brown eyes were pleading. "But, Willis, you didn't have anything to do with it, did you? Faustine said—"

"That lying hell-cat!" I burst out. "What's she told you? Where is she now?"

I paused. A sound had reached my ears. It came from the dark hall, a low monotonous murmur, a woman's voice muttering weirdly in coaxing, reiterated commands, and a man's voice replying in a throaty half-whimper—an eerie mumbling like something forced by necromancy from dead lips.

Instantly I turned, but Lilly clung to me.

"Willis, Willis, you mustn't—"

"Mustn't I?" I grated, rudely shoving her back. "You stay here and keep quiet or I'll tear the roof off this damned place!"

Then I strode softly into the hall and crept toward the door of Faustine's bedroom, from which the queer sounds were coming. Stooping, I applied my eye to the keyhole, and though my range of vision was limited, what I saw was enough to curdle my blood and conjure visions of the witches who dragged the dying from battlefields to use them as horrible mediums of communication with the dead.

For on Faustine's bed, stretched out as if for burial, lay the bulky form of Sam Fleagle, utterly still. His flabby face, the color of a spoiled oyster, was beaded with death sweat, his glassy eyes staring unseeingly at the she-monster poised above him.

Crouched there in loose negligee, Faustine was like a feeding cat. Her vampire-face was thrust forward and down, small teeth gleaming as she articulated words in a husky, commanding whisper.

"Speak, speak, I tell you! What did he say? What did Porter Bruton say? Speak up, or I'll beat you black and blue while you lie there helpless."

And feebly, the thick blubbery lips of Sam Fleagle began to move. "Don't . . . Leave me in peace . . . I don't know . . ."

"You do know!" Sudden savagery blazed in her. Her clawed white hands shot forward, long pointed fingers burying themselves in the gray folds of his throat, while a look of fiendish hate transfixed her painted face. "Tell me, or I'll—"

She got no further because I had stood all I could stand. Kicking the door open, I lunged in.

She whirled, agile as a startled cat, and sprang to meet my rush. White arms shot round me and all the lean, warm, supple strength of her body was exerted against me. The smile that wreathed her face was horrible in its wild, fawning appeal, as her hot breath laved my face in frantic whispers.

"Willis, Willis, go out! You can't interrupt—you mustn't, not now. I'll explain—later—but leave now. Go back to Lilly. Don't leave her alone." Lilly's name coming from her lips broke my spell of madness. I pushed her off, grabbed her thin shoulders instead of her throat, and shook her.

"You won't trick me, you hell-cat!" I snarled. "What have you done to Sam? Poisoned him like you and Macklin poisoned Porter Bruton?"

"But I didn't, I didn't! Oh, Willis, give me time to explain. Go back to Lilly now, and—"

"I'll go when I've choked the truth out of you, when I've—"

Suddenly I stiffened. From the front of the house had come a shrill scream—Lilly's voice in a pulsing jet of terror. Releasing Faustine, I whirled, saw instantly that the front of the house was dark now, heard other sounds mingled with Lilly's cries. Staggering toward the door, my nostrils caught a whiff of that brimstone odor, and as I lurched into the hall, a glowing blotch that seemed wreathed in greenish flame catapulted from the living room into the hall, bearing a wild, screaming bundle that I knew to be my fiancée.

"Lilly, I'm coming!" I yelled and charged toward the monstrous thing now vanishing through the front door of the house.

I reached it before the screen had time to slam back on his exit, but my rashness cost me dearly. As I shot through, I saw too late the dark shapes lurking at the porch edges rise and surge toward me.

The next moment I met the impact of their giant, muscular bodies, slammed my fists madly at a swimming nightmare of gargoyle faces, and then collapsed weakly as a huge fist, like a club covered with brine-soaked leather, smashed against my temple in a blow that hammered me into oblivion.

I woke up in darkness to find myself the core of what seemed to be a bristling, tight-wrapped cocoon, and which proved to be a stout rope wound in galling coils about my body. I rolled over and saw a penciled line of light under a closed door. I made out a whitish bundle near me.

"Lilly?" I whispered hoarsely.

"I don't know where she is." It was Faustine Grenfel's voice that answered.

"Where are we?" I asked, recovering from my surprise.

"In your crematorium, in a closet off from the furnace room," she answered. "The witch-men brought us here."

My brain was a whirling confusion; I couldn't make sense out of anything, least of all why Faustine was here, tied and imprisoned too.

"That's odd," I said, "because I thought they were your pals—yours and Macklin's. How do they happen to be working with this devil masquerading as Porter Bruton?"

"Masquerading?" she asked. "I wish I thought so. The witch-men don't. That's why they obey him in terror. They knew he was dead and burned, yet they saw him come back and kill their master. They don't understand a magic that terrible. I no longer have any influence over them at all."

"Then you admit you were Macklin's accomplice in whatever it was he did to Porter Bruton?"

"Of course. And I'll tell you why. Porter Bruton murdered my father!"

"Murdered your father?"

"Yes. Poisoned him with nitrobenzine, and when that didn't kill quickly enough, shoved him from the window."

"But I thought you were in love with Porter."

"So did he," she said. "And I was, until I began to suspect what he had done. You see, he wanted to steal Father's secret because he was in love with Lilly and hoped to win her from you."

"Yes," I said, "but what's that got to do with this madness you've been spreading among those crazed students?"

Faustine sighed.

"Oh, they aren't crazed," she said. "They're just a lot of silly sheep; they'll come out of it. What I did was done to discover the witness to my father's murder. You see, I was the first one to rush up to the laboratory after he had fallen from the window and, as I reached the upper hall, someone—I couldn't identify him—went scuttling away from the keyhole. Later, when I suspected Porter of murdering Father and faking that note, I remembered the incident.

"So when Dennis Macklin came back and I told him, he suggested the scheme to find out who the witness to the murder had been. With his help, I treated those kids to a lot of faked witchcraft, and I got the boys I suspected off one at a time, doped them with sodium amytal—you know it's used sometimes as a truth serum—and while they were half-conscious, questioned them until I found the one who had seen it.

"It turned out to be Willy Richmond. He'd seen the crime, but had been too scared of Porter to tell. We had already slipped Father's body out of the mausoleum and had had his vital organs chemically analyzed and found the nitrobenzine. But, of course, that wasn't proof enough."

"But once you had Richmond's confession, why didn't you go to the police?"

"The testimony of a spy at a keyhole," she said, "might not have sounded convincing to a jury. We were taking no chances with Porter's paying for that hellish crime. Once we had the proof, Dennis got him into the cemetery and delivered an ultimatum. Porter, of course, didn't know that I had helped get the proof. Dennis told him that he would give him the chance to kill himself—otherwise, he would stand trial for the crime. By killing himself he could save not only his own name, but his father would be spared the scandal. Porter agreed to take that way out."

"But what *did* he do?"

"I don't know," she said. "When I saw his face at that window to-night, I suspected some sort of trickery. That's why I lured Sam Fleagle off, drugged him and questioned him. I thought maybe he, and even you and Tom Carlin, might have aided in some hoax. But I got nothing out of him. But Porter must have intended some trick, or he wouldn't have written me that note. Thinking I was still in love with him, he counted on me to interrupt that cremation—"

"Wait a minute!" I said. "It could have been done—granted that his father and Sam Fleagle were working with him. While Tom and I were taking you out, he could have crawled out of the coffin and substituted that body that was stolen from a pauper's grave last night. I suppose he figured that if you failed him, his father could still cause some scene to get us away. Then later, of course, Sam Fleagle faked his voice to scare me—"

"But old Dr. Bruton," she interrupted, "can you believe that he would have—"

Her voice broke off as a sound from the outer room reached our ears. It was the opening and closing of a door, and then muffled voices, one which I recognized as Sam Fleagle's.

"You tricked me into it, lied to me. Now there's been murder, and by God, you'll answer—" Fleagle was growling.

Worming myself forward, I butted my head against the door. It must not have been closed tightly, for it swung open a few inches, and I stared out to see Sam Fleagle, wild-haired and with a dazed look from the drug Faustine had administered still in his eyes, holding old Dr. Bruton by the collar as a terrier might hold a rat.

"But I didn't know, Sam," Dr. Bruton was gasping. "I didn't know—"

"Sam!" I called. "Come here and get these ropes off me!"

The crematorium superintendent whirled, goggled a moment, then released old Bruton and started toward me. But he hadn't taken three steps when the door behind him swung open. Framed in its dark rectangle stood the grisly specter of Porter Bruton. Behind him loomed the shadowy forms and wide-eyed faces of Macklin's witch-men.

Sam had heard it, and he heeled round again, as the fiend, followed by his fear-enslaved henchmen, stepped into the room. I saw him clearly then, and knew that there could no longer be any doubt that he was really Porter Bruton. I could see now that the burning and blackening was not real, being a skillful camouflage of colored putty, greasepaint, collodion, and phosphorescent paint to cause the glow. But there was no comfort in that. The fiend alive was more terrible and dangerous than his ghost might have been.

With a curse, Sam Fleagle sprang at him. But quick as a flash, the murderer whirled, snatched from the hands of one of the witch-men a fire extinguisher, and leveled it at Sam's rushing figure. At a pressure of the plunger a white jet leaped out, caught Sam Fleagle in mid-rush, and as the murderous spray spurted against his face and chest, he fell back with the scream of a tortured animal, flailing his thick arms, stumbling, crumpling to the floor, a writhing, burning mass of agony.

Deliberately then the killer stepped nearer, aimed another blast at his shrieking victim, and at the same time I identified that acrid, brimstone smell and knew what had happened to Macklin, too. That fire extinguisher was loaded with sulphuric acid!

The stark brutality of the act had apparently stunned old Bruton, but now he came out of his daze, made a stumbling step toward his son.

"Porter, Porter," he quavered, "are you mad? When I was forced into helping you, it was only to save your life. And even though I suspected that your story that Grenfel's death was the accidental result of a struggle was a lie, my father's love could not deny you.

"I helped you fake death with that drug, and signed your death certificate. I guarded your body from observation, bribed this poor man you have just killed to help me substitute the stolen body for yours and later fake your cry from the flames. But you swore that once your life was saved, you'd leave and never come back. Is this my reward—this orgy of murder?"

Porter stared at him coldly, his travesty of a face twisted in a sneer.

"This orgy of murder, as you call it," he said, "was as necessary as the other. These people knew too much, and I couldn't leave tattling tongues behind me. But I'm nearly through now. I've got money and a car ready to carry me to the border, and most important of all, I've got locked in my head the secret that Grenfel died for. In another land, under another name, that secret will make me the greatest scientist in the world. I'm perfectly safe, because I'm officially dead. And the only ones who knew my secret are dead, too—or soon will be. All but Lilly, who shall go with me."

"My God! You won't take her?"

Porter Bruton leered. "She's drugged and safely hidden in a coffin in a certain locked mausoleum, waiting like the sleeping princess for me to come and carry her away. And don't think she won't go; she won't be able to help it. She'll stay with me, too, if it means drugging her for the rest of her life."

For a moment the old man stood aghast. Then a wild look came over his quivering face.

"You beast!" he shrilled. "I'll strangle you with my own hands!" And he sprang.

Agile as a bullfighter, Porter Bruton leaped aside, and as his father lurched past him, he brutally slugged his father with the fire extinguisher, coldly watching him crumple, twitching, to the floor.

I cursed under my breath. Through it all I had been fighting with the coils of rope that bound me. But even the burst of savage strength which the revelation of Lilly's doom inspired was not enough to free me. And now the monster turned to lock the door and bark a command at the witch-men, one of whom started toward the closet where Faustine and I lay helpless.

Rolling over on my back, I flung myself upright and with a desperate heave got my knees under me and straightened to my feet. But swaying there, I realized that I was still as helpless as ever. Then I thought of the switchboard on the left wall. Maybe if I could switch the lights off there would be some bare chance to escape in the confusion.

Blindly I lunged toward the switchboard, felt my head butt a handle, felt the blue flames crackle in my hair. But it wasn't the right switch; the lights stayed on. And now the big witch-man sprang in and dragged me back.

I struggled, writhed, butted at him with my head, but it was no use. Flinging me over his shoulder, he carried me out and dumped me to the floor. There I lay, panting, staring up into Porter Bruton's leering face. Death was only moments away, I knew, and a fight was not even possible. Wildly I began pleading with him for Lilly.

It was futile. The deadly coldness of his eyes told me that, and when a sudden scraping sound on the cement floor caused me to fling my head around, I realized the doom that awaited me. One of the men was dragging a coffin from the storeroom!

Blind panic gripped me then. As the second man darted toward me I began to squirm and heave and pitch like a caterpillar in an ant bed. Now the other man joined his mate, and the two of them laid hands on me. But my last buckling leap had thrown me across the corpse of Sam Fleagle, and my hands, behind my back, seized his coat and clung.

The acid with which his clothes and corroding tissues were saturated burned into my wrists and arms. But I didn't mind; it was the thought of that coffin, of where it was going that drove my brain toward madness.

But Bruton grew impatient.

"Get him in there! We've got the girl to deal with, too!" he growled, and striding over, he slammed the empty extinguisher against my head.

It didn't knock me out. I don't believe anything could have knocked me out then. But it stunned me for the moment necessary for them to lift me and fling me into the coffin. When they slammed the lid tight and I felt myself lifted, felt the carriage moving beneath me and suddenly heard the motors begin to sing their weird tune and heard the flames blast into the oven chamber, I tasted hell.

Then I felt it—the first blast of that terrific heat. Bruton had started the fire before shoving me in, wanting to hear me scream, I suppose. And scream I did. Yet even then, the thought of Lilly, lying drugged at the mercy of this fiend, was more agonizing than my own fate.

The carriage slammed against the front of the oven; the awful heat, blasting through the coffin walls, set the blood in my head boiling. I shrieked, beat my head against the coffin lid; and as I heaved up, the coils of the rope, eaten through by the acid, parted. My arms came free—came free too late to help me, adding instead a final fillip of ironic horror to what seemed my certain doom.

But something had happened. That last heave must have jolted the coffin sideward, for hands lifted it to steady it, and in the brief instant in which I felt them tense for the forward shove, I flung my whole weight sideward and slammed head and shoulders against the coffin's side.

It tottered—and fell! Crashing edgewise to the floor, the catches of the lid came loose, and I was scrambling out, flinging myself upright to meet Porter Bruton's charge.

He swung at me with the fire extinguisher, but I ducked the blow. My weight thudded against him and my clawed hands caught his throat. He fell backward and I went down on top of him. Before his men could spring to his aid, I bellowed into his purpling face.

"Keep them off or I'll strangle you before they can drag me away!" I shouted.

I let up a little on the throat pressure, and he gasped a command that caused the men to freeze in their tracks. Then he snarled at me.

"All right, kill me! But they'll kill you then, and Faustine, too. And what will happen to Lilly? Think of her, waking up buried alive in that coffin in the locked mausoleum!"

My hands, my whole rage-quivering body went rigid at that. It was the most horrible moment of all. To have miraculously escaped the flames, only to be faced with this ghastly choice! But then, was there a choice? Even if Lilly died in the shrieking delirium of the buried-alive, it was better than a lifetime of drugged slavery to this fiend.

With an animal snarl, I fell on him again, and this time my hate-steeled fingers sank to the bone in his throat. He screamed, and the men sprang. I ducked, pressed harder, knowing it was the end, knowing I must kill before I was killed.

But before they reached me, four rapid blasts of gunfire punctuated the din, followed by high-pitched howls of pain. I straightened, saw with incredulous eyes the witch-men groveling on the floor while Tom Carlin, smoking gun in hand, was lunging toward me.

"Tom, how did you happen—" I began.

"The lights," he said. "Didn't you mean to signal?"

"Lights?" I blinked. "I tried to cut them off, but—"

"But you got the wrong switch," Tom said with a flash of sudden understanding. "You idiot, I'm talking about the lights that flood the grounds and building. I saw them on and came to see what was wrong."

Things got a little shaky and confused after that, but one thought was still dominant in my mind. Tom told me later how I stumbled up with a mumbled, "Get Faustine to explain—" and staggered out.

I'm glad no one saw me then, for I must have looked the part of a mad ghoul, roving through the dark graveyard with an axe I had picked up somewhere. But I found what I sought—in the Grenfel vault—and when I smashed the coffin-lock and lifted her limp body out and held it against me to feel that faint heartbeat, sanity seemed to return to me for the first time in hours.

She came out of it all right, though we never learned exactly what he had used to drug her—perhaps the same drug he used on himself. Dr. Bruton hinted of some African drug which Porter had mixed with other chemicals. But Porter never told because he took cyanide before he could be brought to trial—and this time he really died.

Old Dr. Bruton was excused for his part in the plot. He had not dreamed, when he aided in the deception, that his son had planned more than an escape to save his life. And his attack on the fiend at the last had redeemed him.

Dead Sam Fleagle had been likewise a blind tool of the killer, having fallen for a tale that Porter was trying to escape murder at the hands of Macklin, and had allowed himself to be bribed into stealing the pauper's corpse and helping with the substitution.

Oakvale is a quiet suburb again, though to say it has completely recovered from the horror might not be strictly true. Business isn't so good at the crematorium, though Lilly and I, staid married people now, assure ourselves that things will soon pick up.

That, however, isn't what bothers me. What bothers me is myself. I let morbid thoughts prey on my mind too much. You see we never did know just what it was that Professor Grenfel had discovered. The chances are he was simply crazed from overwork when he made that statement about the dead not really being dead at all until they're killed in graves and ovens and with embalmers' knives.

And Porter Bruton may have deluded himself into believing it, and that he knew the secret, too. But that's not the point. The point is that if you can't quit thinking about it, you'd better get out of the business I'm in. So it's pretty likely that I'll sell out my interest to Tom Carlin, and try my hand at something else.

THE DANCE OF THE DEAD

Johann Wolfgang von Goethe

Johann Wolfgang von Goethe has been called "the greatest of all German poets and the outstanding figure of world literature since the Renaissance." Besides being a poet, he was also a dramatist, novelist, lawyer, and scientist. His complete works fill more than 150 volumes. While he wrote in almost every field of science and his discoveries contributed to the theory of evolution, he is best known as the author of *Faust*, which he worked on for over thirty years and which has been described as "one of the greatest poetic and philosophic creations the world possesses."

In this poem he illustrates the *Totentanz*, or the *danse macabre*, where the dead rise out of their graves at night to dance, prompting the cemetery's caretaker to make the mistake of stealing a shroud from one of the dancers.

◆ ◆ ◆

The warder he gazes at dead o' the night
   On the graveyards under him lying,
The moon into clearness throws all by her light,
   The night with the daylight is vying.
There's a stir in the graves, and forth from their tombs

The form of a man, then a woman next looms
    In garments long trailing and snowy.

They stretch themselves out, and with eager delight
    Join the bones for the revel and dancing—
Young and old, rich and poor, the lady and knight,
    Their trains are a hindrance to dancing.
And since here by shame they no longer are bound,
They shuffle them off, and lo, strewn lie around
    Their garments on each little hillock.

Here rises a shank, and a leg wobbles there
    With lewd diabolical gesture;
And clatter and rattle of bones you might hear,
    As of one beating sticks to a measure.
This seems to the warder a laughable game:
Then the tempter, low whispering, up to him came:
    "In one of their shrouds go and wrap thee."

'Twas done soon as said; then he gained in wild flight
    Concealment behind the church portal,
The moon all the while throws her bright beams of light
    On the dance where they revel and sport all.
First one, then another, dispersed all are they,
And donning their shrouds steal the specters away,
    And under the graves all is quiet.

But one of them stumbles and fumbles along,
    'Midst the tombstones groping intently;
But none of his comrades have done him this wrong,
    His shroud in the breeze 'gins to scent he.
He rattles the door of the tower, but can find

No entrance,—good luck to the warder behind!—
    'Tis barred with blest crosses of metal.

His shroud he must have, or rest can he ne'er;
    And so, without further preambles,
The old Gothic carving he grips then and there,
    From turret to pinnacle scrambles.
Alas for the warder! all's over, I fear;
From buttress to buttress in dev'lish career
    He climbs like a long-legged spider.

The warder he trembles, and pale doth he look,
    That shroud he would gladly be giving,
When piercing transfixed it a sharp-pointed hook!
    He thought his last hour he was living.
Clouds cover already the vanishing moon,
With thunderous clang beats the clock a loud *One*—
    Below lies the skeleton, shattered.

THE COFFIN-MAKER

Alexander Pushkin

Many scholars consider Alexander Pushkin to be Russia's greatest poet and the founder of modern Russian literature. Some say he is more popular in Russia than Shakespeare is in the West. Many of his works gave voice to the suffering of the Russian people, but his political views got him into considerable trouble and his work was often censored. It took him five years to get permission to present his masterpiece—his drama *Boris Godunov*. His career was cut short at the age of thirty-seven, when he was killed in a duel.

◆   ◆   ◆

The last of the effects of the coffin-maker, Adrian Prokhoroff, were placed upon the hearse, and a couple of sorry-looking jades dragged themselves along for the fourth time from Basmannaia to Nikitskaia, whither the coffin-maker was removing with all his household. After locking up the shop, he posted upon the door a placard announcing that the house was to be let or sold, and then made his way on foot to his new abode. On approaching the little yellow house, which had so long captivated his imagination, and which at last he had bought for a considerable sum, the old coffin-maker was astonished to find that his heart did not rejoice. When he crossed the unfamiliar threshold and found his new home in the greatest confusion, he sighed for his old hovel, where for eighteen years the strictest order had prevailed. He began to scold his two daughters and the servant for their slowness, and then set to work to help them himself. Order was soon established; the ark with the sacred images, the cupboard with the crockery, the table, the sofa, and the bed occupied the corners reserved for them in the back room; in the kitchen and parlor were placed the articles comprising the stock-in-trade of the master—coffins of all colors and of all sizes, together with cupboards containing mourning hats, cloaks and torches.

Over the door was placed a sign representing a fat Cupid with an inverted torch in his hand and bearing this inscription, "Plain and colored coffins sold and lined here; coffins also let out on hire, and old ones repaired."

The girls retired to their bedroom; Adrian made a tour of inspection of his quarters, and then sat down by the window and ordered the tea-urn to be prepared.

The enlightened reader knows that Shakespeare and Walter Scott have both represented their gravediggers as merry and facetious individuals, in order that the contrast might more forcibly strike our imagination. Out of respect for the truth, we cannot follow their example, and we are compelled to confess that the disposition of our coffin-maker was in perfect harmony with his gloomy occupation. Adrian Prokhoroff was usually gloomy and thoughtful. He rarely opened his mouth, except to scold his daughters when he found them standing idle and gazing out of the window at the passersby, or to demand for his wares an exorbitant price from those who had the misfortune—and sometimes the good fortune—to need them.

Hence it was that Adrian, sitting near the window and drinking his seventh cup of tea, was immersed as usual in melancholy reflections. He thought of the pouring rain which, just a week before, had commenced to beat down during the funeral of the retired brigadier. Many of the cloaks had shrunk in consequence of the downpour, and many of the hats had been put quite out of shape. He foresaw unavoidable expenses, for his old stock of funeral dresses was in a pitiable condition. He hoped to compensate himself for his losses by the burial of old Trukhina, the shopkeeper's wife, who for more than a year had been upon the point of death. But Trukhina lay dying at Rasgouliai, and Prokhoroff was afraid that her heirs, in spite of their promise, would not take the trouble to send so far for him, but would make arrangements with the nearest undertaker.

These reflections were suddenly interrupted by three Masonic knocks at the door.

"Who is there?" asked the coffin-maker.

The door opened, and a man, who at the first glance could be recognized as a German artisan, entered the room, and with a jovial air advanced towards the coffin-maker.

"Pardon me, respected neighbor," said he in that Russian dialect which to this day we cannot hear without a smile; "Pardon me for disturbing you.... I wished to make your acquaintance as soon as possible. I am a shoemaker, my name is Gottlieb Schultz, and I live across the street, in that little house just facing your windows. Tomorrow I am going to celebrate my silver wedding, and I have come to invite you and your daughters to dine with us."

The invitation was cordially accepted. The coffin-maker asked the shoemaker to seat himself and take a cup of tea, and thanks to the open-hearted disposition of Gottlieb Schultz, they were soon engaged in friendly conversation.

"How is business with you?" asked Adrian.

"Just so-so," replied Schultz. "I cannot complain. My wares are not like yours: the living can do without shoes, but the dead cannot do without coffins."

"Very true," observed Adrian, "but if a living person hasn't anything to buy shoes with, you cannot find fault with him, he goes about barefooted; but a dead beggar gets his coffin for nothing."

In this manner the conversation was carried on between them for some time; at last the shoemaker rose and took leave of the coffin-maker, renewing his invitation.

The next day, exactly at twelve o'clock, the coffin-maker and his daughters issued from the doorway of their newly purchased residence, and directed their steps towards the abode of their neighbor. I will not stop to describe the Russian caftan of Adrian Prokhoroff, nor the European clothes of Akoulina and Daria, deviating in this respect from the usual custom of modern novelists. But I do not think it superfluous to observe that they both had on the yellow cloaks and red shoes which they were accustomed to don on solemn occasions only.

The shoemaker's little dwelling was filled with guests, consisting chiefly of German artisans with their wives and foremen. Of the Russian officials there was present but one, Yourko the Finn, a watchman, who, in spite of his humble calling, was the special object of the host's attention. For twenty-five years he had faithfully discharged the duties of postilion of Pogorelsky. The conflagration of 1812, which destroyed the ancient capital, destroyed also his little yellow watch-house. But immediately after the expulsion of the enemy, a new one appeared in its place, painted grey and with white Doric columns, and Yourko began again to pace to and fro before it, with his axe and grey coat of mail. He was known to the greater part of the Germans who lived near the Nikitskaia Gate, and some of them had even spent the night from Sunday to Monday beneath his roof.

Adrian immediately made himself acquainted with him, as with a man whom, sooner or later, he might have need of, and when the guests took their places at the table, they sat down beside each other. Herr Schultz and his wife, and their daughter Lotchen, a young girl of seventeen, did the honors of the table and helped the cook to serve. The beer flowed in streams; Yourko ate like four, and Adrian in no way yielded to him; his daughters, however, stood upon their dignity. The conversation, which was carried on in German, gradually grew more and more boisterous. Suddenly the host requested a moment's attention, and uncorking a sealed bottle, he said with a loud voice in Russian, "To the health of my good Louise!"

The champagne foamed. The host tenderly kissed the fresh face of his partner, and the guests drank noisily to the health of the good Louise.

"To the health of my amiable guests!" exclaimed the host, uncorking a second bottle; and the guests thanked him by draining their glasses once more.

Then followed a succession of toasts. The health of each individual guest was drunk; they drank to the health of Moscow and to quite a dozen little German towns; they drank to the health of all corporations in general and of each in particular; they drank to the health of the masters and foremen. Adrian drank with enthusiasm and became so merry, that he proposed a facetious toast to himself. Suddenly one of the guests, a fat baker, raised his glass and exclaimed, "To the health of those for whom we work, our customers!"

This proposal, like all the others, was joyously and unanimously received. The guests began to salute each other; the tailor bowed to the shoemaker, the shoemaker to the tailor, the baker to both, the whole company to the baker, and so on. In the midst of these mutual congratulations, Yourko exclaimed, turning to his neighbor, "Come, little father! Drink to the health of your corpses!"

Everybody laughed, but the coffin-maker considered himself insulted, and frowned. Nobody noticed it, the guests continued to drink, and the bell had already rung for vespers when they rose from the table.

The guests dispersed at a late hour, the greater part of them in a very merry mood. The fat baker and the bookbinder, whose face seemed as if bound in red morocco, linked their arms in those of Yourko and conducted him back to his little watch-house, thus observing the proverb, "One good turn deserves another."

The coffin-maker returned home drunk and angry.

"Why is it," he exclaimed aloud, "why is it that my trade is not as honest as any other? Is a coffin-maker brother to the hangman? Why did those heathens laugh? Is a coffin-maker a buffoon? I wanted to invite them to my new dwelling and give them a feast, but now I'll do nothing of the kind. Instead of inviting them, I will invite those for whom I work: the orthodox dead."

"What is the matter, little father?" said the servant, who was engaged at that moment in taking off his boots; "Why do you talk such nonsense? Make the sign of the cross! Invite the dead to your new house! What folly!"

"Yes, by the Lord! I will invite them," continued Adrian, "and that, too, for tomorrow! . . . Do me the favor, my benefactors, to come and feast with me tomorrow evening; I will regale you with what God has sent me."

With these words the coffin-maker turned into bed and soon began to snore.

It was still dark when Adrian was awakened out of his sleep. Trukhina, the shopkeeper's wife, had died during the course of that very night, and a special messenger was sent off on horseback by her bailiff to carry the news to Adrian. The coffin-maker gave him ten kopeks to buy brandy with, dressed himself as hastily as possible, took a droshky and set out for Rasgouliai.

Before the door of the house in which the deceased lay, the police had already taken their stand, and the trades-people were passing backwards and forwards, like ravens that smell a dead body. The deceased lay upon a table, yellow as wax, but not yet disfigured by decomposition. Around her stood her relatives, neighbors and domestic servants. All the windows were open; tapers were burning; and the priests were reading the prayers for the dead. Adrian went up to the nephew of Trukhina, a young shopman in a fashionable coat, and informed him that the coffin, wax candles, pall, and the other funeral accessories would be immediately delivered with all possible exactitude. The heir thanked him in an absent-minded manner, saying that he would not bargain about the price, but would rely upon him acting in everything according to his conscience. The coffin-maker, in accordance with his usual custom, vowed that he would not charge him too much, exchanged significant glances with the bailiff, and then departed to commence operations.

The whole day was spent in passing to and fro between Rasgouliai and the Nikitskaia Gate. Towards evening everything was finished, and he returned home on foot, after having dismissed his driver. It was a moonlight night. The coffin-maker reached the Nikitskaia Gate in safety. Near the Church of the Ascension he was hailed by our acquaintance Yourko, who, recognizing the coffin-maker, wished him goodnight. It was late. The coffin-maker was just approaching his house, when suddenly he fancied he saw someone approach his gate, open the wicket, and disappear within.

"What does that mean?" thought Adrian. "Who can be wanting me again? Can it be a thief come to rob me? Or have my foolish girls got lovers coming after them? It means no good, I fear!"

And the coffin-maker thought of calling his friend Yourko to his assistance. But at that moment, another person approached the wicket and was about to enter, but seeing the master of the house hastening towards him, he stopped and took off his three-cornered hat. His face seemed familiar to Adrian, but in his hurry he had not been able to examine it closely.

"You are favoring me with a visit," said Adrian, out of breath. "Walk in, I beg of you."

"Don't stand on ceremony, little father," replied the other, in a hollow voice; "you go first, and show your guests the way."

Adrian had no time to spend upon ceremony. The wicket was open; he ascended the steps, followed by the other. Adrian thought he could hear people walking about in his rooms.

"What the devil does all this mean!" he thought to himself, and he hastened to enter. But the sight that met his eyes caused his legs to give way beneath him.

The room was full of corpses. The moon, shining through the windows, lit up their yellow and blue faces, sunken mouths, dim, half-closed eyes, and protruding noses. Adrian, with horror, recognized in them people that he himself had buried, and in the guest who entered with him, the brigadier who had been buried during the pouring rain. They all, men and women, surrounded the coffin-maker, with bowings and salutations, except one poor fellow lately buried gratis, who, conscious and ashamed of his rags, did not venture to approach, but meekly kept aloof in a corner. All the others were decently dressed: the female corpses in caps and ribbons, the officials in uniforms, but with their beards unshaven, the tradesmen in their holiday caftans.

"You see, Prokhoroff," said the brigadier in the name of all the honorable company, "we have all risen in response to your invitation. Only those who were unable to come stayed at home; those who have crumbled to pieces and have nothing left but fleshless bones. But even of these there was one who hadn't the patience to remain behind so much did he want to come and see you...."

At this moment a little skeleton pushed his way through the crowd and approached Adrian. His fleshless face smiled affably at the coffin-maker. Shreds of green and red cloth and rotten linen hung on him here and there as on a pole, and the bones of his feet rattled inside his big jackboots, like pestles in mortars.

"You do not recognize me, Prokhoroff," said the skeleton. "Don't you remember the retired sergeant of the Guards, Peter Petrovitch Kourilkin, the same to whom, in the year 1799, you sold your first coffin, and that, too, a cheap one instead of oak?"

With these words the corpse stretched out his bony arms towards him; but Adrian, collecting all his strength, shrieked and pushed him from him. Peter Petrovitch staggered, fell, and crumbled all to pieces. Among the corpses arose a murmur of indignation; all stood up for the honor of their companion, and they overwhelmed Adrian with such threats and imprecations, that the poor host, deafened by their shrieks and almost crushed to death, lost his presence of mind, fell upon the bones of the retired sergeant of the Guards, and swooned away.

For some time the sun had been shining upon the bed on which lay the coffin-maker. At last he opened his eyes and saw before him the servant attending to the tea-urn. With horror, Adrian recalled all the incidents of the previous day. Trukhina, the brigadier, and the sergeant, Kourilkin, rose vaguely before his imagination. He waited in silence for the servant to open the conversation and inform him of the events of the night.

"How you have slept, little father Adrian Prokhorovitch!" said Aksinia, handing him his dressing-gown. "Your neighbor, the tailor, has been here, and the watchman also called to inform you that today is his name-day; but you were so sound asleep, that we did not wish to wake you."

"Did anyone come for me from the late Trukhina?"

"The late? Is she dead, then?"

"What a fool you are! Didn't you yourself help me yesterday to prepare the things for her funeral?"

"Have you taken leave of your senses, little father, or have you not yet recovered from the effects of yesterday's drinking-bout? What funeral was there yesterday? You spent the whole day feasting at the German's, and then came home drunk and threw yourself upon the bed, and have slept till this hour, when the bells have already rung for mass."

"Really!" said the coffin-maker, greatly relieved.

"Yes, indeed," replied the servant.

"Well, since that is the case, make the tea as quickly as possible and call my daughters."

FOR THE BLOOD IS THE LIFE

F. Marion Crawford

The title of this story comes from the Bible. In the Book of Deuteronomy, it says, "Only be sure that thou eat not the blood: for the blood is the life; and thou mayest not eat the life with the flesh." While the Bible may say not to consume blood, that never stopped a vampire ... particularly since the primary thing a vampire needs is life.

◆ ◆ ◆

We had dined at sunset on the broad roof of the old tower, because it was cooler there during the great heat of summer. Besides, the little kitchen was built at one corner of the great square platform, which made it more convenient than if the dishes had to be carried down the steep stone steps broken in places and everywhere worn with age. The tower was one of those built all down the west coast of Calabria by the Emperor Charles V early in the sixteenth century, to keep off the Barbary pirates, when the unbelievers were allied with Francis I against the Emperor and the Church. They have gone to ruin, a few still stand intact, and mine is one of the largest.

How it came into my possession ten years ago, and why I spend a part of each year in it, are matters which do not concern this tale. The tower stands in one of the loneliest spots in Southern Italy, at the extremity of a curving, rocky promontory, which forms a small but safe natural harbor at the southern extremity of the Gulf of Policastro, and just north of Cape Scalea, the birthplace of Judas Iscariot, according to the old local legend. The tower stands alone on this hooked spur of the rock, and there is not a house to be seen within three miles of it. When I go there I take a couple of sailors, one of whom is a fair cook, and when I am away it is in the charge of a gnome-like little being who was once a miner and who attached himself to me long ago.

My friend, who sometimes visits me in my summer solitude, is an artist by profession, a Scandinavian by birth, and a cosmopolitan by force of circumstances. We had dined at sunset; the sunset glow had reddened and faded again, and the evening purple steeped the vast chain of the mountains that embrace the deep gulf to eastward and rear themselves higher and higher toward the south. It was hot, and we sat at the landward corner of the platform, waiting for the night breeze to come down from the lower hills. The color sank out of the air, there was a little interval of deep-grey twilight, and a lamp sent a yellow streak from the open door of the kitchen, where the men were getting their supper.

Then the moon rose suddenly above the crest of the promontory, flooding the platform and lighting up every little spur of rock and knoll of grass below us, down to the edge of the motionless water. My friend lighted his pipe and sat looking at a spot on the hillside. I knew that he was looking at it, and for a long time past I had wondered whether he would ever see anything there that would fix his attention. I knew that spot well. It was clear that he was interested at last, though it was a long time before he spoke. Like most painters, he trusts to his own eyesight, as a lion trusts his strength and a stag his speed, and he is always disturbed when he cannot reconcile what he sees with what he believes that he ought to see.

"It's strange," he said. "Do you see that little mound just on this side of the boulder?"

"Yes," I said, and I guessed what was coming.

"It looks like a grave," observed Holger.

"Very true. It does look like a grave."

"Yes," continued my friend, his eyes still fixed on the spot. "But the strange thing is that I see the body lying on the top of it. Of course," continued Holger, turning his head on one side as artists do, "it must be an effect of light. In the first place, it is not a grave at all. Secondly, if it were, the body would be inside and not outside. Therefore, it's an effect of the moonlight. Don't you see it?"

"Perfectly; I always see it on moonlight nights."

"It doesn't seem it interests you much," said Holger.

"On the contrary, it does interest me, though I am used to it. You're not so far wrong, either. The mound is really a grave."

"Nonsense!" cried Holger incredulously. "I suppose you'll tell me that what I see lying on it is really a corpse!"

"No," I answered, "it's not. I know, because I have taken the trouble to go down and see."

"Then what is it?" asked Holger.

"It's nothing."

"You mean that it's an effect of light, I suppose?"

"Perhaps it is. But the inexplicable part of the matter is that it makes no difference whether the moon is rising or setting, or waxing or waning. If there's any moonlight at all, from east or west or overhead, so long as it shines on the grave you can see the outline of the body on top."

Holger stirred up his pipe with the point of his knife, and then used his finger for a stopper. When the tobacco burned well, he rose from his chair.

"If you don't mind," he said, "I'll go down and take a look at it."

He left me, crossed the roof, and disappeared down the dark steps. I did not move, but sat looking down until he came out of the tower below. I heard him humming an old Danish song as he crossed the open space in the bright moonlight, going straight to the mysterious mound. When he was ten paces from it, Holger stopped short, made two steps forward, and then three or four backward, and then stopped again.

I knew what that meant. He had reached the spot where the Thing ceased to be visible—where, as he would have said, the effect of light changed.

Then he went on till he reached the mound and stood upon it. I could see the Thing still, but it was no longer lying down; it was on its knees now, winding its white arms round Holger's body and looking up into his face. A cool breeze stirred my hair at that moment, as the night wind began to come down from the hills, but it felt like a breath from another world.

The Thing seemed to be trying to climb to its feet helping itself up by Holger's body while he stood upright, quite unconscious of it and apparently looking toward the tower, which is very picturesque when the moonlight falls upon it on that side.

"Come along!" I shouted. "Don't stay there all night!"

It seemed to me that he moved reluctantly as he stepped from the mound, or else with difficulty. That was it. The Thing's arms were still round his waist, but its feet could not leave the grave. As he came slowly forward it was drawn and lengthened like a wreath of mist, thin and white, till I saw distinctly that Holger shook himself, as a man does who feels a chill. At the same instant a little wail of pain came to me on the breeze—it might have been the cry of the small owl that lives among the rocks—and the misty presence floated swiftly back from Holger's advancing figure and lay once more at its length upon the mound.

Again I felt the cool breeze in my hair, and this time an icy thrill of dread ran down my spine. I remembered very well that I had once gone down there alone in the moonlight; that presently, being near, I had seen nothing; that, like Holger, I had gone and had stood upon the mound; and I remembered how when I came back, sure that there was nothing there, I had felt the sudden conviction that there was something after all if I would only look back, a temptation I had resisted as unworthy of a man of sense, until, to get rid of it, I had shaken myself just as Holger did.

And now I knew that those white, misty arms had been round me, too; I knew it in a flash, and I shuddered as I remembered that I had heard the night owl then, too. But it had not been the night owl. It was the cry of the Thing.

I refilled my pipe and poured out a cup of strong southern wine; in less than a minute Holger was seated beside me again.

"Of course there's nothing there," he said, "but it's creepy, all the same. Do you know, when I was coming back I was so sure that there was something behind me that I wanted to turn around and look? It was an effort not to."

He laughed a little, knocked the ashes out of his pipe, and poured himself out some wine. For a while neither of us spoke, and the moon rose higher and we both looked at the Thing that lay on the mound.

"You might make a story about that," said Holger after a long time.

"There is one," I answered. "If you're not sleepy, I'll tell it to you."

"Go ahead," said Holger, who likes stories.

Old Alario was dying up there in the village beyond the hill. You remember him, I have no doubt. They say that he made his money by selling sham jewelry in South America, and escaped with his gains when he was found out. Like all those fellows, if they bring anything back with them, he at once set to work to enlarge his house, and as there are no masons here, he sent all the way to Paola for two workmen. They were a rough-looking pair of scoundrels—a Neapolitan who had lost one eye and a Sicilian with an old scar half an inch deep across his left cheek. I often saw them, for on Sundays they used to come down here and fish off the rocks. When Alario caught the fever that killed him the masons were still at work. As he had agreed that part of their pay should be their board and lodging, he made them sleep in the house. His wife was dead, and he had an only son called Angelo, who was a much better sort than himself. Angelo was to marry the daughter of the richest man in the village, and, strange to say, though the marriage was arranged by their parents, the young people were said to be in love with each other.

For that matter, the whole village was in love with Angelo, and among the rest a wild, good-looking creature called Cristina, who was more like a gipsy than any girl I ever saw about here. She had very red lips and very black eyes, she was built like a greyhound, and had the tongue of the devil. But Angelo did not care a straw for her. He was rather a simpleminded fellow, quite different from his old scoundrel of a father, and under what I should call normal circumstances I really believe that he would never have looked at any girl except the nice plump little creature, with a fat dowry, whom his father meant him to marry. But things turned up which were neither normal nor natural.

On the other hand, a very handsome young shepherd from the hills above Maratea was in love with Cristina, who seems to have been quite indifferent to him. Cristina had no regular means of subsistence, but she was a good girl and willing to do any work or go on errands to any distance for the sake of a loaf of bread or a mess of beans, and permission to sleep under cover. She was especially glad when she could get something to do about the house of Angelo's father. There is no doctor in the village, and when the neighbors saw that old Alario was dying they sent Cristina to Scalea to fetch one. That was late in the afternoon, and if they had waited so long, it was because the dying miser refused to allow any such extravagance while he was able to speak. But while Cristina was gone, matters grew rapidly worse, the priest was brought to the bedside, and when he had done what he could he gave it as his opinion to the bystanders that the old man was dead, and left the house.

You know these people. They have a physical horror of death. Until the priest spoke, the room had been full of people. The words were hardly out of his mouth before it was empty. It was night now. They hurried down the dark steps and out into the street.

Angelo, as I have said, was away, Cristina had not come back—the simple woman-servant who had nursed the sick man fled with the rest, and the body was left alone in the flickering light of the earthen oil lamp.

Five minutes later two men looked in cautiously and crept forward toward the bed. They were the one-eyed Neapolitan mason and his Sicilian companion. They knew what they wanted. In a moment they had dragged from under the bed a small but heavy iron-bound box, and long before anyone thought of coming back to the dead man they had left the house and the village under cover of darkness. It was easy enough, for Alario's house is the last toward the gorge which leads down here, and the thieves merely went out by the back door, got over the stone wall, and had nothing to risk after that except that possibility of meeting some belated countryman, which was very small indeed, since few of the people use that path. They had a mattock and shovel, and they made their way without accident.

I am telling you this story as it must have happened, for, of course, there were no witnesses to this part of it. The men brought the box down by the gorge, intending to bury it on the beach in the wet sand, where it would have been much safer. But the paper would have rotted if they had been obliged to leave it there long, so they dug their hole down there, close to that boulder. Yes, just where the mound is now.

Cristina did not find the doctor in Scalea, for he had been sent for from a place up the valley, half-way to San Domenico. If she had found him he would have come on his mule by the upper road, which is smoother but much longer. But Cristina took the short cut by the rocks, which passes about fifty feet above the mound, and goes round that corner. The men were digging when she passed, and she heard them at work. It would not have been like her to go by without finding out what the noise was, for she was never afraid of anything in her life, and, besides, the fishermen sometimes come ashore here at night to get a stone for an anchor or to gather sticks to make a little fire.

The night was dark and Cristina probably came close to the two men before she could see what they were doing. She knew them, of course, and they knew her, and understood instantly that they were in her power. There was only one thing to be done for their safety, and they did it. They knocked her on the head, they dug the hole deep, and they buried her quickly with the iron-bound chest. They must have understood that their only chance of escaping suspicion lay in getting back to the village before their absence was noticed, for they returned immediately, and were found half an hour later gossiping quietly with the man who was making Alario's coffin. He was a crony of theirs, and had been working at the repairs in the old man's house. So far as I have been able to make out, the only persons who were supposed to know where Alario kept his treasure were Angelo and the one woman-servant I have mentioned. Angelo was away; it was the woman who discovered the theft.

It was easy enough to understand why no one else knew where the money was. The old man kept his door locked and the key in his pocket when he was out, and did not let the woman enter to clean the place unless he was there himself. The whole village knew that he had money somewhere, however, and the masons had probably discovered the whereabouts of the chest by climbing in at the window in his absence. If the old man had not been delirious until he lost consciousness he would have been in frightful agony of mind for his riches. The faithful woman-servant forgot their existence only for a few moments when she fled with the rest, overcome by the horror of death. Twenty minutes had not passed before she returned with the two hideous old hags who are always called in to prepare the dead for burial. Even then she had not at first the courage to go near the bed with them, but she made a pretence of dropping something, went down on her knees as if to find it, and looked under the bedstead. The walls of the room were newly white-washed down to the floor and she saw at a glance that the chest was gone. It had been there in the afternoon; it had therefore been stolen in the short interval since she had left the room.

There are no carabineers stationed in the village; there is not so much as a municipal watchman, for there is no municipality. There never was such a place, I believe. Scalea is supposed to look after it in some mysterious way, and it takes a couple of hours to get anybody from there. As the old woman had lived in the village all her life, it did not even occur to her to apply to any civil authority for help. She simply set up a howl and ran through the village in the dark, screaming out that her dead master's house had been robbed. Many of the people looked out, but at first no one seemed inclined to help her. Most of them, judging her by themselves, whispered to each other that she had probably stolen the money herself.

The first man to move was the father of the girl whom Angelo was to marry; having collected his household, all of whom felt a personal interest in the wealth which was to have come into the family, he declared it to be his opinion that the chest had been stolen by the two journeymen masons who lodged in the house. He headed a search for them, which naturally began in Alario's house and ended in the carpenter's workshop, where the thieves were found discussing a measure of wine with the carpenter over the half-finished coffin, by the light of one earthen lamp filled with oil and tallow.

The search-party at once accused the delinquents of the crime, and threatened to lock them up in the cellar till the carabineers could be fetched from Scalea. The two men looked at each other for one moment, and then without the slightest hesitation they put out the single light, seized the unfinished coffin between them, and using it as a sort of battering ram, dashed upon their assailants in the dark. In a few moments they were beyond pursuit.

That is the end of the first part of the story. The treasure had disappeared, and as no trace of it could be found the people supposed that the thieves had succeeded in carrying it off. The old man was buried, and when Angelo came back at last he had to borrow money to pay for the miserable funeral, and had some difficulty in doing so. He hardly needed to be told that in losing his inheritance he had lost his bride. In this part of the world marriages are made on strictly business principles, and if the promised cash is not forthcoming on the appointed day, the bride or the bridegroom whose parents have failed to produce it may as well take themselves off, for there will be no wedding. Poor Angelo knew that well enough. His father had been possessed of hardly any land, and now that the hard cash which he had brought from South America was gone, there was nothing left but debts for the building materials that were to have been used for enlarging and improving the old house. Angelo was beggared, and the nice plump little creature who was to have been his, turned up her nose at him in the most approved fashion.

As for Cristina, it was several days before she was missed, for no one remembered that she had been sent to Scalea for the doctor, who had never come. She often disappeared in the same way for days together, when she could find a little work here and there at the distant farms among the hills. But when she did not come back at all, people began to wonder, and at last made up their minds that she had connived with the masons and had escaped with them.

I paused and emptied my glass.

"That sort of thing could not happen anywhere else," observed Holger, filling his everlasting pipe again. "It is wonderful what a natural charm there is about murder and sudden death in a romantic country like this. Deeds that would be simply brutal and disgusting anywhere else become dramatic and mysterious because this is Italy, and we are living in a genuine tower of Charles V built against Barbary pirates."

"There's something in that," I admitted. Holger is the most romantic man in the world inside of himself, but he always thinks it necessary to explain why he feels anything.

"I suppose they found the poor girl's body with the box," he said presently.

"As it seems to interest you," I answered, "I'll tell you the rest of the story."

The moon had risen by this time; the outline of the Thing on the mound was clearer to our eyes than before.

The village very soon settled down to its small dull life. No one missed old Alario, who had been away so much on his voyages to South America that he had never been a familiar figure in his native place. Angelo lived in the half-finished house, and because he had no money to pay the old woman-servant, she would not stay with him, but once in a long time she would come and wash a shirt for him for old acquaintance' sake. Besides the house, he had inherited a small patch of ground at some distance from the village; he tried to cultivate it, but he had no heart in the work, for he knew he could never pay the taxes on it and on the house, which would certainly be confiscated by the Government, or seized for the debt of the building material, which the man who had supplied it refused to take back.

Angelo was very unhappy. So long as his father had been alive and rich, every girl in the village had been in love with him; but that was all changed now. It had been pleasant to be admired and courted, and in-vited to drink wine by fathers who had girls to marry. It was hard to be stared at coldly, and sometimes laughed at because he had been robbed of his inheritance. He cooked his miserable meals for himself, and from being sad became melancholy and morose.

At twilight, when the day's work was done, instead of hanging about in the open space before the church with young fellows of his own age, he took to wandering in lonely places on the outskirts of the village till it was quite dark. Then he slunk home and went to bed to save the ex-pense of a light. But in those lonely twilight hours he began to have strange waking dreams. He was not always alone, for often when he sat on the stump of a tree, where the narrow path turns down the gorge, he was sure that a woman came up noiselessly over the rough stones, as if her feet were bare; and she stood under a clump of chestnut trees only half a dozen yards down the path, and beckoned to him without speak-ing. Though she was in the shadow he knew that her lips were red, and that when they parted a little and smiled at him she showed two small sharp teeth. He knew this at first rather than saw it, and he knew that it was Cristina, and that she was dead. Yet he was not afraid; he only wondered whether it was a dream, for he thought that if he had been awake he should have been frightened.

Besides, the dead woman had red lips, and that could only happen in a dream. Whenever he went near the gorge after sunset she was already there waiting for him, or else she very soon appeared, and he began to be sure of her blood-red mouth, but now each feature grew distinct, and the pale face looked at him with deep and hungry eyes.

It was the eyes that grew dim. Little by little he came to know that someday the dream would not end when he turned away to go home, but would lead him down the gorge out of which the vision rose. She was nearer now when she beckoned to him. Her cheeks were not livid like those of the dead, but pale with starvation, with the furious and unappeased physical hunger of her eyes that devoured him. They feasted on his soul and cast a spell over him, and at last they were close to his own and held him. He could not tell whether her breath was as hot as fire, or as cold as ice; he could not tell whether her red lips burned his or froze them, or whether her five fingers on his wrists seared scorching scars or bit his flesh like frost; he could not tell whether he was awake or asleep, whether she was alive or dead, but he knew that she loved him, she alone of all creatures, earthly or unearthly, and her spell had power over him.

When the moon rose high that night the shadow of that Thing was not alone down there upon the mound.

Angelo awoke in the cool dawn, drenched with dew and chilled through flesh, and blood, and bone. He opened his eyes to the faint grey light, and saw the stars were still shining overhead. He was very weak, and his heart was beating so slowly that he was almost like a man fainting. Slowly he turned his head on the mound, as on a pillow, but the other face was not there. Fear seized him suddenly, a fear unspeakable and unknown; he sprang to his feet and fled up the gorge, and he never looked behind him until he reached the door of the house on the outskirts of the village.

Drearily he went to his work that day, and wearily the hours dragged themselves after the sun, till at last it touched the sea and sank, and the great sharp hills above Maratea turned purple against the dove-colored eastern sky.

Angelo shouldered his heavy hoe and left the field. He felt less tired now than in the morning when he had begun to work, but he promised himself that he would go home without lingering by the gorge, and eat the best supper he could get himself, and sleep all night in his bed like a Christian man. Not again would he be tempted down the narrow way by a shadow with red lips and icy breath; not again would he dream that dream of terror and delight.

He was near the village now; it was half an hour since the sun had set, and the cracked church bell sent little discordant echoes across the rocks and ravines to tell all good people that the day was done. Angelo stood still a moment where the path forked, where it led toward the village on the left, and down to the gorge on the right, where a clump of chestnut trees overhung the narrow way.

He stood still a minute, lifting his battered hat from his head and gazing at the fast-fading sea westward, and his lips moved as he silently repeated the familiar evening prayer. His lips moved, but the words that followed them in his brain lost their meaning and turned into others, and ended in a name that he spoke aloud—Cristina!

With the name, the tension of his will relaxed suddenly, reality went out and the dream took him again, and bore him on swiftly and surely like a man walking in his sleep, down, down, by the steep path in the gathering darkness. And as she glided beside him, Cristina whispered strange, sweet things in his ear, which somehow, if he had been awake, he knew that he could not quite have understood; but now they were the most wonderful words he had ever heard in his life. And she kissed him also, but not upon his mouth. He felt her sharp kisses upon his white throat, and he knew that her lips were red. So the wild dream sped on through twilight and darkness and moonrise, and all the glory of the summer's night.

But in the chilly dawn he lay as one half dead upon the mound down there, recalling and not recalling, drained of his blood, yet strangely longing to give those red lips more. Then came the fear, the awful name-less panic, the mortal horror that guards the confines of the world we see not, neither know of as we know of other things, but which we feel when its icy chill freezes our bones and stirs our hair with the touch of a ghostly hand. Once more Angelo sprang from the mound and fled up the gorge in the breaking day, but his step was less sure this time, and he panted for breath as he ran; and when he came to the bright spring of water that rises halfway up the hillside, he dropped upon his knees and hands and plunged his whole face in and drank as he had never drunk before—for it was the thirst of the wounded man who has lain bleeding all night upon the battlefield.

She had him fast now, and he could not escape her, but would come to her every evening at dusk until she had drained him of his last drop of blood. It was in vain that when the day was done he tried to take another turning and to go home by a path that did not lead near the gorge. It was in vain that he made promises to himself each morning at dawn when he climbed the lonely way up from the shore to the vil-lage. It was all in vain, for when the sun sank burning into the sea, and the coolness of the evening stole out as from a hiding-place to delight the weary world, his feet turned toward the old way, and she was wait-ing for him in the shadow under the chestnut trees; and then all hap-pened as before, and she fell to kissing his white throat even as she flitted lightly down the way, winding one arm about him.

And as his blood failed, she grew more hungry and more thirsty every day, and every day when he awoke in the early dawn it was harder to rouse himself to the effort of climbing the steep path to the village; and when he went to his work his feet dragged painfully, and there was hardly strength in his arms to wield the heavy hoe. He scarcely spoke to anyone now, but the people said he was "consuming himself" for love of the girl he was to have married when he lost his inheritance; and they laughed heartily at the thought, for this is not a very romantic country.

At this time Antonio, the man who stays here to look after the tower, returned from a visit to his people, who live near Salerno. He had been away all the time since before Alario's death and knew nothing of what had happened. He has told me that he came back late in the afternoon and shut himself up in the tower to eat and sleep, for he was very tired. It was past midnight when he awoke, and when he looked out toward the mound, he saw something, and he did not sleep again that night. When he went out again in the morning it was broad daylight, and there was nothing to be seen on the mound but loose stones and driven sand. Yet he did not go very near it; he went straight up the path to the village and directly to the house of the old priest.

"I have seen an evil thing this night," he said; "I have seen how the dead drink the blood of the living. And the blood is the life."

"Tell me what you have seen," said the priest in reply.

Antonio told him everything he had seen.

"You must bring your book and your holy water tonight," he added. "I will be here before sunset to go down with you, and if it pleases your reverence to sup with me while we wait, I will make ready."

"I will come," the priest answered, "for I have read in old books of these strange beings which are neither quick nor dead, and which lie ever fresh in their graves, stealing out in the dusk to taste life and blood."

Antonio cannot read, but he was glad to see that the priest understood the business; for, of course, the books must have instructed him as to the best means of quieting the half-living Thing forever.

So Antonio went away to his work, which consists largely in sitting on the shady side of the tower, when he is not perched upon a rock with a fishing-line catching nothing. But on that day he went twice to look at the mound in the bright sunlight, and he searched round and round it for some hole through which the being might get in and out; but he found none. When the sun began to sink and the air was cooler in the shadows, he went up to fetch the old priest, carrying a little wicker basket with him; and in this they placed a bottle of holy water, and the basin, and sprinkler, and the stole which the priest would need; and they came down and waited in the door of the tower till it should be dark. But while the light still lingered very grey and faint, they saw something moving, just there, two figures, a man's that walked, and a woman's that flitted beside him, and while her head lay on his shoulder she kissed his throat.

The priest has told me that, too, and that his teeth chattered and he grasped Antonio's arm. The vision passed and disappeared into the shadow. Then Antonio got the leathern flask of strong liquor, which he kept for great occasions, and poured such a draught as made the old man feel almost young again; and gave the priest his stole to put on and the holy water to carry, and they went out together toward the spot where the work was to be done.

Antonio says that in spite of the rum his own knees shook together, and the priest stumbled over his Latin. For when they were yet a few yards from the mound the flickering light of the lantern fell upon Angelo's white face, unconscious as if in sleep, and on his upturned throat, over which a very thin red line of blood trickled down into his collar; and the flickering light of the lantern played upon another face that looked up from the feast, upon two deep, dead eyes that saw in spite of death—upon parted lips, redder than life itself—upon two gleaming teeth on which glistened a rosy drop.

Then the priest, good old man, shut his eyes tight and showered holy water before him, and his cracked voice rose almost to a scream; and then Antonio, who is no coward after all, raised his pick in one hand and the lantern in the other, as he sprang forward, not knowing what the end should be; and then he swears that he heard a woman's cry, and the Thing was gone, and Angelo lay alone on the mound unconscious, with the red line on his throat and the beads of deathly sweat on his cold forehead.

They lifted him, half-dead as he was, and laid him on the ground close by; then Antonio went to work, and the priest helped him, though he was old and could not do much; and they dug deep, and at last Antonio, standing in the grave, stooped down with his lantern to see what he might see.

His hair used to be dark brown, with grizzled streaks about the temples; in less than a month from that day he was as grey as a badger. He was a miner when he was young, and most of these fellows have seen ugly sights now and then, when accidents have happened, but he had never seen what he saw that night—that Thing which is neither alive nor dead, that Thing that will abide neither above ground nor in the grave.

Antonio had brought something with him which the priest had not noticed—a sharp stake shaped from a piece of tough old driftwood. He had it with him now, and he had his heavy pick, and he had taken the lantern down into the grave. I don't think any power on earth could make him speak of what happened then, and the old priest was too frightened to look in. He says he heard Antonio breathing like a wild beast, and moving as if he were fighting with something almost as strong as himself; and he heard an evil sound also, with blows, as of something violently driven through flesh and bone; and then, the most awful sound of all—a woman's shriek, the unearthly scream of a woman neither dead nor alive, but buried deep for many days.

And he, the poor old priest, could only rock himself as he knelt there in the sand, crying aloud his prayers and exorcisms to drown these dreadful sounds. Then suddenly a small iron-bound chest was thrown up and rolled over against the old man's knee, and in a moment more Antonio was beside him, his face as white as tallow in the flickering light of the lantern, shoveling the sand and pebbles into the grave with furious haste, and looking over the edge till the pit was half full; and the priest said that there was much fresh blood on Antonio's hands and on his clothes.

I had come to the end of my story. Holger finished his wine and leaned back in his chair.

"So Angelo got his own again," he said. "Did he marry the prim and plump young person to whom he had been betrothed?"

"No; he had been badly frightened. He went to South America, and has not been heard of since."

"And that poor thing's body is there still, I suppose," said Holger. "Is it quite dead yet, I wonder?"

I wonder, too. But whether it be dead or alive, I should hardly care to see it, even in broad daylight. Antonio is as grey as a badger, and he has never been quite the same man since that night.

THE ADVENTURE OF THE GERMAN STUDENT

Washington Irving

Washington Irving is best known for his famous stories "Rip Van Winkle" and "The Legend of Sleepy Hollow." His work played a major role in the development of the American short story. He was also the first American writer to achieve fame both at home and abroad. This story is an excellent example of his talent.

◆ ◆ ◆

On a stormy night, in the tempestuous times of the French Revolution, a young German was returning to his lodgings, at a late hour, across the old part of Paris. The lightning gleamed, and the loud claps of thunder rattled through the lofty narrow streets—but I should first tell you something about this young German.

Gottfried Wolfgang was a young man of good family. He had studied for some time at Göttingen, but being of a visionary and enthusiastic character, he had wandered into those wild and speculative doctrines which have so often bewildered German students. His secluded life, his intense application, and the singular nature of his studies, had an effect on both mind and body. His health was impaired; his imagination diseased. He had been indulging in fanciful speculations on spiritual essences, until, like Swedenborg, he had an ideal world of his own around him. He took up a notion, I do not know from what cause, that there was an evil influence hanging over him; an evil genius or spirit seeking to ensnare him and ensure his perdition. Such an idea working on his melancholy temperament produced the most gloomy effects. He became haggard and desponding. His friends discovered the mental malady preying upon him, and determined that the best cure was a change of scene; he was sent, therefore, to finish his studies amidst the splendors and gayeties of Paris.

Wolfgang arrived at Paris at the breaking out of the revolution. The popular delirium at first caught his enthusiastic mind, and he was captivated by the political and philosophical theories of the day: but the scenes of blood which followed shocked his sensitive nature, disgusted him with society and the world, and made him more than ever a recluse. He shut himself up in a solitary apartment in the Pays Latin, the quarter of students. There, in a gloomy street not far from the monastic walls of the Sorbonne, he pursued his favorite speculations. Sometimes he spent hours together in the great libraries of Paris, those catacombs of departed authors, rummaging among their hoards of dusty and obsolete works in quest of food for his unhealthy appetite. He was, in a manner, a literary ghoul, feeding in the charnel-house of decayed literature.

Wolfgang, though solitary and recluse, was of an ardent temperament, but for a time it operated merely upon his imagination. He was too shy and ignorant of the world to make any advances to the fair, but he was a passionate admirer of female beauty, and in his lonely chamber would often lose himself in reveries on forms and faces which he had seen, and his fancy would deck out images of loveliness far surpassing the reality.

While his mind was in this excited and sublimated state, a dream produced an extraordinary effect upon him. It was of a female face of transcendent beauty. So strong was the impression made, that he dreamt of it again and again. It haunted his thoughts by day, his slumbers by night; in fine, he became passionately enamored of this shadow of a dream. This lasted so long that it became one of those fixed ideas which haunt the minds of melancholy men, and are at times mistaken for madness.

Such was Gottfried Wolfgang, and such his situation at the time I mentioned. He was returning home late on a stormy night, through some of the old and gloomy streets of the Marais, the ancient part of Paris. The loud claps of thunder rattled among the high houses of the narrow streets. He came to the Place de Graève, the square where public executions are performed. The lightning quivered about the pinnacles of the ancient Hôtel de Ville, and shed flickering gleams over the open space in front. As Wolfgang was crossing the square, he shrank back with horror at finding himself close by the guillotine. It was the height of the reign of terror, when this dreadful instrument of death stood ever ready, and its scaffold was continually running with the blood of the virtuous and the brave. It had that very day been actively employed in the work of carnage, and there it stood in grim array, amidst a silent and sleeping city, waiting for fresh victims.

Wolfgang's heart sickened within him, and he was turning shuddering from the horrible engine, when he beheld a shadowy form, cowering as it were at the foot of the steps which led up to the scaffold. A succession of vivid flashes of lightning revealed it more distinctly. It was a female figure, dressed in black. She was seated on one of the lower steps of the scaffold, leaning forward, her face hid in her lap, and her long disheveled tresses hanging to the ground, streaming with the rain which fell in torrents. Wolfgang paused. There was something awful in this solitary monument of woe. The female had the appearance of being above the common order. He knew the times to be full of vicissitude, and that many a fair head, which had once been pillowed on down, now wandered houseless. Perhaps this was some poor mourner whom the dreadful axe had rendered desolate, and who sat here heart-broken on the strand of existence, from which all that was dear to her had been launched into eternity.

He approached, and addressed her in the accents of sympathy. She raised her head and gazed wildly at him. What was his astonishment at beholding, by the bright glare of the lightning, the very face which had haunted him in his dreams. It was pale and disconsolate, but ravishingly beautiful.

Trembling with violent and conflicting emotions, Wolfgang again accosted her. He spoke something of her being exposed at such an hour of the night, and to the fury of such a storm, and offered to conduct her to her friends. She pointed to the guillotine with a gesture of dreadful signification.

"I have no friend on earth!" said she.

"But you have a home," said Wolfgang.

"Yes—in the grave!"

The heart of the student melted at the words.

"If a stranger dare make an offer," said he, "without danger of being misunderstood, I would offer my humble dwelling as a shelter; myself as a devoted friend. I am friendless myself in Paris, and a stranger in the land; but if my life could be of service, it is at your disposal, and should be sacrificed before harm or indignity should come to you."

There was an honest earnestness in the young man's manner that had its effect. His foreign accent, too, was in his favor; it showed him not to be a hackneyed inhabitant of Paris. Indeed, there is an eloquence in true enthusiasm that is not to be doubted. The homeless stranger confided herself implicitly to the protection of the student.

He supported her faltering steps across the Pont Neuf, and by the place where the statue of Henry the Fourth had been overthrown by the populace. The storm had abated, and the thunder rumbled at a distance. All Paris was quiet; that great volcano of human passion slumbered for a while, to gather fresh strength for the next day's eruption. The student conducted his charge through the ancient streets of the Pays Latin, and by the dusky walls of the Sorbonne, to the great dingy hotel which he inhabited. The old portress who admitted them stared with surprise at the unusual sight of the melancholy Wolfgang, with a female companion.

On entering his apartment, the student, for the first time, blushed at the scantiness and indifference of his dwelling. He had but one chamber—an old-fashioned saloon—heavily carved, and fantastically furnished with the remains of former magnificence, for it was one of those hotels in the quarter of nobility. It was lumbered with books and papers, and all the usual apparatus of a student, and his bed stood in a recess at one end.

When lights were brought, and Wolfgang had a better opportunity of contemplating the stranger, he was more than ever intoxicated by her beauty. Her face was pale, but of a dazzling fairness, set off by a profusion of raven hair that hung clustering about it. Her eyes were large and brilliant, with a singular expression approaching almost to wildness. As far as her black dress permitted her shape to be seen, it was of perfect symmetry. Her whole appearance was highly striking, though she was dressed in the simplest style. The only thing approaching to an ornament which she wore, was a broad black band round her neck, clasped by diamonds.

The perplexity now commenced with the student on how to dispose of the helpless being thus thrown upon his protection. He thought of abandoning his chamber to her, and seeking shelter for himself elsewhere. Still he was so fascinated by her charms, there seemed to be such a spell upon his thoughts and senses, that he could not tear himself from her presence. Her manner, too, was singular and unaccountable. She spoke no more of the guillotine. Her grief had abated. The attentions of the student had first won her confidence, and then, apparently, her heart. She was evidently an enthusiast like himself, and enthusiasts soon understand each other.

In the infatuation of the moment, Wolfgang avowed his passion for her. He told her the story of his mysterious dream, and how she had possessed his heart before he had even seen her. She was strangely affected by his recital, and acknowledged to have felt an impulse towards him equally unaccountable. It was the time for wild theory and wild actions. Old prejudices and superstitions were done away; everything was under the sway of the "Goddess of Reason." Among other rubbish of the old times, the forms and ceremonies of marriage began to be considered superfluous bonds for honorable minds. Social compacts were the vogue. Wolfgang was too much of a theorist not to be tainted by the liberal doctrines of the day.

"Why should we separate?" said he. "Our hearts are united; in the eye of reason and honor we are as one. What need is there of sordid forms to bind high souls together?"

The stranger listened with emotion: she had evidently received illumination at the same school.

"You have no home nor family," continued he. "Let me be everything to you, or rather let us be everything to one another. If form is necessary, form shall be observed—there is my hand. I pledge myself to you forever."

"Forever?" said the stranger, solemnly.

"Forever!" repeated Wolfgang.

The stranger clasped the hand extended to her: "Then I am yours," murmured she, and sank upon his bosom.

The next morning the student left his bride sleeping, and sallied forth at an early hour to seek more spacious apartments suitable to the change in his situation. When he returned, he found the stranger lying with her head hanging over the bed, and one arm thrown over it. He spoke to her, but received no reply. He advanced to awaken her from her uneasy posture. On taking her hand, it was cold—there was no pulsation—her face was pallid and ghastly. In a word, she was a corpse.

Horrified and frantic, he alarmed the house. A scene of confusion ensued. The police were summoned. As the officer of police entered the room, he started back on beholding the corpse.

"Great heaven!" cried he, "how did this woman come here?"

"Do you know anything about her?" said Wolfgang eagerly.

"Do I?" exclaimed the officer. "She was guillotined yesterday."

He stepped forward, undid the black collar round the neck of the corpse, and the head rolled on the floor!

The student burst into a frenzy. "The fiend! the fiend has gained possession of me!" shrieked he; "I am lost forever."

They tried to soothe him, but in vain. He was possessed with the frightful belief that an evil spirit had reanimated the dead body to ensnare him. He went distracted, and died in a mad-house.

Here the old gentleman with the haunted head finished his narrative.

"And is this really a fact?" said the inquisitive gentleman.

"A fact not to be doubted," replied the other. "I had it from the best authority. The student told it me himself. I saw him in a mad-house in Paris."

THE TOMB OF SARAH

F. G. Loring

F. G. Loring was an electrical engineer, a commander in the British Navy, and an author, but he is best known for this creepy tale.

✦ ✦ ✦

My father was the head of a celebrated firm of church restorers and decorators about sixty years ago. He took a keen interest in his work, and made an especial study of any old legends or family histories that came under his observation. He was necessarily very well read and thoroughly well posted in all questions of folklore and medieval legend. As he kept a careful record of every case he investigated the manuscripts he left at his death have a special interest. From amongst them I have selected the following, as being a particularly weird and extraordinary experience. In presenting it to the public I feel it is superfluous to apologize for its supernatural character.

MY FATHER'S DIARY

1841.—*June 17th.* Received a commission from my old friend Peter Grant to enlarge and restore the chancel of his church at Hagarstone, in the wilds of the West Country.

July 5th. Went down to Hagarstone with my head man, Somers. A very long and tiring journey.

July 7th. Got the work well started. The old church is one of special interest to the antiquarian, and I shall endeavor while restoring it to alter the existing arrangements as little as possible. One large tomb, however, must be moved bodily ten feet at least to the southward. Curiously enough, there is a somewhat forbidding inscription upon it in Latin, and I am sorry that this particular tomb should have to be moved. It stands amongst the graves of the Kenyons, an old family which has been extinct in these parts for centuries. The inscription on it runs thus:

SARAH.

1630.

For the sake of the dead and the welfare
of the living, let this sepulchre remain untouched and its
occupant undisturbed till the coming of Christ.
In the name of the Father, the Son, and
the Holy Ghost.

July 8th. Took counsel with Grant concerning the "Sarah Tomb." We are both very loath to disturb it, but the ground has sunk so beneath it that the safety of the church is in danger; thus we have no choice. However, the work shall be done as reverently as possible under our own direction.

Grant says there is a legend in the neighborhood that it is the tomb of the last of the Kenyons, the evil Countess Sarah, who was murdered in 1630. She lived quite alone in the old castle, whose ruins still stand three miles from here on the road to Bristol. Her reputation was an evil one even for those days. She was a witch or were-woman, the only companion of her solitude being a familiar in the shape of a huge Asiatic wolf. This creature was reputed to seize upon children, or failing these, sheep and other small animals, and convey them to the castle, where the Countess used to suck their blood. It was popularly supposed that she could never be killed. This, however, proved a fallacy, since she was strangled one day by a mad peasant woman who had lost two children, she declaring that they had both been seized and carried off by the Countess's familiar. This is a very interesting story, since it points to a local superstition very similar to that of the Vampire, existing in Slavonic and Hungarian Europe.

The tomb is built of black marble, surmounted by an enormous slab of the same material. On the slab is a magnificent group of figures. A young and handsome woman reclines upon a couch; round her neck is a piece of rope, the end of which she holds in her hand. At her side is a gigantic dog with bared fangs and lolling tongue. The face of the reclining figure is a cruel one: the corners of the mouth are curiously lifted, showing the sharp points of long canine or dog teeth. The whole group, though magnificently executed, leaves a most unpleasant sensation.

If we move the tomb it will have to be done in two pieces, the covering slab first and then the tomb proper. We have decided to remove the covering slab tomorrow.

July 9th.—6 P.M. A very strange day.

By noon everything was ready for lifting off the covering stone, and after the men's dinner we started the jacks and pulleys. The slab lifted easily enough, though it fitted closely into its seat and was further secured by some sort of mortar or putty, which must have kept the interior perfectly air-tight.

None of us were prepared for the horrible rush of foul, moldy air that escaped as the cover lifted clear of its seating. And the contents that gradually came into view were more startling still. There lay the fully dressed body of a woman, wizened and shrunk and ghastly pale as if from starvation. Round her neck was a loose cord, and, judging by the scars still visible, the story of death of strangulation was true enough.

The most horrible part, however, was the extraordinary freshness of the body. Except for the appearance of starvation, life might have been only just extinct. The flesh was soft and white, the eyes were wide open and seemed to stare at us with a fearful understanding in them. The body itself lay on mold, without any pretence to coffin or shell.

For several moments we gazed with horrible curiosity, and then it became too much for my workmen, who implored us to replace the covering slab. That, of course, we would not do; but I set the carpenters to work at once to make a temporary cover while we moved the tomb to its new position. This is a long job, and will take two or three days at least.

July 9th.—9 P.M. Just at sunset we were startled by the howling of, seemingly, every dog in the village. It lasted for ten minutes or a quarter of an hour, and then ceased as suddenly as it began. This, and a curious mist that has risen round the church, makes me feel rather anxious about the "Sarah Tomb." According to the best-established traditions of the Vampire-haunted countries, the disturbance of dogs or wolves at sunset is supposed to indicate the presence of one of these fiends, and local fog is always considered to be a certain sign. The Vampire has the power of producing it for the purpose of concealing its movements near its hiding-place at any time.

I dare not mention or even hint my fears to the Rector, for he is, not unnaturally perhaps, a rank disbeliever in many things that I know, from experience, are not only possible but even probable. I must work this out alone at first, and get his aid without his knowing in what direction he is helping me. I shall now watch till midnight at least.

10:15 P.M. As I feared and half expected. Just before ten there was another outburst of the hideous howling. It was commenced most distinctly by a particularly horrible and blood-curdling wail from the vicinity of the churchyard. The chorus lasted only a few minutes, however, and at the end of it I saw a large dark shape, like a huge dog, emerge from the fog and lope away at a rapid canter towards the open country. Assuming this to be what I fear, I shall see it return soon after midnight.

12:30 P.M. I was right. Almost as midnight struck I saw the beast returning. It stopped at the spot where the fog seemed to commence, and lifting up its head, gave tongue to that particularly horrible long-drawn wail that I had noticed as preceding the outburst earlier in the evening.

Tomorrow I shall tell the Rector what I have seen; and if, as I expect, we hear of some neighboring sheepfold having been raided, I shall get him to watch with me for this nocturnal marauder. I shall also examine the "Sarah Tomb" for something which he may notice without any previous hint from me.

July 10th. I found the workmen this morning much disturbed in mind about the howling of the dogs. "We doan't like it, zur," one of them said to me—"we doan't like it; there was zummat abroad last night that was unholy." They were still more uncomfortable when the news came round that a large dog had made a raid upon a flock of sheep, scattering them far and wide, and leaving three of them dead with torn throats in the field.

When I told the Rector of what I had seen and what was being said in the village, he immediately decided that we must try and catch or at least identify the beast I had seen. "Of course," said he, "it is some dog lately imported into the neighborhood, for I know of nothing about here nearly as large as the animal you describe, though its size may be due to the deceptive moonlight."

This afternoon I asked the Rector, as a favor, to assist me in lifting the temporary cover that was on the tomb, giving as an excuse the reason that I wished to obtain a portion of the curious mortar with which it had been sealed. After a slight demur he consented, and we raised the lid. If the sight that met our eyes gave me a shock, at least it appalled Grant.

"Great God!" he exclaimed; "the woman is alive!"

And so it seemed for a moment. The corpse had lost much of its starved appearance and looked hideously fresh and alive. It was still wrinkled and shrunken, but the lips were firm, and of the rich red hue of health. The eyes, if possible, were more appalling than ever, though fixed and staring. At one corner of the mouth I thought I noticed a slight dark-colored froth, but I said nothing about it then.

"Take your piece of mortar, Harry," gasped Grant, "and let us shut the tomb again. God help me! Parson though I am, such dead faces frighten me!"

Nor was I sorry to hide that terrible face again; but I got my bit of mortar, and I have advanced a step towards the solution of the mystery.

This afternoon the tomb was moved several feet towards its new position, but it will be two or three days yet before we shall be ready to replace the slab.

10:15 P.M. Again the same howling at sunset, the same fog enveloping the church, and at ten o'clock the same great beast slipping silently out into the open country. I must get the Rector's help and watch for its return. But precautions we must take, for if things are as I believe, we take our lives in our hands when we venture out into the night to way-lay the Vampire. Why not admit it at once? For that the beast I have seen is the Vampire of that evil thing in the tomb I can have no reasonable doubt.

Not yet come to its full strength, thank Heaven! after the starvation of nearly two centuries, for at present it can only maraud as wolf apparently. But, in a day or two, when full power returns, that dreadful woman in new strength and beauty will be able to leave her refuge. Then it would not be sheep merely that would satisfy her disgusting lust for blood, but victims that would yield their life-blood without a murmur to her caressing touch—victims that, dying of her foul embrace, themselves must become Vampires in their turn to prey on others.

Mercifully my knowledge gives me a safeguard; for that little piece of mortar that I rescued today from the tomb contains a portion of the Sacred Host, and who holds it, humbly and firmly believing in its virtue, may pass safely through such an ordeal as I intend to submit myself and the Rector to tonight.

12:30 P.M. Our adventure is over for the present, and we are back safe.

After writing the last entry recorded above, I went off to find Grant and tell him that the marauder was out on the prowl again. "But, Grant," I said, "before we start out tonight I must insist that you will let me prosecute this affair in my own way; you must promise to put yourself completely under my orders, without asking any questions as to the why and wherefore."

After a little demur, and some excusable chaff on his part at the serious view I was taking of what he called a "dog hunt," he gave me his promise. I then told him that we were to watch tonight and try and track the mysterious beast, but not to interfere with it in any way. I think, in spite of his jests, that I impressed him with the fact that there might be, after all, good reason for my precautions.

It was just after eleven when we stepped out into the still night.

Our first move was to try and penetrate the dense fog round the church, but there was something so chilly about it, and a faint smell so disgustingly rank and loathsome, that neither our nerves nor our stomachs were proof against it. Instead, we stationed ourselves in the dark shadow of a yew tree that commanded a good view of the wicket entrance to the churchyard.

At midnight the howling of the dogs began again, and in a few minutes we saw a large grey shape, with green eyes shining like lamps, shamble swiftly down the path towards us.

The Rector started forward, but I laid a firm hand upon his arm and whispered a warning "Remember!" Then we both stood very still and watched as the great beast cantered swiftly by. It was real enough, for we could hear the clicking of its nails on the stone flags. It passed within a few yards of us, and seemed to be nothing more nor less than a great grey wolf, thin and gaunt, with bristling hair and dripping jaws. It stopped where the mist commenced, and turned round. It was truly a horrible sight, and made one's blood run cold. The eyes burnt like fires, the upper lip was snarling and raised, showing the great canine teeth, while round the mouth clung and dripped a dark-colored froth.

It raised its head and gave tongue to its long wailing howl, which was answered from afar by the village dogs. After standing for a few moments it turned and disappeared into the thickest part of the fog.

Very shortly afterwards the atmosphere began to clear, and within ten minutes the mist was all gone, the dogs in the village were silent, and the night seemed to reassume its normal aspect. We examined the spot where the beast had been standing and found, plainly enough upon the stone flags, dark spots of froth and saliva.

"Well, Rector," I said, "will you admit now, in view of the things you have seen today, in consideration of the legend, the woman in the tomb, the fog, the howling dogs, and, last but not least, the mysterious beast you have seen so close, that there is something not quite normal in it all? Will you put yourself unreservedly in my hands and help me, *whatever I may do*, to first make assurance doubly sure, and finally take the necessary steps for putting an end to this horror of the night?" I saw that the uncanny influence of the night was strong upon him, and wished to impress it as much as possible.

"Needs must," he replied, "when the Devil drives; and in the face of what I have seen I must believe that some unholy forces are at work. Yet, how can they work in the sacred precincts of a church? Shall we not call rather upon Heaven to assist us in our need?"

"Grant," I said solemnly, "that we must do, each in his own way. God helps those who help themselves, and by His help and the light of my knowledge we must fight this battle for Him and the poor lost soul within."

We then returned to the rectory and to our rooms, though I have sat up to write this account while the scene is fresh in my mind.

July 11th. Found the workmen again very much disturbed in their minds, and full of a strange dog that had been seen during the night by several people, who had hunted it. Farmer Stotman, who had been watching his sheep—the same flock that had been raided the night before—had surprised it over a fresh carcass and tried to drive it off, but its size and fierceness so alarmed him that he had beaten a hasty retreat for a gun. When he returned the animal was gone, though he found that three more sheep from his flock were dead and torn.

The "Sarah Tomb" was moved today to its new position; but it was a long, heavy business, and there was not time to replace the covering slab. For this I was glad, as in the prosaic light of day the Rector almost disbelieves the events of the night, and is prepared to think everything to have been magnified and distorted by our imagination.

As, however, I could not possibly proceed with my war of extermination against this foul thing without assistance, and as there is nobody else I can rely upon, I appealed to him for one more night—to convince him that it was no delusion, but a ghastly, horrible truth, which must be fought and conquered for our own sakes, as well as that of all those living in the neighborhood.

"Put yourself in my hands, Rector," I said, "for tonight at least. Let us take those precautions which my study of the subject tells me are the right ones. Tonight you and I must watch in the church; and I feel assured that tomorrow you will be as convinced as I am, and be equally prepared to take those awful steps which I know to be proper, and I must warn you that we shall find a more startling change in the body lying there than you noticed yesterday."

My words came true; for on raising the wooden cover once more the rank stench of a slaughterhouse arose, making us feel positively sick. There lay the Vampire, but how changed from the starved and shrunken corpse we saw two days ago for the first time! The wrinkles had almost disappeared, the flesh was firm and full, the crimson lips grinned horribly over the long pointed teeth, and a distinct smear of blood had trickled down one corner of the mouth. We set our teeth, however, and hardened our hearts. Then we replaced the cover and put what we had collected into a safe place in the vestry. Yet even now Grant could not believe that there was any real or pressing danger concealed in that awful tomb, as he raised strenuous objections to any apparent desecration of the body without further proof. This he shall have tonight. God grant that I am not taking too much on myself! If there is any truth in old legends it would be easy enough to destroy the Vampire now; but Grant will not have it.

I hope for the best of this night's work, but the danger in waiting is very great.

6 P.M. I have prepared everything: the sharp knives, the pointed stake, fresh garlic, and the wild dog-roses. All these I have taken and concealed in the vestry, where we can get at them when our solemn vigil commences.

If either or both of us die with our fearful task undone, let those reading my record see that this is done. I lay it upon them as a solemn obligation. "That the Vampire be pierced through the heart with the stake, then let the Burial Service be read over the poor clay at last released from its doom. Thus shall the Vampire cease to be, and a lost soul rest."

July 12th. All is over. After the most terrible night of watching and horror one Vampire at least will trouble the world no more. But how thankful should we be to a merciful Providence that that awful tomb was not disturbed by anyone not having the knowledge necessary to deal with its dreadful occupant! I write this with no feelings of self-complacency, but simply with a great gratitude for the years of study I have been able to devote to this special subject.

And now to my tale.

Just before sunset last night the Rector and I locked ourselves into the church, and took up our position in the pulpit. It was one of those pulpits, to be found in some churches, which is entered from the vestry, the preacher appearing at a good height through an arched opening in the wall.

This gave us a sense of security—which we felt we needed—a good view of the interior, and direct access to the implements which I had concealed in the vestry.

The sun set and the twilight gradually deepened and faded. There was, so far, no sign of the usual fog, nor any howling of the dogs. At nine o'clock the moon rose, and her pale light gradually flooded the aisles, and still no sign of any kind from the "Sarah Tomb." The Rector had asked me several times what he might expect, but I was determined that no words or thought of mine should influence him, and that he should be convinced by his own senses alone.

By half-past ten we were both getting very tired, and I began to think that perhaps after all we should see nothing that night. However, soon after eleven we observed a light mist rising from the "Sarah Tomb." It seemed to scintillate and sparkle as it rose, and curled in a sort of pillar or spiral.

I said nothing, but I heard the Rector give a sort of gasp as he clutched my arm feverishly.

"Great Heaven!" he whispered, "it is taking shape."

And, true enough, in a very few moments we saw standing erect by the tomb the ghastly figure of the Countess Sarah!

She looked thin and haggard still, and her face was deadly white; but the crimson lips looked like a hideous gash in the pale cheeks, and her eyes glared like red coals in the gloom of the church.

It was a fearful thing to watch as she stepped unsteadily down the aisle, staggering a little as if from weakness and exhaustion. This was perhaps natural, as her body must have suffered much physically from her long incarceration, in spite of the unholy forces which kept it fresh and well.

We watched her to the door, and wondered what would happen; but it appeared to present no difficulty, for she melted through it and disappeared.

"Now, Grant," I said, "do you believe?"

"Yes," he replied, "I must. Everything is in your hands, and I will obey your commands to the letter, if you can only instruct me how to rid my poor people of this unnameable terror."

"By God's help I will," said I; "but you shall be yet more convinced first, for we have a terrible work to do, and much to answer for in the future, before we leave the church again this morning. And now to work, for in its present weak state the Vampire will not wander far, but may return at any time, and must not find us unprepared."

We stepped down from the pulpit and, taking dog-roses and garlic from the vestry, proceeded to the tomb. I arrived first and, throwing off the wooden cover, cried, "Look! It is empty!" There was nothing there! Nothing except the impress of the body in the loose damp mold!

I took the flowers and laid them in a circle round the tomb, for legend teaches us that Vampires will not pass over these particular blossoms if they can avoid it.

Then, eight or ten feet away, I made a circle on the stone pavement, large enough for the Rector and myself to stand in, and within the circle I placed the implements that I had brought into the church with me.

"Now," I said, "from this circle, which nothing unholy can step across, you shall see the Vampire face to face, and see her afraid to cross that other circle of garlic and dog-roses to regain her unholy refuge. But on no account step beyond the holy place you stand in, for the Vampire has a fearful strength not her own, and, like a snake, can draw her victim willingly to his own destruction."

Now so far my work was done, and, calling the Rector, we stepped into the Holy Circle to await the Vampire's return.

Nor was this long delayed. Presently a damp, cold odor seemed to pervade the church, which made our hair bristle and flesh to creep. And then, down the aisle with noiseless feet came That which we watched for.

I heard the Rector mutter a prayer, and I held him tightly by the arm, for he was shivering violently.

Long before we could distinguish the features we saw the glowing eyes and the crimson sensual mouth. She went straight to her tomb, but stopped short when she encountered my flowers. She walked right round the tomb seeking a place to enter, and as she walked she saw us. A spasm of diabolical hate and fury passed over her face; but it quickly vanished, and a smile of love, more devilish still, took its place. She stretched out her arms towards us. Then we saw that round her mouth gathered a bloody froth, and from under her lips long pointed teeth gleamed and champed.

She spoke: a soft soothing voice, a voice that carried a spell with it, and affected us both strangely, particularly the Rector. I wished to test as far as possible, without endangering our lives, the Vampire's power.

Her voice had a soporific effect, which I resisted easily enough, but which seemed to throw the Rector into a sort of trance. More than this: it seemed to compel him to her in spite of his efforts to resist.

"Come!" she said—"come! I give sleep and peace—sleep and peace— sleep and peace."

She advanced a little towards us; but not far, for I noted that the Sacred Circle seemed to keep her back like an iron hand.

My companion seemed to become demoralized and spellbound. He tried to step forward and, finding me detain him, whispered, "Harry, let go! I must go! She is calling me! I must! I must! Oh, help me! help me!" And he began to struggle.

It was time to finish.

"Grant!" I cried, in a loud, firm voice, "in the name of all that you hold sacred, have done and play the man!" He shuddered violently and gasped, "Where am I?" Then he remembered, and clung to me convulsively for a moment.

At this a look of damnable hate changed the smiling face before us, and with a sort of shriek she staggered back.

"Back!" I cried. "Back to your unholy tomb! No longer shall you molest the suffering world! Your end is near."

It was fear that now showed itself in her beautiful face—for it was beautiful in spite of its horror—as she shrank back, back and over the circlet of flowers, shivering as she did so. At last, with a low mournful cry, she appeared to melt back again into her tomb.

As she did so the first gleams of the rising sun lit up the world, and I knew all danger was over for the day.

Taking Grant by the arm, I drew him with me out of the circle and led him to the tomb. There lay the Vampire once more, still in her living death as we had a moment before seen her in her devilish life. But in the eyes remained that awful expression of hate, and cringing, appalling fear.

Grant was pulling himself together.

"Now," I said, "will you dare the last terrible act and rid the world for ever of this horror?"

"By God!" he said solemnly, "I will. Tell me what to do."

"Help me to lift her out of her tomb. She can harm us no more," I replied.

With averted faces we set to our terrible task, and laid her out upon the flags.

"Now," I said, "read the Burial Service over the poor body, and then let us give it its release from this living hell that holds it."

Reverently the Rector read the beautiful words, and reverently I made the necessary responses. When it was over I took the stake and, without giving myself time to think, plunged it with all my strength through the heart.

As though really alive, the body for a moment writhed and kicked convulsively, and an awful heart-rending shriek woke the silent church; then all was still.

Then we lifted the poor body back; and, thank God! the consolation that legend tells is never denied to those who have to do such awful work as ours came at last. Over the face stole a great and solemn peace; the lips lost their crimson hue, the prominent sharp teeth sank back into the mouth, and for a moment we saw before us the calm, pale face of a most beautiful woman, who smiled as she slept. A few minutes more, and she faded away to dust before our eyes as we watched. We set to work and cleaned up every trace of our work, and then departed for the rectory. Most thankful were we to step out of the church, with its horrible associations, into the rosy warmth of the summer morning.

With the above end the notes in my father's diary, though a few days later this further entry occurs:—

July 15th. Since the 12th everything has been quiet and as usual. We replaced and sealed up the "Sarah Tomb" this morning. The workmen were surprised to find the body had disappeared, but took it to be the natural result of exposing it to the air.

One odd thing came to my ears today. It appears that the child of one of the villagers strayed from home the night of the 11th inst., and was found asleep in a coppice near the church, very pale and quite exhausted. There were two small marks on her throat, which have since disappeared.

What does this mean? I have, however, kept it to myself, as, now that the Vampire is no more, no further danger either to that child or any other is to be apprehended. It is only those who die of the Vampire's embrace that become Vampires at death in their turn.

TEIG O'KANE AND THE CORPSE

Douglas Hyde

Douglas Hyde was an Irish scholar of the Gaelic language and the founder of the Gaelic League, which played a significant role in the preservation of Irish culture. He went on to become Ireland's first president. This story, translated from one of his books, was included in a volume by W. B. Yeats, who described it as a "magnificent story."

In it, Teig O'Kane encounters a group of fairies, but these fairies are not the Tinkerbell-type fairies that most people are familiar with. The fairies of Irish folklore that people actually believed in were extremely dangerous shape-shifting spirits who often did terrible things to people. The term had a much broader sense and encompassed a wide variety of spirits, from poltergeist-like creatures to water horses. People generally didn't mention them at all, for fear of attracting them. When they did speak of them, they usually used euphemisms, such as "the good people" or "the little people," to keep from pissing them off. Folks did a lot of things to avoid fairies because some of them really enjoyed tormenting people, which is what happens to Teig O'Kane in this tale.

✦   ✦   ✦

There was once a grown-up lad in the County Leitrim, and he was strong and lively, and the son of a rich farmer. His father had plenty of money, and he did not spare it on the son. Accordingly, when the boy grew up he liked sport better than work, and, as his father had no other children, he loved this one so much that he allowed him to do in everything just as it pleased himself. He was very extravagant, and he used to scatter the gold money as another person would scatter the white. He was seldom to be found at home, but if there was a fair, or a race, or a gathering within ten miles of him, you were dead certain to find him there. And he seldom spent a night in his father's house, but he used to be always out rambling, and, like Shawn Bwee long ago, there was "grádh gach cailin i mbrollach a léine," "the love of every girl in the breast of his shirt," and it's many's the kiss he got and he gave, for he was very handsome, and there wasn't a girl in the country but would fall in love with him, only for him to fasten his two eyes on her, and it was for that someone made this *rann* on him—

"Feuch an rógaire 'g iarraidh póige,
     Ni h-iongantas mór é a bheith mar atá
Ag leanamhaint a gcómhnuidhe d'árnán na gráineóige
     Anuas 's anios's nna chodladh 'sa' lá."

"Look at the rogue, it's for kisses he's rambling,
     It isn't much wonder, for that was his way;
He's like an old hedgehog, at night he'll be scrambling
     From this place to that, but he'll sleep in the day."

At last he became very wild and unruly. He wasn't to be seen day nor night in his father's house, but always rambling or going on his *kailee* (night-visit) from place to place and from house to house, so that the old people used to shake their heads and say to one another, "it's easy seen what will happen to the land when the old man dies; his son will run through it in a year, and it won't stand him that long itself."

He used to be always gambling and card-playing and drinking, but his father never minded his bad habits, and never punished him. But it happened one day that the old man was told that the son had ruined the character of a girl in the neighborhood, and he was greatly angry, and he called the son to him, and said to him, quietly and sensibly— "Avic [my son]," says he, "you know I loved you greatly up to this, and I never stopped you from doing your choice thing whatever it was, and I kept plenty of money with you, and I always hoped to leave you the house and land, and all I had after myself would be gone; but I heard a story of you today that has disgusted me with you. I cannot tell you the grief that I felt when I heard such a thing of you, and I tell you now plainly that unless you marry that girl I'll leave house and land and everything to my brother's son. I never could leave it to anyone who would make so bad a use of it as you do yourself, deceiving women and coaxing girls. Settle with yourself now whether you'll marry that girl and get my land as a fortune with her, or refuse to marry her and give up all that was coming to you; and tell me in the morning which of the two things you have chosen."

"Och! *Domnoo Sheery!* father, you wouldn't say that to me, and I such a good son as I am. Who told you I wouldn't marry the girl?" says he.

But his father was gone, and the lad knew well enough that he would keep his word too; and he was greatly troubled in his mind, for as quiet and as kind as the father was, he never went back of a word that he had once said, and there wasn't another man in the country who was harder to bend than he was.

The boy did not know rightly what to do. He was in love with the girl indeed, and he hoped to marry her some time or other, but he would much sooner have remained another while as he was, and follow on at his old tricks—drinking, sporting and playing cards; and, along with that, he was angry that his father should order him to marry, and should threaten him if he did not do it.

"Isn't my father a great fool," says he to himself. "I was ready enough, and only too anxious, to marry Mary; and now since he threatened me, faith I've a great mind to let it go another while."

His mind was so much excited that he remained between two notions as to what he should do. He walked out into the night at last to cool his heated blood, and went on to the road. He lit a pipe, and as the night was fine he walked and walked on, until the quick pace made him begin to forget his trouble. The night was bright, and the moon half full. There was not a breath of wind blowing, and the air was calm and mild. He walked on for nearly three hours, when he suddenly remembered that it was late in the night, and time for him to turn. "Musha! I think I forgot myself," says he; "it must be near twelve o'clock now."

The word was hardly out of his mouth, when he heard the sound of many voices, and the trampling of feet on the road before him. "I don't know who can be out so late at night as this, and on such a lonely road," said he to himself.

He stood listening, and he heard the voices of many people talking through other, but he could not understand what they were saying.

"Oh, wirra!" says he, "I'm afraid. It's not Irish or English they have; it can't be they're Frenchmen!"

He went on a couple of yards farther, and he saw well enough by the light of the moon a band of little people coming towards him, and they were carrying something big and heavy with them.

"Oh, murder!" says he to himself, "sure it can't be that they're the good people that's in it!"

Every *rib* of hair that was on his head stood up, and there fell a shaking on his bones, for he saw that they were coming to him fast.

He looked at them again, and perceived that there were about twenty little men in it, and there was not a man at all of them higher than about three feet or three feet and a half, and some of them were grey, and seemed very old. He looked again, but he could not make out what was the heavy thing they were carrying until they came up to him, and then they all stood round about him. They threw the heavy thing down on the road, and he saw on the spot that it was a dead body.

He became as cold as the Death, and there was not a drop of blood running in his veins when an old little grey *maneen* came up to him and said, "Isn't it lucky we met you, Teig O'Kane?"

Poor Teig could not bring out a word at all, nor open his lips, if he were to get the word for it, and so he gave no answer.

"Teig O'Kane," said the little grey man again, "isn't it timely you met us?"

Teig could not answer him.

"Teig O'Kane," says he, "the third time, isn't it lucky and timely that we met you?"

But Teig remained silent, for he was afraid to return an answer, and his tongue was as if it was tied to the roof of his mouth.

The little grey man turned to his companions, and there was joy in his bright little eye. "And now," says he, "Teig O'Kane hasn't a word, we can do with him what we please. Teig, Teig," says he, "you're living a bad life, and we can make a slave of you now, and you cannot withstand us, for there's no use in trying to go against us. Lift that corpse."

Teig was so frightened that he was only able to utter the two words, "I won't"; for as frightened as he was, he was obstinate and stiff, the same as ever.

"Teig O'Kane won't lift the corpse," said the little *maneen*, with a wicked little laugh, for all the world like the breaking of a *lock* of dry *kippeens* [a bundle of twigs], and with a little harsh voice like the striking of a cracked bell. "Teig O'Kane won't lift the corpse—make him lift it"; and before the word was out of his mouth they had all gathered round poor Teig, and they all talking and laughing through other.

Teig tried to run from them, but they followed him, and a man of them stretched out his foot before him as he ran, so that Teig was thrown in a heap on the road. Then before he could rise up the fairies caught him, some by the hands and some by the feet, and they held him tight, in a way that he could not stir, with his face against the ground. Six or seven of them raised the body then, and pulled it over to him, and left it down on his back. The breast of the corpse was squeezed against Teig's back and shoulders, and the arms of the corpse were thrown around Teig's neck. Then they stood back from him a couple of yards, and let him get up. He rose, foaming at the mouth and cursing, and he shook himself, thinking to throw the corpse off his back. But his fear and his wonder were great when he found that the two arms had a tight hold round his own neck, and that the two legs were squeezing his hips firmly, and that, however strongly he tried, he could not throw it off, any more than a horse can throw off its saddle. He was terribly frightened then, and he thought he was lost. "Ochone! forever," said he to himself, "it's the bad life I'm leading that has given the good people this power over me. I promise to God and Mary, Peter and Paul, Patrick and Bridget, that I'll mend my ways for as long as I have to live, if I come clear out of this danger—and I'll marry the girl."

The little grey man came up to him again, and said he to him, "Now, Teig*een*," says he, "you didn't lift the body when I told you to lift it, and see how you were made to lift it; perhaps when I tell you to bury it you won't bury it until you're made to bury it!"

"Anything at all that I can do for your honor," said Teig, "I'll do it," for he was getting sense already, and if it had not been for the great fear that was on him, he never would have let that civil word slip out of his mouth.

The little man laughed a sort of laugh again. "You're getting quiet now, Teig," says he. "I'll go bail but you'll be quiet enough before I'm done with you. Listen to me now, Teig O'Kane, and if you don't obey me in all I'm telling you to do, you'll repent it. You must carry with you this corpse that is on your back to Teampoll-Démus, and you must bring it into the church with you, and make a grave for it in the very middle of the church, and you must raise up the flag stones and put them down again the very same way, and you must carry the clay out of the church and leave the place as it was when you came, so that no one could know that there had been anything changed. But that's not all. Maybe that the body won't be allowed to be buried in the church; perhaps some other man has the bed, and, if so, it's likely he won't share it with this one. If you don't get leave to bury it in Teampoll-Démus, you must carry it to Carrick-fhad-vic-Orus, and bury it in the churchyard there; and if you don't get it into that place, take it with you to Teampoll-Ronan; and if that churchyard is closed on you, take it to Imlogue-Fada; and if you're not able to bury it there, you've no more to do than to take it to Kill-Breedya, and you can bury it there without hindrance. I cannot tell you what one of those churches is the one where you will have leave to bury that corpse under the clay, but I know that it will be allowed you to bury him at some church or other of them. If you do this work rightly, we will be thankful to you, and you will have no cause to grieve; but if you are slow or lazy, believe me we shall take satisfaction of you."

When the grey little man had done speaking, his comrades laughed and clapped their hands together. "Glic! Glic! Hwee! Hwee!" they all cried; "go on, go on, you have eight hours before you till daybreak, and if you haven't this man buried before the sun rises, you're lost." They struck a fist and a foot behind on him, and drove him on in the road. He was obliged to walk, and to walk fast, for they gave him no rest.

He thought himself that there was not a wet path, or a dirty *boreen* [lane], or a crooked contrary road in the whole county, that he had not walked that night. The night was at times very dark, and whenever there would come a cloud across the moon he could see nothing, and then he used often to fall. Sometimes he was hurt, and sometimes he escaped, but he was obliged always to rise on the moment and to hurry on. Sometimes the moon would break out clearly, and then he would look behind him and see the little people following his back. And he heard them speaking amongst themselves, talking and crying out, and screaming like a flock of sea-gulls; and if he was to save his soul he never understood as much as one word of what they were saying.

He did not know how far he had walked, when at last one of them cried out to him, "Stop here!" He stood, and they all gathered round him.

"Do you see those withered trees over there?" says the old boy to him again. "Teampoll-Démus is amongst those trees, and you must go in there by yourself, for we cannot follow you or go with you. We must remain here. Go on boldly."

Teig looked from him, and he saw a high wall that was in places half broken down, and an old grey church on the inside of the wall, and about a dozen withered old trees scattered here and there round it. There was neither leaf nor twig on any of them, but their bare crooked branches were stretched out like the arms of an angry man when he threatens. He had no help for it, but was obliged to go forwards. He was a couple of hundred yards from the church, but he walked on, and never looked behind him until he came to the gate of the churchyard. The old gate was thrown down, and he had no difficulty in entering. He turned then to see if any of the little people were following him, but there came a cloud over the moon, and the night became so dark that he could see nothing. He went into the churchyard, and he walked up the old grassy pathway leading to the church. When he reached the door, he found it locked. The door was large and strong, and he did not know what to do. At last he drew out his knife with difficulty, and stuck it in the wood to try if it were not rotten, but it was not.

"Now," said he to himself, "I have no more to do; the door is shut, and I can't open it."

Before the words were rightly shaped in his own mind, a voice in his ear said to him, "Search for the key on the top of the door, or on the wall."

He started. "Who is that speaking to me?" he cried, turning round; but he saw no one. The voice said in his ear again, "Search for the key on the top of the door, or on the wall."

"What's that?" said he, and the sweat running from his forehead; "who spoke to me?"

"It's I, the corpse, that spoke to you!" said the voice.

"Can you talk?" said Teig.

"Now and again," said the corpse.

Teig searched for the key, and he found it on the top of the wall. He was too much frightened to say any more, but he opened the door wide, and as quickly as he could, and he went in, with the corpse on his back. It was as dark as pitch inside, and poor Teig began to shake and tremble.

"Light the candle," said the corpse.

Teig put his hand in his pocket, as well as he was able, and drew out a flint and steel. He struck a spark out of it, and lit a burnt rag he had in his pocket. He blew it until it made a flame, and he looked round him. The church was very ancient, and part of the wall was broken down. The windows were blown in or cracked, and the timber of the seats was rotten. There were six or seven old iron candlesticks left there still, and in one of these candlesticks Teig found the stump of an old candle, and he lit it. He was still looking round him on the strange and horrid place in which he found himself, when the cold corpse whispered in his ear, "Bury me now, bury me now; there is a spade and turn the ground."

Teig looked from him, and he saw a spade lying beside the altar. He took it up, and he placed the blade under a flag stone that was in the middle of the aisle, and leaning all his weight on the handle of the spade, he raised it. When the first flag was raised it was not hard to raise the others near it, and he moved three or four of them out of their places. The clay that was under them was soft and easy to dig, but he had not thrown up more than three or four shovelfuls, when he felt the iron touch something soft like flesh. He threw up three or four more shovelfuls from around it, and then he saw that it was another body that was buried in the same place.

"I am afraid I'll never be allowed to bury the two bodies in the same hole," said Teig, in his own mind. "You corpse, there on my back," says he, "will you be satisfied if I bury you down here?" But the corpse never answered him a word.

"That's a good sign," said Teig to himself. "Maybe he's getting quiet." And he thrust the spade down in the earth again. Perhaps he hurt the flesh of the other body, for the dead man that was buried there stood up in the grave, and shouted an awful shout. "Hoo! hoo!! hoo!!! Go! go!! go!!! or you're a dead, dead, dead man!" And then he fell back in the grave again. Teig said afterwards, that of all the wonderful things he saw that night, that was the most awful to him. His hair stood upright on his head like the bristles of a pig, the cold sweat ran off his face, and then came a tremor over all his bones, until he thought that he must fall.

But after a while he became bolder, when he saw that the second corpse remained lying quietly there, and he threw in the clay on it again, and he smoothed it overhead, and he laid down the flags carefully as they had been before. "It can't be that he'll rise up any more," said he.

He went down the aisle a little farther, and drew near to the door, and began raising the flags again, looking for another bed for the corpse on his back. He took up three or four flags and put them aside, and then he dug the clay. He was not long digging until he laid bare an old woman without a thread upon her but her shirt. She was more lively than the first corpse, for he had scarcely taken any of the clay away from about her, when she sat up and began to cry, "Ho, you *bodach* (clown)! Ha, you *bodach*! Where has he been that he got no bed?"

Poor Teig drew back, and when she found that she was getting no answer, she closed her eyes gently, lost her vigor and fell back quietly and slowly under the clay. Teig did to her as he had done to the man—he threw the clay back on her, and let the flags down overhead.

He began digging again near the door, but before he had thrown up more than a couple of shovelfuls, he noticed a man's hand laid bare by the spade. "By my soul, I'll go no farther, then," said he to himself; "what use is it for me?" And he threw the clay in again on it, and settled the flags as they had been before.

He left the church then, and his heart was heavy enough, but he shut the door and locked it, and left the key where he found it. He sat down on a tombstone that was near the door, and began thinking. He was in great doubt what he should do. He laid his face between his two hands, and cried for grief and fatigue, since he was dead certain at this time that he never would come home alive. He made another attempt to loosen the hands of the corpse that were squeezed round his neck, but they were as tight as if they were clamped; and the more he tried to loosen them, the tighter they squeezed him. He was going to sit down once more, when the cold, horrid lips of the dead man said to him, "Carrick-fhad-vic-Orus," and he remembered the command of the people to bring the corpse with him to that place if he should be unable to bury it where he had been.

He rose up, and looked about him. "I don't know the way," he said.

As soon as he had uttered the word, the corpse stretched out suddenly its left hand that had been tightened round his neck, and kept it pointing out, showing him the road he ought to follow. Teig went in the direction that the fingers were stretched, and passed out of the churchyard. He found himself on an old rutty, stony road, and he stood stiff again, not knowing where to turn. The corpse stretched out its bony hand a second time, and pointed out to him another road—not the road by which he had come when approaching the old church. Teig followed that road, and whenever he came to a path or road meeting it, the corpse always stretched out its hand and pointed with its fingers, showing him the way he was to take.

Many was the cross-road he turned down, and many was the crooked *boreen* he walked, until he saw from him an old burying-ground at last, beside the road, but there was neither church nor chapel nor any other building in it. The corpse squeezed him tightly, and he stood. "Bury me, bury me in the burying-ground," said the voice.

Teig drew over towards the old burying-place, and he was not more than about twenty yards from it, when, raising his eyes, he saw hundreds and hundreds of ghosts—men, women, and children—sitting on the top of the wall round about, or standing on the inside of it, or running backwards and forwards, and pointing at him, while he could see their mouths opening and shutting as if they were speaking, though he heard no word, nor any sound amongst them at all.

He was afraid to go forwards, so he stood where he was, and the moment he stood, all the ghosts became quiet, and ceased moving. Then Teig understood that it was trying to keep him from going in, that they were. He walked a couple of yards forwards, and immediately the whole crowd rushed together towards the spot to which he was moving, and they stood so thickly together that it seemed to him that he never could break through them, even though he had a mind to try. But he had no mind to try it. He went back broken and dispirited, and when he had gone a couple of hundred yards from the burying-ground, he stood again, for he did not know what way he was to go. He heard the voice of the corpse in his ear, saying "Teampoll-Ronan," and the skinny hand was stretched out again, pointing him out the road.

As tired as he was, he had to walk, and the road was neither short nor even. The night was darker than ever, and it was difficult to make his way. Many was the toss he got, and many a bruise they left on his body. At last he saw Teampoll-Ronan from him in the distance, standing in the middle of the burying-ground. He moved over towards it, and thought he was all right and safe, when he saw no ghosts nor anything else on the wall, and he thought he would never be hindered now from leaving his load off him at last. He moved over to the gate, but as he was passing in, he tripped on the threshold. Before he could recover himself, something that he could not see seized him by the neck, by the hands, and by the feet, and bruised him, and shook him, and choked him, until he was nearly dead; and at last he was lifted up, and carried more than a hundred yards from that place, and then thrown down in an old dyke, with the corpse still clinging to him.

He rose up, bruised and sore, but feared to go near the place again, for he had seen nothing the time he was thrown down and carried away.

"You corpse, up on my back," said he, "shall I go over again to the churchyard?"—but the corpse never answered him. "That's a sign you don't wish me to try it again," said Teig.

He was now in great doubt as to what he ought to do, when the corpse spoke in his ear, and said, "Imlogue-Fada."

"Oh, murder!" said Teig, "must I bring you there? If you keep me long walking like this, I tell you I'll fall under you."

He went on, however, in the direction the corpse pointed out to him.

He could not have told, himself, how long he had been going, when the dead man behind suddenly squeezed him, and said, "There!"

Teig looked from him, and he saw a little low wall, that was so broken down in places that it was no wall at all. It was in a great wide field, in from the road; and only for three or four great stones at the corners, that were more like rocks than stones, there was nothing to show that there was either graveyard or burying-ground there.

"Is this Imlogue-Fada? Shall I bury you here?" said Teig.

"Yes," said the voice.

"But I see no grave or gravestone, only this pile of stones," said Teig.

The corpse did not answer, but stretched out its long fleshless hand, to show Teig the direction in which he was to go. Teig went on accordingly, but he was greatly terrified, for he remembered what had happened to him at the last place. He went on, "with his heart in his mouth," as he said to himself afterwards; but when he came to within fifteen or twenty yards of the little low square wall, there broke out a flash of lightning, bright yellow and red, with blue streaks in it, and went round about the wall in one course, and it swept by as fast as the swallow in the clouds, and the longer Teig remained looking at it the faster it went, till at last it became like a bright ring of flame round the old graveyard, which no one could pass without being burnt by it. Teig never saw, from the time he was born, and never saw afterwards, so wonderful or so splendid a sight as that was. Round went the flame, white and yellow and blue sparks leaping out from it as it went, and although at first it had been no more than a thin, narrow line, it increased slowly until it was at last a great broad band, and it was continually getting broader and higher, and throwing out more brilliant sparks, till there was never a color on the ridge of the earth that was not to be seen in that fire; and lightning never shone and flame never flamed that was so shining and so bright as that.

Teig was amazed; he was half dead with fatigue, and he had no courage left to approach the wall. There fell a mist over his eyes, and there came a *soorawn* [vertigo] in his head, and he was obliged to sit down upon a great stone to recover himself. He could see nothing but the light, and he could hear nothing but the whirr of it as it shot round the paddock faster than a flash of lightning.

As he sat there on the stone, the voice whispered once more in his ear, "Kill-Breedya"; and the dead man squeezed him so tightly that he cried out. He rose again, sick, tired, and trembling, and went forwards as he was directed. The wind was cold, and the road was bad, and the load upon his back was heavy, and the night was dark, and he himself was nearly worn out, and if he had had very much farther to go he must have fallen dead under his burden.

At last the corpse stretched out its hand, and said to him, "Bury me there."

"This is the last burying-place," said Teig in his own mind; "and the little grey man said I'd be allowed to bury him in some of them, so it must be this; it can't be but they'll let him in here."

The first faint streak of the *ring of day* was appearing in the east, and the clouds were beginning to catch fire, but it was darker than ever, for the moon was set, and there were no stars.

"Make haste, make haste!" said the corpse; and Teig hurried forwards as well as he could to the graveyard, which was a little place on a bare hill, with only a few graves in it. He walked boldly in through the open gate, and nothing touched him, nor did he either hear or see anything. He came to the middle of the ground, and then stood up and looked round him for a spade or shovel to make a grave. As he was turning round and searching, he suddenly perceived what startled him greatly—a newly-dug grave right before him. He moved over to it, and looked down, and there at the bottom he saw a black coffin. He clambered down into the hole and lifted the lid, and found that (as he thought it would be) the coffin was empty. He had hardly mounted up out of the hole, and was standing on the brink, when the corpse, which had clung to him for more than eight hours, suddenly relaxed its hold of his neck, and loosened its shins from round his hips, and sank down with a *plop* into the open coffin.

Teig fell down on his two knees at the brink of the grave, and gave thanks to God. He made no delay then, but pressed down the coffin lid in its place, and threw in the clay over it with his two hands; and when the grave was filled up, he stamped and leaped on it with his feet, until it was firm and hard, and then he left the place.

The sun was fast rising as he finished his work, and the first thing he did was to return to the road, and look out for a house to rest himself in. He found an inn at last, and lay down upon a bed there, and slept till night. Then he rose up and ate a little, and fell asleep again till morning. When he awoke in the morning he hired a horse and rode home. He was more than twenty-six miles from home where he was, and he had come all that way with the dead body on his back in one night.

All the people at his own home thought that he must have left the country, and they rejoiced greatly when they saw him come back. Everyone began asking him where he had been, but he would not tell anyone except his father.

He was a changed man from that day. He never drank too much; he never lost his money over cards; and especially he would not take the world and be out late by himself of a dark night.

He was not a fortnight at home until he married Mary, the girl he had been in love with; and it's at their wedding the sport was, and it's he was the happy man from that day forwards, and it's all I wish that we may be as happy as he was.

THE NAME ON THE STONE

Lafcadio Hearn

Lafcadio Hearn was a journalist and author who is famous for his many books on Japan, the Caribbean, and New Orleans. He grew up in Greece, Ireland, England, Wales, and France and then spent the first half of his adult life in the United States and the latter half living in Japan, where he became a Buddhist and a Japanese citizen, adopting the name Yakumo Koizumi. While he is primarily associated with Japan, he is also very well-known for his writings on New Orleans and its culture. This impressionistic sketch was written for his New Orleans newspaper column.

◆ ◆ ◆

"As surely as the wild bird seeks the summer, you will come back," she whispered. "Is there a drop of blood in your veins that does not grow ruddier and warmer at the thought of me? Does not your heart beat quicker at this moment because I am here? It belongs to me—it obeys me in spite of your feeble will—it will remain my slave when you are gone. You have bewitched yourself at my lips; I hold you as a bird is held by an invisible thread; and my thread, invisible and intangible, is stronger than your will. Fly: but you can no longer fly beyond the circle in which my wish confines you. Go: but I shall come to you in dreams of the night; and you will be awakened by the beating of your own heart to find yourself alone with darkness and memory. Sleep in whose arms you will, I shall come like a ghost between you; kiss a thousand lips, but it will be I that shall receive them. Though you circle the earth in your wanderings, you will never be able to leave my memory behind you; and your pulse will quicken at recollections of me whether you find yourself under Indian suns or Northern lights. You lie when you say you do not love me!—your heart would fling itself under my feet could it escape from its living prison! You will come back."

And having vainly sought rest through many vainly spent years, I returned to her. It was a night of wild winds and fleeting shadows and strange clouds that fled like phantoms before the storm and across the face of the moon.

"You are a cursed witch," I shrieked, "but I have come back!"

And she, placing a finger—white as the waxen tapers that are burned at the feet of the dead—upon my lips, only smiled and whispered, "Come with me."

And I followed her.

The thunder muttered in the east; the horizon pulsated with lightnings; the night-birds screamed as we reached the iron gates of the burial-ground, which swung open with a groan at her touch.

Noiselessly she passed through the ranges of the graves; and I saw the mounds flame when her feet touched them—flame with a cold white dead flame, like the fire of the glow-worm.

Was it an illusion of broken moonlight and flying clouds, or did the dead rise and follow us like a bridal train? And was it only the vibration of the thunder, or did the earth quake when I stood upon *that* grave?

"Look not behind you even for an instant," she muttered, "or you are lost."

But there came to me a strange desire to read the name graven upon the moss-darkened stone; and even as it came the storm unveiled the face of the moon.

And the dark shadow at my side whispered, "Read it not!"

And the moon veiled herself again. "I cannot go! I cannot go!" I whispered passionately, "until I have read the name upon this stone."

Then a flash of lightning in the east revealed to me the name; and an agony of memory came upon me; and I shrieked it to the flying clouds and the wan lights of heaven!

Again the earth quaked under my feet; and a white Shape rose from the bosom of the grave like an exhalation and stood before me: I felt the caress of lips shadowy as those of the fair phantom women who haunt the dreams of youth; and the echo of a dead voice, faint as the whisper of a summer wind, murmured—"Love, love is stronger than Death!— I come back from the eternal night to save thee!"

THE VAMPIRE OF CROGLIN GRANGE

(as recorded by Augustus Hare)

This is one of the most popular "true" vampire stories. The narrative was told to Augustus Hare in 1874 by Edward Rowe Fisher-Rowe, late captain of the Fourth Dragoon Guards. Hare quoted it in his book *The Story of My Life*, with little comment other than saying it is a "really extraordinary story" connected with Captain Fisher's own family. A number of people have tried to determine how much of this story is true. Certain elements of the story indicate that it is from the 1600s, while others place it in the 1800s.

Croglin Grange—now known as Croglin Low Hall—is a rural farmhouse in what is now Cumbria, in northwestern England. Croglin, which means "crooked river," is the name of a brook that flows about 350 yards to the northwest of the hall.

The people featured in the account—Amelia, Michael, and Edward Cranswell—subleased the house from the Fishers in the mid to late 1800s, but it's noted in the narrative that it was a single-story house, although by then the house had two floors. According to local tradition, the second story was built in the 1720s, and it was at this time that Croglin Grange became known as Croglin Low Hall. The Fishers leased the house from 1809 up until this story was told to Augustus Hare.

Some suggest the church and graveyard in the story are the ones in Ainstable, a mile and a half to the northeast, but there were a small church and graveyard very close to Croglin Grange, though they were destroyed by Oliver Cromwell's brother-in-law in the mid 1600s during the English Civil War. The window next to the front door, which

312 The Book of the Living Dead

tradition says is the one through which the vampire entered, is now bricked up, along with at least four other windows. It's suggested this was done to avoid a window tax that began to be levied in 1696.

There are indications that this story was associated with the house at least as far back as the early 1800s, which would support an earlier date. Augustus Hare probably wrote Captain Fisher's narrative down from memory and may have introduced some of the confusing elements from his personal knowledge of the house. At any rate, here is what Hare quoted the captain as saying.

♦   ♦   ♦

Fisher may sound a very plebeian name, but this family is of a very ancient lineage, and for many hundreds of years they have possessed a very curious old place in Cumberland, which bears the weird name of Croglin Grange. The great characteristic of the house is that never at any period of its very long existence has it been more than one story high, but it has a terrace from which large grounds sweep away towards the church in the hollow, and a fine distant view.

When, in lapse of years, the Fishers outgrew Croglin Grange in family and fortune, they were wise enough not to destroy the long-standing characteristic of the place by adding another story to the house, but they went away to the south, to reside at Thorncombe near Guildford, and they let Croglin Grange.

They were extremely fortunate in their tenants, two brothers and a sister. They heard their praises from all quarters. To their poorer neighbors they were all that is most kind and beneficent, and their neighbors of a higher class spoke of them as a most welcome addition to the little society of the neighborhood. On their part, the tenants were greatly delighted with their new residence. The arrangement of the house, which would have been a trial to many, was not so to them. In every respect Croglin Grange was exactly suited to them.

The winter was spent most happily by the new inmates of Croglin Grange, who shared in all the little social pleasures of the district, and made themselves very popular. In the following summer, there was one day which was dreadfully, annihilatingly hot. The brothers lay under the trees with their books, for it was too hot for any active occupation. The sister sat in the veranda and worked, or tried to work, for in the intense sultriness of that summer day, work was next to impossible. They dined early, and after dinner they still sat out on the veranda, enjoying the cool air which came with the evening, and they watched the sun set, and the moon rise over the belt of trees which separated the grounds from the churchyard, seeing it mount the heavens till the whole lawn was bathed in silver light, across which the long shadows from the shrubbery fell as if embossed, so vivid and distinct were they.

When they separated for the night, all retiring to their rooms on the ground-floor (for, as I said, there was no upstairs in that house), the sister felt that the heat was still so great that she could not sleep, and having fastened her window, she did not close the shutters—in that very quiet place it was not necessary—and, propped against the pillows, she still watched the wonderful, the marvelous beauty of that summer night. Gradually she became aware of two lights, two lights which flickered in and out in the belt of trees which separated the lawn from the churchyard, and, as her gaze became fixed upon them, she saw them emerge, fixed in a dark substance, a definite ghastly *something*, which seemed every moment to become nearer, increasing in size and substance as it approached. Every now and then it was lost for a moment in the long shadows which stretched across the lawn from the trees, and then it emerged larger than ever, and still coming on—on. As she watched it, the most uncontrollable horror seized her. She longed to get away, but the door was close to the window, and the door was locked on the inside, and while she was unlocking it she must be for an instant nearer to *it*. She longed to scream, but her voice seemed paralyzed, her tongue glued to the roof of her mouth.

Suddenly—she could never explain why afterwards—the terrible object seemed to turn to one side, seemed to be going round the house, not to be coming to her at all, and immediately she jumped out of bed and rushed to the door, but as she was unlocking it she heard scratch, scratch, scratch upon the window, and saw a hideous brown face with flaming eyes glaring in at her. She rushed back to the bed, but the creature continued to scratch, scratch, scratch upon the window. She felt a sort of mental comfort in the knowledge that the window was securely fastened on the inside.

Suddenly the scratching sound ceased, and a kind of pecking sound took its place. Then, in her agony, she became aware that the creature was unpicking the lead! The noise continued, and a diamond pane of glass fell into the room. Then a long bony finger of the creature came in and turned the handle of the window, and the window opened, and the creature came in; and it came across the room, and her terror was so great that she could not scream, and it came up to the bed, and it twisted its long, bony fingers into her hair, and it dragged her head over the side of the bed, and—it bit her violently in the throat.

As it bit her, her voice was released, and she screamed with all her might and main. Her brothers rushed out of their rooms, but the door was locked on the inside. A moment was lost while they got a poker and broke it open. Then the creature had already escaped through the window, and the sister, bleeding violently from a wound in the throat, was lying unconscious over the side of the bed.

One brother pursued the creature, which fled before him through the moonlight with gigantic strides, and eventually seemed to disappear over the wall into the churchyard. Then he rejoined his brother by the sister's bedside. She was dreadfully hurt, and her wound was a very definite one, but she was of strong disposition, not even given to romance or superstition, and when she came to herself she said, "What has happened is most extraordinary and I am very much hurt. It seems inexplicable, but of course there *is* an explanation, and we must wait for it. It will turn out that a lunatic has escaped from some asylum and found his way here."

The wound healed, and she appeared to get well, but the doctor who was sent for would not believe that she could bear so terrible a shock so easily, and insisted that she must have change, mental and physical; so her brothers took her to Switzerland.

Being a sensible girl, when she went abroad she threw herself at once into the interests of the country she was in. She dried plants, she made sketches, she went up mountains, and as autumn came on, she was the person who urged that they should return to Croglin Grange.

"We have taken it," she said, "for seven years, and we have only been there one; and we shall always find it difficult to let a house which is only one story high, so we had better return there; lunatics do not escape every day."

As she urged it, her brothers wished nothing better, and the family returned to Cumberland. From there being no upstairs in the house it was impossible to make any great change in their arrangements. The sister occupied the same room, but it is unnecessary to say she always closed the shutters, which, however, as in many old houses, always left one top pane of the window uncovered. The brothers moved, and occupied a room together, exactly opposite that of their sister, and they always kept loaded pistols in their room.

The winter passed most peacefully and happily. In the following March, the sister was suddenly awakened by a sound she remembered only too well—scratch, scratch, scratch upon the window, and, looking up, she saw, climbed up to the topmost pane of the window, the same hideous brown shriveled face, with glaring eyes, looking in at her.

This time she screamed as loud as she could. Her brothers rushed out of their room with pistols, and out of the front door. The creature was already scudding away across the lawn. One of the brothers fired and hit it in the leg, but still with the other leg it continued to make way, scrambled over the wall into the churchyard, and seemed to disappear into a vault which belonged to a family long extinct.

The next day the brothers summoned all the tenants of Croglin Grange, and in their presence the vault was opened. A horrible scene revealed itself. The vault was full of coffins; they had been broken open, and their contents, horribly mangled and distorted, were scattered over the floor. One coffin alone remained intact. Of that the lid had been lifted, but still lay loose upon the coffin. They raised it, and there, brown, withered, shriveled, mummified, but quite entire, was the same hideous figure which had looked in at the windows of Croglin Grange, with the marks of a recent pistol-shot in the leg: and they did the only thing that can lay a vampire—they burnt it.

THURNLEY ABBEY

Perceval Landon

Here is an interesting gothic tale, which horror author M. R. James described as "a horrid one . . . almost too horrid." It's the perfect story to read when you're alone in bed on a dark, candlelit night.

✦ ✦ ✦

Three years ago I was on my way out to the East, and as an extra day in London was of some importance, I took the Friday evening mail-train to Brindisi instead of the usual Thursday morning Marseilles express. Many people shrink from the long forty-eight-hour train journey through Europe, and the subsequent rush across the Mediterranean on the nineteen-knot *Isis* or *Osiris*; but there is really very little discomfort on either the train or the mail-boat, and unless there is actually nothing for me to do, I always like to save the extra day and a half in London before I say goodbye to her for one of my longer tramps. This time—it was early, I remember, in the shipping season, probably about the beginning of September—there were few passengers, and I had a compartment in the P. & O. Indian express to myself all the way from Calais. All Sunday I watched the blue waves dimpling the Adriatic, and the pale rosemary along the cuttings; the plain white towns, with their flat roofs and their bold "duomos," and the grey-green gnarled olive orchards of Apulia. The journey was just like any other. We ate in the dining-car as often and as long as we decently could. We slept after luncheon; we dawdled the afternoon away with yellow-backed novels; sometimes we exchanged platitudes in the smoking-room, and it was there that I met Alastair Colvin.

Colvin was a man of middle height, with a resolute, well-cut jaw; his hair was turning grey; his moustache was sun-whitened, otherwise he was clean-shaven—obviously a gentleman, and obviously also a preoccupied man. He had no great wit. When spoken to, he made the usual remarks in the right way, and I dare say he refrained from banalities only because he spoke less than the rest of us; most of the time he buried himself in the Wagon-lit Company's time-table, but seemed unable to concentrate his attention on any one page of it. He found that I had been over the Siberian railway, and for a quarter of an hour he discussed it with me. Then he lost interest in it, and rose to go to his compartment. But he came back again very soon, and seemed glad to pick up the conversation again.

Of course this did not seem to me to be of any importance. Most travelers by train become a trifle infirm of purpose after thirty-six hours' rattling. But Colvin's restless way I noticed in somewhat marked contrast with the man's personal importance and dignity; especially ill suited was it to his finely made large hand with strong, broad, regular nails and its few lines. As I looked at his hand I noticed a long, deep, and recent scar of ragged shape. However, it is absurd to pretend that I thought anything was unusual. I went off at five o'clock on Sunday afternoon to sleep away the hour or two that had still to be got through before we arrived at Brindisi.

Once there, we few passengers transhipped our hand baggage, verified our berths—there were only a score of us in all—and then, after an aimless ramble of half an hour in Brindisi, we returned to dinner at the Hotel International, not wholly surprised that the town had been the death of Virgil. If I remember rightly, there is a gaily painted hall at the International—I do not wish to advertise anything, but there is no other place in Brindisi at which to await the coming of the mails—and after dinner I was looking with awe at a trellis overgrown with blue vines, when Colvin moved across the room to my table. He picked up *Il Secolo*, but almost immediately gave up the pretence of reading it. He turned squarely to me and said, "Would you do me a favor?"

One doesn't do favors to stray acquaintances on Continental expresses without knowing something more of them than I knew of Colvin. But I smiled in a noncommittal way, and asked him what he wanted. I wasn't wrong in part of my estimate of him; he said bluntly, "Will you let me sleep in your cabin on the *Osiris*?" And he colored a little as he said it.

Now, there is nothing more tiresome than having to put up with a stable-companion at sea, and I asked him rather pointedly, "Surely there is room for all of us?" I thought that perhaps he had been partnered off with some mangy Levantine, and wanted to escape from him at all hazards.

Colvin, still somewhat confused, said, "Yes; I am in a cabin by myself. But you would do me the greatest favor if you would allow me to share yours."

This was all very well, but, besides the fact that I always sleep better when alone, there had been some recent thefts on board English liners, and I hesitated, frank and honest and self-conscious as Colvin was. Just then the mail-train came in with a clatter and a rush of escaping steam, and I asked him to see me again about it on the boat when we started. He answered me curtly—I suppose he saw the mistrust in my manner—"I am a member of White's." I smiled to myself as he said it, but I remembered in a moment that the man—if he were really what he claimed to be, and I make no doubt that he was—must have been sorely put to it before he urged the fact as a guarantee of his respectability to a total stranger at a Brindisi hotel.

That evening, as we cleared the red and green harbor-lights of Brindisi, Colvin explained. This is his story in his own words.

———

"When I was traveling in India some years ago, I made the acquaintance of a youngish man in the Woods and Forests. We camped out together for a week, and I found him a pleasant companion. John Broughton was a light-hearted soul when off duty, but a steady and capable man in any of the small emergencies that continually arise in that department. He was liked and trusted by the natives, and though a trifle over-pleased with himself when he escaped to civilization at Simla or Calcutta, Broughton's future was well assured in Government service, when a fair-sized estate was unexpectedly left to him, and he joyfully shook the dust of the Indian plains from his feet and returned to England. For five years he drifted about London. I saw him now and then. We dined together about every eighteen months, and I could trace pretty exactly the gradual sickening of Broughton with a merely idle life. He then set out on a couple of long voyages, returned as restless as before, and at last told me that he had decided to marry and settle down at his place, Thurnley Abbey, which had long been empty. He spoke about looking after the property and standing for his constituency in the usual way. Vivien Wilde, his fiancée, had, I suppose, begun to take him in hand. She was a pretty girl with a deal of fair hair and rather an exclusive manner; deeply religious in a narrow school, she was still kindly and high-spirited, and I thought that Broughton was in luck. He was quite happy and full of information about his future.

"Among other things, I asked him about Thurnley Abbey. He confessed that he hardly knew the place. The last tenant, a man called Clarke, had lived in one wing for fifteen years and seen no one. He had been a miser and a hermit. It was the rarest thing for a light to be seen at the Abbey after dark. Only the barest necessities of life were ordered, and the tenant himself received them at the side-door. His one half-caste manservant, after a month's stay in the house, had abruptly left without warning, and had returned to the Southern States. One thing Broughton complained bitterly about: Clarke had willfully spread the rumor among the villagers that the Abbey was haunted, and had even condescended to play childish tricks with spirit-lamps and salt in order to scare trespassers away at night. He had been detected in the act of this tomfoolery, but the story spread, and no one, said Broughton, would venture near the house except in broad daylight. The haunted-ness of Thurnley Abbey was now, he said with a grin, part of the gospel of the countryside, but he and his young wife were going to change all that. Would I propose myself any time I liked? I, of course, said I would, and equally, of course, intended to do nothing of the sort without a definite invitation.

"The house was put in thorough repair, though not a stick of the old furniture and tapestry were removed. Floors and ceilings were relaid: the roof was made watertight again, and the dust of half a century was scoured out. He showed me some photographs of the place. It was called an Abbey, though as a matter of fact it had been only the infir-mary of the long-vanished Abbey of Clouster some five miles away. The larger part of the building remained as it had been in pre-Reformation days, but a wing had been added in Jacobean times, and that part of the house had been kept in something like repair by Mr. Clarke. He had in both the ground and first floors set a heavy timber door, strongly barred with iron, in the passage between the earlier and the Jacobean parts of the house, and had entirely neglected the former. So there had been a good deal of work to be done.

"Broughton, whom I saw in London two or three times about this period, made a deal of fun over the positive refusal of the workmen to remain after sundown. Even after the electric light had been put into every room, nothing would induce them to remain, though, as Broughton observed, electric light was death on ghosts. The legend of the Abbey's ghosts had gone far and wide, and the men would take no risks. They went home in batches of five and six, and even during the daylight hours there was an inordinate amount of talking between one and another, if either happened to be out of sight of his companion. On the whole, though nothing of any sort or kind had been conjured up even by their heated imaginations during their five months' work upon the Abbey, the belief in the ghosts was rather strengthened than otherwise in Thurnley because of the men's confessed nervousness, and local tradition declared itself in favor of the ghost of an immured nun.

"'Good old nun!' said Broughton.

"I asked him whether in general he believed in the possibility of ghosts, and, rather to my surprise, he said that he couldn't say he entirely disbelieved in them. A man in India had told him one morning in camp that he believed that his mother was dead in England, as her vision had come to his tent the night before. He had not been alarmed, but had said nothing, and the figure vanished again. As a matter of fact, the next possible dak-walla brought on a telegram announcing the mother's death. 'There the thing was,' said Broughton. But at Thurnley he was practical enough. He roundly cursed the idiotic selfishness of Clarke, whose silly antics had caused all the inconvenience. At the same time, he couldn't refuse to sympathize to some extent with the ignorant workmen. 'My own idea,' said he, 'is that if a ghost ever does come in one's way, one ought to speak to it.'

"I agreed. Little as I knew of the ghost world and its conventions, I had always remembered that a spook was in honor bound to wait to be spoken to. It didn't seem much to do, and I felt that the sound of one's own voice would at any rate reassure oneself as to one's wakefulness. But there are few ghosts outside Europe—few, that is, that a white man can see—and I had never been troubled with any. However, as I have said, I told Broughton that I agreed.

"So the wedding took place, and I went to it in a tall hat which I bought for the occasion, and the new Mrs. Broughton smiled very nicely at me afterwards. As it had to happen, I took the Orient Express that evening and was not in England again for nearly six months. Just before I came back I got a letter from Broughton. He asked if I could see him in London or come to Thurnley, as he thought I should be better able to help him than anyone else he knew. His wife sent a nice message to me at the end, so I was reassured about at least one thing. I wrote from Budapest that I would come and see him at Thurnley two days after my arrival in London, and as I sauntered out of the Pannonia into the

Kerepesi Utcza to post my letters, I wondered of what earthly service I could be to Broughton. I had been out with him after tiger on foot, and I could imagine few men better able at a pinch to manage their own business. However, I had nothing to do, so after dealing with some small accumulations of business during my absence, I packed a kit-bag and departed to Euston.

"I was met by Broughton's great limousine at Thurnley Road station, and after a drive of nearly seven miles we echoed through the sleepy streets of Thurnley village, into which the main gates of the park thrust themselves, splendid with pillars and spread-eagles and tom-cats rampant atop of them. I never was a herald, but I know that the Broughtons have the right to supporters—Heaven knows why! From the gates a quadruple avenue of beech-trees led inwards for a quarter of a mile. Beneath them a neat strip of fine turf edged the road and ran back until the poison of the dead beech-leaves killed it under the trees. There were many wheel-tracks on the road, and a comfortable little pony trap jogged past me laden with a country parson and his wife and daughter. Evidently there was some garden party going on at the Abbey. The road dropped away to the right at the end of the avenue, and I could see the Abbey across a wide pasturage and a broad lawn thickly dotted with guests.

"The end of the building was plain. It must have been almost mercilessly austere when it was first built, but time had crumbled the edges and toned the stone down to an orange-lichened grey wherever it showed behind its curtain of magnolia, jasmine, and ivy. Farther on was the three-storied Jacobean house, tall and handsome. There had not been the slightest attempt to adapt the one to the other, but the kindly ivy had glossed over the touching-point. There was a tall fleche in the middle of the building, surmounting a small bell tower. Behind the house there rose the mountainous verdure of Spanish chestnuts all the way up the hill.

"Broughton had seen me coming from afar, and walked across from his other guests to welcome me before turning me over to the butler's care. This man was sandy-haired and rather inclined to be talkative. He could, however, answer hardly any questions about the house; he had, he said, only been there three weeks. Mindful of what Broughton had told me, I made no inquiries about ghosts, though the room into which I was shown might have justified anything. It was a very large low room with oak beams projecting from the white ceiling. Every inch of the walls, including the doors, was covered with tapestry, and a remarkably fine Italian four-post bedstead, heavily draped, added to the darkness and dignity of the place. All the furniture was old, well made, and dark. Underfoot there was a plain green pile carpet, the only new thing about the room except the electric light fittings and the jugs and basins. Even the looking-glass on the dressing-table was an old pyramidal Venetian glass set in heavy *repoussé* frame of tarnished silver.

"After a few minutes' cleaning up, I went downstairs and out upon the lawn, where I greeted my hostess. The people gathered there were of the usual country type, all anxious to be pleased and roundly curious as to the new master of the Abbey. Rather to my surprise, and quite to my pleasure, I rediscovered Glenham, whom I had known well in old days in Barotseland: he lived quite close, as, he remarked with a grin, I ought to have known. 'But,' he added, 'I don't live in a place like this.' He swept his hand to the long, low lines of the Abbey in obvious admiration, and then, to my intense interest, muttered beneath his breath, 'Thank God!' He saw that I had overheard him, and turning to me said decidedly, 'Yes, "thank God," I said, and I meant it. I wouldn't live at the Abbey for all Broughton's money.'

"'But surely,' I demurred, 'you know that old Clarke was discovered in the very act of setting light on his bug-a-boos?'

"Glenham shrugged his shoulders. 'Yes, I know about that. But there is something wrong with the place still. All I can say is that Broughton is a different man since he has lived there. I don't believe that he will remain much longer. But—you're staying here?—well, you'll hear all about it to-night. There's a big dinner, I understand.' The conversation turned off to old reminiscences, and Glenham soon after had to go.

"Before I went to dress that evening I had twenty minutes' talk with Broughton in his library. There was no doubt that the man was altered, gravely altered. He was nervous and fidgety, and I found him looking at me only when my eye was off him. I naturally asked him what he wanted of me. I told him I would do anything I could, but that I couldn't conceive what he lacked that I could provide. He said with a lusterless smile that there was, however, something, and that he would tell me the following morning. It struck me that he was somehow ashamed of himself, and perhaps ashamed of the part he was asking me to play. However, I dismissed the subject from my mind and went up to dress in my palatial room. As I shut the door a draught blew out the Queen of Sheba from the wall, and I noticed that the tapestries were not fastened to the wall at the bottom. I have always held very practical views about spooks, and it has often seemed to me that the slow waving in firelight of loose tapestry upon a wall would account for ninety-nine per cent. of the stories one hears. Certainly the dignified undulation of this lady with her attendants and huntsmen—one of whom was untidily cutting the throat of a fallow deer upon the very steps on which King Solomon, a grey-faced Flemish nobleman with the order of the Golden Fleece, awaited his fair visitor—gave color to my hypothesis.

"Nothing much happened at dinner. The people were very much like those of the garden party. A young woman next me seemed anxious to know what was being read in London. As she was far more familiar than I with the most recent magazines and literary supplements, I found salvation in being myself instructed in the tendencies of modern fiction. All true art, she said, was shot through and through with melancholy. How vulgar were the attempts at wit that marked so many modern books! From the beginning of literature it had always been tragedy that embodied the highest attainment of every age. To call such works morbid merely begged the question. No thoughtful man—she looked sternly at me through the steel rim of her glasses—could fail to agree with me. Of course, as one would, I immediately and properly said that I slept with Pett Ridge and Jacobs under my pillow at night, and that if *Jorrocks* weren't quite so large and cornery, I would add him to the company. She hadn't read any of them, so I was saved—for a time. But I remember grimly that she said that the dearest wish of her life was to be in some awful and soul-freezing situation of horror, and I remember that she dealt hardly with the hero of Nat Paynter's vampire story, between nibbles at her brown-bread ice. She was a cheerless soul, and I couldn't help thinking that if there were many such in the neighborhood, it was not surprising that old Glenham had been stuffed with some nonsense or other about the Abbey. Yet nothing could well have been less creepy than the glitter of silver and glass, and the subdued lights and cackle of conversation all round the dinner-table.

"After the ladies had gone I found myself talking to the rural dean. He was a thin, earnest man, who at once turned the conversation to old Clarke's buffooneries. But, he said, Mr. Broughton had introduced such a new and cheerful spirit, not only into the Abbey, but, he might say, into the whole neighborhood, that he had great hopes that the ignorant superstitions of the past were from henceforth destined to oblivion.

"Thereupon his other neighbor, a portly gentleman of independent means and position, audibly remarked 'Amen,' which damped the rural dean, and we talked to partridges past, partridges present, and pheasants to come. At the other end of the table Broughton sat with a couple of his friends, red-faced hunting men. Once I noticed that they were discussing me, but I paid no attention to it at the time. I remembered it a few hours later.

"By eleven all the guests were gone, and Broughton, his wife, and I were alone together under the fine plaster ceiling of the Jacobean drawing-room. Mrs. Broughton talked about one or two of the neighbors, and then, with a smile, said that she knew I would excuse her, shook hands with me, and went off to bed. I am not very good at analyzing things, but I felt that she talked a little uncomfortably and with a suspicion of effort, smiled rather conventionally, and was obviously glad to go. These things seem trifling enough to repeat, but I had throughout the faint feeling that everything was not quite square. Under the circumstances, this was enough to set me wondering what on earth the service could be that I was to render—wondering also whether the whole business were not some ill-advised jest in order to make me come down from London for a mere shooting-party.

"Broughton said little after she had gone. But he was evidently laboring to bring the conversation round to the so-called haunting of the Abbey. As soon as I saw this, of course I asked him directly about it. He then seemed at once to lose interest in the matter. There was no doubt about it: Broughton was somehow a changed man, and to my mind he had changed in no way for the better. Mrs. Broughton seemed no sufficient cause. He was clearly very fond of her, and she of him. I reminded him that he was going to tell me what I could do for him in the morning, pleaded my journey, lighted a candle, and went upstairs with him. At the end of the passage leading into the old house he grinned weakly and said, 'Mind, if you see a ghost, do talk to it; you said you would.' He stood irresolutely a moment and then turned away. At the door of his dressing-room he paused once more: 'I'm here,' he called out, 'if you should want anything. Good night,' and he shut the door.

"I went along the passage to my room, undressed, switched on a lamp beside my bed, read a few pages of *The Jungle Book*, and then, more than ready for sleep, turned the light off and went fast asleep.

"Three hours later I woke up. There was not a breath of wind outside. There was not even a flicker of light from the fireplace. As I lay there, an ash tinkled slightly as it cooled, but there was hardly a gleam of the dullest red in the grate. An owl cried among the silent Spanish chestnuts on the slope outside. I idly reviewed the events of the day, hoping that I should fall off to sleep again before I reached dinner. But at the end I seemed as wakeful as ever. There was no help for it. I must read my *Jungle Book* again till I felt ready to go off, so I fumbled for the pear at the end of the cord that hung down inside the bed, and I switched on the bedside lamp. The sudden glory dazzled me for a moment. I felt under my pillow for my book with half-shut eyes. Then, growing used to the light, I happened to look down to the foot of my bed.

"I can never tell you really what happened then. Nothing I could ever confess in the most abject words could even faintly picture to you what I felt. I know that my heart stopped dead, and my throat shut automatically. In one instinctive movement I crouched back up against the head-boards of the bed, staring at the horror. The movement set my heart going again, and the sweat dripped from every pore. I am not a particularly religious man, but I had always believed that God would never allow any supernatural appearance to present itself to man in such a guise and in such circumstances that harm, either bodily or mental, could result to him. I can only tell you that at the moment both my life and my reason rocked unsteadily on their seats."

The other *Osiris* passengers had gone to bed. Only he and I remained leaning over the starboard railing, which rattled uneasily now and then under the fierce vibration of the over-engined mail-boat. Far over, there were the lights of a few fishing-smacks riding out the night, and a great rush of white combing and seething water fell out and away from us overside.

At last Colvin went on:

"Leaning over the foot of my bed, looking at me, was a figure swathed in a rotten and tattered veiling. This shroud passed over the head, but left both eyes and the right side of the face bare. It then followed the line of the arm down to where the hand grasped the bed-end. The face was not entirely that of a skull, though the eyes and the flesh of the face were totally gone. There was a thin, dry skin drawn tightly over the features, and there was some skin left on the hand. One wisp of hair crossed the forehead. It was perfectly still. I looked at it, and it looked at me, and my brains turned dry and hot in my head. I had still got the pear of the electric lamp in my hand, and I played idly with it; only I dared not turn the light out again. I shut my eyes, only to open them in a hideous terror the same second. The thing had not moved. My heart was thumping, and the sweat cooled me as it evaporated. Another cinder tinkled in the grate, and a panel creaked in the wall.

"My reason failed me. For twenty minutes, or twenty seconds, I was able to think of nothing else but this awful figure, till there came, hurtling through the empty channels of my senses, the remembrances that Broughton and his friends had discussed me furtively at dinner. The dim possibility of its being a hoax stole gratefully into my unhappy mind, and once there, one's pluck came creeping back along a thousand tiny veins. My first sensation was one of blind unreasoning thankfulness that my brain was going to stand the trial. I am not a timid man, but the best of us needs some human handle to steady him in time of extremity, and in this faint but growing hope that after all it might be only a brutal hoax, I found the fulcrum that I needed. At last I moved.

"How I managed to do it I cannot tell you, but with one spring towards the foot of the bed I got within arm's-length and struck out one fearful blow with my fist at the thing. It crumbled under it, and my hand was cut to the bone. With a sickening revulsion after my terror, I dropped half-fainting across the end of the bed. So it was merely a foul trick after all. No doubt the trick had been played many a time before: no doubt Broughton and his friends had had some large bet among themselves as to what I should do when I discovered the gruesome thing. From my state of abject terror I found myself transported into an insensate anger. I shouted curses upon Broughton. I dived rather than climbed over the bed-end of the sofa. I tore at the robed skeleton—how well the whole thing had been carried out, I thought—I broke the skull against the floor, and stamped upon its dry bones. I flung the head away under the bed, and rent the brittle bones of the trunk in pieces. I snapped the thin thigh-bones across my knee, and flung them in different directions. The shin-bones I set up against a stool and broke with my heel. I raged like a Berserker against the loathly thing, and stripped the ribs from the backbone and slung the breastbone against the cupboard. My fury increased as the work of destruction went on. I tore the frail rotten veil into twenty pieces, and the dust went up over every-thing, over the clean blotting-paper and the silver inkstand. At last my work was done. There was but a raffle of broken bones and strips of parchment and crumbling wool. Then, picking up a piece of the skull—it was the cheek and temple bone of the right side, I remember—I opened the door and went down the passage to Broughton's dressing-room. I remember still how my sweat-dripping pyjamas clung to me as I walked. At the door I kicked and entered.

"Broughton was in bed. He had already turned the light on and seemed shrunken and horrified. For a moment he could hardly pull himself together. Then I spoke. I don't know what I said. Only I know that from a heart full and over-full with hatred and contempt, spurred on by shame of my own recent cowardice, I let my tongue run on. He answered nothing. I was amazed at my own fluency. My hair still clung lankily to my wet temples, my hand was bleeding profusely, and I must have looked a strange sight. Broughton huddled himself up at the head of the bed just as I had. Still he made no answer, no defense. He seemed preoccupied with something besides my reproaches, and once or twice moistened his lips with his tongue. But he could say nothing though he moved his hands now and then, just as a baby who cannot speak moves its hands.

"At last the door into Mrs. Broughton's rooms opened and she came in, white and terrified. 'What is it? What is it? Oh, in God's name! what is it?' she cried again and again, and then she went up to her husband and sat on the bed in her night-dress, and the two faced me. I told her what the matter was. I spared her husband not a word for her presence there. Yet he seemed hardly to understand. I told the pair that I had spoiled their cowardly joke for them. Broughton looked up.

"'I have smashed the foul thing into a hundred pieces,' I said. Brough-ton licked his lips again and his mouth worked. 'By God!' I shouted, 'it would serve you right if I thrashed you within an inch of your life. I will take care that not a decent man or woman of my acquaintance ever speaks to you again. And there,' I added, throwing the broken piece of the skull upon the floor beside his bed, 'there is a souvenir for you, of your damned work to-night!'

"Broughton saw the bone, and in a moment it was his turn to frighten me. He squealed like a hare caught in a trap. He screamed and screamed till Mrs. Broughton, almost as bewildered as myself, held on to him and coaxed him like a child to be quiet. But Broughton—and as he moved I thought that ten minutes ago I perhaps looked as terribly ill as he did—thrust her from him, and scrambled out of bed on to the floor, and still screaming put out his hand to the bone. It had blood on it from my hand. He paid no attention to me whatever. In truth I said nothing. This was a new turn indeed to the horrors of the evening. He rose from the floor with the bone in his hand and stood silent. He seemed to be listening. 'Time, time, perhaps,' he muttered, and almost at the same moment fell at full length on the carpet, cutting his head against the fender. The bone flew from his hand and came to rest near the door. I picked Broughton up, haggard and broken, with blood over his face. He whispered hoarsely and quickly, 'Listen, listen!' We listened.

"After ten seconds' utter quiet, I seemed to hear something. I could not be sure, but at last there was no doubt. There was a quiet sound as one moving along the passage. Little regular steps came towards us over the hard oak flooring. Broughton moved to where his wife sat, white and speechless, on the bed, and pressed her face into his shoulder.

"Then, the last thing that I could see as he turned the light out, he fell forward with his own head pressed into the pillow of the bed. Something in their company, something in their cowardice, helped me, and I faced the open doorway of the room, which was outlined fairly clearly against the dimly lighted passage. I put out one hand and touched Mrs. Broughton's shoulder in the darkness. But at the last moment I too failed. I sank on my knees and put my face in the bed. Only we all heard. The footsteps came to the door and there they stopped. The piece of bone was lying a yard inside the door. There was a rustle of moving stuff, and the thing was in the room. Mrs. Broughton was silent: I could hear Broughton's voice praying, muffled in the pillow: I was cursing my own cowardice. Then the steps moved out again on the oak boards of the passage, and I heard the sounds dying away. In a flash of remorse I went to the door and looked out. At the end of the corridor I thought I saw something that moved away. A moment later the passage was empty. I stood with my forehead against the jamb of the door almost physically sick.

"'You can turn the light on,' I said, and there was an answering flare. There was no bone at my feet. Mrs. Broughton had fainted. Broughton was almost useless, and it took me ten minutes to bring her to. Broughton only said one thing worth remembering. For the most part he went on muttering prayers. But I was glad afterwards to recollect that he had said that thing. He said in a colorless voice, half as a question, half as a reproach, 'You didn't speak to her.'

"We spent the remainder of the night together. Mrs. Broughton actually fell off into a kind of sleep before dawn, but she suffered so horribly in her dreams that I shook her into consciousness again. Never was dawn so long in coming. Three or four times Broughton spoke to himself. Mrs. Broughton would then just tighten her hold on his arm, but she could say nothing. As for me, I can honestly say that I grew worse as the hours passed and the light strengthened. The two violent reactions had battered down my steadiness of view, and I felt that the foundations of my life had been built upon the sand. I said nothing, and after binding up my hand with a towel, I did not move. It was better so. They helped me and I helped them, and we all three knew that our reason had gone very near to ruin that night. At last, when the light came in pretty strongly, and the birds outside were chattering and singing, we felt that we must do something. Yet we never moved. You might have thought that we should particularly dislike being found as we were by the servants: yet nothing of that kind mattered a straw, and an overpowering listlessness bound us as we sat, until Chapman, Broughton's man, actually knocked and opened the door. None of us moved. Broughton, speaking hardly and stiffly, said, 'Chapman, you can come back in five minutes.' Chapman was a discreet man, but it would have made no difference to us if he had carried his news to the 'room' at once.

"We looked at each other and I said I must go back. I meant to wait outside till Chapman returned. I simply dared not re-enter my bedroom alone. Broughton roused himself and said that he would come with me. Mrs. Broughton agreed to remain in her own room for five minutes if the blinds were drawn up and all the doors left open.

"So Broughton and I, leaning stiffly one against the other, went down to my room. By the morning light that filtered past the blinds we could see our way, and I released the blinds. There was nothing wrong with the room from end to end, except smears of my own blood on the end of the bed, on the sofa, and on the carpet where I had torn the thing to pieces."

Colvin had finished his story. There was nothing to say. Seven bells stuttered out from the fo'c'sle, and the answering cry wailed through the darkness. I took him downstairs.

"Of course I am much better now, but it is a kindness of you to let me sleep in your cabin."

A CURIOUS DREAM

Containing a Moral

Mark Twain

In spite of having virtually no formal education, Mark Twain—whose real name was Samuel Clemens—went on to become one of America's greatest authors. William Faulkner labeled him "the father of American literature." Twain's classic works include "The Celebrated Jumping Frog of Calaveras County," *The Adventures of Tom Sawyer, The Adventures of Huckleberry Finn, A Connecticut Yankee in King Arthur's Court,* and *Pudd'nhead Wilson.* He came to prominence during a period when America was still strongly divided into North and South, but oddly he was a blend of the two, with a heavy dose of the West thrown in.

After the Civil War broke out, he formed a Confederate militia with some friends, but after two weeks they disbanded—or "resigned," as he called it—and went to the Nevada Territory with his brother, who had just been appointed as secretary to the territory's governor. Here he tried his hand as a prospector and miner. Unsuccessful, he turned to writing and created his pen name, soon becoming America's favorite humorist and an international celebrity. He remains tremendously popular today.

In this story he writes about some very unhappy corpses.

◆　◆　◆

Night before last I had a singular dream. I seemed to be sitting on a doorstep—in no particular city perhaps—ruminating, and the time of night appeared to be about twelve or one o'clock. The weather was balmy and delicious. There was no human sound in the air, not even a footstep. There was no sound of any kind to emphasize the dead stillness, except the occasional hollow barking of a dog in the distance and the fainter answer of a further dog. Presently up the street I heard a bony clack-clacking, and guessed it was the castanets of a serenading party. In a minute more a tall skeleton, hooded, and half-clad in a tattered and moldy shroud, whose shreds were flapping about the ribby lattice-work of its person, swung by me with a stately stride, and disappeared in the grey gloom of the starlight. It had a broken and worm-eaten coffin on its shoulder and a bundle of something in its hand. I knew what the clack-clacking was then; it was this party's joints working together, and his elbows knocking against his sides as he walked. I may say I was surprised. Before I could collect my thoughts and enter upon any speculations as to what this apparition might portend, I heard another one coming—for I recognized his clack-clack. He had two-thirds of a coffin on his shoulder, and some foot- and headboards under his arm. I mightily wanted to peer under his hood and speak to him, but when he turned and smiled upon me with his cavernous sockets and his projecting grin as he went by, I thought I would not detain him. He was hardly gone when I heard the clacking again, and another one issued from the shadowy half-light. This one was bending under a heavy gravestone, and dragging a shabby coffin after him by a string. When he got to me he gave me a steady look for a moment or two, and then rounded to and backed up to me, saying, "Ease this down for a fellow, will you?"

I eased the gravestone down till it rested on the ground, and in doing so noticed that it bore the name of "John Baxter Copmanhurst," with "May 1839," as the date of his death. Deceased sat wearily down by me, and wiped his os frontis with his major maxillary—chiefly from former habit I judged, for I could not see that he brought away any perspiration.

"It is too bad, too bad," said he, drawing the remnant of the shroud about him and leaning his jaw pensively on his hand. Then he put his left foot up on his knee and fell to scratching his ankle bone absently with a rusty nail which he got out of his coffin.

"What is too bad, friend?"

"Oh, everything, everything. I almost wish I never had died."

"You surprise me. Why do you say this? Has anything gone wrong? What is the matter?"

"Matter! Look at this shroud—rags. Look at this gravestone, all battered up. Look at that disgraceful old coffin. All a man's property going to ruin and destruction before his eyes, and ask him if anything is wrong? Fire and brimstone!"

"Calm yourself, calm yourself," I said. "It *is* too bad—it is certainly too bad, but then I had not supposed that you would much mind such matters, situated as you are."

"Well, my dear sir, I *do* mind them. My pride is hurt, and my comfort is impaired—destroyed, I might say. I will state my case—I will put it to you in such a way that you can comprehend it, if you will let me," said the poor skeleton, tilting the hood of his shroud back, as if he were clearing for action, and thus unconsciously giving himself a jaunty and festive air very much at variance with the grave character of his position in life—so to speak—and in prominent contrast with his distressful mood.

"Proceed," said I.

"I reside in the shameful old graveyard a block or two above you here, in this street—there, now, I just expected that cartilage would let go!—third rib from the bottom, friend, hitch the end of it to my spine with a string, if you have got such a thing about you, though a bit of silver wire is a deal pleasanter, and more durable and becoming, if one keeps it polished—to think of shredding out and going to pieces in this way, just on account of the indifference and neglect of one's posterity!"— and the poor ghost grated his teeth in a way that gave me a wrench and a shiver—for the effect is mightily increased by the absence of muffling flesh and cuticle. "I reside in that old graveyard, and have for these thirty years; and I tell you things are changed since I first laid this old tired frame there, and turned over, and stretched out for a long sleep, with a delicious sense upon me of being *done* with bother, and grief, and anxiety, and doubt, and fear, for ever and ever, and listening with comfortable and increasing satisfaction to the sexton's work, from the startling clatter of his first spadeful on my coffin till it dulled away to the faint patting that shaped the roof of my new home—delicious! My! I wish you could try it tonight!" and out of my reverie deceased fetched me with a rattling slap with a bony hand.

"Yes, sir, thirty years ago I laid me down there, and was happy. For it was out in the country, then—out in the breezy, flowery, grand old woods, and the lazy winds gossiped with the leaves, and the squirrels capered over us and around us, and the creeping things visited us, and the birds filled the tranquil solitude with music. Ah, it was worth ten years of a man's life to be dead then!

"Everything was pleasant. I was in a good neighborhood, for all the dead people that lived near me belonged to the best families in the city. Our posterity appeared to think the world of us.

"They kept our graves in the very best condition; the fences were always in faultless repair, headboards were kept painted or whitewashed, and were replaced with new ones as soon as they began to look rusty or decayed; monuments were kept upright, railings intact and bright, the rosebushes and shrubbery trimmed, trained, and free from blemish, the walks clean and smooth and graveled. But that day is gone by. Our descendants have forgotten us. My grandson lives in a stately house built with money made by these old hands of mine, and I sleep in a neglected grave with invading vermin that gnaw my shroud to build them nests withal! I and friends that lie with me founded and secured the prosperity of this fine city, and the stately bantling of our loves leaves us to rot in a dilapidated cemetery which neighbors curse and strangers scoff at. See the difference between the old time and this—for instance: Our graves are all caved in, now; our headboards have rotted away and tumbled down; our railings reel this way and that with one foot in the air, after a fashion of unseemly levity; our monuments lean wearily, and our gravestones bow their heads discouraged; there be no adornments any more—no roses, nor shrubs, nor graveled walks, nor anything that is a comfort to the eye; and even the paintless old board fence that did make a show of holding us sacred from companionship with beasts and the defilement of heedless feet, has tottered till it overhangs the street, and only advertises the presence of our dismal resting-place and invites yet more derision to it. And now we cannot hide our poverty and tatters in the friendly woods, for the city has stretched its withering arms abroad and taken us in, and all that remains of the cheer of our old home is the cluster of lugubrious forest trees that stand, bored and weary of a city life, with their feet in our coffins, looking into the hazy distance and wishing they were there. I tell you it is disgraceful!

"You begin to comprehend—you begin to see how it is. While our descendants are living sumptuously on our money, right around us in the city, we have to fight hard to keep skull and bones together. Bless you, there isn't a grave in our cemetery that doesn't leak—not one. Every time it rains in the night we have to climb out and roost in the trees—and sometimes we are wakened suddenly by the chilly water trickling down the back of our necks. Then I tell you there is a general heaving up of old graves and kicking over of old monuments, and scampering of old skeletons for the trees! Bless me, if you had gone along there some such nights after twelve you might have seen as many as fifteen of us roosting on one limb, with our joints rattling drearily and the wind wheezing through our ribs! Many a time we have perched there for three or four dreary hours, and then come down, stiff and chilled through and drowsy, and borrowed each other's skulls to bale out our graves with—if you will glance up in my mouth, now as I tilt my head back, you can see that my head-piece is half full of old dry sediment—how top-heavy and stupid it makes me sometimes! Yes, sir, many a time if you had happened to come along just before the dawn you'd have caught us baling out the graves and hanging our shrouds on the fence to dry. Why, I had an elegant shroud stolen from there one morning—think a party by the name of Smith took it, that resides in a plebeian graveyard over yonder—I think so because the first time I ever saw him he hadn't anything on but a check-shirt, and the last time I saw him, which was at a social gathering in the new cemetery, he was the best dressed corpse in the company—and it is a significant fact that he left when he saw me; and presently an old woman from here missed her coffin—she generally took it with her when she went anywhere, because she was liable to take cold and bring on the spasmodic rheumatism that originally killed her if she exposed herself to the night air much. She was named Hotchkiss—Anna Matilda Hotchkiss—you might know her? She has two upper front teeth, is tall, but a good deal inclined to stoop, one rib on the left side gone, has one shred of rusty hair hanging from the left side of her head, and one little tuft just above and a little forward of her right ear, has her under jaw wired on one side where it had worked loose, small bone of left forearm gone—lost in a fight—has a kind of swagger in her gait and a 'gallus' way of going with her arms akimbo and her nostrils in the air—has been pretty free and easy, and is all damaged and battered up till she looks like a queensware crate in ruins—maybe you have met her?"

"God forbid!" I involuntarily ejaculated, for somehow I was not looking for that form of question, and it caught me a little off my guard. But I hastened to make amends for my rudeness, and say, "I simply meant I had not had the honor—for I would not deliberately speak discourteously of a friend of yours. You were saying that you were robbed—and it was a shame, too—but it appears by what is left of the shroud you have on that it was a costly one in its day. How did—"

A most ghastly expression began to develop among the decayed features and shriveled integuments of my guest's face, and I was beginning to grow uneasy and distressed, when he told me he was only working up a deep, sly smile, with a wink in it, to suggest that about the time he acquired his present garment a ghost in a neighboring cemetery missed one. This reassured me, but I begged him to confine himself to speech thenceforth, because his facial expression was uncertain. Even with the most elaborate care it was liable to miss fire. Smiling should especially be avoided. What *he* might honestly consider a shining success was likely to strike me in a very different light. I said I liked to see a skeleton cheerful, even decorously playful, but I did not think smiling was a skeleton's best hold.

"Yes, friend," said the poor skeleton, "the facts are just as I have given them to you. Two of these old graveyards—the one that I resided in and one further along—have been deliberately neglected by our descendants of today until there is no occupying them any longer. Aside from the osteological discomfort of it—and that is no light matter this rainy weather—the present state of things is ruinous to property. We have got to move or be content to see our effects wasted away and utterly destroyed. Now, you will hardly believe it, but it is true, nevertheless, that there isn't a single coffin in good repair among all my acquaintance—now that is an absolute fact. I do not refer to low people who come in a pine box mounted on an express wagon, but I am talking about your high-toned, silver mounted burial-case, your monumental sort, that travel under black plumes at the head of a procession and have choice of cemetery lots—I mean folks like the Jarvises, and the Bledsoes and Burlings, and such. They are all about ruined. The most substantial people in our set, they were. And now look at them—utterly used up and poverty-stricken. One of the Bledsoes actually traded his monument to a late bar-keeper for some fresh shavings to put under his head. I tell you it speaks volumes, for there is nothing a corpse takes so much pride in as his monument. He loves to read the inscription. He comes after awhile to believe what it says himself, and then you may see him sitting on the fence night after night enjoying it. Epitaphs are cheap, and they do a poor chap a world of good after he is dead, especially if he had hard luck while he was alive. I wish they were used more. Now, I don't complain, but confidentially I *do* think it was a little shabby in my descendants to give me nothing but this old slab of a gravestone—and all the more that there isn't a compliment on it. It used to have

GONE TO HIS JUST REWARD

on it, and I was proud when I first saw it, but by-and-by I noticed that whenever an old friend of mine came along he would hook his chin on the railing and pull a long face and read along down till he came to that, and then he would chuckle to himself and walk off, looking satisfied and comfortable. So I scratched it off to get rid of those fools. But a dead man always takes a deal of pride in his monument. Yonder goes half-a-dozen of the Jarvises, now, with the family monument along. And Smithers and some hired specters went by with his a while ago. Hello, Higgins, goodbye, old friend! That's Meredith Higgins—died in '44— belongs to our set in the cemetery—fine old family—great-grandmother was an Injun—I am on the most familiar terms with him—he didn't hear me was the reason he didn't answer me. And I am sorry, too, because I would have liked to introduce you. You would admire him. He is the most disjointed, swaybacked, and generally distorted old skeleton you ever saw, but he is full of fun. When he laughs it sounds like rasping two stones together, and he always starts it off with a cheery screech like raking a nail across a window-pane. Hey, Jones! That is old Columbus Jones—shroud cost four hundred dollars—entire trousseau, including monument, twenty-seven hundred. This was in the spring of '26. It was enormous style for those days. Dead people came all the way from the Alleghenies to see his things—the party that occupied the grave next to mine remembers it well. Now do you see that individual going along with a piece of a headboard under his arm, one leg-bone below his knee gone, and not a thing in the world on? That is Barstow Dalhousie and next to Columbus Jones he was the most sumptuously outfitted person that ever entered our cemetery.

"We are all leaving. We cannot tolerate the treatment we are receiving at the hands of our descendants. They open new cemeteries, but they leave us to our ignominy. They mend the streets, but they never mend anything that is about us or belongs to us. Look at that coffin of mine—yet I tell you in its day it was a piece of furniture that would have attracted attention in any drawing-room in this city. You may have it if you want it—I can't afford to repair it. Put a new bottom in her, and part of a new top, and a bit of fresh lining along the left side, and you'll find her about as comfortable as any receptacle of her species you ever tried. No thanks—no, don't mention it—you have been civil to me, and I would give you all the property I have got before I would seem ungrateful. Now this winding-sheet is a kind of a sweet thing in its way, if you would like to—No? Well, just as you say, but I wished to be fair and liberal—there's nothing mean about *me*. Goodbye, friend, I must be going. I may have a good way to go tonight—don't know. I only know one thing for certain, and that is, that I am on the emigrant trail, now, and I'll never sleep in that crazy old cemetery again. I will travel till I find respectable quarters, if I have to hoof it to New Jersey. All the boys are going. It was decided in public conclave, last night, to emigrate, and by the time the sun rises there won't be a bone left in our old habitations. Such cemeteries may suit my surviving friends, but they do not suit the remains that have the honor to make these remarks. My opinion is the general opinion. If you doubt it, go and see how the departing ghosts upset things before they started. They were almost riotous in their demonstrations of distaste. Hello, here are some of the Bledsoes, and if you will give me a lift with this tombstone I guess I will join company and jog along with them—mighty respectable old family, the Bledsoes, and used to always come out in six-horse hearses, and all that sort of thing fifty years ago when I walked these streets in daylight. Goodbye, friend."

And with his gravestone on his shoulder he joined the grisly procession, dragging his damaged coffin after him, for notwithstanding he pressed it upon me so earnestly, I utterly refused his hospitality. I suppose that for as much as two hours these sad outcasts went clacking by, laden with their dismal effects, and all that time I sat pitying them. One or two of the youngest and least dilapidated among them inquired about midnight trains on the railways, but the rest seemed unacquainted with that mode of travel, and merely asked about common public roads to various towns and cities, some of which are not on the map now, and vanished from it and from the earth as much as thirty years ago, and some few of them never *had* existed anywhere but on maps, and private ones in real estate agencies at that. And they asked about the condition of the cemeteries in these towns and cities, and about the reputation the citizens bore as to reverence for the dead.

This whole matter interested me deeply, and likewise compelled my sympathy for these homeless ones. And it all seeming real, and I not knowing it was a dream, I mentioned to one shrouded wanderer an idea that had entered my head to publish an account of this curious and very sorrowful exodus, but said also that I could not describe it truthfully, and just as it occurred, without seeming to trifle with a grave subject and exhibit an irreverence for the dead that would shock and distress their surviving friends. But this bland and stately remnant of a former citizen leaned him far over my gate and whispered in my ear, and said, "Do not let that disturb you. The community that can stand such grave-yards as those we are emigrating from can stand anything a body can say about the neglected and forsaken dead that lie in them."

At that very moment a cock crowed, and the weird procession vanished and left not a shred or a bone behind. I awoke, and found myself lying with my head out of the bed and "sagging" downwards considerably—a position favorable to dreaming dreams with morals in them, maybe, but not poetry.

NOTE—The reader is assured that if the cemeteries in his town are kept in good order, this Dream is not leveled at his town at all, but is leveled particularly and venomously at the *next* town.

THE STORY OF BAELBROW

E. and H. Heron

E. and H. Heron were pseudonyms for Hesketh Prichard and his mother, Katherine Prichard. Hesketh was an adventurer, an explorer, a big-game hunter, and a major in the British Army who founded a training school for snipers. He was also a journalist and an author. When writing fiction, he often worked with his mother. Hesketh actually did most of the writing, while Kate polished things up and made suggestions. One of their more popular creations was Flaxman Low, who is featured in this story. Flaxman Low is a scientist who investigates paranormal phenomena; sort of a Sherlock Holmes of the supernatural.

◆ ◆ ◆

It is a matter for regret that so many of Mr. Flaxman Low's reminiscences should deal with the darker episodes of his career. Yet this is almost unavoidable, as the more purely scientific and less strongly marked cases would not, perhaps, contain the same elements of interest for the general public however valuable and instructive they might be to the expert student. It has also been considered better to choose the completer cases, those that ended in something like satisfactory proof, rather than the many instances where the thread broke abruptly amongst surmisings, which it was never possible to subject to convincing tests.

North of a low-lying strip of country on the East Anglian coast, the promontory of Bael Ness thrusts a blunt nose into the sea. On the ness, backed by pinewoods, stands a square, comfortable stone mansion, known to the countryside as Baelbrow. It has faced the east winds for close upon three hundred years, and during the whole period has been the home of the Swaffam family, who were never in any wise put out of conceit of their ancestral dwelling by the fact that it had always been haunted. Indeed, the Swaffams were proud of the Baelbrow Ghost, which enjoyed a wide notoriety, and no one dreamt of complaining of its behavior until Professor Jungvort, of Nuremberg, laid information against it, and sent an urgent appeal for help to Mr. Flaxman Low.

The Professor, who was well acquainted with Mr. Low, detailed the circumstances of his tenancy of Baelbrow, and the unpleasant events that had followed thereupon.

It appeared that Mr. Swaffam, senior, who spent a large portion of his time abroad, had offered to lend his house to the Professor for the summer season. When the Jungvorts arrived at Baelbrow, they were charmed with the place. The prospect, though not very varied, was at least extensive, and the air exhilarating. Also the Professor's daughter enjoyed frequent visits from her betrothed—Harold Swaffam—and the Professor was delightfully employed in overhauling the Swaffam library.

The Jungvorts had been duly told of the ghost, which lent distinction to the old house, but never in any way interfered with the comfort of the inmates. For some time they found this description to be strictly true, but with the beginning of October came a change. Up to this time and as far back as the Swaffam annals reached, the ghost had been a shadow, a rustle, a passing sigh—nothing definite or troublesome. But early in October strange things began to occur, and the terror culminated when a housemaid was found dead in a corridor three weeks later. Upon this the Professor felt that it was time to send for Flaxman Low.

Mr. Low arrived upon a chilly evening when the house was already beginning to blur in the purple twilight, and the resinous scent of the pines came sweetly on the land breeze. Jungvort welcomed him in the spacious, fire-lit hall. He was a stout German with a quantity of white hair, round eyes emphasized by spectacles, and a kindly, dreamy face. His life-study was philology, and his two relaxations: chess and the smoking of a big Bismarck-bowled meerschaum.

"Now, Professor," said Mr. Low when they had settled themselves in the smoking-room, "how did it all begin?"

"I will tell you," replied Jungvort, thrusting out his chin, and tapping his broad chest, and speaking as if an unwarrantable liberty had been taken with him. "First of all, it has shown itself to me!"

Mr. Flaxman Low smiled and assured him that nothing could be more satisfactory.

"But not at all satisfactory!" exclaimed the Professor. "I was sitting here alone, it might have been midnight—when I hear something come creeping like a little dog with its nails, tick-tick, upon the oak flooring of the hall. I whistle, for I think it is the little 'Rags' of my daughter, and afterwards opened the door, and I saw"—he hesitated and looked hard at Low through his spectacles—"something that was just disappearing into the passage which connects the two wings of the house. It was a figure, not unlike the human figure, but narrow and straight. I fancied I saw a bunch of black hair, and a flutter of something detached, which may have been a handkerchief. I was overcome by a feeling of repulsion. I heard a few, clicking steps, then it stopped, as I thought, at the Museum door. Come, I will show you the spot."

The Professor conducted Mr. Low into the hall. The main staircase, dark and massive, yawned above them, and directly behind it ran the passage referred to by the Professor. It was over twenty feet long, and about midway led past a deep arch containing a door reached by two steps. Jungvort explained that this door formed the entrance to a large room called the Museum, in which Mr. Swaffam senior, who was something of a dilettante, stored the various curios he picked up during his excursions abroad. The Professor went on to say that he immediately followed the figure, which he believed had gone into the Museum, but he found nothing there except the cases containing Swaffam's treasures.

"I mentioned my experience to no one. I concluded that I had seen the ghost. But two days after, one of the female servants, coming through the passage in the dark, declared that a man leapt out at her from the embrasure of the Museum door, but she released herself and ran screaming into the servants' hall. We at once made a search but found nothing to substantiate her story.

"I took no notice of this, though it coincided pretty well with my own experience. The week after, my daughter Lena came down late one night for a book. As she was about to cross the hall, something leapt upon her from behind and she fainted! Since then she has been ill and the doctor says 'run down.'" Here the Professor spread out his hands. "So she leaves for a change tomorrow. Since then other members of the household have been attacked in much the same manner, with always the same result, they faint and are weak and useless when they recover.

"But, last Wednesday, the affair became a tragedy. By that time the servants had refused to come through the passage except in a crowd of three or four—most of them preferring to go round by the terrace to reach this part of the house. But one maid, named Eliza Freeman, said she was not afraid of the Baelbrow Ghost, and undertook to put out the lights in the hall one night. When she had done, and was returning through the passage past the Museum door, she appears to have been attacked, or at any rate frightened. In the grey of the morning they found her lying beside the steps dead. There was a little blood upon her sleeve but no mark upon her body except a small raised pustule under the ear. The doctor said the girl was extraordinarily anemic, and that she probably died from fright, her heart being weak. I was surprised at this, for she had always seemed to be a particularly strong and active young woman."

"Can I see Miss Jungvort tomorrow before she goes?" asked Low, as the Professor signified he had nothing more to tell.

The Professor was rather unwilling that his daughter should be questioned, but he at last gave his permission, and next morning Low had a short talk with the girl before she left the house. He found her a very pretty girl, though listless and startlingly pale, and with a frightened stare in her light brown eyes. Mr. Low asked if she could describe her assailant.

"No," she answered, "I could not see him, for he was behind me. I only saw a dark, bony hand, with shining nails, and a bandaged arm pass just under my eyes before I fainted."

"Bandaged arm? I have heard nothing of this."

"Tut-tut, mere fancy!" put in the Professor impatiently.

"I saw the bandages on the arm," repeated the girl, turning her head wearily away, "and I smelt the antiseptics it was dressed with."

"You have hurt your neck," remarked Mr. Low, who noticed a small circular patch of pink under her ear.

She flushed and paled, raising her hand to her neck with a nervous jerk, as she said in a low voice, "It has almost killed me. Before he touched me, I knew he was there! I felt it!"

When they left her the Professor apologized for the unreliability of her evidence, and pointed out the discrepancy between her statement and his own.

"She says she sees nothing but an arm, yet I tell you it had no arms! Preposterous! Conceive a wounded man entering this house to frighten the young women! I do not know what to make of it! Is it a man, or is it the Baelbrow Ghost?"

During the afternoon when Mr. Low and the Professor returned from a stroll on the shore, they found a dark-browed young man with a bull neck, and strongly marked features, standing sullenly before the hall fire. The Professor presented him to Mr. Low as Harold Swaffam. Swaffam seemed to be about thirty, but was already known as a far-seeing and successful member of the Stock Exchange.

"I am pleased to meet you, Mr. Low," he began, with a keen

glance, "though you don't look sufficiently high-strung for one of your profession."

Mr. Low merely bowed.

"Come, you don't defend your craft against my insinuations?" went on Swaffam. "And so you have come to rout out our poor old ghost from Baelbrow? You forget that he is an heirloom, a family possession! What's this about his having turned rabid, eh, Professor?" he ended, wheeling round upon Jungvort in his brusque way.

The Professor told the story over again. It was plain that he stood rather in awe of his prospective son-in-law.

"I heard much the same from Lena, whom I met at the station," said Swaffam. "It is my opinion that the women in this house are suffering from an epidemic of hysteria. You agree with me, Mr. Low?"

"Possibly. Though hysteria could hardly account for Freeman's death."

"I can't say as to that until I have looked further into the particulars," Swaffam continued. "I have not been idle since I arrived. I have examined the Museum. No one has entered it from the outside, and there is no other way of entrance except through the passage. The flooring is laid, I happen to know, on a thick layer of concrete. And there the case for the ghost stands at present." After a few moments of dogged reflection, he swung round on Mr. Low, in a manner that seemed peculiar to him when about to address any person. "What do you say to this plan, Mr. Low? I propose to drive the Professor over to Ferryvale, to stop there for a day or two at the hotel, and I will also dispose of the servants who still remain in the house for, say, forty-eight hours. Meanwhile you and I can try to go further into the secret of the ghost's new pranks?"

Flaxman Low replied that this scheme exactly met his views. But the Professor protested against being sent away. Harold Swaffam however was a man who liked to arrange things in his own fashion, and within forty-five minutes he and Jungvort departed in the dogcart.

The evening was lowering, and Baelbrow, like all houses built in exposed situations, was extremely susceptible to the changes of the weather. Therefore, before many hours were over, the place was full of creaking noises as the screaming gale battered at the shuttered windows, and the tree-branches tapped and groaned against walls.

Harold Swaffam, on his way back, was caught in the storm and drenched to the skin. It was, therefore, settled that after he had changed his clothes he should have a couple of hours' rest on the smoking-room sofa, while Mr. Low kept watch in the hall.

The early part of the night passed over uneventfully. A light burned faintly in the great wainscotted hall, but the passage was dark. There was nothing to be heard but the wild moan and whistle of the wind coming in from the sea, and the squalls of rain dashing against the windows. As the hours advanced, Mr. Low lit a lantern that lay at hand, and, carrying it along the passage, tried the Museum door. It yielded, and the wind came muttering through to meet him. He looked round at the shutters and behind the big cases which held Mr. Swaffam's treasures, to make sure that the room contained no living occupant but himself.

Suddenly he fancied he heard a scraping noise behind him, and turned round, but discovered nothing to account for it. Finally, he laid the lantern on a bench so that its light should fall through the door into the passage, and returned again to the hall, where he put out the lamp, and then once more took up his station by the closed door of the smoking-room.

A long hour passed, during which the wind continued to roar down the wide hall chimney, and the old boards creaked as if furtive footsteps were gathering from every corner of the house. But Flaxman Low heeded none of these; he was waiting for a certain sound.

After a while, he heard it—the cautious scraping of wood on wood. He leant forward to watch the Museum door. Click, click came the curious dog-like tread upon the tiled floor of the Museum till the thing, whatever it was, paused and listened behind the open door. The wind lulled at the moment, and Low listened also, but no further sound was to be heard, only slowly across the broad ray of light falling through the door grew a stealthy shadow.

Again the wind rose, and blew in heavy gusts about the house, till even the flame in the lantern flickered, but when it steadied once more, Flaxman Low saw that the silent form had passed through the door, and was now on the steps outside. He could just make out a dim shadow in the dark angle of the embrasure.

Presently, from the shapeless shadow came a sound Mr. Low was not prepared to hear. The thing sniffed the air with the strong, audible inspiration of a bear, or some large animal. At the same moment, carried on the draughts of the hall, a faint, unfamiliar odor reached his nostrils. Lena Jungvort's words flashed back upon him—this, then, was the creature with the bandaged arm!

Again, as the storm shrieked and shook the windows, a darkness passed across the light. The thing had sprung out from the angle of the door, and Flaxman Low knew that it was making its way towards him through the illusive blackness of the hall. He hesitated for a second; then he opened the smoking-room door.

Harold Swaffam sat up on the sofa, dazed with sleep.

"What has happened? Has it come?"

Low told him what he had just seen. Swaffam listened half-smilingly.

"What do you make of it now?" he said.

"I must ask you to defer that question for a little," replied Low.

"Then you mean me to suppose that you have a theory to fit all these incongruous items?"

"I have a theory, which may be modified by further knowledge," said Low. "Meantime, am I right in concluding from the name of this house that it was built on a barrow or burying-place?"

"You are right, though that has nothing to do with the latest freaks of our ghost," returned Swaffam decidedly.

"I also gather that Mr. Swaffam has lately sent home one of the many cases now lying in the Museum?" went on Mr. Low.

"He sent one, certainly, last September."

"And you have opened it," asserted Low.

"Yes; though I flattered myself I had left no trace of my handiwork."

"I have not examined the cases," said Low. "I inferred that you had done so from other facts."

"Now, one thing more," went on Swaffam, still smiling. "Do you imagine there is any danger—I mean to men like ourselves?"

"Certainly; the gravest danger to any person who moves about this part of the house alone after dark," replied Low.

Harold Swaffam leant back and crossed his legs.

"To go back to the beginning of our conversation, Mr. Low, may I remind you of the various conflicting particulars you will have to reconcile before you can present any decent theory to the world?"

"I am quite aware of that."

"First of all, our original ghost was a mere misty presence, rather guessed at from vague sounds and shadows—now we have something that is tangible, and that can, as we have proof, kill with fright. Next Jungvort declares the thing was a narrow, long and distinctly armless object, while Miss Jungvort has not only seen the arm and hand of a human being, but saw them clearly enough to tell us that the nails were gleaming and the arm bandaged. She also felt its strength. Jungvort, on the other hand, maintained that it clicked along like a dog—you bear out this description with the additional information that it sniffs like a wild beast. Now what can this thing be? It is capable of being seen, smelt, and felt, yet it hides itself successfully in a room where there is no cavity or space sufficient to afford covert to a cat! You still tell me that you believe that you can explain?"

"Most certainly," replied Flaxman Low with conviction.

"I have not the slightest intention or desire to be rude, but as a mere matter of common sense, I must express my opinion plainly. I believe the whole thing to be the result of excited imaginations, and I am about to prove it. Do you think there is any further danger tonight?"

"Very great danger tonight," replied Low.

"Very well, as I said, I am going to prove it. I will ask you to allow me to lock you up in one of the distant rooms, where I can get no help from you, and I will pass the remainder of the night walking about the passage and hall in the dark. That should give proof one way or the other."

"You can do so if you wish, but I must at least beg to be allowed to look on. I will leave the house and watch what goes on from the window in the passage, which I saw opposite the Museum door. You cannot, in all fairness, refuse to let me be a witness."

"I cannot, of course," returned Swaffam. "Still, the night is too bad to turn a dog out into, and I warn you that I shall lock you out."

"That will not matter. Lend me a macintosh, and leave the lantern lit in the Museum, where I placed it."

Swaffam agreed to this. Mr. Low gives a graphic account of what followed. He left the house and was duly locked out, and after groping his way round the house, found himself at length outside the window of the passage, which was almost opposite to the door of the Museum. The door was still ajar and a thin band of light cut out into the gloom. Further down the hall gaped black and void. Low, sheltering himself as well as he could from the rain, waited for Swaffam's appearance. Was the terrible yellow watcher balancing itself upon its lean legs in the dim corner opposite, ready to spring out with its deadly strength upon the passer-by?

Presently Low heard a door bang inside the house, and the next moment Swaffam appeared with a candle in his hand, an isolated spread of weak rays against the vast darkness behind. He advanced steadily down the passage, his dark face grim and set, and as he came Mr. Low experienced that tingling sensation, which is so often the forerunner of some strange experience. Swaffam passed on towards the other end of the passage. There was a quick vibration of the Museum door as a lean shape with a shrunken head leapt out into the passage after him. Then all together came a hoarse shout, the noise of a fall and utter darkness.

In an instant, Mr. Low had broken the glass, opened the window, and swung himself into the passage. There he lit a match and as it flared he saw by its dim light a picture painted for a second upon the obscurity beyond.

Swaffam's big figure lay with outstretched arms, face downwards, and as Low looked a crouching shape extricated itself from the fallen man, raising a narrow vicious head from his shoulder.

The match spluttered feebly and went out, and Low heard a flying step click on the boards, before he could find the candle Swaffam had dropped. Lighting it, he stooped over Swaffam and turned him on his back. The man's strong color had gone, and the wax-white face looked whiter still against the blackness of hair and brows, and upon his neck under the ear, was a little raised pustule from which a thin line of blood was streaked up to the angle of his cheekbone.

Some instinctive feeling prompted Low to glance up at this moment. Half extended from the Museum doorway were a face and bony neck— a high-nosed, dull-eyed, malignant face, the eye-sockets hollow, and the darkened teeth showing. Low plunged his hand into his pocket, and a shot rang out in the echoing passageway and hall. The wind sighed through the broken panes, a ribbon of stuff fluttered along the polished flooring, and that was all, as Flaxman Low half dragged, half carried Swaffam into the smoking-room.

It was some time before Swaffam recovered consciousness. He listened to Low's story of how he had found him with a red angry gleam in his somber eyes.

"The ghost has scored off me," he said with an odd, sullen laugh, "but now I fancy it's my turn! But before we adjourn to the Museum to examine the place, I will ask you to let me hear your notion of things. You have been right in saying there was real danger. For myself I can only tell you that I felt something spring upon me, and I knew no more. Had this not happened I am afraid I should never have asked you a second time what your idea of the matter might be," he ended with a sort of sulky frankness.

"There are two main indications," replied Low. "This strip of yellow bandage, which I have just now picked up from the passage floor, and the mark on your neck."

"What's that you say?" Swaffam rose quickly and examined his neck in a small glass beside the mantelshelf.

"Connect those two, and I think I can leave you to work it out for yourself," said Low.

"Pray let us have your theory in full," requested Swaffam shortly.

"Very well," answered Low good-humouredly—he thought Swaffam's annoyance natural under the circumstances. "The long, narrow figure which seemed to the Professor to be armless is developed on the next occasion. For Miss Jungvort sees a bandaged arm and a dark hand with gleaming—which means, of course, gilded—nails. The clicking sound of the footstep coincides with these particulars, for we know that sandals made of strips of leather are not uncommon in company with gilt nails and bandages. Old and dry leather would naturally click upon your polished floors."

"Bravo, Mr. Low! So you mean to say that this house is haunted by a mummy!"

"That is my idea, and all I have seen confirms me in my opinion."

"To do you justice, you held this theory before tonight—before, in fact, you had seen anything for yourself. You gathered that my father had sent home a mummy, and you went on to conclude that I had opened the case."

"Yes. I imagine you took off most of, or rather all, the outer bandages, thus leaving the limbs free, wrapped only in the inner bandages which were swathed round each separate limb. I fancy this mummy was preserved by the Theban method with aromatic spices which left the skin olive-colored, dry and flexible, like tanned leather, the features remaining distinct, and the hair, teeth and eyebrows perfect."

"So far, good," said Swaffam. "But now, how about the intermittent vitality? The pustule on the neck of those whom it attacks? And where is our old Baelbrow Ghost to come in?"

Swaffam tried to speak in a rallying tone, but his excitement and lowering temper were visible enough, in spite of the attempts he made to suppress them.

"To begin at the beginning," said Flaxman Low, "everybody who, in a rational and honest manner, investigates the phenomena of spiritism will, sooner or later, meet in them some perplexing element, which is not to be explained by any of the ordinary theories. For reasons into which I need not now enter, this present case appears to me to be one of these. I am led to believe that the ghost which has for so many years given dim and vague manifestations of its existence in this house is a vampire."

Swaffam threw back his head with an incredulous gesture.

"We no longer live in the middle ages, Mr. Low! And besides how could a vampire come here?" he said scoffingly.

"It is held by some authorities on these subjects that under certain conditions a vampire may be self-created. You tell me that this house is built upon an ancient barrow, in fact, on a spot where we might naturally expect to find such an elemental psychic germ. In those dead human systems were contained all the seeds for good and evil. The power which causes these psychic seeds or germs to grow is thought, and from being long dwelt on and indulged, a thought might finally gain a mysterious vitality, which could go increasing more and more by attracting to itself suitable and appropriate elements from its environment. For a long period this germ remained a helpless intelligence, awaiting the opportunity to assume some material form, by means of which to carry out its desires. The invisible is the real; the material only subserves its manifestation. The impalpable reality already existed, when you provided for it a physical medium for action by unwrapping the mummy's form. Now, we can only judge of the nature of the germ by its manifestation through matter. Here we have every indication of a vampire intelligence touching into life and energy the dead human frame. Hence the mark on the neck of its victims, and their bloodless and anemic condition. For a vampire, as you know, sucks blood."

Swaffam rose, and took up the lamp.

"Now, for proof," he said bluntly. "Wait a second, Mr. Low. You say you fired at this appearance?" And he took up the pistol which Low had laid down on the table.

"Yes, I aimed at a small portion of its foot which I saw on the step."

Without more words, and with the pistol still in his hand, Swaffam led the way to the Museum.

The wind howled round the house, and the darkness, which precedes the dawn, lay upon the world, when the two men looked upon one of the strangest sights it has ever been given to men to shudder at.

Half in and half out of an oblong wooden box in a corner of the great room, lay a lean shape in its rotten yellow bandages, the scraggy neck surmounted by a mop of frizzled hair. The toe strap of a sandal and a portion of the right foot had been shot away.

Swaffam, with a working face, gazed down at it, then seizing it by its tearing bandages, he flung it into the box, where it fell into life-like posture, its wide, moist-lipped mouth gaping up at them.

For a moment Swaffam stood over the thing; then with a curse he raised the revolver and shot into the grinning face again and again with a deliberate vindictiveness. Finally he rammed the thing down into the box, and clubbing the weapon, smashed the head into fragments with a vicious energy that colored the whole horrible scene with a suggestion of murder done.

Then, turning to Low, he said, "Help me to fasten the cover on it."

"Are you going to bury it?"

"No, we must rid the earth of it," he answered savagely. "I'll put it into the old canoe and burn it."

The rain had ceased when in the daybreak they carried the old canoe down to the shore. In it they placed the mummy case with its ghastly occupant, and piled logs about it. The sail was raised and the pile lighted, and Low and Swaffam watched it creep out on the ebb-tide, at first a twinkling spark, then a flare of waving fire, until far out to sea the history of that dead thing ended 3,000 years after the priests of Amen had laid it to rest in its appointed pyramid.

THE HERO OF THE TOMB

Sir Walter Scott

Sir Walter Scott is one of Scotland's most famous authors. He is credited as the inventor of the historical novel and the first to portray peasant characters sympathetically and realistically. His works include *Ivanhoe, Rob Roy, Woodstock,* and the story-poem *The Lady of the Lake.* It's said he was the first English-language author to achieve international success. His death in 1832 marks the end of the Romantic Age of English literature.

Scott was very interested in folk tales, myths, and legends. This one is from his book *Letters on Demonology and Witchcraft.* He said his source was *Gesta Danorum* by Danish historian Saxo Grammaticus (c. 1150–1220).

✦ ✦ ✦

To incur the highest extremity of danger became accounted a proof of that insuperable valor for which every Northman desired to be famed; and their annals afford numerous instances of encounters with ghosts, witches, furies, and fiends, whom the Kiempe, or champions, compelled to submit to their mere mortal strength, and yield to their service the weapons or other treasures which they guarded in their tombs.

The Norsemen were the more prone to these superstitions, because it was a favorite fancy of theirs that, in many instances, the change from life to death altered the temper of the human spirit from benignant to malevolent; or perhaps, that when the soul left the body, its departure was occasionally supplied by a wicked demon, who took the opportunity to enter and occupy its late habitation. Upon such a supposition the wild fiction that follows is probably grounded; which, extravagant as it is, possesses something striking to the imagination.

Saxo Grammaticus tells us of the fame of two Norse princes or chiefs, who had formed what was called a brotherhood in arms, implying not only the firmest friendship and constant support during all the adventures which they should undertake in life, but binding them by a solemn compact, that after the death of either, the survivor should descend alive into the sepulcher of his brother in arms, and consent to be buried along with him. The task of fulfilling this dreadful compact fell upon Asmund, his companion, Assueit, having been slain in battle.

The tomb was formed after the ancient northern custom in what was called the age of hills, that is, when it was usual to bury persons of distinguished merit or rank on some conspicuous spot, which was crowned with a mound. With this purpose a deep narrow vault was constructed, to be the apartment of the future tomb, over which the sepulchral heap was to be piled. Here they deposited arms, trophies, poured forth, perhaps, the blood of victims, introduced into the tomb the warhorses of the champions, and when these rites had been duly paid, the body of Assueit was placed in the dark and narrow house, while his faithful brother in arms entered and sat down by the corpse, without a word or look which testified regret or unwillingness to fulfill his fearful engagement.

The soldiers who had witnessed this singular interment of the dead and living, rolled a huge stone to the mouth of the tomb, and piled so much earth and stones above the spot as made a mound visible from a great distance, and then, with loud lamentation for the loss of such undaunted leaders, they dispersed themselves like a flock which has lost its shepherd.

Years passed away after years, and a century had elapsed, ere a noble Swedish rover, bound upon some high adventure, and supported by a gallant band of followers, arrived in the valley which took its name from the tomb of the brethren in arms.

The story was told to the strangers, whose leader determined on opening the sepulcher, partly because, as already hinted, it was reckoned a heroic action to brave the anger of departed heroes by violating their tombs; partly to attain the arms and swords of proof with which the deceased had done their great actions.

He set his soldiers to work, and soon removed the earth and stones from one side of the mound, and laid bare the entrance. But the stoutest of the rovers started back, when, instead of the silence of a tomb, they heard within horrid cries, the clash of swords, the clang of armor, and all the noise of a mortal combat between two furious champions.

A young warrior was let down into the profound tomb by a cord, which was drawn up shortly after, in hopes of news from beneath. But when the adventurer descended, someone threw him from the cord, and took his place in the noose. When the rope was pulled up, the soldiers, instead of their companion, beheld Asmund, the survivor of the brethren in arms.

He rushed into the open air, his sword drawn in his hand, his armor half torn from his body, the left side of his face almost scratched off, as by the talons of some wild beast. He had no sooner appeared in the light of day, than, with the improvisatory poetic talent, which these champions often united with heroic-strength and bravery, he poured forth a string of verses containing the history of his hundred years' conflict within the tomb.

It seems that no sooner was the sepulcher closed than the corpse of the slain Assueit arose from the ground, inspired by some ravenous ghoul, and having first torn to pieces and devoured the horses which had been entombed with them, threw himself upon the companion who had just given him such a sign of devoted friendship, in order to treat him in the same manner.

The hero, no way discountenanced by the horrors of his situation, took to his arms, and defended himself manfully against Assueit, or rather against the evil demon who tenanted that champion's body. In this manner the living brother waged a preternatural combat, which had endured during a whole century, when Asmund, at last obtaining the victory, prostrated his enemy, and by driving, as he boasted, a stake through his body, had finally reduced him to the state of quiet becoming a tenant of the tomb.

Having chanted the triumphant account of his contest and victory, this mangled conqueror fell dead before them. The body of Assueit was taken out of the tomb, burnt, and the ashes dispersed to heaven; while that of the victor, now lifeless, and without a companion, was deposited there, so that it was hoped his slumbers might remain undisturbed.

The precautions taken against Assueit's reviving a second time, remind us of those adopted in the Greek islands, and in the Turkish provinces, against the Vampire. It affords also a derivation of the ancient English law in case of suicide, when a stake was driven through the body, originally to keep it secure in the tomb.

THE CROSS-ROADS

Amy Lowell

Amy Lowell was an American Imagist poet who posthumously won a Pulitzer Prize. She was a major champion of free verse, and because she often didn't use line breaks, much of her poetry looks like prose. She called it "polyphonic prose" and this remarkable vampire poem is an excellent example.

◆　◆　◆

A bullet through his heart at dawn. On the table a letter signed with a woman's name. A wind that goes howling round the house, and weeping as in shame. Cold November dawn peeping through the windows, cold dawn creeping over the floor, creeping up his cold legs, creeping over his cold body, creeping across his cold face. A glaze of thin yellow sunlight on the staring eyes. Wind howling through bent branches. A wind which never dies down. Howling, wailing. The gazing eyes glitter in the sunlight. The lids are frozen open and the eyes glitter.

The thudding of a pick on hard earth. A spade grinding and crunching. Overhead, branches writhing, winding, interlacing, unwinding, scattering; tortured twinings, tossings, creakings. Wind flinging branches apart, drawing them together, whispering and whining among them. A waning, lopsided moon cutting through black clouds. A stream of pebbles and earth and the empty spade gleams clear in the moonlight, then is rammed again into the black earth. Tramping of feet. Men and horses. Squeaking of wheels.

"Whoa! Ready, Jim?"

"All ready."

Something falls, settles, is still. Suicides have no coffin.

"Give us the stake, Jim. Now."

Pound! Pound!

"He'll never walk. Nailed to the ground."

An ash stick pierces his heart, if it buds the roots will hold him. He is a part of the earth now, clay to clay. Overhead the branches sway, and writhe, and twist in the wind. He'll never walk with a bullet in his heart, and an ash stick nailing him to the cold, black ground.

Six months he lay still. Six months. And the water welled up in his body, and soft blue spots checkered it. He lay still, for the ash stick held him in place. Six months! Then her face came out of a mist of green. Pink and white and frail like Dresden china, lilies-of-the-valley at her breast, puce-colored silk sheening about her. Under the young green leaves, the horse at a foot-pace, the high yellow wheels of the chaise scarcely turning, her face, rippling like grain a-blowing, under her puce-colored bonnet; and burning beside her, flaming within his correct blue coat and brass buttons, is someone. What has dimmed the sun? The horse steps on a rolling stone; a wind in the branches makes a moan. The little leaves tremble and shake, turn and quake, over and over, tearing their stems. There is a shower of young leaves, and a sudden-sprung gale wails in the trees.

The yellow-wheeled chaise is rocking—rocking, and all the branches are knocking—knocking. The sun in the sky is a flat, red plate, the branches creak and grate. She screams and cowers, for the green foliage is a lowering wave surging to smother her. But she sees nothing. The stake holds firm. The body writhes, the body squirms. The blue spots widen, the flesh tears, but the stake wears well in the deep, black ground. It holds the body in the still, black ground.

Two years! The body has been in the ground two years. It is worn away; it is clay to clay. Where the heart molders, a greenish dust, the stake is thrust. Late August it is, and night; a night flauntingly jeweled with stars, a night of shooting stars and loud insect noises. Down the road to Tilbury, silence—and the slow flapping of large leaves. Down the road to Sutton, silence—and the darkness of heavy-foliaged trees. Down the road to Wayfleet, silence—and the whirring scrape of insects in the branches. Down the road to Edgarstown, silence—and stars like stepping-stones in a pathway overhead. It is very quiet at the cross-roads, and the sign-board points the way down the four roads, endlessly points the way where nobody wishes to go.

A horse is galloping, galloping up from Sutton. Shaking the wide, still leaves as he goes under them. Striking sparks with his iron shoes; silencing the katydids. Dr. Morgan riding to a child-birth over Tilbury way; riding to deliver a woman of her first-born son. One o'clock from Wayfleet bell tower, what a shower of shooting stars! And a breeze all of a sudden, jarring the big leaves and making them jerk up and down. Dr. Morgan's hat is blown from his head, the horse swerves, and curves away from the sign-post. An oath—spurs—a blurring of grey mist. A quick left twist, and the gelding is snorting and racing down the Tilbury road with the wind dropping away behind him.

The stake has wrenched, the stake has started, the body, flesh from flesh, has parted. But the bones hold tight, socket and ball, and clamping them down in the hard, black ground is the stake, wedged through ribs and spine. The bones may twist, and heave, and twine, but the stake holds them still in line. The breeze goes down, and the round stars shine, for the stake holds the fleshless bones in line.

Twenty years now! Twenty long years! The body has powdered itself away; it is clay to clay. It is brown earth mingled with brown earth. Only flaky bones remain, lain together so long they fit, although not one bone is knit to another. The stake is there too, rotted through, but upright still, and still piercing down between ribs and spine in a straight line.

Yellow stillness is on the cross-roads, yellow stillness is on the trees. The leaves hang drooping, wan. The four roads point four yellow ways, saffron and gamboge ribbons to the gaze. A little swirl of dust blows up Tilbury road, the wind which fans it has not strength to do more; it ceases, and the dust settles down. A little whirl of wind comes up Tilbury road. It brings a sound of wheels and feet. The wind reels a moment and faints to nothing under the sign-post. Wind again, wheels and feet louder. Wind again—again—again. A drop of rain, flat into the dust. Drop!—Drop! Thick heavy raindrops, and a shrieking wind bending the great trees and wrenching off their leaves.

Under the black sky, bowed and dripping with rain, up Tilbury road, comes the procession. A funeral procession, bound for the graveyard at Wayfleet. Feet and wheels—feet and wheels. And among them one who is carried.

The bones in the deep, still earth shiver and pull. There is a quiver through the rotted stake. Then stake and bones fall together in a little puffing of dust.

Like meshes of linked steel the rain shuts down behind the procession, now well along the Wayfleet road.

He wavers like smoke in the buffeting wind. His fingers blow out like smoke, his head ripples in the gale. Under the sign-post, in the pouring rain, he stands, and watches another quavering figure drifting down the Wayfleet road. Then swiftly he streams after it. It flickers among the trees. He licks out and winds about them. Over, under, blown, contorted. Spindrift after spindrift; smoke following smoke. There is a wailing through the trees, a wailing of fear, and after it laughter—laughter—laughter, skirling up to the black sky. Lightning jags over the funeral procession. A heavy clap of thunder. Then darkness and rain, and the sound of feet and wheels.

A DEAD LOVE

Lafcadio Hearn

He knew no rest; for all his dreams were haunted by her; and when he sought love, she came as the dead come between the living. So that, weary of his life, he passed away at last in the fevered summer of a tropical city; dying with her name upon his lips. And his face was no more seen in the palm-shadowed streets; but the sun rose and sank as before.

And that vague phantom life, which sometimes lives and thinks in the tomb where the body molders, lingered and thought within the narrow marble bed where they laid him with the pious hope—*que en paz descansa!*

Yet so weary of his life had the wanderer been that he could not even find the repose of the dead. And while the body sank into dust the phantom man found no rest in the darkness, and thought to himself, "I am even too weary to rest!"

There was a fissure in the wall of the tomb. And through it, and through the meshes of the web that a spider had spun across it, the dead looked, and saw the summer sky blazing like amethyst; the palms swaying in the breezes from the sea; the flowers in the shadows of the sepulchers; the opal fires of the horizon; the birds that sang; and the river that rolled its whispering waves between tall palms and vast-leaved plants to the heaving emerald of the Spanish Main. The voices of women and sounds of argentine laughter and of footsteps and of music, and of merriment, also came through the fissure in the wall of the tomb—

sometimes also the noise of the swift feet of horses, and afar off the drowsy murmur made by the toiling heart of the city. So that the dead wished to live again; seeing that there was no rest in the tomb.

And the gold-born days died in golden fire—and the moon whitened nightly the face of the earth; and the perfume of the summer passed away like a breath of incense; but the dead in the sepulcher could not wholly die. The voices of life entered his resting-place; the murmur of the world spoke to him in the darkness; the winds of the sea called to him through the crannies of the tomb. So that he could not rest. And yet for the dead there is no consolation of tears!

The stars in their silent courses looked down through the crannies of the tomb and passed on; the birds sang above him and flew to other lands; the lizards ran noiselessly above his bed of stone and as noiselessly departed; the spider at last ceased to renew her web of magical silk; the years came and went as before, but for the dead there was no rest!

And it came to pass that after many tropical moons had waxed and waned, and the summer was come, with a presence sweet as a fair woman's—making the drowsy air odorous about her—that she whose name was uttered by his lips when the Shadow of Death fell upon him, came to that city of palms, and to the ancient place of burial, and even to the tomb that was nameless.

And he knew the whisper of her robes; and from the heart of the dead man a flower sprang and passed through the fissure in the wall of the tomb and blossomed before her and breathed out its soul in passionate sweetness.

But she, knowing it not, passed by; and the sound of her footsteps died away forever!

SALT IS NOT FOR SLAVES

G. W. Hutter

Not all zombies want to eat your brains. Sometimes it's the zombies
who are the victims.

◆ ◆ ◆

Several times before I had noticed the old woman. She always squatted
on her low stool as far as possible from the servants, as if her age did
not separate her enough from the young, rollicking workers. Her years
were impossible to reckon. She seemed as old as the island; and a
definite, tangible part of it. Hayti's mountains and valleys appeared
impressed on her face; and the darkness and mystery of history mirrored in her eyes; eyes which were startling in their strength and intensity; eyes which suggested timelessness more than anything I had ever
seen—animate or inanimate. They were incredible in her stooped, bent
old body.

She sat immovable save for the quick motions of her long fingers as
she sliced pineapples or plucked doves and guineas for the hotel dinner.
Her hands worked automatically— she did not need her eyes, which
were staring ceaselessly up to the heights of the dark green mountains
in the distance.

As I gazed out of my glassless window, waiting for the tropic sun to
drop low enough to permit the evening plunge in the concrete "basin"

in the rear garden, I heard a commotion and a violent outburst of Creole. 'Tit Jean, terror-stricken, was scrambling away from the old woman as fast as his little legs could carry him. On the ground by the old woman's stool lay several empty salt cellars, their contents strewn over the grass.

Madame appeared just as the old woman was overtaking the cause of her fury. "Marie!" she shouted imperatively. The old woman turned, slunk back to her stool, picked it up and resumed her work at the end of the garden.

'Tit Jean was sobbing at the foot of the stairs when I descended in my bathrobe. I asked him the trouble. "Marie, *pas bonne*," he declared.

When I asked him why Marie was no good, he told me in Creole, broken by sobs, that when he accidentally tripped in passing her stool, she had tried to kill him because a little salt had fallen on her. Yes, that was everything he had done. Her rage was as inexplicable to me as it had been to him, and I gave him the only comfort I knew—a five centime piece. This seemed to make his world rosy once more.

He smiled, motioned me to come behind the door and then, in a voice so low that I was forced to bend my head to his level, he whispered, "Voodoo!"

He nodded his head meaningly towards the garden. When I laughed, terror leaped into his round eyes. I had heard many stories of voodoo in Hayti, but I could not connect the trivial incident of a small boy accidentally spilling a bit of table salt with any of them. 'Tit Jean, however, was silent. He would say no more. Voodoo was too real and serious a matter with him to be discussed laughingly with a foreigner.

I walked past the old woman. She looked through me as if I did not exist.

I entered the small boarded enclosure of the "basin," stripped off the bathrobe; and the heat of the day was soon forgotten in the invigorating buoyancy of clear mountain water.

As I walked, dripping wet, by the uplifted eyes, I said, "*Bon soir.*"

"*Bon soir, Monsieur*," she replied. Even though she hardly glanced at me as she spoke and there was little cordiality in her voice, I felt encouraged. At least she was approachable and I might draw her into conversation.

I was still thinking of her after I had dressed and was seated at dinner. 'Tit Jean was not himself as he served me. He could hardly wait for me to empty the spoon of guava jelly on my guinea; he was in such a hurry to leave the single table I occupied in the corner of the porch. The whites of his eyes showed plainly as I smiled at his uneasiness to be away from me and serve the other guests—they would not ask cynical questions about voodoo.

As I sipped my after-dinner coffee, I glanced up at the black mountains. I imagined I heard the beat of a tom-tom and I remembered old Marie's gaze directed up to these mountains—seeing all and seeing nothing. 'Tit Jean saw me as I looked at the distant hills, and remained in a corner until I had left the table.

A squawk of a loudspeaker drew me into the large park spreading out before the hotel. A radio concert was being given from the local station and the town had assembled before an enormous receiving set placed in the bandstand. The chatter of Creole was completely stilled by the strains of "Bye, Bye, Blackbird," and the native favorite, "Yes, Sir, That's My Baby."

Standing in a group, their faces beaming with delight, were the servants from the hotel. They were all there, I noticed, except old Marie. Now was a good chance to see the old woman, I thought. Obviously the servants' work was done for the night and I could catch her alone in the garden. I left the spellbound crowd in the park and paused on my way back to the hotel in a cafe to buy a large bag of tobacco.

Marie was sitting on her stool as I had hoped. Casually I strolled around the garden and stopped beside her.

"Would you care for some tobacco?" I asked in French. She reached her bony hand for the bag. "*Oui, Monsieur*. You are very kind."

She began to fill the large calabash pipe which had stuck from her apron pocket. I continued my stroll for a few minutes and then sat down on the outside rim of the "basin" a few yards from her stool.

She was again staring straight ahead at the mountains.

I lit a cigarette and we both smoked silently. A second cigarette—still another, but not·a word from her. She remained motionless—staring.

"You like to look at the hills, Marie?" I began awkwardly. Without turning she said, "No, *Monsieur.*"

"Then why do you stare at them?" I was determined to get some returns from my tobacco.

She took three long puffs before she replied very slowly, "It is because I cannot help but stare at my life. That large mountain is my life. It began at the topmost point and it ends at the bottom. From this seat I can see everything by casting my eyes to the top; and today, *Monsieur,* I have not raised them very high."

"You were born on the mountain?" I prodded her.

"That I do not know—but many years I spent there as a girl. My master's villa was the only one there. That, also, was many years ago.

"My master was rich and powerful and had many slaves. They say he chose the site for his villa because it was the highest point in all Hayti, and from the door of his home he could look down on his lands extending from Port-au-Prince up to the Cape. His lands were so many that he needed hundreds of slaves to till them and gather in the crops. In some years his coffee alone required a fleet of ships to carry it to France. But he had no mercy for his slaves. He drove them hard, and when they could endure it no more they dropped from exhaustion. Then he sent them up to the slave quarters at the villa just like broken-down horses to be patched up for work again.

"I was always there. I was a house servant. When I grew old enough I loved Tresaint. Tresaint was a big, strong, young man, whom his master trusted. He, like me, was there always, and the master made him the overseer of the other slaves. When business called the master away,

Tresaint was left in charge of everything. The key to the salt even was left with him."

"The salt?" I asked wonderingly.

"Yes, the salt. Years before—almost the first thing I remember—the master called us before him, the six men and me, and gave his command about the salt. 'Slaves,' he said, 'you are to be under my roof always. There is one order you must not disobey. You shall eat no salt. You will grow strong. You will suffer no sickness; but let one grain of salt pass your lips and you die.' He looked very stern and grim as he said it, and we knew that it was true.

"We did not ask why. The master was to be obeyed, not questioned. We also knew his powers—powers not in slaves and lands—but other and more mysterious ones he had at his command. That is why we put even the thought of salt from our minds, and grew strong and healthy. Sometimes the quarters were filled with a hundred slaves stricken with the fever of the low rice fields, or with their legs swollen the size of large burros, and all around us were dying like flies; but none of us was sick a day.

"Yes," Marie went on, "all of the men were strong, but Tresaint was the strongest of the six. When he held me in his arms I felt as if he would break every bone in my body, but I loved him for it.

"No slave in the country was as well-off as Tresaint, but he was not happy. Always the misery of the worn-out slaves oppressed him. The harsh words and treatment he dealt out to them seemed to hurt him as well. He must treat them severely when the master was around, but when he was away on one of his trips the others would know at once through Tresaint's kindly manner.

"Strange rumors came to our ears, brought by incoming slaves. They said there was a man in the north of the island around the Cape who was preaching freedom. He taught that the slaves should rise up and throw off the yoke of the French. That they were human beings—not animals—and that they themselves should rule their country. This man was a slave himself. His name was Christophe."

I gasped. Surely that couldn't have been true! Christophe became Emperor Henry of Hayti in 1804. This would make the old woman almost a hundred and fifty years old. It was impossible. Then I looked in Marie's face—a rock in the moonlight. She seemed centuries older than anything I had ever seen before. She spoke so surely, seemed so certain of what she was saying. I was confused and undecided.

A creaking of shoes at the garden entrance, a babble of Creole and laughter, and the servants were back from the concert. When they saw Marie and me, their talking and laughter stopped. They went quietly to their rooms strewn back of the kitchen along the edge of garden.

The lights in the hotel were flicked out. Everything was quiet. Marie was puffing rhythmically at her pipe.

"And Tresaint—" I urged her on. "Was he interested in these tales of Christophe?"

"Yes, he was interested. He was too interested. That was the cause of everything." Marie spoke earnestly. "Christophe, he said, was the savior of Hayti. France, herself, had thrown off the yoke of her kings and now Hayti should throw off the yoke of France. The slave should rule his own country. All of this Tresaint would tell me until I became worried for fear that the master would learn of his trusted overseer's burning thoughts.

"Finally there came a time when the master himself was aroused. Christophe had persuaded scores of slaves on the master's lands near the Cape to leave their fields of bondage and flee to him. This news sent the master into a mighty rage. He left the villa at once to sail to the Cape.

"Before the master's carriage had reached Port-au-Prince a great change had come over the villa. Shouts, singing and laughter filled the house. Tresaint, who had always been lenient when the master was away, now became the master himself and treated the slaves as if they were the master's guests. He opened up the wine cellar and invited them in. He did not give them the *tafia* in the tin mugs which was kept for the slaves, but he rolled out a keg of the finest rum. Rum that was many years old; and he served it to them in the villa's finest glasses. They skipped and danced about and dropped ashes from the master's cigars on the marble floors.

"I was frightened, but Tresaint would not listen to me. He was encouraging them into complete lawlessness. He left the slaves in the main salon. Bare feet which before had known only the feel of rocks and sod plopped delightedly across smooth marble. Soon he appeared, his huge arms hugging bottles and bottles of champagne. With a blow from a sword snatched down from the wall, he cut off the necks—the wine popping and gurgling to the floor. When every slave had a bottle, Tresaint mounted the mahogany table in the hall.

"'Friends,' he shouted, 'drink to the health of your new masters—yourselves! We shall be slaves no longer. The day of freedom has come. Drink!' He drained the upraised jagged bottle with one long draught and dashed it in a thousand pieces on the floor.

"The glass cut my feet as I ran to him.

"'Tresaint! Tresaint! Listen to me,' I begged. 'The master will kill you surely when he returns. Stop this foolish wildness before it is too late.'

"But the idea of freedom was as strong in his head as the fumes of the liquor. He laughed at my fears and pushed me aside.

"'Women are cowards,' he announced to the cheering crowd, 'but I am a man. I am no longer afraid of anybody—not even the master. Lose all fear and you shall be free. The master put fear into us from the start. You five men who have been with me here know what this key means.' He held out the smallest key that dangled on the chain around his neck.

"I was terrified. I knew the key. It was to the chest that was filled with salt! What madness was he up to now?

"He saw the terror on my face and called, 'And you too, Marie! You were placed in the master's power at the same time—all by his command about the salt. We shall eat no salt. Why? Because the master forbade it and we are not to question his command. Bah!'

"He threw the key at my feet.

"'We will show the master's power is gone. Marie, fetch some salt. We will eat it and be forever free.'

"I picked up the key and stumbled out of the room, on past the closet that contained the forbidden chest. From the back gallery I dropped the key beside an orange-tree. I hoped this ruse would delay Tresaint in his madness. That in a little while he would come to his senses again when the rum and the wine wore off and would thank me for preventing him carrying out his rash deed.

"I crouched in the corner of the gallery.

"'Marie! Marie!' his voice thundered out from the house, but I did not answer.

"In a few minutes he came out to where I was.

"'Where is the key?' he asked.

"I told him I did not know.

"'That doesn't matter. The chest is not so strong that I cannot open it.'

"He put his arm around me.

"'You are too timid,' he said.

"I returned his embrace with all my strength. I tried to draw him down on a bench while I pleaded and cajoled with him to stay with me. I pointed out the truth of the master's curse on the salt. I showed him how we had been strong and healthy always just as the master had foretold and that to disobey him would cause our death. If the master's predictions had worked one way they would work the other. But he would not hear me. I called on his love for me, but all to no avail. He left me stricken dumb with terror.

"Sounds of blows on wood, a shout of triumph and Tresaint's voice floated out: 'Here, my friends, in one hand you have the salt, in the other the wine to wash the curse away.'

"A moment of silence as I shivered in the heat of midday and then more shouts. They were dancing around in the marble salon, yelling exultantly.

"How long I remained frozen to my seat I do not know, but gradually there beat into my ears a curious sound. The pattering of bare feet was all I heard; the shouts and singing had disappeared.

"Fearfully I crept into the room. Along the sides of the wall were stretched out the slaves from the quarters, stupefied by drink. In the centre were Tresaint and the five others skipping around with waving arms without uttering a sound. The marble floor was covered with jagged pieces of bottles.

"I stood in amazement looking at their bare feet. They seemed unaware of the glass, unaware of everything. Great gashes were in their feet. As he lifted his feet ceaselessly across the floor, two of Tresaint's toes dangled like broken palm leaves. The wounds had a strange unnatural appearance. There was no sign of blood.

"Horrified I looked in Tresaint's face. His eyes did not move, his nostrils and mouth gave no sign of breathing. And as I looked I saw his face set in rigidity, the flesh seemed to drop away leaving nothing but cheek bones and eyes. His ribs stood out through the torn shirt—bare.

"I screamed in horror. He was dead! They were all dead! They were corpses treading a fantastic dance of death.

"My screams awoke the drunken slaves from their stupor. Opening their eyes, without rising from the floor, they saw what I had seen. The truth was plain to them. They cried in terror at the dead dancing bodies. They scrambled to their feet and fled out of the house and down the road. The whole mountainside shook with their yells of horror as they raced away. I was left alone with these prancing shells of men.

"For some reason, I do not know what, unless it was for the love I had borne him, I was impelled to touch him who had been so close to me. I reached for his hand as he passed by in his endless mad dance.

"The fingers closed cold around my hand. The two arms pressed me against the body which stopped still. I could hear and feel my own heartbeat—nothing more. It was as if I was being enfolded by the cool marble of the villa.

"He placed a hand over my heart, then quickly on one of the other forms. He turned his unseeing eyes full from my face to the others. Then those eyes, which had been as glassy and dead as the eyes of a fish two days from the bay, mirrored such horror as the world had never seen. From the dead caverns of the throat came a cry. Half shriek and half groan of such force and terror that my blood froze.

"The others took up the cry. I was mad from horror."

Marie was living again those dead days. Her body was shaking with emotion. Her voice rose and fell, reflecting all the horror of her story.

She arose from her stool, stepping fantastically in the moonlight, to show how that macabre measure was trod by the moving dead in the glass covered marble of the salon.

I was too engrossed to interrupt. She talked on:

"Those shrieks of horror meant that they knew they were dead. It was their spirits crying out—crying to be released from their dead bodies.

"My hand was still held by the lifeless fingers—fingers without blood, but with all the strength of iron bands.

"With one accord the forms rushed through the villa, bounding me along with them. Down the road they tore. My feet did not seem to touch the ground. I felt as if I were being whisked through the air. I screamed at the top of my lungs, but so mighty were their cries that my ears never received a sound coming from my lips.

"Down, down the road we flew. A sight to strike terror into the bravest heart. For miles the screams could be heard and we met nothing on the road, but deserted burros. The travelers had heard the fearful noises and the dust that the leaping spirits raised in the afternoon sun had sent them scurrying from the approaching horror, to a safe retreat from the roadside. God, *Monsieur*, it was such a sight that would strike you dead. Six dead men racing and falling down the road, dragging along a woman more gripped by fear and horror than death itself holds. Heads like death; bodies stripped of clothes, the rags fluttering behind them; skeleton ribs showing the dust of the road through their gaunt gaps; the fleshless arms raised, threshing the air; and above all the shrill, deep unearthly yells that came from still throats. On down the road!"

Marie had worked herself up into a fearful pitch of excitement. She arose from her stool.

"Like this they ran!" And with that she threw open her dress, lifted her arms and began bounding around the garden. Her dress trailed after her as she ran, her arms clutched wildly at the air, and from her throat came a low horrible cry.

There in the moonlight I myself saw that mad race down the mountain. She was no longer an old woman of more than a hundred years, she became a deathless spirit.

I jumped to my feet, throbbing with excitement. She dashed up and caught my hand in a viselike grip. I had become part of the mad cavalcade.

She ran on, pulling me by her side. I was the living being dragged along by death. I shuddered and wrenched my hand loose from her cold clutch.

She was too wrought up to resume her seat. She continued to move about spasmodically as she spoke:

"On down the road we came—never stopping. On, on, near the city. The other slaves had run down before us and spread the news that dead men were dancing in the master's villa. Crowds filled the roads out from the city. They had heard us coming. They wanted to see with their own eyes. As we bounded around a curve into their midst, they shouted in horror. They had not expected so terrifying a sight. Screaming they turned in their tracks and rushed down the road before us. Like a herd of wild cattle from the hills they stampeded into the city, shoving one another wildly, tripping and falling—all screaming in terror at the oncoming spectacle. Such confusion, fright and horror as no one could picture.

"On in the city we came, heralded by the crazed multitude. Old men throwing away their crutches and running lamely away. Mothers with babies clutched to their breasts, fleeing as if from death itself. The very animals in the town were overcome with terror. Droves of burros charged wildly around the Champ de Mars; horses, deserted by their drivers, crashed their empty carriages against the palms as the crazed beasts sought to escape the tumult. Goats, dogs and fowls sensed the terror and added their voices to the bedlam of the humans. Still on, on, I was dragged. I was as powerless as a baby in that grip of death. Those long strong bones that had only a few hours before been the hand of my lover jerked me along as if I were one of the rags that fluttered behind the crazed spirits.

"My whole soul had gone out in horror. I thought there was no feeling left in me. Drained by terror as I was, I saw before me a sight that seemed to draw all the horror of the fear-stricken city into my own breast. Directly in front of me were the gates to the cemetery!

"The spirits' screams grew wilder and louder than ever. There seemed a note of triumph to the din as I was whisked through the gate.

"On over the graves we went. My mouth was open wide, but no sound came. My eyes felt as if they had fallen on my cheeks; my throat as if it were being clutched by the ghosts of the countless dead as I was yanked from one grave to another.

"With one last effort I tore at the bones around my hand. It was like tearing at the marble tombstones. My eyes could see no more. They closed.

"My body swung through the air and bounded over the ground like this—" The old woman hurtled herself on the grass, turning over several times.

I rushed to her side. It was a violent jolt to an old woman of her years. But she lay there as she fell and continued talking. Spellbound I drank in every word.

"*Oui, Monsieur*, I lay like this. I do not know how long and then I noticed that the cries seemed far away—and different. They were the cries from the frightened city, not the wailing screams of the spirits.

I lifted my right hand—it was free. I opened my eyes. There beside me were the bodies, perfectly still, lying peacefully on their backs all in a row. That which had once been Tresaint was nearest me. I reached out fearfully and touched the hand. It was stiff in death.

"I staggered over the graves and out through the cemetery. Some of the braver of the town people did not run when they saw me approaching. They knew that the spirits' shrieks had ceased and that I was alive. They went into the cemetery, on back into the corner where the bodies lay.

"As they lifted up the corpses they discovered a curious looseness to the earth. There were six graves under the covering of sod. Each body had lain evenly over a waiting grave. The spirits had known that, *Monsieur*, and that is why they had rushed down the mountain to set themselves at rest, to release themselves from the dead bodies. That which was Tresaint had tried to drag me to the grave with him, but when he found only the six graves he had flung me aside. There would have been seven graves in the cemetery yonder at the foot of the mountain if I had eaten of the salt.

"Ah! If Tresaint had listened to my warnings my lover would be with me now."

"But the salt, Marie?" I enquired. "By obeying the master—is that what keeps you well and strong?"

"What else could it be?" she answered earnestly. "As surely as the rains come from the sea, if I never tasted salt I should live to be as old as the mountains and as strong."

"Then you will never die?" I asked, struck by the earnestness in the old woman's voice.

"*Monsieur*, have you a match?"

Wonderingly I made a light as she ran her thin fingers over the grass near her head.

"Would you taste this for me?" She dropped a few grains of salt she had pinched between her fingers into my hand.

I made as if I tasted it. "It is salt," I said in a low voice. I was becoming strangely upset—so in sympathy with the old woman's story that I was afraid of a grain of salt.

"Yes," she said, "I thought so. That is why I have told you all this. Everyone who knew my story died many years ago, but now I wanted someone to learn it before I go."

"But you said you would never go unless you tasted—salt." I hesitated on the word. My voice was jumpy. The old woman's strange calm and cryptic remarks after her delirious running around the garden had upset me more than I cared to admit.

"Oh! but I have—this afternoon." Her voice became sharp and venomous. "That little imp of the Evil One threw some in my mouth. He said he stumbled and accidentally a few grains hit my tongue—but," her voice became low again, "but what difference does it make how it happened? I have eaten and the curse is upon me. Perhaps a little more will hasten the time."

She licked her hands hungrily, then ran her tongue over the grass.

I shuddered and rose to my feet.

"Good night, Marie," I called weakly as I walked to the hotel door.

"*Adieu, Monsieur,*" she answered.

I climbed the stairs to my room. Why did she say farewell instead of good night? I did not want an answer. "Don't be such a fool," I told myself, "as to be worrying over some voodoo spell of over a hundred years ago."

I undressed and got into bed, but I could not sleep. I arose and poured a stiff drink of rum from a bottle on the washstand. With the drink and a cigarette I felt that I could get to sleep. I reached for my matches. Then I remembered I had left them in the garden. The moon had gone down and the night was inky black, but I thought I could find them by locating the stool and feeling around in the grass.

I slipped on my shoes and bathrobe, and groped my way down the back stairs. As I opened the door I hoped that old Marie had gone to her room. The dark was thick enough to cut with a knife. I hesitated a moment to get my bearings. I did want a cigarette.

Then out straight in front where I was looking I saw a faint glow. She was still there. The glow brightened and the huge bowl of the calabash pipe took shape before my eyes. And then the face! Plainer than in the moonlight!

Great drops of perspiration rolled down my chilled forehead. I was rooted in horror. My heart pounded the roof of my mouth.

That face! The flesh melted away under my terrified gaze. Nothing was left, but the grim bones of the dead.

As I watched, stricken with cold terror, old Marie fell headlong on the cool grass of the garden. I knew she was dead, and I knew how it was she had died.

A THOUSAND DEATHS

Jack London

Jack London was the author of the adventure classics *The Call of the Wild* and *White Fang*. He was born in San Francisco, the illegitimate son of a traveling astrologer. As a child, poverty forced him to work ten-hour days in a canning factory for ten cents an hour. At the age of fourteen he borrowed money to buy a small boat and joined in raids on privately owned oyster fields, before switching to the other side, working for law enforcement. When he was seventeen he signed aboard a ship bound for Japan. On his return he became a hobo, traveling throughout the United States, with ninety days in prison for vagrancy.

London's education came primarily from books. At the age of nineteen he began high school and the following year he attended a semester at the University of California. In 1897 he left for the Klondike to take part in the gold rush there. On returning to San Francisco, he tried to make a living by writing, but had little luck until his adventure stories set in the Yukon began to be published. Those were a tremendous success. An active socialist with Marxist leanings, he claimed he only wrote for money, saying, "If I could have my choice about it, I never would put pen to paper—except to write a socialist essay to tell the bourgeois world how much I despise it." But this didn't slow him down, for he wrote close to fifty books in seventeen years. After enduring a divorce, continuing financial difficulties, severe health problems, and his heavy drinking, he finally died from an overdose of morphine at the age of forty. Some believe his death was a suicide, while others are convinced it was accidental. His stories remain tremendously popular, largely for capturing the American ideal of rugged individualism.

This story is an excellent foray into the realm of science fiction, along the lines of Jules Verne and H. G. Wells.

❖   ❖   ❖

I had been in the water about an hour, and cold, exhausted, with a terrible cramp in my right calf, it seemed as though my hour had come. Fruitlessly struggling against the strong ebb tide, I had beheld the maddening procession of the water-front lights slip by, but now I gave up attempting to breast the stream and contented myself with the bitter thoughts of a wasted career, now drawing to a close.

It had been my luck to come of good, English stock, but of parents whose account with the bankers far exceeded their knowledge of child-nature and the rearing of children. While born with a silver spoon in my mouth, the blessed atmosphere of the home circle was to me unknown. My father, a very learned man and a celebrated antiquarian, gave no thought to his family, being constantly lost in the abstractions of his study; while my mother, noted far more for her good looks than her good sense, sated herself with the adulation of the society in which she was perpetually plunged. I went through the regular school and college routine of a boy of the English bourgeoisie, and as the years brought me increasing strength and passions, my parents suddenly became aware that I was possessed of an immortal soul, and endeavored to draw the curb. But it was too late; I perpetrated the wildest and most audacious folly, and was disowned by my people, ostracized by the society I had so long outraged, and with the thousand pounds my father gave me, with the declaration that he would neither see me again nor give me more, I took a first-class passage to Australia.

Since then my life had been one long peregrination—from the Orient to the Occident, from the Arctic to the Antarctic—to find myself at last, an able seaman at thirty, in the full vigor of my manhood, drowning in San Francisco bay because of a disastrously successful attempt to desert my ship.

My right leg was drawn up by the cramp, and I was suffering the keenest agony. A slight breeze stirred up a choppy sea, which washed into my mouth and down my throat, nor could I prevent it. Though I still contrived to keep afloat, it was merely mechanical, for I was rapidly becoming unconscious. I have a dim recollection of drifting past the sea-wall, and of catching a glimpse of an upriver steamer's starboard light; then everything became a blank.

I heard the low hum of insect life, and felt the balmy air of a spring morning fanning my cheek. Gradually it assumed a rhythmic flow, to whose soft pulsations my body seemed to respond. I floated on the gentle bosom of a summer's sea, rising and falling with dreamy pleasure on each crooning wave. But the pulsations grew stronger; the humming, louder; the waves, larger, fiercer—I was dashed about on a stormy sea. A great agony fastened upon me. Brilliant, intermittent sparks of light flashed athwart my inner consciousness; in my ears there was the sound of many waters; then a sudden snapping of an intangible something, and I awoke.

The scene, of which I was protagonist, was a curious one. A glance sufficed to inform me that I lay on the cabin floor of some gentleman's yacht, in a most uncomfortable posture. On either side, grasping my arms and working them up and down like pump handles, were two peculiarly clad, dark-skinned creatures. Though conversant with most aboriginal types, I could not conjecture their nationality. Some attachment had been fastened about my head, which connected my respiratory organs with the machine I shall next describe. My nostrils, however, had been closed, forcing me to breathe through my mouth. Foreshortened by the obliquity of my line of vision, I beheld two tubes, similar to small hosing but of different composition, which emerged from my mouth and went off at an acute angle from each other. The first came to an abrupt termination and lay on the floor beside me; the second traversed the floor in numerous coils, connecting with the apparatus I have promised to describe.

In the days before my life had become tangential, I had dabbled not a little in science, and, conversant with the appurtenances and general paraphernalia of the laboratory, I appreciated the machine I now beheld. It was composed chiefly of glass, the construction being of that crude sort which is employed for experimentative purposes. A vessel of water was surrounded by an air chamber, to which was fixed a vertical tube, surmounted by a globe. In the centre of this was a vacuum gauge. The water in the tube moved upwards and downwards, creating alternate inhalations and exhalations, which were in turn communicated to me through the hose. With this, and the aid of the men who pumped my arms, so vigorously, had the process of breathing been artificially carried on, my chest rising and falling and my lungs expanding and contracting, till nature could be persuaded to again take up her wonted labor.

As I opened my eyes the appliance about my head, nostrils and mouth was removed. Draining a stiff three fingers of brandy, I staggered to my feet to thank my preserver, and confronted—my father. But long years of fellowship with danger had taught me self-control, and I waited to see if he would recognize me. Not so; he saw in me no more than a runaway sailor and treated me accordingly.

Leaving me to the care of the assistants, he fell to revising the notes he had made on my resuscitation. As I ate of the handsome fare served up to me, confusion began on deck, and from the chanteys of the sailors and the rattling of blocks and tackles I surmised that we were getting under way. What a lark! Off on a cruise with my recluse father into the wide Pacific! Little did I realize, as I laughed to myself, which side the joke I was to be on. Aye, had I known, I would have plunged overboard and welcomed the dirty fo'c'sle from which I had just escaped.

I was not allowed on deck till we had sunk the Farallones and the last pilot boat. I appreciated this forethought on the part of my father and made it a point to thank him heartily, in my bluff seaman's manner. I could not suspect that he had his own ends in view, in thus keeping my presence secret to all save the crew. He told me briefly of my rescue by his sailors, assuring me that the obligation was on his side, as my appearance had been most opportune. He had constructed the apparatus for the vindication of a theory concerning certain biological phenomena, and had been waiting for an opportunity to use it.

"You have proved it beyond all doubt," he said; then added with a sigh, "But only in the small matter of drowning."

But, to take a reef in my yarn—he offered me an advance of two pounds on my previous wages to sail with him, and this I considered handsome, for he really did not need me. Contrary to my expectations, I did not join the sailors' mess, for'ard, being assigned to a comfortable stateroom and eating at the captain's table. He had perceived that I was no common sailor, and I resolved to take this chance for reinstating myself in his good graces. I wove a fictitious past to account for my education and present position, and did my best to come in touch with him. I was not long in disclosing a predilection for scientific pursuits, nor he in appreciating my aptitude. I became his assistant, with a corresponding increase in wages, and before long, as he grew confidential and expounded his theories, I was as enthusiastic as himself.

The days flew quickly by, for I was deeply interested in my new studies, passing my waking hours in his well-stocked library, or listening to his plans and aiding him in his laboratory work. But we were forced to forego many enticing experiments, a rolling ship not being exactly the proper place for delicate or intricate work. He promised me, however, many delightful hours in the magnificent laboratory for which we were bound. He had taken possession of an uncharted South Sea island, as he said, and turned it into a scientific paradise.

We had not been on the island long, before I discovered the horrible mare's nest I had fallen into. But before I describe the strange things which came to pass, I must briefly outline the causes which culminated in as startling an experience as ever fell to the lot of man.

Late in life, my father had abandoned the musty charms of antiquity and succumbed to the more fascinating ones embraced under the general head of biology. Having been thoroughly grounded during his youth in the fundamentals, he rapidly explored all the higher branches as far as the scientific world had gone, and found himself on the no man's land of the unknowable. It was his intention to pre-empt some of this unclaimed territory, and it was at this stage of his investigations that we had been thrown together. Having a good brain, though I say it myself, I had mastered his speculations and methods of reasoning, becoming almost as mad as himself. But I should not say this. The marvelous results we afterwards obtained can only go to prove his sanity. I can but say that he was the most abnormal specimen of cold-blooded cruelty I have ever seen.

After having penetrated the dual mysteries of physiology and psychology, his thought had led him to the verge of a great field, for which, the better to explore, he began studies in higher organic chemistry, pathology, toxicology and other sciences and sub-sciences rendered kindred as accessories to his speculative hypotheses. Starting from the proposition that the direct cause of the temporary and permanent arrest of vitality was due to the coagulation of certain elements and compounds in the protoplasm, he had isolated and subjected these various substances to innumerable experiments. Since the temporary arrest of vitality in an organism brought coma, and a permanent arrest death, he held that by artificial means this coagulation of the protoplasm could be retarded, prevented, and even overcome in the extreme states of solidification. Or, to do away with the technical nomenclature, he argued that death, when not violent and in which none of the organs had suffered injury, was merely suspended vitality; and that, in such instances, life could be induced to resume its functions by the use of proper methods. This, then, was his idea: To discover the method—and by practical experimentation prove the possibility—of renewing vitality in a structure from which life had seemingly fled. Of course, he recognized the futility of such endeavor after decomposition had set in; he must have organisms which but the moment, the hour, or the day before, had been quick with life. With me, in a crude way, he had proved this theory. I was really drowned, really dead, when picked from the water of San Francisco bay—but the vital spark had been renewed by means of his aerotherapeutical apparatus, as he called it.

Now to his dark purpose concerning me. He first showed me how completely I was in his power. He had sent the yacht away for a year, retaining only his two dark assistants, who were utterly devoted to him. He then made an exhaustive review of his theory and outlined the method of proof he had adopted, concluding with the startling announcement that I was to be his subject.

I had faced death and weighed my chances in many a desperate venture, but never in one of this nature. I can swear I am no coward, yet this proposition of journeying back and forth across the borderland of death put the yellow fear upon me. I asked for time, which he granted, at the same time assuring me that but the one course was open—I must submit. Escape from the island was out of the question; escape by suicide was not to be entertained, though really preferable to what it seemed I must undergo; my only hope was to destroy my captors. But this latter was frustrated through the precautions taken by my father. I was subjected to a constant surveillance, even in my sleep being guarded by one or the other of the assistants.

Having pleaded in vain, I announced and proved that I was his son. It was my last card, and I had played all my hopes upon it. But he was inexorable; he was not a father but a scientific machine. I wonder yet how it ever came to pass that he married my mother or begat me, for there was not the slightest grain of emotion in his make-up. Reason was all in all to him, nor could he understand such things as love or sympathy in others, except as petty weaknesses which should be overcome. So he informed me that in the beginning he had given me life, and who had better right to take it away than he? Such, he said, was not his desire, however; he merely wished to borrow it occasionally, promising to return it punctually at the appointed time. Of course, there was a liability of mishaps, but I could do no more than take the chances, since the affairs of men were full of such.

The better to insure success, he wished me to be in the best possible condition, so I was dieted and trained like a great athlete before a decisive contest. What could I do? If I had to undergo the peril, it were best to be in good shape. In my intervals of relaxation he allowed me to assist in the arranging of the apparatus and in the various subsidiary experiments. The interest I took in all such operations can be imagined. I mastered the work as thoroughly as he, and often had the pleasure of seeing some of my suggestions or alterations put into effect. After such events I would smile grimly, conscious of officiating at my own funeral.

He began by inaugurating a series of experiments in toxicology. When all was ready, I was killed by a stiff dose of strychnine and allowed to lie dead for some twenty hours. During that period my body was dead, absolutely dead. All respiration and circulation ceased; but the frightful part of it was, that while the protoplasmic coagulation proceeded, I retained consciousness and was enabled to study it in all its ghastly details.

The apparatus to bring me back to life was an air-tight chamber, fitted to receive my body. The mechanism was simple—a few valves, a rotary shaft and crank, and an electric motor. When in operation, the interior atmosphere was alternately condensed and rarefied, thus communicating to my lungs an artificial respiration without the agency of the hosing previously used. Though my body was inert, and, for all I knew, in the first stages of decomposition, I was cognizant of everything that transpired. I knew when they placed me in the chamber, and though all my senses were quiescent, I was aware of hypodermic injections of a compound to react upon the coagulatory process. Then the chamber was closed and the machinery started. My anxiety was terrible; but the circulation became gradually restored, the different organs began to carry on their respective functions, and in an hour's time I was eating a hearty dinner.

It cannot be said that I participated in this series, nor in the subsequent ones, with much verve; but after two ineffectual attempts of escape, I began to take quite an interest. Besides, I was becoming accustomed. My father was beside himself at his success, and as the months rolled by his speculations took wilder and yet wilder flights. We ranged through the three great classes of poisons, the neurotics, the gaseous and the irritants, but carefully avoided some of the mineral irritants and passed the whole group of corrosives. During the poison regime I became quite accustomed to dying, and had but one mishap to shake my growing confidence. Scarifying a number of lesser blood vessels in my arm, he introduced a minute quantity of that most frightful of poisons, the arrow poison, or curare. I lost consciousness at the start, quickly followed by the cessation of respiration and circulation, and so far had the solidification of the protoplasm advanced, that he gave up all hope. But at the last moment he applied a discovery he had been working upon, receiving such encouragement as to redouble his efforts.

In a glass vacuum, similar but not exactly like a Crookes' tube, was placed a magnetic field. When penetrated by polarized light, it gave no phenomena of phosphorescence nor the rectilinear projection of atoms, but emitted non-luminous rays, similar to the X ray. While the X ray could reveal opaque objects hidden in dense mediums, this was possessed of far subtler penetration. By this he photographed my body, and found on the negative an infinite number of blurred shadows, due to the chemical and electric motions still going on. This was an infallible proof that the rigor mortis in which I lay was not genuine; that is, those mysterious forces, those delicate bonds which held my soul to my body, were still in action. The resultants of all other poisons were unapparent, save those of mercurial compounds, which usually left me languid for several days.

Another series of delightful experiments was with electricity. We verified Tesla's assertion that high currents were utterly harmless by passing 100,000 volts through my body. As this did not affect me, the current was reduced to 2,500, and I was quickly electrocuted. This time he ventured so far as to allow me to remain dead, or in a state of suspended vitality, for three days. It took four hours to bring me back.

Once, he superinduced lockjaw; but the agony of dying was so great that I positively refused to undergo similar experiments. The easiest deaths were by asphyxiation, such as drowning, strangling, and suffocation by gas; while those by morphine, opium, cocaine and chloroform, were not at all hard.

Another time, after being suffocated, he kept me in cold storage for three months, not permitting me to freeze or decay. This was without my knowledge, and I was in a great fright on discovering the lapse of time. I became afraid of what he might do with me when I lay dead, my alarm being increased by the predilection he was beginning to betray towards vivisection. The last time I was resurrected, I discovered that he had been tampering with my breast. Though he had carefully dressed and sewed the incisions up, they were so severe that I had to take to my bed for some time. It was during this convalescence that I evolved the plan by which I ultimately escaped.

While feigning unbounded enthusiasm in the work, I asked and received a vacation from my moribund occupation. During this period I devoted myself to laboratory work, while he was too deep in the vivisection of the many animals captured by the blacks to take notice of my work.

It was on these two propositions that I constructed my theory: First, electrolysis, or the decomposition of water into its constituent gases by means of electricity; and, second, by the hypothetical existence of a force, the converse of gravitation, which Astor has named "apergy." Terrestrial attraction, for instance, merely draws objects together but does not combine them; hence, apergy is merely repulsion. Now, atomic or molecular attraction not only draws objects together but integrates them; and it was the converse of this, or a disintegrative force, which

I wished to not only discover and produce, but to direct at will. Thus, the molecules of hydrogen and oxygen reacting on each other, separate and create new molecules, containing both elements and forming water. Electrolysis causes these molecules to split up and resume their original condition, producing the two gases separately. The force I wished to find must not only do this with two, but with all elements, no matter in what compounds they exist. If I could then entice my father within its radius, he would be instantly disintegrated and sent flying to the four quarters, a mass of isolated elements.

It must not be understood that this force, which I finally came to control, annihilated matter; it merely annihilated form. Nor, as I soon discovered, had it any effect on inorganic structure; but to all organic form it was absolutely fatal. This partiality puzzled me at first, though had I stopped to think deeper I would have seen through it. Since the number of atoms in organic molecules is far greater than in the most complex mineral molecules, organic compounds are characterized by their instability and the ease with which they are split up by physical forces and chemical reagents.

By two powerful batteries, connected with magnets constructed specially for this purpose, two tremendous forces were projected. Considered apart from each other, they were perfectly harmless; but they accomplished their purpose by focusing at an invisible point in mid-air. After practically demonstrating its success, besides narrowly escaping being blown into nothingness, I laid my trap. Concealing the magnets, so that their force made the whole space of my chamber doorway a field of death, and placing by my couch a button by which I could throw on the current from the storage batteries, I climbed into bed.

The assistants still guarded my sleeping quarters, one relieving the other at midnight. I turned on the current as soon as the first man arrived. Hardly had I begun to doze, when I was aroused by a sharp, metallic tinkle. There, on the mid-threshold, lay the collar of Dan, my father's St. Bernard. My keeper ran to pick it up. He disappeared like a gust of wind, his clothes falling to the floor in a heap. There was a slight whiff of ozone in the air, but since the principal gaseous components of his body were hydrogen, oxygen and nitrogen, which are equally colorless and odorless, there was no other manifestation of his departure. Yet when I shut off the current and removed the garments, I found a deposit of carbon in the form of animal charcoal; also other powders, the isolated, solid elements of his organism, such as sulphur, potassium and iron. Resetting the trap, I crawled back to bed. At midnight I got up and removed the remains of the second assistant, and then slept peacefully till morning.

I was awakened by the strident voice of my father, who was calling to me from across the laboratory. I laughed to myself. There had been no one to call him and he had overslept. I could hear him as he approached my room with the intention of rousing me, and so I sat up in bed, the better to observe his translation—perhaps apotheosis were a better term. He paused a moment at the threshold, then took the fatal step. Puff! It was like the wind sighing among the pines. He was gone. His clothes fell in a fantastic heap on the floor. Besides ozone, I noticed the faint, garlic-like odor of phosphorus. A little pile of elementary solids lay among his garments. That was all. The wide world lay before me. My captors were no more.

BIBLIOGRAPHY

Some of these stories have been modified to remove racism and to update spelling and punctuation.

Baudelaire, Charles. "The Metamorphoses of a Vampire," *Les Fleurs du Mal* (*Flowers of Evil*), 1857, trans. by John Richard Stephens.

Burke, Thomas. "The Hollow Man," *Collier's*, October 14, 1933.

Clarke, Harry. Illustrations for Edgar Allan Poe, *Tales of Mystery and Imagination*, New York: Brentano's, 1919.

Clifford, Sir Hugh. "The Ghoul," *The Further Side of Silence*, Garden City, New York: Doubleday, Page & Co., 1916.

Crawford, F. Marion. "For the Blood Is the Life," *Colliers*, December 16, 1905.

Evening Telegram, The. "The Corpse That Ran Away," St. Johns, Newfoundland, August 14, 1888.

Gautier, Théophile. "La Morte Amoureuse" ("The Amorous Corpse" or "The Dead Lover"), *La Chronique de Paris*, June 23, 1836, trans. by Lafcadio Hearn.

Goethe, Johann Wolfgang von. "The Dance of the Dead," *The Poems of Goethe*, Boston: S. E. Cassino, 1882, trans. by Edward Chawner.

Hare, Augustus, quoting Edward Rowe Fisher-Rowe. "The Vampire of Croglin Grange," *The Story of My Life*, London: George Allen, 1896–1900, vol. 4.

Hearn, Lafcadio. "A Dead Love," *Item*, October 21, 1880.

———. "The Name on the Stone," *Item*, October 9, 1880.

Heron, E. and H. (Katherine and Hesketh Prichard). "The Story of Baelbrow," *Pearson's Magazine*, April 1898.

Hutter, G. W. "Salt Is Not for Slaves," *Ghost Stories*, August 1931.

Hyde, Douglas. "Teig O'Kane and the Corpse," in W. B. Yeats, *Fairy and Folk Tales of the Irish Peasantry*, London: W. Scott, 1888.

Irving, Washington. "The Adventure of the German Student," *Tales of a Traveller*, John Murray, 1824. Later published as "The Lady with the Velvet Collar" and "The Tale of the German Student."

Jacobs, W. W. (William Wyman). "The Monkey's Paw," *Harper's Monthly*, September 1902.

Knox, John H. "Wake Not the Dead," *Thrilling Mystery*, January 1940.

Landon, Perceval. "Thurnley Abbey," *Raw Edges*, London: William Heinemann, 1908.

London, Jack. "A Thousand Deaths," *The Black Cat*, May 1899.

Loring, F. G. "The Tomb of Sarah," *Pall Mall Magazine*, December 1900.

Lovecraft, H. P. "Herbert West: Reanimator," *Home Brew*, vol. 1, nos. 1–6, published in six parts, February–July 1922.

> I. "From the Dark," *Home Brew*, February 1922.
>
> II. "The Plague-Daemon," *Home Brew*, March 1922.
>
> III. "Six Shots by Moonlight," *Home Brew*, April 1922.
>
> IV. "The Scream of the Dead," *Home Brew*, May 1922.
>
> V. "The Horror from the Shadows," *Home Brew*, June 1922.
>
> VI. "The Tomb-Legions," *Home Brew*, July 1922.

Lowell, Amy. "The Cross-Roads," *Men, Women and Ghosts*, New York: Macmillan, 1916.

Maupassant, (Henri René Albert) Guy de. "La Main" ("The Hand"), *Le Gaulois*, December 23, 1883. Anonymous translator, *The Complete Short Stories of Guy de Maupassant*, New York: Walter J. Black, 1903. Also published as "The Englishman."

Poe, Edgar Allan. "The Facts of M. Valdemar's Case," *The American Review*, December 1845. Later published as "The Facts in the Case of M. Valdemar."

Pushkin, Alexander. "The Coffin-Maker," 1834, trans. by T. Keane, *The Prose Tales of Alexander Poushkin*, London: G. Bell & Sons, 1916.

Scott, Sir Walter. "The Hero of the Tomb", *Letters on Demonology and Witchcraft*, Edinburgh, Scotland: Ballantyne & Co., 1840, citing Danish historian Saxo Grammaticus (c. 1150–1220), *Gesta Danorum*, vol. 5.

Shelley, Mary. *Frankenstein, or The Modern Prometheus*, London: H. Colburn and R. Bentley, 1831 revised edition, abridged by John Richard Stephens. This novel was originally published in 1818.

Twain, Mark. "A Curious Dream (Containing a Moral), *Buffalo Express*, April 30 and May 7, 1870.